Elyse John is a writer and a poet. She studied literature, writing and French at university, completing a PhD. Her poetry nominations include the Pushcart Prize and several major Australian prizes. She has published a collection of poetry and her poems feature in journals in Australia, Europe and Japan. Inspired by her late brother, she creates work in his memory. She lives in Melbourne, Australia.

ORPHIA

AND

EURYDICIUS

ELYSE JOHN

HarperCollins*Publishers*

HarperCollins*Publishers*
Australia • Brazil • Canada • France • Germany • Holland • India
Italy • Japan • Mexico • New Zealand • Poland • Spain • Sweden
Switzerland • United Kingdom • United States of America

HarperCollins acknowledges the Traditional Custodians
of the land upon which we live and work, and pays respect
to Elders past and present.

First published in Australia in 2023
by HarperCollins*Publishers* Australia Pty Limited
Gadigal Country
Level 19, 201 Elizabeth Street, Sydney NSW 2000
ABN 36 009 913 517
harpercollins.com.au

A catalogue record for this book is available from the National Library of Australia

ISBN 978 1 4607 6304 9 (paperback)
ISBN 978 1 4607 1726 4 (ebook)
ISBN 978 1 4607 4802 2 (audiobook)

Cover design and illustration by Andrew Davis
Typeset in Plantin Std by Kirby Jones

For John –
every day
I wish I could bring you back

Someone will remember us,
I say,
even in another time

– Sappho

I sharpened my spear with poetry and hardened my arm with the memory of lyre strings. Each line grew in my mind with glimmering force, a shoot pushing out of loam, promising petal and seed. The goddesses surged through me as my sandals swept the dust.

I leapt and thrust. The raw passion of a couplet streamed into my spear-hand and coursed through my fingers until my skin sparked with words, and Demetrius tottered.

He flung the pieces of his broken shield to the ground and met my spear in a crunch of bicep, and as my invocation cooled within me, I felt the poetry ebb.

'I yield.'

Bitterness tinged his voice. Removing my helmet, I heard applause patter against my cheeks, not the deluge of clapping that followed the young men's victories but a trickle. I imagined the echoes of twining voices: the incantation of women weaving verse.

How long had I wanted to thread words? Twenty of my twenty-three years, perhaps? Or had I begun dreaming of poetry before I could speak, when my ears alone could yearn?

Men performed poems, of course. Men, everyone knew, were capable of creating the kinds of stories where striving, suffering and joy tussled in the breast of a hero – only men could sing of great deeds, my tutor said.

The scuff of leather against soil drew my gaze ahead. A pair of red sandals cut through the crowd, parting the watching youths.

'My prince,' I said.

The man before me folded his arms, waiting while I dropped to my knees.

'Rise, sun-girl. You love this, do you not? Jabbing at a different one of them each month.'

I said nothing.

'If you were a real warrior – fit to be a hero – you would challenge me, not pick at scraps. Or do you need your father to descend from the skies and protect you first?'

A murmur ran through the crowd. This was something different, something that could break the pattern of blow after blow, week after week.

'It is not the place of a warrior-in-training to challenge Prince Ixion,' I said.

'Yet you grip a man's spear and stride across my father's land, hefting your shield. You dare to compete in the tournament of the Whispering Isle.'

Scorn rang in Ixion's words. As I stood with my back straight, I considered the wisdom of silence. I recalled my father's declaration when he left me on the rocks of the island's southern tip: *One by one, you will beat the sons of the great men on this island. Only when you defeat the king's son with your spear may you sing farewell to these black rocks.*

Around me, the men picked up their weapons and began to trudge down the dusty path towards the palace.

I had long noted the way they left a gap between my elbow and theirs when we walked to the training field; how a bottle of wine might be passed around the table but never quite make its way to me during a festival dinner; how jokes would die on their lips when I entered a palace courtyard, giving way to murmurs. My father had told me that the Whispering Isle was named after the trees that rustled in the wind along the eastern shore, but I suspected otherwise.

Only one of the men would walk with me, and I heard his voice as I entered the palace grounds. He chewed an apple. 'For a girl who just won her twenty-sixth tournament, you don't look happy.'

'A full tablet of victories by day brings an empty bowl by night,' I said.

'Are we dealing in proverbs, now? Here's one I thought up. The sun only nourishes those who walk below it.'

'The sun can wither every living thing, as you well know.' I guessed why Jason had chosen to mention the sun, but I had no mind to speak of my father. Not now. I pretended to swipe the apple from Jason's hand, prompting a shove in return, and he laughed as we walked through the maze of the front garden. A hedge snaked around us, giving way here and there to small fountains, while vines draped the walls and rose-pink stone glowed in the afternoon light; from each angle, the garden announced its bright power.

Demetrius joined us outside the palace. 'The king sends for you, sun-girl.'

'Well, that is unfortunate.' Jason grinned at me. 'The bread has only just been baked, and the wine poured.'

'Save some for me, or I'll snatch your figs in the morning,' I said.

My jesting tone masked the drumbeat of my heart as I passed along the corridors. The chill of the stairwell seeped into me, a flame guttering atop a single torch, unable to spread its light to the corners. Two soldiers outside the throne room nodded; whether in greeting or out of habit, I could not say.

The stone felt cold, and dust smeared my greaves. I knelt for a long moment. When I looked up, the bronze dragons snarled with teeth bared, flanking the throne. Between the statues, King Dorus beckoned, his lips pressed into a line like the edge of a closed door.

'Your presence honours us, it seems, Lady Orphia.'

In the past month, I had not forgotten the iron in his voice.

'I am grateful to compete in the tournament, my king.' I cast my eyes down.

'I do not mean those petty monthly games.' He glanced towards a dim corner of the hall, and a figure stepped forward, shaking the shadows from its shoulders. It sparked and coruscated until Dorus shielded his gaze. My eyes adjusted first and I met our guest with an embrace, feeling the warmth of his skin.

'I wondered if the day would come when I could smile to look upon my daughter.' Apollo stepped back, his eyes raking my figure. 'You wield a spear well.'

'Fearsome enough for you?' I said.

He answered me with a show of teeth. A white blaze filled the throne room, driving the soldiers backwards.

I did not ask any of the questions I had stored for him. If I spoke on, I might risk showing my father how much I wished for his approval, or how much I wished to know why he had left me on this island – and I would sooner gnaw on rocks.

'You have kept your part of the bargain, Dorus. She fights powerfully,' Apollo said.

'I have tried, Lord Apollo, but I cannot see why you insist on training her. The spear is no tool for a young woman.' The king shifted on his throne.

'Let us ask my daughter what she thinks.' Apollo turned his face to me.

'I do not mind training.'

'And do you think it worth risking the ire of every lord on this island, as you throw their sons in the dust like hog carcasses?' Dorus said.

'I kill no one.' The words came out like stiffened twigs.

'Tell me what you like of my tournaments, child.' Apollo took my hand in his. I looked up into his face and saw the clean-shaven cheeks that so many poets had praised, and the laurel circlet, perched upon his head in place of a crown. Something about him radiated in a way that even burnished gold could not. I sought myself there, but saw nothing of my muscular form and nervous eyes, only a sharp grace beyond anything I could aspire to; a beauty that burned.

For a moment, I weighed the risk of inflaming Dorus' wrath, and I remembered how I had once walked past the eastern courtyard to find two washer-women scrubbing the stones.

Both had crouched naked. Their mouths had been bound in cloth.

A crowd of soldiers had watched them, pointing. The pair had spoken against the king, Jason had explained; it was not the only punishment for women who disagreed, either.

I knew what risk I would be taking, if I spoke.

Yet I could not bring myself to lie. I *did* like the tournaments, but not because of the clash of spear and shield. Just as I weighed Dorus' wrath, I weighed the pain of concealing my desire forever.

'Winning may purchase respect,' I said, 'but it is more gratifying to feel the rhythm of a fight in each breath, and in the skid of sandals. All manner of phrases throng in my head when I fight.'

'You sound more like a poet than a warrior,' Apollo said.

My fingers tightened around his palm.

I felt a sea-wind whipping through me, driving me to imagine women fighting off monsters, sailing under the stars on great quests, and searching for an equal love, full of kindness and passion alike.

Was it not natural for women to rail and rejoice on the scale of artists – to ache with the passion of heroes? If not, then why did I seek poetry? Why did I fly towards it like a bee seeking an open crocus?

'Perhaps I do sound like a poet.' My voice came out as little more than a whisper. 'Is it impossible to believe that your daughter could weave golden stories?'

'Listen to her. She grows drunk on victory,' Dorus said.

Apollo let go of my hand, regarding me. The hair on the back of my neck quivered. I felt him rummage through my memories, turning them over until he found the moments in the drinking-hall: the times I had snuck in, clad in a plain white chiton that draped to the ankles, disguised enough to sit up the back. He saw me waiting as the visiting poet took his place in front of the crowd. I felt him watch me as I leaned forward, listening to the lyre.

'I see what has happened here,' Apollo said softly. 'Note these words, my child. I do not repeat a command. You will no longer listen to poets who stop by the Whispering Isle. You will not study or practise poetry. You will not seek out a lyre.'

'But—'

'You will think nothing of music and verse.'

'Those are your gifts, Lord Apollo, are they not?' Dorus interjected. 'Strange, that they should be forbidden to her.'

The old man was not on my side, I knew. He merely wanted me to stop fighting in the tournaments. My father did not strike Dorus, however; his words echoed within me, like a spear tapping stone. *You will think nothing of music and verse.*

I tried to pretend I could accept them.

'There is much you do not understand, Dorus.' Apollo's gaze sharpened. 'Remember why your fields flourish. Remember why your orchards bear fruit and your cows yield milk, and why this island heaves with skilful washer-women. Remember the bargain we made.'

The look that passed between them quivered with things unsaid.

I knew better than to ask a question.

Could my father forbid me from dreaming of poetry? Surely, it was like forbidding an almond tree from flowering: the branches might stay bare in the winter, but come spring, the tree would do what was in its nature, and creation swelled in mine. I pictured women speaking in defiance; women holding up shields to sea serpents and dragons; women hoping and sighing and desiring, in stories ripe to become poems. Something stirred inside me, calling me to braid and entangle words.

My father's very aura seemed to burn. He reached out and cupped my jaw in his smooth fingers.

'Do not forget my orders.' He tilted my chin and smiled, and there was no mercy in it. 'The next time I see you, you will have defeated the king's son in combat.'

Gold lingered in the air after he vanished. It floated down to cover the stones with a myriad of tiny flecks. I watched it fall.

That which is repressed only swells and grows, like a barley stalk pushing through soil. Not a day passed when I did not think about poetry, and not a night passed when I did not wake from a dream of a sea battle or a tussle with a monster; the phrases I had heard in the drinking-hall metamorphosed into scenes in which a heroine rescued her beloved, or a goddess cast a spell upon a slavering chimera. Storytelling slipped over me like armour. I spent my days training with the spear and shield, talking with Jason in the gardens or climbing the rocks down by the ocean, looking out on the churning waves, yet at night, in the recesses of my mind, there pooled a spirit that refused to quieten.

All my life, I had listened to poems created by others. Although I knew the risk, the desire to weave my own stories thickened in me: I wanted to speak of women whose eyes blazed and lips flamed. I wanted to tell the world about artists whose voices led them to joy.

Demetrius did not challenge me again. The sons of the north coast took his place – brawny Lysippus, swift-footed Ariston, and Damon the smiling swordsman – and I beat them month by month, calling upon sparkling descriptions of Hera, Athena and Aphrodite, imagining the goddesses guiding my arm. The wives of the island remained shut up in their houses, and the washer-women were sworn to speak to no one but their masters, so the immortal women of Mt Olympus kept me company instead.

I was rising to my task, I told myself. By the time Apollo next graced the island, I would be warrior enough to take on the best-trained bully on the island. I would defeat Prince Ixion, and then I would call my father's name until he returned.

Perhaps, if I triumphed, he would heed my desire for poetry. Or perhaps he would melt my flesh until blackened bones dropped onto the dirt.

One morning, as I was practising with my spear beside the olive grove, Jason's voice carried from the path. My ears pricked up. Jason usually saved his company for times when food or wine was involved, or at the very least, when some maiden or pretty youth was visiting the palace and he might beg me to help him approach the guest.

'What is it?' I said.

'You'll want to see for yourself.'

The drinking-hall thronged with bodies. We elbowed our way through blue and white chitons to where the crowd thinned near the front of the hall, and I caught a glimpse of a figure in a hooded cloak. One of the lords moved in front of them, cutting off my view, but before I lost sight of the hooded figure, I saw an aulos in their hand, the instrument's holes exposed.

I stared at Jason.

'So what if you're forbidden from poetry?' He grinned. 'We don't often get a woman to sing.'

A woman. My eyes darted back to the cloaked guest. I thought of the quiet rage in my father's voice as he ordered me to avoid poetry. But this ... this was worth risking his fury, was it not?

Had I dreamed her into life, or had my imaginings of bold women always been true, like a blurry shape on the horizon that turns into a full storm cloud?

The crowd took seats upon the floor or propped themselves against the pillars. Ringlets tumbled from the visitor's hood – locks the colour of ripened wheat, framing a face with laughing eyes. Her gaze roved across the noblemen before falling upon me, and we held each other's stare for a long time.

'Do you think he knows?' Jason said, beside me. I did not need to ask who he meant. King Dorus had denounced travelling women as evil influences and banned them from his palace and grounds. Women who wandered the roads were whores and tricksters, Dorus said.

'Perhaps she is an exceptional musician.' As I spoke, the woman took off her cloak and laid it on the floor, and the crowd began to whisper. She glowed, but not in the way that my father did. Hers was not a searing aura but a reddening in the cheeks and a brightness to the skin, the health of a woman whose very gaze promised bounty.

Raising the aulos, she blew a few notes, the reedy sound transmuting into musical gold. The noblemen fell silent. She

played a melody that wound around my bones, lowering the
aulos' pipe when the last note petered out and letting her eyes
find mine.

'I grace the Whispering Isle with a tale of the Queen of
Heaven. Hear me, and you will be blessed to witness the might
of ox-eyed Hera, whose chariot sails through the skies, drawn
by peacocks. Feel the earth shake as she lands. See her crush
those who incur her wrath.'

Whispers ran through the hall. I felt my body fix itself to the
spot like a tree taking root. I could not move my legs, nor fold
my arms: I could not expend a moment's energy on anything
but her.

'Hear of Queen Hera's labour for our Greek soldiers.
Of her work to send the father of the gods to sleep, so that
we could fight the Trojans without his perilous meddling. Of
her efforts to frighten the river from harming great Achilles,
first of all warriors. Close your eyes, and let your soul be
charmed by my poem, abandoning the stone weight of your
cares.'

The men closed their eyes. Jason, too, and the other youths:
they followed her command. But I could not draw my gaze
from the visitor. Now, we stared at one another freely as she
set the aulos down, straightened her back, spread her arms and
began to recite her verses, her brown eyes still laughing and her
wheat-like hair fluttering around her face as if the very force of
her words made it move.

I needed to witness this. Not only her story, but her power.
I felt her poems reverberate within me. The Queen of Heaven
plummeted from the sky, the gem-bright blues and greens
of peacock feathers framing her, each bird opening its tail
in salute to the goddess, and I felt Hera's rage and joy; saw
Achilles surging onto the battlefield outside the gates of Troy;
smelled the burning ashes as the goddess scorched the ground

where the Trojan army stood. My heart swelled like a leather pouch that brims with wine.

As soon as the poet finished her verses, men clustered around her, and I strode from the hall. Jason called after me, but I did not stop. My feet flew down the corridors to my chamber, where I picked up a sack and slid out the instrument; it did not matter that I had scarcely played the lyre since I won it from a wool-trader's son, making him swear not to tell anyone. I knew that carved horseshoe of tortoise-shell with its arms reaching to meet the crossbar. I knew the strings that hung from that bar. I knew the sound they made when I ran a pick across them, humming and vibrating, their melodies gentle but quickening.

I was no longer satisfied with listening. After what I had just heard, I could not accept that only men could speak great poems. I would simply refuse to agree.

Words tumbled from my lips, and I did not know where I was, nor what I did, my mind directed by something I could not name, conjuring stories I seemed to have breathed into existence long ago. Perhaps I had carried them inside me during every fight. As I spoke, I strummed the lyre faster and faster, my pick drawing notes to match my images, and together the words and the music etched the poem into my memory. Surging ahead, I added another verse, and then another, composing as I thought, letting my mind blaze with scenes.

At last, I sank back in my chair in a kind of stupor, poring over the story I had coloured into life. A great romance between equals, a tragedy, and a quest to a grim and depthless place flared in my head. A woman surged through each obstacle, the hero of the story. Little errors appeared where I had rushed, constellations of poor phrases occasionally obscuring the better ones; there was no elegance, that was certain. This tale lacked the regal phrasing that the woman in the drinking-hall had employed, yet in forming this poem, I had imbued the women with rational thought, gifted the men with vulnerability, and conjured monsters of a strange and crag-sharp beauty ... I had created this story, where before there had been only a blank tablet of imagination.

In these lines, I perceived something of myself that had never been there in my spear-thrusts. Even in the most skilful of my leaps and blows, when I had pictured the goddesses and hoped for their strength, I had not felt this. It made my fingers tremble.

By the time I returned to the drinking-hall, no trace of poet, cloak or aulos remained. Jason told me that the visitor had looked him in the eyes and spoken of his father, Aeson, who she said was still imprisoned in a dungeon in Iolcus, gnawing on rat-bones and wasting away. She had told Jason that he would not create poetry, but would inspire poets – 'and that is better, would you not say?' Jason added.

I made a noncommittal grunt.

'She left before Prince Ixion could reach the drinking-hall,' Jason said. 'The guards said they lost her outside. They claimed she simply disappeared. Imagine that!'

Often, in the days that followed, I envisaged her striding out into the night, walking the paths of the island and vanishing where the cliffs dropped down to the ocean. I pictured her ringlets flying around her face as she slipped between the foaming mares.

All winter, I engraved poems in my mind and repeated them in my chamber. I practised in a low tone, half whispering. One day I looked up to find a washer-woman listening to me, her woollen garments tumbling from her hands as she gaped.

'Excuse me,' I said. 'I was recalling the words of a great man.'

She nodded, wiping tear-filled eyes. 'Let me help you,' I said, picking up the clothes. She retreated, but not before I glimpsed the mark on her wrist: a purplish splotch, dark and painful looking, like a stain.

I had seen bruises like that before. They bloomed on wives and daughters too.

As she scuttled away with the garments, she cast a look at me, like a pigeon's darting glance. I felt a warm surge of assurance that she would not tell on me.

The next day, I wrapped my lyre in a cloak of black wool and buried it inside the hollow of an old laurel tree in the grounds. I hoped that my father would not be tempted to look into the trunk. Training kept my thoughts away; I fought hand-to-hand with the young men and cleansed my scrapes and cuts each evening, enjoying the sight of the hair-fine scar on my thigh, and if the words I had written of love and defiance called to me, I pushed them down.

Summer brought sweat to our necks and herons to the skies, under a ripple of grey clouds. All through the palace hedges, tiny midges and mosquitoes flitted from leaf to leaf. I won two more fights, defeating a pair of eager contenders, but despite my victories, I could not sleep. Even when Jason saturated all the competitors with the wine he had stolen, I lay open-eyed, my mind heavy with thoughts of Hera and her peacock-driven chariot, and of all the women who might take up her lead: women whose stories I could speak into being.

That night, I recalled my poems and thought of the lyre encased in the laurel tree, smothered in thick cloth, still humming.

Zeno of the house of Theon bowed to me beside the black rocks, before the last tournament of the hot months. Meeting his gaze, I bowed back. Even Prince Ixion feared Zeno, for he had grown in stature and worked like a bull in the training yard – graceless, but steady – and the young men spoke of his prowess behind their cups. What was it that Jason had told me, last week? *Between Prince Ixion and Lady Orphia, the men say that there is only Zeno.*

I cleaned my greaves and honed my spear-tip. The crowd had already gathered when I reached the rocks, and the dusty patch of ground in the middle lay empty. The ring of youths seemed thicker than usual. We bowed again, Zeno looming over me.

Then it was underway. My muscles ached from the battering his spear gave my shield; he was heavier, but I pivoted and ducked, leapt and turned, until he shouted at me, a raw cry. When he nearly impaled me, I pretended to stumble in the dirt.

Similes and metaphors surged through my blood. I channelled all of my poetry: every phrase, every syllable, every rhythmic pulse of the goddesses' voices, and I prayed that it would be enough.

Zeno closed in. A moment later, he saw my spear's new path. The hard iron pierced his neck before he could twist away.

Blood flecked my nose and cheeks. Zeno gasped, his mouth opening and closing like a fish when it is pulled from the water. I felt all of the light leave me.

There was no jostling of shoulders as I walked home; no friendly congratulations as there would have been if Zeno had triumphed. In the great hall that night, King Dorus stood, raising his cup to me, and every man copied him. *Your first kill,* nobody needed to say.

I felt the weight of the moment, and I felt a dark liquid trickling through me, soaking into my skin and into the coldest places in my marrow. I sensed the stain, even though it hid.

As I took in the king's scowl, I wondered again what bargain Dorus had made with Apollo – why my father had left me on this outcrop of black stone, amongst gulls and spotted wolves.

Guards flanked Ixion as he swaggered into my chamber two days later, the door still rattling from his knock.

'This is it, truly? By Zeus, you must be frugal.'

'May I be of service to my prince?'

He drew closer to my bed. I did not move from where I perched on the corner, staring straight at him.

'Not so dangerous now, are you?'

His fingers brushed my cheek. They stroked their way down and traced along the line of my jaw, pressing into the bone, lingering on my lips. I had been the only unmarried girl living in Dorus' palace for all my twenty-three years, but it was easy to forget about my ripening body when no one dared to touch me. Under Ixion's falcon-eyed gaze, I became newly aware of my long black hair, and of my torso that, despite its muscle, did not belong to a son or a brother or an heir ... I could feel the shape of Ixion's thumb against my upper lip, icy and firm, as if it was draining the blood from me.

'Zeno was of a noble house. He deserved better than you.'

Guilt stirred in my chest. I wanted to declare that I had never wanted to fight. I wanted to explain that I did not want to be the person who killed Zeno – that I did not want to be a person who killed at all. Ixion removed his thumb and rubbed it on his wrist, smirking, as if he were wiping away a smudge of dirt.

'Perhaps he should not have challenged me, then,' I said.

Ixion stepped to the table and calmly swept his hand along its surface, sending pins and cups and bottles flying. I could have answered him with the dagger in my drawer. Instead, I watched him march out, aware of the golden clasp on his cloak.

All afternoon I paced in my chamber. Think of the goddesses, I told myself. I tried to picture the Muses who lived on Mt Parnassus and inspired artists, but they had been discussed so quickly by my tutor – their images were blurry in my mind, barely formed women standing on a distant peak. My thoughts slipped from Athena to Aphrodite to Artemis like a cat slipping through alleyways. Yet there was one goddess I had been drawn to my whole life, a goddess whose power animated and terrified by turns.

I had felt Hera's magic flowing from the words of the strange poet. Her wrath surged through my veins, pulsing with the force it had unleashed upon the Trojan army. Apollo had told me that he created me from marble – that I stemmed from no woman – yet in times like this, it was Hera, protector of all women, whose strength encouraged me.

I knew that I needed to speak poetry. If I did not, the energy inside me would burst free, and there would be blood on the palace stones – Ixion's, or mine.

The palace slept while I slipped through the corridors. Shadows crossed the floor between slices of torchlight, and when I passed through courtyards, my feet disappeared into the darkness. The guards on the front doors started as I approached.

'Why must the summer make it hard to sleep?' I said.

'True enough,' the man on the left remarked.

'I could believe all the air has been sucked from my chamber.'

'Stay close to the palace, Lady Orphia.' The men parted their spears.

I walked to the left and looped my path back around the walls, coming to where the laurel tree stood. The black woollen cloak felt soft to my touch. Only a fine coating of dust showed that it had waited months. I hesitated, glancing around, then clasped the bundle to my chest and padded out of the grounds, towards the smell of salt.

Dappled moonlight guided me to the shore. Beyond a tufting of scrub, bright red poppies pushed up between bone-like rock formations, giving way to a swathe of pebbles and then the ocean. I sat down on a rock. The emptiness of this place rolled over me, here, far from the black crags where we fought our tournaments. I remembered rumours that this beach was home to sea serpents in the summer, though I found no sign of scales.

Perhaps I had driven them away.

I gripped the lyre tighter. A breeze blew the scent of myrtos flowers to the rocks. The longer I sat, the more plants I could smell: sweet reeds, the mild notes of herbs and the fragrant waft of heliotrope mingling around me. Every one of them welcomed me.

Still I waited, the perfume thickening, until an orb rose over the water before me, transforming the waves into pure silver. 'Great Hera,' I said, softly, 'if you are there, give me this one moment. Let my father slumber on.'

I did not wait for her response. The cloak unwrapped easily and the lyre inside it lay unharmed, waiting only for my fingers to grasp it. The tortoiseshell shone too brightly for me to think, at first, under the pearlescent light of the moon, but after a moment I recalled my poems and began to strum.

Something landed on the instrument. It was a dragonfly, I realised. Its body glittered, a tiny sapphire sitting atop one string, before the creature took flight again. Lucky insect. If it had landed on the black rocks when the men were gathered, some laughing son of a noble house would have crushed it.

I put my finger to that same string and began to play. A picture came to me, painted by every phrase and simile, yet I needed to release it from my head. The moon poured its glow over the lyre, and the sound of the strings blended with the lapping of waves against pebbles.

'Tell me, Muse, of the terror of Helen, whom the gods, the titans, and even men abandoned, when a prince of Troy strode with blade unsheathed to her door. What darkness swaddled her, then? As a Trojan prow carved the waters, pulling her nearer to their shore, what faces did she perceive in the dance of torchlight? Did they shine like gorgons' teeth? Did they smell of crushed barley and broken grapes? Of figs split at the seam?'

How easy it was to continue, with my lyre in my hand and no one watching me. The strange visitor with her aulos and her diamond-sharp words had set my poetry flowing, but now, it turned into something distinct from her … under the sky's bright orb, with the perfume of flowers and herbs filling my lungs, it became part of my own being.

I was aware of my voice, too; the sound of it; its soft but steady rhythm, its dark honey timbre. Listening silently was the province of the past.

'Tell me of how Helen stoppered her fear, even while she smiled, and buried it in a place where men could not seize it.'

I did not look up from the lyre until I had spoken the last line. Something in the air had changed. A fresh smell permeated even the salty breeze. Soil, I realised.

Branches glimmered in the moonlight. On the slope leading down to the beach, an olive tree stood, dirt flung around the base of its trunk. Had it been there before? The longer I looked at it, the more certain I became that the soil was newly scattered.

Something brushed my arm. I looked down to find a flower nudging me, bright red petals swaying at the end of a stalk that had twisted towards me. It tapped my elbow again. Then a tap came at my other elbow, and all around me I saw poppies pushing themselves up between the rocks, curving their stalks in my direction.

My poem had done this. My story of a woman who was loathed and abused – a woman who had been carried off, yet never ceded her strength – had called soft plants to me.

Fear should have forced me to leave. Magic was the death of order, the bane of kings, the ruin of heroes. It was unnatural for mortals to try to create it. Our tutors had told us that since we could hold a spear: even mortals created by a god, like me, were not supposed to attempt the work of immortals.

Slowly, I raised my lyre again. 'Tell me, Muse,' I said, 'of the terror of Helen, whom the gods, the titans, and even men abandoned ...'

A rattle, not from behind me, but from before me. White pieces of stone whirled up and stopped, quivering in the air, a mosaic of pebbles hanging over the water. They were dancing, I realised.

'... when a prince of Troy strode with blade unsheathed to her door. What darkness swaddled her, then?'

The buzz of hundreds of wings cut me off as jewelled bodies mingled with the pebbles, the dragonflies darting and cavorting amongst them. A reedy sound followed. On my right, I saw dirt spray up as a spindly trunk and branches pushed through the earth, revealing a pine tree, and then another. A smile tugged my mouth upwards.

It should have been terrifying. The sight of stones and roots shaking off their constraints should have silenced me.

'As a Trojan prow carved the waters, pulling her nearer to their shore, what faces did she perceive in the dance of torchlight? Did they shine like gorgons' teeth?'

Somehow, I wanted to keep weaving the poem. I wanted desperately to tell Helen's story; to bring it alive in words that *did* enchant.

The dragonflies buzzed up into the air and the pebbles fell to the ground. The breeze built to a headwind, the violence of the gust forcing my body to tense. It buffeted me for a few seconds before turning back on itself and striking the ocean's surface. Water rose in a spout from the spot: a thick column, like one of the pillars of the palace at Mt Olympus that poets sang of; and before my eyes, the column split into smaller pieces, which reshaped themselves as horses, racing across the ocean and leaping towards me, evanescing as they reached the pebbles.

The sound of my laughter mingled with the foam.

'Is this why you forbid me poetry, father?' I asked.

It was a safe question. I knew that he could not hear me beneath the moonlight.

Amongst fresh bark and petals, surrounded by the fluttering of insects, I performed the first poem that I had spoken aloud in my chamber. Waves galloped towards me again, and blood-red blooms curled their stalks around me. Pine trees pushed through soil. The land reached to me, and I reached back, not with my hands, but with my words. I was not afraid – or so I told myself. The equal love between woman and man, the tragedy and the heroic quest swirled together on my tongue, binding the poem.

Leaving the rocks at the nearing of the dawn, I uttered another prayer to Hera.

That night I felt something thrumming within me, a strange rhythm, and I nourished it. It could stop boulders and silence nightingales' song even as it created. Darkness mingled with the rivers of golden words; I slept, to the chirps of crickets and the hoots of owls, and when the dawn broke, only a few leaves tangled in my hair reminded me of last night. Yet I could still feel the pine trunks rising, and with them, the possibility that I could raise things of grace from the hard ground.

Discovery is not always worsened by the discoverer. If it had been Jason who found me in the orchard, we might have laughed and wrestled, chapping our hands from our blows. If it had been another youth meandering amongst the peaches, we might have nodded and parted ways.

The tread that caused me to break off my recitation crunched over twigs. I scrambled to hide my lyre behind my back.

'Remember.' A man dragged a struggling woman into the orchard, pulling her by the arm. 'You're not permitted to squeal. Lord Apollo gave you to my father.'

'My prince—'

Ixion pushed the woman to the ground and she whimpered. I recognised the washer-woman who had heard me practising in my chamber. The bruise on her wrist stood out, dark and unmistakeable.

'Take your gown off,' Ixion said.

'My prince, I don't …'

'Don't what? My family owns you, woman. What will you say to that?'

I stepped out from behind a tree. 'You know very well that she cannot speak against you. Yet I can speak for her.'

The look Ixion turned on me was python venom, distilled into a glance.

'She exists like you or I, with thoughts and feelings and a voice. My father may pass women around like silent things, and so may you, but we are not silent in our souls. Our minds are often in conversation.' I looked at the woman and gestured to the palace. 'Go, my friend. Lady Orphia says you may return now.'

She slipped away from the orchard, keeping her head down. I faced Ixion, telling myself not to retreat; his look made it clear he was moments away from lashing out.

'I've seen her wrist,' I said. 'You've done more than drag her around, haven't you?' His silence was louder than a reply. 'How many times did she try to get away?'

Ixion gave a short bark of a laugh. 'And you're going to defend her?'

I made to stride past him, but he snatched the lyre from me, examined it, and threw it back with a smile. 'How do you think Lord Apollo will punish you for this? Your head on a spike? Poison dripped into your mouth? Perhaps he'll save his plague-tipped arrows for you – I hear he once fired them into a Theban encampment for fun.'

Tendrils of fear curled around my mind. There was no hope of beating him to Dorus and arguing my case; he was the swifter runner, and he knew it. His smirk told me there was little point in arguing with him.

'I challenge you to combat with spear and shield,' I said.

Silence filled the orchard. Even the birds ceased their song.

'Tomorrow, by the black rocks,' I added.

Ixion mustered a thin smile. 'If I win, you will speak nothing of today.'

'And if I win, you will not speak of *this* to anyone.' I tapped my lyre.

He hesitated for a moment, then nodded. 'There is no chance of that.'

When his last footfall had sounded in the orchard, a finch began to sing, its melody cheerful and swift. In my heart, a more sombre tune began.

All the way back to the palace I thought about what I had done, and the more I thought, the more fear encircled my mind. Most of all, I feared for the washer-woman – would Ixion rape her and strike her, because I had dared to intervene? To my shame, I also worried for myself. I had trained harder since my father's last visit, keeping Ixion's moves in mind while I wove and ducked with the other young men, but it was still not enough. I had grasped my first spear at eight, and Ixion had been trained by the best teachers on the island from the time he could walk. His armour was fashioned by the finest smith. His spear-head sang against any shield.

Perhaps I had another weapon.

Ever since the night I had slipped out of the palace grounds, I had been yearning to slip back to the beach and compose again.

Whispers followed me at dinner, and at breakfast, when Jason slumped into the chair beside me.

'Were you going to tell me?' he muttered.

'I did not wish to speak of it.'

'No one can speak of anything else. It's hard to tell who they'd prefer to lose.'

'If we trip and spear each other at the same time,' I said, 'we could please everyone.'

Two hours later, the youths smiled and chattered in their usual ring at the black rocks, munching on peaches and apples. A hush stole through the group. As I approached, a warm wind licked my heels.

I felt a swelling unease, and turned my thoughts to the visiting poet and her confident stance; to the projection of her voice, the crystalline transparency of every vowel. She would not fear this.

'Ready, piglet?' Ixion said. 'Ready to be crushed?'

'You sound so cheerful about fighting me. Almost as if you love beating women.'

Ixion shot me a glance that seethed with entitled fury, then turned his back. Casually, he removed his helmet and threw it into the crowd, where a youth caught it and grinned. I had no choice but to do the same. The fight would be ruled unequal if we did not wear the same protection, and if I asked the prince to don his helmet, I would look weak. He was counting on my compliance.

Slowly, I lifted my spear. Doubt gripped my mind in the spreading silence. I waited for Ixion to face me again, and at last he began to prowl around me, drawing an invisible ring with his feet.

I stepped towards him and he darted back. We danced a while in this manner, the young men jostling, pointing at us, no doubt comparing our moves. The first thrust came at my jaw. The point of the prince's spear stabbed within a half-inch of my face, and I jumped sideways.

Ixion smirked, just as he had in the orchard. 'Where is your spirit, sun-girl? Aren't you tasked with conquering every one of us? Knocking us on our manly arses?'

I made to thrust, but he was already leaping out of the path of my spear, knocking me with the butt-end of his own as he evaded me. Laughter streamed from the men.

'Did your father not show you how to triumph over a *real* opponent?'

There was no way I could keep up with his pace. I ceased my efforts to match his manoeuvres and waited until he came within my radius – weighting my move with all of my arm's momentum, I swung, landing my fist on his cheekbone. The hard resistance told me I had aimed true. With a low sound that was almost a snarl, Ixion thrust faster.

I felt the warmth of a few drops of blood on my neck. This should be the moment to swing back, but again, I waited, and when he drew near I struck him with the butt-end of my spear. I saw him stumble, clutching his jaw.

His speed, his superior training, his lithe moves, against my muscle and judgement: together we might dance this way for hours. Perhaps I would even land enough blows to lay him in the dust, and my father would descend, scattering gold in his wake, to bestow one of his hard-edged smiles upon me. *Would it be worth it?* I asked myself, dodging another of Ixion's jabs.

I had been raised to ask *how* I could beat the king's son. I had never been taught to ask *why* this task was allotted to me.

My father could have trained me in the art of poetry, but he forced me to fight. I did not wish to let a spear speak on my behalf any more. Apollo and Ixion might try to silence me, but I felt a powerful urge to let words flow: sweet words, sharp words, curious and questing words. For a long time, roots had curled inside me, folding back upon themselves; now they were beginning to push outwards, seeking new soil.

Ixion's nostrils flared. I read his face and found other signs of rage. An understanding came upon me: this, I could use. I punched and ducked. 'Tell me, my prince, are you strong?'

'Stronger than you.' He swung hard, and my feint made him overstep, teetering.

'How can you be sure? What is strength, according to you?'

'Fight me. Don't prattle like a damned philosopher.'

'But to fight, one must understand the source of strength. It is not a strong arm, nor fine armour.' I sidestepped his spear. 'Nor a sharpened point.' He leapt again, but missed, his thrust too quick. 'You like to use brutish strength against women; surely, you wish to know where real strength comes from.'

'Where?' he snapped.

This time, I did not need to peruse the scenes in my mind, for the words burst forth. 'It is that which is born of curiosity, which seeks to discover the queer, fragrant things of the world, and to create. It flows like a river, not from the hills, but from somewhere inside you. In its softness it can move the hard peaks of granite and the deep-rooted trees of the forest. You cannot rein it in, any more than you can stop your own blood.'

As I spoke, I felt the land listening. Beneath my feet, a tremor began, specks of dirt rising to swirl around my ankles.

Ixion's eyes found mine. Somewhere in the middle of my speech, he had stopped thrusting. Now, seeing the dust resettle itself, he laughed. 'What could Orphia – of no real house – know of strength?'

'I know the woman you abused is stronger than you will ever be.'

'Piglet.' He spat at my feet. 'Raise your spear.'

The command vibrated with anger. I let it reach me, absorbing its virulence. It pooled within me, in the same place that poetry sprang from, and I began to speak. I told of Ixion's jealousy as he watched me defeat the other young men, and his anger as I confronted him in the orchard: the words spun forth in golden rivulets, weaving a pattern so delicate he could not see he was ensnared. He poured his fury at me, and I bound him with it.

'Witness the strength of poetry,' I said, 'and behold what Orphia of no real house can work in this world.'

I raised my hands. It was easier, now, with the knowledge that I could bend the earth. Dust sprayed the faces around me and shot up into the air, showering Ixion. He coughed. The geyser of dirt collapsed and he shouted something, but a rumble cut him off. The soil shifted, tiny green stalks pushing through its surface, and one of the youths whimpered as a stalk pierced the sole of his sandal. I looked around. Hundreds of plants thrust up, hungry for air.

And for flesh. The thought came to me untempered, and somewhere, a scream sounded.

All the while, I felt Ixion's anger and resentment, and I mixed it with the golden rivers of my poetry and let it flow out. Roots and stems welcomed my voice, and soil parted.

When the plants stopped growing, I saw that the men were staring at me.

A moment later, a crack rang out. The black rocks seemed to freeze in the air as they split – and when they fell, it was quicker than even I had thought possible. My words sent the rocks rolling. More screams followed, from those not able to evade the tumbling stone, and I tried to steer the debris away from them. I glimpsed Ixion staggering towards me.

'Sorcery won't save you now. Ready your spear, piglet,' he shouted.

I do not know exactly what I said. I remember calling out in silent prayer to the goddess whose power I had always sensed, and feeling the might of Hera flowing through me in a torrent, the words silver and rich. I remember moving towards Ixion as I spoke, bearing down upon his sneering form as if Hera worked through me.

The line that separated him from me seemed to dissolve like salt in water, and a raw, pulsating force flew from me, until he flinched and stumbled, falling to his knees amongst the shards. For the first time, I noticed Jason listening with his mouth open, twin streams trickling down his cheeks.

'You cannot win,' Ixion shouted. 'My father will not allow it.'

'It was never my desire to win or lose.' Using the force of my words, I twisted the jagged end of a stalk upward, into his heel. 'But since you threatened me, I choose to fight as myself, for all the women washing and cleaning and scrubbing – for all the women silenced on this island. I have a tongue. I have a voice. Even your father cannot take that from me.'

I left him there, pierced through the skin, writhing. As I walked away, I turned back to glance at the cliff. A gap had opened in the rock, and I could see the ocean below, stretching out in a gilded infinity. The breadth of it stole the air from my lungs.

Voices dipped and rose beyond the door. When it opened at last, I jumped up from the stone floor to see my father's aura blazing, filling the frame.

'We will be another hour, child. Take a walk to divert yourself.' His words were leaping flames. The soldiers at the door shifted away from him, avoiding his eyes.

I thought of speaking up, then: telling him that I had only come to blows with Ixion because I had defended a woman. But Apollo had given the washer-women to Dorus as a gift.

A gift could not refuse to be used.

The dining hall fell silent when I entered. Hands fell from mouths, and grapes dropped onto plates. No eye found mine. I hurried out again and walked until I reached a courtyard; here, a few men stood in a cluster, and all refrained from greeting me. I turned my gaze down and walked on.

The old laurel threw shadows over me as I slumped beneath it, and my tutor's stories welled up in my head: Glaucus, the son of a king, crashing his chariot after he had insulted Aphrodite, his horses turning on him and devouring his body; Pentheus, ruler of Thebes, torn limb from limb, his head ripped off by his own mother, after he had dared imprison the god Dionysus. I recalled the tale of the weaver Arachne, who had tried to hang herself after boasting that her craftwork was better than Athena's, before being transformed into a spider by the goddess. This was what it meant to cross an immortal: death, or something worse. And while men became tragedies, women became examples.

I had heard my opponents talk of a woman called Niobe who had claimed to be more important than the titaness Leto; while she had seven daughters and seven sons, Leto only had Apollo and Artemis, she gloated: one of each. Niobe's boasts carried to Mt Olympus, reaching the immortals. The next day, she found her children stabbed to death, and in her grief, she ran to a nearby mountain and transformed into stone. Sometimes, one of the men said, Niobe still cried. When melted ice ran down from the summit of the mountain, her tears were flowing.

Awe and relish had mingled in the speaker's voice, and I had leaned in to learn who had inflicted such a punishment.

Apollo, the man had said, dropping his voice as he spoke the name. The great lord Apollo, god of the sun and raven, of medicine and the plague, who can enchant with his lyre: he killed Niobe's sons and daughters one by one.

Remember the bargain we made, my father had told Dorus.

I had made an agreement with Apollo, too. I had promised not to study or practise poetry, not even to think of music and verse; and I had let the stories flow through me all the same, without a thought of Niobe and her horrible fate. The thrill of expressing myself had driven me into fresh imaginings, until I could not see the risk I took. Yet I thought of the pebbles quivering in the air above the galloping horses of the waves, of the black rocks splitting and the shoots thrusting up through the soil, and I did not regret it, not even now.

The courtyard was empty when I returned, leaving the way clear to the small fountain in the corner, and I drank and washed my face. When I turned, Jason was approaching, leading a man I had not seen before.

Jason slapped me on the shoulder. 'They'll never forget today.' His eyes were no longer shining, and only the slight redness in his cheeks told me he knew I had seen his tears. He smiled at me, the way only Jason could smile, full of honey and hemlock at once, while the man beside him bowed. Neither of them recoiled from me – that was something, at least.

'I suppose the prince is angry,' I said.

'Never mind Ixion.' Jason smirked. 'He can smoulder in private. If you're looking for a distraction, try Eurydicius. He arrived a few weeks ago.'

His companion gazed at me. His eyes had not lifted from my face since Jason greeted me, and now I saw them flick over my hair and down to my arms, taking in the curves of my biceps before returning to my face and lingering on my frown, with neither fear nor disgust but something entirely new. What was it that the poets had called the regard of the sculptor Pygmalion when he had become entranced with his statue Galatea? *Veneration.* But Eurydicius was not looking at me purely with worshipful desire ... it was something more than that.

I took in his slender figure, the soft blonde strands that fell across his brow and framed his face with thick locks, and the brightness of his golden irises, which seemed to radiate a queer light. Something about his manner gave me pause.

'Lady Orphia,' he said. 'Jason has told me much of your prowess with the spear.'

'Eurydicius, was it?'

'Yes; though you would not have heard of my house unless you follow the deeds of cattle-raisers.' He gave a gentle laugh. 'My father sent me here to win the patronage of King Dorus.

I make shields, you see, to keep warriors safe. They may not be so fine as the deeds of princes, but my inventions have brought us some little gold and grain.'

The brightness in those eyes did not only come from the colour, I realised. His gaze did not dip out of fear; nor did he study me as a portrait to be gossiped of later, over cups of wine. His expression smoothed out his countenance, while he watched me without advancing.

What I was looking at, I realised, was a man who appreciated my manner. The desire in his eyes mingled with awe and something surprisingly soft.

Respect. That was the word.

He was looking at me the way men looked at famous men, even though it was quite obvious that I was a woman.

'I should like to hear more of your craft,' I said.

'Watch her,' Jason said. 'She is the daughter of a god. You should be afraid, Eurydicius. She can split boulders with her words. She could probably split you in two.'

Eurydicius smiled. It softened his features further. I could see no puffing-out of his chest, no hint of a swagger. My legs felt a little off balance as I shifted on the spot.

Jason excused himself, claiming that he needed to meet his tutor. The warm breeze of the mid-afternoon gusted through the courtyard, and behind us, the fountain tinkled.

'If I may ask, Lady Orphia ...' Eurydicius began.

'You may.'

'Is it true that you use your poetry to do magic?'

'Use it? No. Poetry is not a thing to be used. But I am no longer afraid to say that I compose verses and dare to speak them aloud.'

'I have no right to ask ... but could I hear a poem?'

His voice came softly, as a stream in a forest glade. It touched me with the lightest of splashes, each word a droplet leaping. Such a stream lived under the shade of a canopy, but it would be silvered by a little sun, its beauty declared even in dappled light.

'One of my poems?' I said.

Eurydicius nodded. Even his nod seemed gentle, as if he could not do anything with the roughness of a warrior, missing that fear of ignominy which led men to challenge each other. Something about his manner made my stomach swirl, though I could not say why.

It would be a risk to recite a poem while my father and Dorus were still deciding my punishment ... but I could feel a flush in my cheeks as Eurydicius looked at me. I could not very well run to my chamber for the lyre, so I called up the rivers of golden words inside me, summoning the kind of poem I most liked to create: one where the women were bold, intelligent, curious, and not at all as the world expected them to be.

'Tell me, Muse, of Pandora: the woman forged by the smith-god Hephaestus on Zeus' command, sent into the world with a jar. Her fingers itched to touch the lid.'

Her spirit flowed through me, honey-rich and inquisitive, questing. Phrases rushed swifter and swifter through my veins.

'Ailments, death, and despair: Zeus had dropped these, one by one, into the narrow mouth of that clay jar. He whispered a spell and sprinkled venom over his creations. O, Muse, how little did Pandora know! When her eager fingers pulled the lid off and loosed a host of ills upon the world, she blamed herself – she never guessed that Zeus had designed those cruelties well before he made her, and realised that he lacked a woman to blame.' I paused, letting the silence punctuate my story. 'Yet as Pandora cried over the jar, one of her tears fell on the last evil at the bottom of the baked clay. Her compassion transformed it into a soft and radiant power, streaming out. The darkest atrocity became hope.'

Exhaling after the verses had ended, I watched Eurydicius. The breeze had tangled a few strands of his hair and the tress dangled in the breeze, maiden-like, though he did not seem to notice. His golden eyes focused only on me.

'Well?' I said. 'Will it do?'

He seemed to struggle with words.

'You may tell me if it is not to your taste. Bad wine should not be praised.'

'It is a nectar beyond any I have ever drunk.' His voice had thickened. 'In truth, Lady Orphia, I was excited to hear your poetry – I had heard gossip of your talent, and I longed to hear an artist speak shining words. But I was not ready for the boldness of your speech. Pandora stands before me; I see her, I understand her as I never did before. I feel as if I have listened to a goddess perform.'

'Boldness.' I smiled. 'Is that an insult of the veiled kind?'

'It is the greatest compliment I can think of, for a poet. You weave words so audaciously that they echo and reverberate, like a song made of gold.'

I had not meant to take his hand, but something about his look encouraged me, and I seized it, kissing the back of his palm. It was his turn to flush, and yet he did not approach me. He wanted to be kissed, I realised. He did not desire to lead.

That made my stomach swirl even more rapidly.

Behind him, I saw one of Dorus' soldiers enter the courtyard.

'Pleasant to meet you, Eurydicius,' I said. 'Since we may never meet again, good luck with plying your shields.'

I left him with a little smile and walked over to the guard, refusing to let my gaze linger.

3

There comes a place in any maze where the path twists away from the light: where you can either turn back or advance to where the glow may not accompany you. I found myself in such a place when Dorus' door opened. A bloodied face appeared, blocking my way. The shards of rock had scratched deeply and Ixion's right cheek made a map of red lines, drawn by magic.

'Come to gloat?' Ixion said.

'My child,' Apollo said, before I could reply, 'Prince Ixion has been telling me of your fight this morning.'

So that was what the promises of princes were worth. There was no chance that he had omitted the part where I spoke poetry, shattering rock and twisting plants through the soil. My father had never glowed with such anger, and I thought that my skin might blister and peel from my body; maybe Niobe's children had felt this heat when they woke in their beds to find him clutching a dagger, looming over them.

'When I sculpted you from marble and breathed life into you, I knew you would be like this.' A diamond edge sharpened my father's stare. 'Part mortal. Let it not concern me, I told myself, because half-breeds are obedient. They know to defer to a god's power. I gave you a place to live, away from the world; a place of safety; a place to train and grow. And you have rewarded me with rebellion.'

'I only wished—'

'Did you think because you hid your lyre in a laurel, I would not see it?' He laughed, and that too was like diamonds, hard and exquisite. 'Laurel is *my* tree. It answers to me alone.'

It is one thing to be betrayed by a prince. It is quite another to be betrayed by wood and leaf. Yet the anger I felt for the laurel faded as I looked at my father, thinking of all the times I had disguised myself in a cloak while creeping into the drinking-hall. I thought of the poems I had remembered and kept hidden from Apollo's view, a norm that I had allowed myself to accept.

How long did it take before concealment became a part of your very being?

'If I rebel,' I said, 'it is because you hold me down. The spear, the shield, the armour: they are all chains. I am bound to this island and this king.'

'I give you the opportunity to be the best warrior of your generation – a new Achilles. And yet you ask to be a poet. Do you think so little of what gods may know? Of prophecy?'

'Prophecy?' I felt something ripple out from that word, like the kind of wave that warns a storm is coming. A look passed over Apollo's face; one I could not quite read. It soon melted away.

'Never mind that. A father owes no reason to his daughter. He tells her the law, and she obeys.'

'I did not ask for poetry. It came to me, through you.' My face was hot, and not only because he was nearby. 'If the god of poetry and music breathed life into me, he cannot be surprised that I move stones when I speak.'

He did not reply for a moment. Something shifted at our side. I had forgotten that Ixion and Dorus were standing there, and I glanced over to see Ixion's mouth hanging open; in my father's glow, his skin shone with sweat.

'The poetry comes unbidden, then?' Apollo spoke softly.

I nodded.

'Like golden rivers within you, mingling with darker waters?'

How had he known? It did not matter; I nodded again. 'Sometimes, it becomes a torrent, and I cannot hold back the flow,' I said.

He did not speak aloud, but I heard his reply all the same, quietly calm in my head. *Show me.* How easy he made it sound, for me to cast aside his rebuke and call up elegant phrases, as if nothing had passed between us.

Sifting through poems, I dedicated myself to the task, aware that my future dangled upon the outcome. I settled on the story of Pandora that I had just told to Eurydicius, for it seemed important to show him not only how I spoke, but the stories that drove me. I repeated the lines slowly, bringing the story into the world with rhythm and sound, letting my voice rise and fall with each verse. Myrtos flowers climbed through the open window and shot towards me on their soft stalks. They lengthened and trembled, but I kept my gaze fixed upon my father until I felt a tap at my elbow. I looked down to see pure white petals dancing against my arm.

Apollo stared at me as if I were a marketplace statue, newly painted in bright colours.

'I will consider what to do with you, my child.'

'Forgive me, lord Apollo, but this is no matter for consideration.' Dorus' voice was full of splinters. 'In working sorcery upon my son, your daughter has dishonoured her hosts.'

Again, I heard my father's voice in my head. *And what of these shattering rocks? Are you to blame for the prince's scars?*

'I did not intend to hurt anyone.' It only clicked into place as I spoke. Living a truth was different from stepping back and identifying it. 'The world around me ... it responds to me, if I mean it to or not. Magic flows through my poetry, and whether I speak my verses aloud or in my heart, I am called to words and their music. It is as if the gods have made me a painter, favoured to reimagine their scenes. Yet it is not an accident of fate. The desire of my heart and my mind entwine in every word I speak; I choose to be a poet, father. And not only for myself.'

'For who, then?'

'For all the women who cannot speak freely upon this sun-touched earth.'

Apollo paced for a moment. As he turned his gaze to me, I could feel him delving into my mind, ruffling my memories for a moment before withdrawing. Dorus stepped towards him, halting when he came too close to the heat.

'Lady Orphia, you will take your belongings and remove yourself from the Whispering Isle,' the king declared. 'Your time here has ended. Whatever gifts and tributes must be made to your father, I will raise them.' He turned to Apollo. 'She will not ensorcell these halls.'

Ixion made a satisfied noise. I was not looking at him. My gaze sought only my father's beardless face: that smooth skin, like the gold of a fine chalice, and the eyes that seemed so soulful at rest but moved dangerously, threatening to pierce you. All my father's heat turned on Dorus. There was a difference between frustration and fury, and now I knew which had been directed at me – and for the first time in my life, I pitied Dorus.

'Tell me, mortal. Tell me how you have appraised the conditions of your wealth. Do you think so little of the young warriors I bade journey here to train with your son? Of the fame I have brought to your isle? How about the fat cows in the pastures, the women I sent to perform your chores, and the figs and barley I persuaded Demeter to bless you with?' Apollo laughed, and that sound was sharper than chastisement. 'Do you take so lightly the fact that no curse has ever touched these black rocks – no spell ravaged them?'

'There is magic aplenty, now, it seems.' Dorus shot a glance at me.

'All these riches I lavished upon you, and you needed only to fulfil your side of the bargain: see that my daughter trains and keep her safe. Such a small price for what you have reaped; but you have grown tired of paying it, I see.'

Keep me safe from what? I thought.

Apollo rose a few feet into the air and hovered, looking down at Dorus. The force of his presence struck me in the chest, as it must have struck the others, invisibly crushing our ribs. It seemed that the king would remain still, his stare locked on Apollo. At last, though, something in Dorus seemed to buckle.

Before he could speak, Ixion interjected. 'I will not tolerate her sorcery, father.'

He took hold of Dorus' wrist and pulled the two of them together. The rage in his eyes thickened. Slowly, Dorus nodded. 'My son will have his recompense. A future king of the Whispering Isle will not bear dishonour.'

'Very well,' Apollo said. 'I grant your wish.'

A gust of wind slammed into the wall outside, rushed through the window and scattered the petals, leaving the flower-heads bare. The air swirled around us, building until it formed a spiral. I thought of whirlpools in the sea, of the monster Charybdis bringing hundreds of sailors to their deaths. All the while, I struggled to keep my footing.

'You no longer have charge of my daughter,' Apollo said. 'And I lift my protection from this isle.'

The spiral of air raced to Ixion and struck him in the back. He cried out and pushed against it. A twig might as soon have pushed against a hurricane – the wind picked him up, carried him through the window, and flung him into the sky, where he vanished into a cloud's dark heart.

Dorus whimpered. I could not speak, the breath eddying in my lungs.

'You should be proud, Dorus. His fame will live eternally,' Apollo said.

The king choked out a cry, clutching his throne.

Apollo watched him with a smile. He seemed to know that Dorus would not find words. 'Prince Ixion will be bound to a fiery wheel that is always spinning,' he added. 'That will be recompense. Remember your son's face, for you will not look upon it in this life or the next.'

My father beckoned to me, and made a clicking noise with his tongue. 'Come, my child.'

I knew that it was not a request.

I looked for anger in my father's face – for the desire to lash out at me, to punish me for betraying his orders – and I found nothing of the sort. That made me more worried than if I had glimpsed a spark of fury.

Gathering my strength, I willed myself to follow him. In the doorway I looked back and saw Dorus clutching the throne, staring at the open window through which Ixion had disappeared; he did not seem to see us. White petals covered the stones around his feet, and the light that filtered into the room tinged him with a pinkish glow, like a sunset's departure.

The palace dropped away, the rooves of its buildings diminishing into an artist's sketch, too small even for a painting. As we rose into the bright air, I thought of the lyre that I had been forced to leave behind, and of my chamber, bare but familiar; the firm bed that I had lain on only this morning, my clothes still folded upon it. I thought of Jason, chewing a peach somewhere in the palace grounds, never to see me again or laugh at my victories, never to sprinkle snide remarks into his congratulations as he had been wont to do. And I thought of the soft way that Eurydicius had asked to hear one of my poems, and the smile he had bestowed upon me, yielding like his voice, a dissolving wave. Still we rose. The island that had been my entire world now reduced to a miniature, whittled from black stone and floating in an expanse of sparkling water.

It was hard to tell how my father's magic worked. Perhaps that was the nature of it. I did not speak until we neared the clouds.

'Prince Ixion mentioned a story about you, once.' I glanced at Apollo. 'It involved you firing plague-tipped arrows—'

'Into a Theban camp, and watching the disease spread?'

He held my gaze. Nausea nested in the pit of my stomach; there had been no surprise in that reply. So Ixion was really bound to a flaming wheel, then.

My father only smiled as we broke the layer of cloud. His aura flared around him, undimmed by the sun.

We passed into the white swirls, and in the second before it disappeared from view, I caught a glimpse of the island, glowing brighter than the coals in a royal fireplace. Tongues of orange flame danced on every tree, flower and building.

'Father!' I shouted.

'Wisdom means knowing when to be silent, my child.'

'You cannot do this! Not to Jason! And those women – those women did nothing but labour for their masters!'

'If you wish to survive where I am taking you, then you must learn one thing. There are no limits to what a god can do.'

In his voice, I heard anger, at last.

I stared down. The black rocks blazed brighter than the palace. The sight of it hit me in the chest, for every part of my childhood was turning to smoke: even the laurel tree would be dead, soon. My pulse stuttered in my neck.

'Do not gaze for long. We are headed to where pain is memory, and memory weighs less than an ivy leaf.' My father's voice simmered.

I closed my eyes. I imagined Jason's face melting into a slurry of flesh and bone. I pictured the washer-women screaming as they died. I tried to imagine Eurydicius diving into the sea, a sheaf of blonde hair disappearing into the water before the island ignited, fleeing a bonfire of beautiful and painful things. Air struck my cheeks and the scent of cinders whirled around me until the miasma thinned and cleared.

When I opened my eyes, I saw only white light.

How can one describe orchards and fountains and blooms that enchant with their very presence, daubed in colours that are not of this world? It is a hard task to put words to the sight that confronted me. Plums, peaches, apricots, figs, and fruits that I did not recognise surrounded me – shockingly green ovals with spiked cases and star-shaped silver objects dangled from branches – vines sparkled, their leaves shimmering in shades of iridescent purple.

My sandals touched soil, but a ball of pain filled my stomach before I could orient myself. I wanted to cry, yet I could only open my mouth in silence, trying to purge the thought of what had happened, as images of the washer-women, of Jason, of everyone who had shown me a little kindness on the Whispering Isle visited me again. I saw each person blazing until their bones alone survived, and those too were blackened, charred.

My body quivered, as if my frame could not withstand this agony.

My father's grip propelled me along the path, hard and unyielding. The route wound onward in a series of curves, hedges unfolding in patterns to our right, dotted with sculptures and fountains that gleamed. Every so often, a stone arch rose amidst the fruits and flowers, and far from breaking the harmony of the garden, these monuments only sweetened it.

I could not accept such beauty without thinking of the place I had just left. The memory of the burning island refused to fade, and the thought of Eurydicius diving into the water lingered in my mind, sharpening.

As I followed my father over this new summit, unease shadowed me. A lioness cleaned her paws under one arch and a peacock fanned its tail out beneath another, fixing its black eyes upon my face. I stumbled, treading on a flower that gave off a puff of glittering gold dust. Drawing a deep lungful of air, I discerned a scent so delicate that it was a note between notes, something so fine that it could barely be sensed; many of these half-notes and quarter-notes of blossoms reached me together, and the whole garden grew into a song, repeating in new iterations.

'Mt Olympus,' I said.

My father glanced at me, his gaze as hard as his grip. 'You are a visitor, only.'

Light struck the buildings on the horizon. I raised my eyes, taking in the swirls of colour in the walls, finding myself unable to say more. The contrast with the sight of my former life burning chafed; it was impossible to ignore the stillness, the heavy layer of peace that hung here.

I thought of bones amongst the black rocks, of chitons turned to ash.

My father moved at a pace that left me no time to contemplate. We reached the nearest wall and I reached out to stroke one of the rainbows within the stone.

'We do not announce our presence, child.'

He yanked my arm away. On his command, I closed my eyes. I felt a rush of air, and the soft thump of my feet landing somewhere new.

'Follow me quickly, and do not speak.'

My head throbbed and my vision seemed to wobble. Somehow, I was supposed to accept the fact that we had passed through a solid wall. Apollo pulled me forward, grumbling.

Time slowed inside the palatial walls, and even as we ran, I drank in my surroundings. In one courtyard lights floated at different heights, radiating a whiteness that set my skin tingling. Waterfalls poured in gardens just beyond open windows; flowers in pots bloomed, blackened, turned to ash, and regrew. Through one door, I glimpsed a hall of glass, its floor luminescent with every colour, rainbows refracting off the panes of the ceiling and bathing the stone tablets stacked on the shelves. There was something wonderful about all those engraved messages lying uncovered, ready for viewing.

Anger rippled through me, for Apollo seemed only to be concerned with yanking me past each wonder. When I slowed to admire a crowd of people in robes standing around a fountain, he shot me a murderous look. 'I told you to follow me.'

I could hardly be blamed if the palace of Mt Olympus brimmed with magic. Still more astonishing was the fact that magic could be performed in the open, for all to appreciate; yet my father did not slow to admire it.

He stopped at last outside what appeared to be a brass door, though I could see no ring or knob. When he pressed his hand to the surface, the door swung back, opening just long enough to admit us to an antechamber. On the single table inside, jugs sparkled, and a youth sitting behind it eyed us over his cup.

I made out the image of a pair of athletes wrestling on the cup's side, their bodies entwined.

'You were not invited.' The young man rose in a fluid movement and folded his arms.

'Polite as always, I see, Ganymede.' My father rested his hands on the table's edge. 'One day someone will teach you a lesson and save us all the trouble. I need no appointment to see him, as you know.'

Our greeter stepped around the table, coming close enough to peruse my features. He wrinkled his nose as he surveyed me from top to toe, and while he did, I took the chance to stare at him, too, for I had never seen such a man, with honeyed skin and hands that moved like a painter's; all the same grace of bearing as a man I had seen recently, but none of the same reticence. Where Eurydicius had been soft in manner, gentle in his words and his silences, this Ganymede was a honed blade beneath silk.

'How curious. A mortal offshoot of a god.' He laughed, the sound tinkling. 'Did you fashion him a new species, as a gift?'

'Lower your voice,' my father snapped. 'No one here has seen her, yet.'

Ganymede approached us, still clutching the cup, blocking our path to the doors on the far side of the chamber.

'You know why I am here,' my father said.

'He would prefer not to be disturbed.'

'You may know my father's body like a well-drawn map, and I've no doubt he maps yours nightly, but I'm certain he does not share his mind with you.' Apollo smiled.

'And how well do you know his mind, lately?'

'Stand aside, Ganymede.'

They faced each other for a moment. Apollo did not appear to move, but Ganymede's pretty face twisted as he yelped and dropped the cup. It had begun to melt: I saw the painted scene disfigured as liquid dripped down from the rim, and by the look of agony on Ganymede's countenance, he was not immune to my father's heat. He glared in Apollo's direction as he stepped aside.

I had scarcely time to take in the peacock carved into the door on the left before my father pressed his palm to the other door. He touched the carving of a bull with curving horns, linking his elbow with mine. Air swirled around us and a force sucked us through the wall, sending my vision wobbling.

This garden was not like the one that we had first landed in, that blend of sweet light and melody and fragrance. I shivered, clutching my upper arms. There was something primal in the vines and thorns that surrounded us, the gnarled oaks, the pale petals that littered the soil like chips of bone: something that drew me on, even as I wanted to leave. We walked together onto the narrow path.

'Do not touch anything.' Apollo spoke loudly. The further we delved, the denser the garden seemed, except for a small clearing where a thin tree rose, its roots spidering over the ground. Its bark looked stiff and blackened. I thought of a tree on the Whispering Isle that had been struck by lightning, killed in an instant and yet forever standing.

'My child.'

I wanted to reach out with a finger and stroke it.

'My child. Look at me.'

But I could only look at the charred branches. My hand extended towards the tree, and if Apollo had not wrenched me backwards, who can say what might have happened?

'Mortals who enter this place usually succumb to its power. But I say you will leave Zeus' garden whole.'

Zeus. Bringer of lightning; bearer of the Aegis, the divine shield. Granting mortals protection or hurling thunderbolts at them; seducing the princess Europa in the form of a bull; abandoning his daughter Persephone to a life of imprisonment in the Underworld. Cloud-gatherer. Chief of the gods and goddesses, who might smite any mortal as a vineyard worker tramples on grapes. We were walking in his garden without permission, as if visiting an old friend.

My eyes sought the blackened tree once more, and this time, I thought of the torched remains of the island. Pain and anguish surged through me again, but with them came another feeling, for I remembered how Apollo had calmly told me, as I watched my life burn, that there were no limits to what a god could do. Suddenly, I no longer simply resented my father – I wanted to scream and rage, to hurl all my fury in his face like a lion in full roar.

We forged ahead, ducking beneath fronds and branches, and I kept quiet. More and more plants seemed to block our way, but then the tangle cleared and I shielded my eyes. The rainbow that arced before us glittered with so many facets that it hurt to behold.

'Remarkable, is it not? Made from no metal, and yet it shines.'

At once, Apollo dropped to his knees. I copied him. The rainbow blazed furiously for a moment and then dissipated, yet I felt its power vibrate through the air.

The speaker made his way over the grass. I ascertained that he used a chair with one large wheel on each side – how did it move, without force? – before I dropped my gaze, trying to breathe quietly.

'Rise, Apollo.' The figure in the chair chuckled as my father stood. 'You arrived exactly when I expected you to. But then, I did see you coming.' Another chuckle.

'Father, I would not bring her unless the time demanded it,' Apollo said.

A sudden warmth flushed my face. This time, I knew it was not my father's aura but the regard of the god in the chair that touched me. I was overwhelmed with the desire to look Zeus in the eyes, and I thought of the blackened tree in the centre of the garden: I felt its presence still. There was another presence I felt too, further away, towards the back of the grassy area.

'A gift, forged by pure sunlight. For you, father.' Apollo opened his palm and a small bowl appeared there, golden and smooth. Zeus reached over and scooped it up.

'Impressive.' The hint of amusement in his voice was hard to miss.

'You remember when I first came to you about the prophecy, no doubt.'

My jaw clenched. I was old enough to know that when men spoke of prophecy, bad things followed. What happened, then, when gods spoke of prophecy? I wished to hear more, and at the same time, every bone in my body hoped that this prophecy did not involve me.

'And you must remember *my* advice on that day,' Zeus replied.

'I have followed it. I sought to protect my daughter by teaching her to fight. Isolating her on the Whispering Isle; enchanting the island just for her.' I had never heard Apollo like this, hesitating between words, weighing each phrase. 'I sent the sons of good men so that she could learn to beat them, father.'

Zeus' mouth had curled up at the corners, and I realised that he knew all this already. He was watching Apollo's expression. His beard twinkled with slivers of onyx and agate, threaded between the strands of white.

'The mortal king brought his punishment upon himself, father, when he banished my daughter. Now that the island is gone, she needs a new place to live – somewhere far-flung, beneath the notice of heroes. You must understand, this is not only a matter of her protection. This touches the Sun God's honour.' Apollo's lip curled. 'My child will not be subject to some seer's spiteful prediction.'

'And do you think you are the only one who would claim her?' a new voice said.

The grass rustled. From behind Zeus, a figure in a hooded cloak approached, and I recognised her at once, though she no longer carried her aulos. Those laughing eyes remained the same. The voice that spoke to me carried clearly, and it took me a few moments to realise that I was not hearing it aloud.

Orphia. A simple word, but one that I had rarely heard.

'Sun-girl' from the men, 'Lady Orphia' from the guards, or 'piglet' from Ixion; those had been my titles. Never my bare name.

Orphia. Nod if you hear me.

To my father, I was always 'my child', the mark of importance that all his progeny were granted. My name sounded inside my mind now.

Ever so slightly, I nodded.

'I do not recall inviting you here, Euterpe,' Apollo snapped.

The poet did not reply, but turned her gaze to me, and I heard her voice in my head again. *Stay calm and wait, Orphia. It is not our wish that you be thrown onto some outcrop for the rest of your days.*

If I could hear her, perhaps she could hear my thoughts. *Who are you?*

I am the aulos and the panpipes. I am the wearer of the other laurel wreath. Do not fret; someone is coming to you.

Hope rattled through my body. I didn't want to hope – it was like chasing a wild boar for your dinner when you could easily have stayed amongst the sheep – and yet the echo and throb of this woman's words made me dare. We gazed at each other for a few seconds before she turned to face Apollo. 'The girl is not your possession to hoard, Sun God.' I felt grace resonate in her voice.

'Of course, a Muse would hope to meddle in the affairs of greater gods,' Apollo said.

A Muse. I could have laughed aloud at my own slow-wittedness. Of course she had slipped in and out of Dorus' palace. My father had spoken her name, but I had not recognised who she was – Euterpe, the Muse of Lyric Poetry; the one who carried an aulos in drawings and statues of the Muses. Had I been so mesmerised by her poetry that I had never realised I was listening to one of the inspirational goddesses of Mt Parnassus?

I should have behaved with more reverence, I thought, trying to project the message.

And that would have been less merry for both of us. Her voice rang in my head again. *I have known who you are for a long time, Orphia. I have been sent from the heart of the web.*

The web?

Beside me, Apollo had begun speaking to Zeus again, pleading his case to transport me away. I knew that I should listen to him.

There is a web woven by the minds of women, supple as a nymph's heartstring. If you come with me, you will enter it. You will be draped in tragedy and pastoral, in the sacred and the profane, in the scroll and the sword; you will wear power like a summer cloak, and you will carry it for all your days.

Euterpe's words scored into my very being. They sent a new rattle of hope through me, though I could scarcely believe it. Could there really be a group of women ready to welcome me with power ... a web of women ... a *community*? I became aware that Apollo had finished speaking, and I felt Zeus' regard pass across my face. His look was not warm, like my father's aura; it was more like the chill that spreads when clouds obscure the sun.

'Interesting, that you all claim such a stake in the girl. Come forward.' He beckoned me. The hair on my arms stood up as I drew close enough to kneel before him. 'A warrior girl. My wife would like that. She has sometimes wished to take a spear to me.' He chuckled. 'Tell me, daughter of Apollo, what do you think of the prophecy?'

My confusion must have been written on my brow, for he chuckled again. I heard my father huff behind me. 'There is no need to provoke her. If I do not share everything with her, it is for her own protection.'

How quickly he had cut himself off, back on the island, when he first mentioned a prophecy. *A father owes no reason to his daughter.*

'Surely, she has the right to know why you hide her from the world,' Euterpe said.

'She is mine. My creation. And I will not have her torn apart by knowledge of her fate.'

The anger in those words touched something hot and sharp inside me and set off a burst of sparks. Who was Apollo to claim possession of me – the father who had scarcely visited the Whispering Isle in all my twenty-three years? And even if he had created me, why did that make me his? Should not every woman belong to herself?

I felt the air quiver, and a tremor ran through the soil beneath us.

'But she is not yours, Apollo,' a deep voice said.

5

I turned, as though looking into a mirror. My own arms with their sculpted muscle, my eyes the colour of flint, my straight spine that had kept me firm in many a fight: they combined in this woman, with a few additions. The lines of smiles and frowns past were etched upon features less weather-touched than mine. A long chiton flecked with gold hung easily from her, and the heavy crown that rested upon her curling hair drew my eye, with a single ruby set into the gilded band. I felt her words as much as I heard them. Rain mingled with stars in her voice, too strong to interrupt, too exquisite for me to capture in a poem.

The majesty of her presence chilled my skin. I did not speak as she strode towards me.

Apollo's swelling aura warned me that he meant to obstruct her path, but he seemed suspended, and could only glower at her. Something rippled inside me as she came to a stop.

'The memory of skin endures,' she proclaimed.

She extended her hand, her fingers brushing my cheek, and without knowing why, I placed my palm over hers. A current crackled through our skin. The garden around us dimmed and I saw a cave fringed with hundreds of crystals, its dark mouth glowing, a white fur nestled in the middle of the ground. It was as if I had fallen into someone else's memory. The same woman who now touched my cheek lay on the fur, cradling something in her arms, and I knew it was a baby even before I came close, just as I knew that this could only be the shadow of the past. The relief she exuded flowed from her in waves, steady, undeniable. Something had been avoided, some great pain averted. She pressed her lips to the baby's brow, and I felt the touch on my own forehead: felt the warm glow of the colourful crystals surround me.

Then darkness, and a chill. Absence; the loneliness of an abyss, not outside of her, but a fissure of the soul. She was keening with pain, this woman, though she never made a sound. The gap within her began to close and her soul re-formed, forging itself with a strength that never left. The woman rose, floated, soared. She reached a group of bright threads and flew to the heart of the cluster, where she bound them to her, tightening the web, her being shining with a lustre beyond any of the other strands. I felt a tear wind a path down my cheek as I watched.

The vision disappeared, and we were in Zeus' garden again, touching palm to palm.

'I wish I could claim all of your blood,' the woman said. 'But half will have to do.'

I stared at her. She gently detached her hand from my own.

'Who are you?' I said, nearly adding the word: *mother*. It felt like a live fish in my mouth.

'Even a warrior girl who lived on an island would have heard of Calliope, chief of the Muses. But I fear your father's memory has been errant at times. He seems to have forgotten that we made you together, and that he stole you from me with neither explanation nor apology.'

When I turned to Apollo, he flinched, and I remembered the youths by the black rocks, backing away from me. 'Sculpting me from marble? What else did you lie to me about?'

'All your life, I have acted to protect you.'

'Only a man could think a woman safer without her mother.'

'If you knew what I knew, my child—'

'Then tell me!' The words erupted from me, and I did not care that they must have carried to the antechamber and through the corridors. Looking at Apollo, I no longer saw the god who had bestowed life upon me, but a liar. I could scarcely comprehend the news that had been flung in my face.

'Such ignorance, belied by rage. But I suppose you cannot be blamed for a dearth of wisdom.' The blaze around him grew, and I kept silent. 'Tell me, my child, do you think that I was happy to receive divine knowledge of your fate? That I long to see my own daughter torn to pieces by the hands of a mob, her body ripped to shreds, her heart's blood flowing in torrents over the ground?'

It sounded too extraordinary to be real. Like a joke, told to warn me off adventuring on my own; but I could see no traces of mirth around Apollo's mouth, and I waited for Calliope or Euterpe to protest this prophecy.

Silence prevailed, and in the stillness, I imagined my own violent end as Apollo had described it. I felt the gristle of my flesh tearing, my bones fracturing and my skull collapsing, a river pouring from my chest like the death-choked Xanthus after Achilles had turned its waters red ... would it be quick, or would my agony linger, like Ixion's must?

'I ask you again, father.' Apollo's gaze swung back to the figure in the chair. 'Let me take her to a new island and continue her training. Already, she has flung the prince of the Whispering Isle down in combat. I believe that she can become one of the greatest heroes of this age, strong enough to fight off that mob – like bronze beaten until it sings.'

My mother – for I had begun to think of her as such – made to open her mouth. Zeus raised a hand, shooting sparks towards her.

We all fell silent. If we had forgotten whose presence we were in, there was no ignoring it now. I prayed to Hera, as I had always done when I felt darkness gather.

Great Queen of Heaven, protector of women, watch over me and I will please you.

'The girl has worked hard. There can be no doubt of that. She has become a warrior that even Hector might fear.' Zeus fixed his gaze upon me. 'But I have looked into her mind, and I see how she defeated the prince you speak of; not with iron and wood, but with a woman's weapon.'

'I see a simple way to resolve this. A harmless demonstration,' Calliope cut in.

No one could have missed the melodies in her voice. Nor could they have failed to notice the effect of ecstasy – or so the poets called it – produced by a blending of notes in every syllable. I could tell that Zeus was listening, for his eyes had become slightly glazed.

'Let us see if she is as powerful as the Muses believe. Those on Olympus lack entertainment of late. I propose a recitation,' Calliope said.

Apollo attempted to interject, but my mother cut him off. *My mother.* It still felt strange to think it, let alone to say it.

'If she were a boy, you would have nourished the arts in her, Apollo, as you do in your sons. Your crime is not that you have hidden her from us. It is that you have hidden her from herself.'

I felt Calliope's words fall inside me and wash through in a glittering rain. I knew their truth at once. Anger sparked inside me again. Zeus seemed to come out of his stupor, wheeling himself towards her. 'Careful, Calliope.'

'If the king of the gods is truly great, he should not fear the chief of the Muses.'

They eyed each other. Calliope lifted her crown from her head and held it before her. 'You have always been enamoured of oaths,' she added, 'so I make this oath to you, great Zeus. I will not aid Orphia in her performance. What she speaks must come from her.'

There it was. My name, again, ringing out, only this time it sounded for all to hear.

I seized that one word. *Orphia*. With it came a promise, bound in invisible thread – a promise that I could be a poet if I proved myself worthy of the task.

Euterpe's voice sounded in my head.

I think you understand that even on Mt Olympus, freedom must be purchased.

Daring to look at her, I nodded, ever so slightly.

'Very well, Calliope,' Zeus said. 'But we will do this in the Hall of Starlight. Let the girl prove herself under the eyes of many Olympians, or not at all.'

A cloud cast a pall over the garden. I felt Zeus' gaze fall upon me and wondered if I might splinter in the face of a single stare. I bowed my head. My mother led the way out of the garden, her crown nestled upon her curls again, and the rest of us followed in single file. Only Zeus did not move. When I turned back, the chair had disappeared, taking the chief of the immortals with it.

6

The tapping began slowly, and at first, it could have been the clink of any bronze cups, yet I could hear an echo ring on, like the flecks of gold that remained whenever my father left. I tried to put names to the immortals who knocked their vessels on the tables: a man with dark curls chuckled; a woman stroked the pure white flowers in her braid; another deity rested their cup against the knife-sharp points of their trident. The gods and goddesses sat encircled by their hangers-on. I yearned to see each of them up close, but Apollo steered me on, and we approached a dais at the end of the hall.

'Kneel,' Apollo muttered.

The movement down to the floor forced my gaze up, and I gasped. I had not noticed them before, but now I could not ignore them: the stars winked in clusters and bright pairs.

A tapestry of indigo sky swirled with black clouds on the ceiling above us, inlaid with gems of white light that dazzled and danced, as if the night sky really stretched across the Hall of Starlight. Allowing myself to stare, I traced the constellations into my memory.

A bang sounded. The dais had been empty when I knelt, but now, Zeus sat atop it. The father of the gods stared down the hall.

'I give you a spectacle. Do not rise – only raise your cups.' His voice could strike any god or goddess down with its power,

I was sure. This was not like Zeus speaking to his son behind locked doors. This was lightning given sound.

The guests ceased their banging and drank, and when Zeus beckoned to me, I rose and took the last few steps towards the dais. As every eye in the hall fell upon me, my lungs threatened to burst with the straining of my breath, each inhalation pressing against their walls.

'Is she not a bit powerful for one of your conquests, Zeus?' the man with dark curls said. He was the only immortal who did not hold a cup, drinking instead from a large bottle. A gaggle of young men around him laughed, the sound like honed teeth.

'A conquest has the grace to look defeated,' another god said. I recognised his winged helmet and sandals, and by the smirk on his face, I did not think Hermes, the messenger god, was speaking for my benefit. 'She looks more like a soldier. Perhaps she would like to conquer you, Dionysus.'

The whole hall rang with laughter, and just as the hands of immortals had made their cups ring incessantly, so too did their voices echo. It set my teeth on edge.

Zeus raised a hand.

'The chief of the Muses would offer you a treat, my friends. Tell them what you have in store, sweet Calliope.' He beckoned to my mother. There was no one who could have called Calliope 'sweet' and received no reply except for Zeus, I was sure. Calliope mounted the dais and squeezed my hand. 'This is Orphia: woman of twenty-three years, poet, and daughter of my own blood. Ready yourselves for her gifts.'

Several of the immortals sitting near the front wore glazed expressions, and I too felt the ecstasy that Calliope's voice left in its wake, buffeting me like a headwind that might blow a ship over a dark ocean into sunlit waters. A ripening pride swelled within me. For the first time, I could truly believe that she was my mother – or perhaps, for the first time, I dared to hope that it was true.

Only one god withstood Calliope's power, limping forward. 'Can she work a forge?'

The question seemed to break the spell. I noticed a woman standing beside the speaker; her lips moved, but no sound came out. In the stories I had heard, Aphrodite, the goddess of love, wore myrtos flowers in her hair, and I could see white blooms peeking from her braid. Her husband gripped her arm, leaving a red mark on her skin.

'Orphia's talent lies with words,' Calliope said. 'I have proposed a test for her. It should be to your liking, Hephaestus, for I know how you adore listening to women.' Some of the immortals laughed, but I looked at Aphrodite and saw her strain to speak again, producing no sound.

'The test is simplicity itself. One of you will pick a subject, and my daughter will create a poem. She will have no more than a minute to prepare,' Calliope declared. 'If what she says moves you, and if you judge it equal to any poem in the world, then she will have earned her place on Mt Parnassus. She will leave this hall with me, and hereafter she shall be trained by my Muses.'

A jug banged on a table: Dionysus threw his vessel down and burst into laughter, joined by several of the gods. Hephaestus glowered at Calliope, and a few others wore disapproving looks, but the mirth of the majority struck me hardest. They did not believe I could spin words. They expected to enjoy a woman's failure, presented like a play for their amusement.

Men shouted as lawmakers in pillared buildings, and spoke like gods in their own homes. What were women but wives shut away, weavers for the marketplace, and slaves carrying water? If men were the voices of Greece, what did that make us?

What were women, if not silence?

I caught Euterpe's gaze, and remembered her remark. Even here, freedom must be purchased. The gods were still laughing at the thought of my words having any impact, and I knew my odds were long, yet a strange thing happened as Calliope took my hand once more. We were back in that cave, in the glow of colourful light, and she held me to her chest. I felt the message of her touch for what it was: faith in me; impossible to understand, yet as real as the olive tree that had pushed through the soil on the island.

Perhaps the gods who laughed so raucously would prefer me to complement their noise with silence, just as, so often, in tents and houses and palaces alike, women were expected to remain wordless. If so, they were too late. I had already discovered what could happen when I spoke.

I met Hermes' stare, and something crystallised inside me.

I faced the immortals assembled in the Hall of Starlight with my head held high. Muttering around the tables told me that my figure inspired puzzlement as well as mirth: how could a woman of no name hope to complete an impossible task? It was the same question Ixion had voiced when our spears clashed. From the left of the dais, I caught the full force of my father's glare.

'Come now, do not leave all the work to us Muses, dear Olympians,' Calliope said. 'A topic.'

Male voices rang through the hall, leaping over each other. I felt weak and small, but I kept my back straight and my feet planted, refusing to shrink. Through the haze of talk, Aphrodite stood and raised her hand – and although Hephaestus made to wrench his wife's arm down, a god spoke across the others.

'I see no reason why infidelity should prevent your wife from speaking,' Zeus said. 'Let Aphrodite break her punishment for a word.'

'One word,' Hephaestus snarled.

We all waited while Aphrodite put a hand to her throat. She stroked it for a moment, then, swallowing, looked me in the eyes. Her voice sounded reedy, as a flute that has not been played for a year sounds, lacking tunefulness yet full of the promise of new songs.

'Beauty,' she whispered.

Heads turned slowly from Aphrodite to the dais. I drew a breath and tasted the ocean on my tongue again, and pictured myself amongst the rocks and the blood-red poppies, looking out over a swathe of pebbles and the foam of the waves. From such foam, the goddess of love had been born, the poets said. Perhaps Aphrodite had heard me that night when the sea turned to horses and myrtos flowers wafted their scent to me, as they did now, their fragrance radiating from the petals in her hair. My poetry seemed like such a flower, a gift that could be easily crushed.

'Take this.' Calliope's voice reached me as if from a great distance. 'A poet should hold her instrument in both hands.'

Something glinted in the starlight. My mother had opened her palm, and an object nestled there, just as when Apollo offered the bowl to Zeus – except that this carved piece of tortoise shell made a familiar sight, its strings evenly placed along its length. Looking at those taut strings, I felt a queer sensation travel through me, as if I were entering epic poems: plunging in and out of stories. I felt the fear and fury of soldiers charging over a Trojan plain, the desperation of Odysseus as he sailed home, and the black sorrow of Athena as she stared down at Pallas' corpse, looking at the dear friend she had impaled on her glinting spear.

My hands trembled as I took the instrument, for it seemed that my poetry was sanctified, my task official. All the poets who visited Dorus' palace had played a lyre while they recited their verses; after losing mine in the blaze, I had not thought to find another so soon. This new lyre hummed with magic, awakening words that were gathering inside me. Calliope handed me a pick made of smooth white stone, and I slipped it between my fingers.

Fear nibbled at my mind. Still, I forced myself to draw my hand across the gut-strings, strumming them once. I thought of splitting rock when I fought Ixion, and of the roots pushing through the soil at the sound of my voice, sedulous in their defence of me. Calliope's faith wrapped me, and I allowed myself to be swaddled.

I pulled the pick firmly across the strings and heard music flow out, golden and swift, driven by a force beyond understanding. Now, I did not need to prepare my words. Lines leapt to my mouth, and I began to speak of the Whispering Isle: of studying in the palace and practising with the spear and shield; of sitting alone in the dining hall, eating in silence while the others bragged and jested. I spoke of fighting by the black rocks until my muscles were strong and my aim true. I spoke of the first time that Jason had shared his wine with me, and how we had laughed when he knocked over the chalice and stained the edge of his chiton – and how quick Jason had been to laugh at others, under the pretence of a light jest – how he had pricked the men until they chafed. My words flowed to Dorus and his cold contempt for me; to Ixion and his hot dislike for me. Verses came one after another, and I strung them together.

If this was magic, this torrent, it carried the story of my life. I did not wish to hide it any longer. Even if they killed me for it, I would show them my power. I had thought to spend my life listening to poetry and composing my own stories of terror, courage and loss, but I had never realised until now that I was living a story of my own: a wonderful and terrible story. A twist came, then, as I recounted Euterpe's visit – I described the change inside me, and the curious way my feet had been drawn to the shore at night. The smell of freshly broken earth. The hum of the dragonflies. The anger that rushed through me when Ixion dragged the bruised washer-woman into the orchard, an anger that turned to determination when I faced him, ringed by men, and turned his own fury back upon him in lines of poetry.

By the time I finished, eyes shone amongst the audience. Cheeks glistened at every table. Several of the gods sniffed, and Aphrodite hid her face in her hands, peeping at me from between her fingers. Something warm surged through my chest: something a little like pride.

Beauty, she had said. Well, I would try to give her beauty. It was not hard, for an image of grace was embossed in my mind so clearly that I might have been gazing upon it. The loss of those you had known was one thing, but there was another kind of loss, too, formed of pieces salvaged from those you had scarcely begun to know. Eurydicius had not shied away from me; he had not swaggered, nor tried to win me like a prize; his voice had been a soft stream, meandering over my consciousness, offering not only awe but respect for my art. Those were the pieces of him that I clutched, even now, after my father had turned the island to ash.

Emotions surged through me: love, grief, pain: they sank into deep-plunging fissures. I nourished the violence of my passion. I would give these immortals a taste of what I had only started to know.

'Tell me, Muse, of a man like water, who came close enough to the sun-girl that she could see him ripple in the light. Tell me of his yielding smile, of the doors that opened in his eyes. Tell me of all the worlds, real and unreal, that they might have explored; and tell me of how he was snatched away.'

I strummed the lyre while phrases flowed. The music hummed beneath the poetry, not loud enough to be heard alone.

While the power of loss coursed through me, I described the glow of Eurydicius' quiet appreciation – a gentle admiration, not a desire to possess me – yet I did not notice the smell of peaches until it surrounded me.

The vines emerged as I spoke, from between the rainbow stones of the walls, through gaps too tiny to be made out. Their fruit dangled in the air as they snaked between the tables, questing towards the dais, not stopping for wood or stone. I sensed the garden's adoration.

It took a few moments for what I had done to come home to me, and scarcely daring to look, I turned my gaze to the immortals.

No one strode towards me in anger. Remarkably, no one demanded that I pay for pulling branches and vines through the walls of the Hall of Starlight. Euterpe wept, her aulos hanging limply from her hand; Apollo stared at me, as if seeing me for the first time; at some point Ganymede had joined the group beside the dais, and his pretty face squinted, his body leaning towards me. I looked to Aphrodite again and noticed that her eyes were bedewed.

I held the lyre tightly. Strumming faster, I picked up my poem mid-verse. Now I unleashed the spirits of love and loss that had been rising, the full force of them rushing from my throat. I would show those laughing gods that I had not been permitted to ripen like the plums on the twisting branches – that my father had stolen a seed from me before it could open. The walls shook as my poem built. Stones jittered, then cracked, their rainbows splintering and shattering as something thrust into the hall; branches pushed forward, thicker now, their wood gnarled, and I recognised the trees of Zeus' garden as they surged towards me, knocking over chairs and scraping the arms of immortals. Cries flew from every side, while the mountain quivered beneath our feet.

'Cease this at once, my child!' Apollo shouted.

I might have paused, mid-verse, if I had not felt a grip on my palm again. Calliope's gaze brimmed with starlight, like the sky above, like her voice with its harmonies, and it held my magic steady. I felt her pride swell as I finished my last line. When the earth stopped shaking, a new rhythm began, and between the twisting branches I saw the immortals applauding, one after the other joining in, their palms slapping faster and faster. Slowly, I turned to face Zeus.

He wiped his cheek, but before it was clean, I glimpsed the droplet of pure silver. I wondered how often the chief of the Olympians shed a tear.

I had only hurled words. Not a spear, not a dagger, not an arrow. Perhaps words were not so slight as gods and men expected them to be.

At a wave of Zeus' hand, the branches and vines retreated through the gaps in the walls. Shards of rainbow stone flew up and re-formed, and for a moment the whole hall was alive with movement, until every trace of a plant disappeared and the walls resealed. The doors at the end of the hall blew open, and the gods turned.

'If you are waiting for an arrival, you will be disappointed.' Calliope stepped forward. 'Those are the doors through which I will be leaving. Let every god remember that a web shines brightly on Mt Parnassus, spun from the Muses, woven by our voices.' I had the feeling that Calliope was speaking to me, as much as to the rest of the hall. She held my hand aloft. 'I come to claim my daughter, Orphia, who has moved you beyond all expectation – to take her into the heart of our web. I will not ask a second time.'

A cold wind blew through the hall. Aphrodite shivered and clutched her shoulders. I saw some of the gods exchange glances, and a few nodded. I did not like to think what would happen if any of them refused my mother. As I felt the love emanating from her touch, my own feelings solidified.

I wanted to follow her. Not only because I wanted to leave my father's lies scattered in the dust from my sandals, but because I wanted to see the world that Calliope and Euterpe had dangled, ever so enticingly, in front of me. A world where women wove words into stories. Could it really exist?

A glow flared from the foot of the dais. When Apollo spoke, fire tinged his words.

'Let every god ask himself if he would really trust a Muse to save his daughter.' He glanced at Zeus. 'Father, you owe it to me. Her custody is my right.'

The remark seemed to crackle between them. It sent a shock through the hall, and I heard the word 'owe' repeated; saw fingers pointed at Apollo. Zeus did not need to move. Without lifting a finger, he exuded something that made my father's aura flicker.

'A test was performed fairly. I owe nothing.' He shot a glance down the hall and the tables in the middle of the floor scraped to either side. 'You may leave if you can, Calliope.'

At once, my mother strode from the dais, my hand still clasped in hers. Euterpe moved to flank me. I heard my father's angry cry from behind us, and then, with a thump, he landed in front of me.

'Think on your fate, my child. Think of your body torn to pieces. Would you walk through life, knowing where you are destined to end?' He stared into my face.

Silence, then. Every eye in the hall watched me struggle with the weight of those words.

'If I must die,' I said, 'I would live, first.'

My mother's smile was unmissable. She stepped forward. 'I will take my leave.'

'Oh, it is not so simple. You may leave *if you can*,' Apollo said. He swelled in his pale cape and spread his arms wide. Hermes rose from his seat, and then Dionysus, Hephaestus, and other gods too, moving so steadily towards us that I knew they had made some commitment to my father prior to this gathering. On either side of me, Calliope and Euterpe drew nearer. I saw the cruel smile on Hephaestus' countenance and a chill ran through me, prompting me to glance at the chief of the immortals.

Zeus stared ahead, unperturbed. I wondered, then, if he had known what the result of his pronouncement would be. My spine felt brittle, as if my body were readying itself for an onslaught.

'It will not be simple for you, either. As it was not when you wooed me.' Calliope's words carried the flint in her eyes.

Before she or Apollo could move to attack, Euterpe's voice cut through my head, reverberating with a new urgency. *Beware. Brace yourselves.*

I began to grope for a fresh prayer to Hera, one that would reach her with its eloquence, and I had only managed to pronounce her name when a quake shook the hall, knocking over jugs, sending cups rolling along the floor. The gods who were closing in on us stopped where they stood, staring at the doors. They seemed to be looking at the empty air until a dash of bright blue appeared, and then, with another quake, a figure came driving her chariot into the hall, the peacocks below it fanning out their tails. The ox-eyed Queen of Heaven leapt from the back of the chariot and flew to land on the dais, drawing herself up, sending shockwaves through the floor.

She stepped slowly towards us, her sapphire gown trailing across the stone platform, her countenance as unyielding as a statue's. I felt all the cold parts of me begin to flame. Just the sight of her, exuding power, set me alight, until I blazed with power too, and my whole flesh felt as if it were aglow. This was the most satisfying burn I could imagine.

'You think to deceive me,' Hera said.

Zeus did not raise his gaze to meet hers. Nearby, Apollo moved, but Hera did not deign to look at him, keeping her attention on Zeus. Even the smallest movement of her feet made the stones beneath me vibrate. I had never felt anything so magnificent; I wanted to throw myself at her feet and tell her that she had inspired me all my life, as she must inspire all women. Yet I had the queer feeling that she already knew.

I could not bow my head. I needed to soak in the confidence of her glance.

'Tell me, husband.' The title rang with scorn from her lips. 'Where is Orphia's audience of goddesses? Where is Artemis?'

'I do not—'

'Does the huntress shun this performance, and take no interest in her own niece? What of Athena? Does the goddess of warfare see no power in Orphia's tongue?'

'Such matters are not my concern,' Zeus said.

'But it was you who sent the message calling us three away on an errand to protect the city of Athens,' Hera said. Euterpe made a little noise of satisfaction, and Apollo's eyes narrowed. 'Oh yes, I know. If you thought that Athens would distract me, husband, you are a fool.' Another tremor rocked the hall as Hera raised a finger to point at Zeus' chest, and I felt my teeth rattle in my head. 'None of you will touch the girl.'

Apollo made to protest, but Hera turned to face him, and he quailed.

'Was it not you, Lord Apollo, who informed Hephaestus of his wife's lover? Convenient that Aphrodite would be silenced before this meeting, is it not? Artemis, Athena, myself ... and now the goddess of love. I am curious as to why the voices of the most powerful goddesses are missing. Could it be that Zeus and Apollo are afraid of them?'

Apollo made to speak again, but Calliope cut across him, the harmonies of her vowels travelling to the far walls.

'I shall tell you, Olympians, what Zeus and Lord Apollo are afraid of. It is not each goddess in turn. It is all of us, united. They fear that we will speak to each other, and share our thoughts as a collective. They fear that the goddesses will stand beside me when I take my own daughter.' Somehow, her voice had grown even more beautiful, and yet terrible, too. 'My husband fears that the goddesses will want Orphia to learn her own greatness. The gods of the sky and sun have worked in the shadows to distract us.'

She took my hand and clasped it in hers. We looked at each other and, as one, we began to stride towards the doors, passing Apollo. He flew to block us again. The movement prompted me to shift to the right, with the instinct of my training, yet I need not have bothered: Apollo froze, his arm outstretched. Hera's laugh rang through the hall, shattering several tables. *Of course,* I thought. *Of course her powers are as great as her husband's; just because no poet has declared it does not mean it is not so.*

Our path cleared, then. The gods seemed to forget that they had been about to cross us. I desperately desired to say something to Hera – to tell her how much I admired her – to ask for her blessing for my future – to tell her that I suspected that the stories about her jealousy were untrue. Calliope pulled me forward, and I kept moving.

We were at the end of the hall when I heard a voice speak my name inside my mind, and I halted. Some instinct made me hesitate, but I forced myself to turn.

The father of the immortals slumped in his chair. A deep peace etched his face with a smile. Before him, the hall was full of frozen gods; Dionysus, Hermes, and even Hephaestus stood where they had been when Hera's gaze had touched them. Hera faced me with unwavering focus.

Through the silence, I heard a single word in my mind.

Orphia.

Was the Queen of Heaven going to trap me forever in the doorway, halfway between freedom and containment? I knew that immortals did not take kindly to mortals running off.

It was hard to ignore prayers in such a golden tongue. Not even my priestesses do me such credit, of late.

I did not dare to reply.

I have seen your future, Orphia.

The words were a knife in my flesh. Hera's eyes held mine over the top of the unmoving gods.

And I have seen other things, which Zeus and Apollo are too hasty to notice. I do not disclose my wisdom to mortals, but perhaps you have earned it, this once. Did you not pray to me every month and worship my might?

It was no longer judicious to stay silent. *Yes, great queen,* I thought. *You have been my star.*

You understand who deserves your loyalty. It is not wise to know too much, so I shall tell you two things only.

I waited.

The first is that you will be happier than all heroes, and yet not happy.

Her promise sounded like a coiled adder. I turned it over in my head, unable to find the venom. Hera folded her arms.

Thank you, great queen, I thought.

The second fact is simpler. I think it will please you more. She smiled, sharp enough to cut glass. *I saved them, your old friend and your new one, and all the washer-women and wives of the island. Know this, Orphia: Jason and Eurydicius dived into the ocean. I sent the women in a different direction. They have all swum to rocky shores.*

My knees wanted to buckle. *Alive*, I thought. *Alive*. The word swept through me in a rush of hot smoke.

But my father ... I began.

If your father finds out, then he may take a lesson from it. The world is not Apollo's dominion, nor Zeus', but mine too. Go, and do with this knowledge what you will.

I could imagine the women cutting through the water, struggling through the briny swell, carried by Hera's magic whenever they faltered. I could picture Jason and Eurydicius swimming swiftly away from the island, inhaling ash and smoke and shouting to each other.

Calliope and Euterpe grabbed my arms as I slumped and hoisted me up, dragging me into the corridor. My last glimpse of the Hall of Starlight showed a tableau of frozen figures, then a quake racked the hall again, rubble dislodging from a hole in the ceiling. Hera mounted her chariot and flew upward, disappearing through the gap in the stars.

An angry buzz of voices began to spread.

Calliope pushed the doors shut. She did not pause to look back.

'Come,' she said.

Jason and Eurydicius are not burnt bones, I told myself, letting my thoughts oscillate. There was no clear path, any more. If there was a road, it would have to be laid one stone at a time, sealed by my own effort.

I followed the two Muses out of the palace. My hands itched to begin the labour, and I moved forward at a stride, pulsing with a new music; and as I placed my sandals firmly on the soft grass, I exhaled into sweetened air.

In all the years I had lived in his palace, I had never once seen Dorus remove his crown, yet now I saw my mother toss hers up and catch it again. She had scarcely chanted a few words before Euterpe pushed me close to her. My teeth knocked; the very fabric of the air seemed to rip, the seams of the garden came undone and all of Mt Olympus peeled back, and then we were gone.

We landed within seconds. A soft hum emanated from the soil beneath my feet. Calliope lowered her crown onto her curls and smiled a panther's smile, while I glanced up into a swirl of white.

Mt Parnassus kept its place cautiously, above the world of mortals yet lower than Mt Olympus, sitting beneath a bank of cloud. Chunks of limestone studded the ground and yellow grass thatched the dirt. The plateau-like summit rose amongst other peaks in a range, clustering with its sisters above the pale blue jewel of the Corinthian Gulf; I heard the voices of this soil harmonise and felt the embrace of the mountain in its breeze.

My head throbbed from our sudden departure, from meeting Hera, from learning that Jason and Eurydicius were alive, and I forced my thoughts to slow their dance. If I was about to enter the world of the Muses, the web of women that Euterpe had described so lyrically, I would need my mind as clear as an unrippled lake.

Calliope placed one hand upon a tall stone. 'The riddle, oread, if you please.'

A gasp jumped into my throat. Where the stone had been, a rock nymph now stood, her feet planted wide. Her scarlet robe trailed in the dirt, but she did not seem to notice, swaggering over to us. A dagger dangled from her belt.

'What comes but once a year, yet flows all year round?'

'Spring,' Calliope replied.

'And from whom do *you* spring?' the oread said.

'Mnemosyne: eternal queen of memory.'

A door appeared – a frame of silver light, shimmering, suspended in the air. I looked back to the nymph, but she had disappeared.

Calliope put her hand against the small of my back and guided me forward. I tried not to stumble as I climbed through.

I followed the path of Calliope's hand as she gestured to the land ahead, and with great difficulty, I managed to stifle my cry.

'See?' Calliope said to Euterpe, who was following us, the glowing doorway closing behind her. 'I told you she would not be afraid. Look how she steps.'

My feet had moved of their own accord. I could not blame them. Where the mountaintop had been bare, a landscape of lush green now unfolded, studded with shimmering pools of water, dark crags, and ancient outcrops of pale pink stone, undulating to the edges of the peak. Poetry lived here. Some unseen hand had written it long ago, in every limestone tooth and every blade of grass. As I moved forward, I tried to record the beauty of this land in my head – not for myself, but for Eurydicius, for if I should ever speak to him again, I wanted to give him a poem of Mt Parnassus that would linger in the crevasses of his mind.

A great lake stretched before us, providing a mirror in which buildings were reflected – so many different shapes that I could not tell which was the largest: the tower, the dome, or the pillared rectangular building that sat in the centre. I could not help but grin at the way the ground sloped down to reveal this walled city. Had there ever been such a stronghold, sprinkled with rose beds and orchards and the glitter of fountains? I hungered to see it all.

'Far better than anything the gods on Mt Olympus have flung down,' Calliope said. 'They have no patience for spells – they make everything at a snap of their fingers. It took us a hundred years, working together, to finish the city wall.' She clapped a hand to my shoulder. 'Have you ever seen the like of our corner-towers? Each one has music in its rock.'

'A hundred years, and she still needs to brag to you,' Euterpe said, her eyes smiling. 'Let us go down to the palace, Calliope. Passing through the air will empty a girl's stomach.'

I was glad of her interjection, for I was still not sure that I had the right words to convey how I felt. Yet something inside me hurled its rapturous feelings at the world below – a world under the rule of goddesses.

Calliope called out in a language that I did not understand. She looked down at the lake, then glanced at Euterpe. 'They are lazing again.'

'With you home, they would not dare.' Euterpe smiled. 'Look to your left.'

We turned, and my face split with a grin. The breeze ruffled their golden-brown plumage as they swooped to the ground. The gryphons I had seen on painted vases as a child stood proud and haughty, as if they feared nothing and risked all; yet here, a pair of gryphons nestled into my mother's side, and one of them rubbed its beak against her palm. She patted the creature on the forehead, and it chirped.

'I thought gryphons guarded treasure, not served the Muses as steeds.' My voice came out a little higher than I intended.

'A steed would be more reliable. You will have to take your chances on Fury, Orphia.' She gave her gryphon a soft thump on the back. 'Let us hope that she does not chase breakfast on the way.' My mother beckoned to me. The gryphon crouched lower while she swung onto its back, and then she gestured to the spot in front of her. I hesitated, reminding myself that I had faced my father several times while his aura blazed – but even he had never sported talons.

Euterpe mounted the other gryphon so smoothly that I would have been envious, if I had not been struggling to keep my balance. We soared upward, moving so fast that the breeze slapped my cheeks, and soon I could see every rock and glimmering pool atop Mt Parnassus. As we crossed the smooth glass of the lake, a feeling of freedom hit me in the chest. Here lay a world beyond the one I had lived in, a realm I had only begun to sense but which was swiftly expanding before me. *Halt*, my father would have said. *Conceal yourself.* I looked ahead to the shore.

We climbed a little before dropping towards the city of the Muses, and I gaped as I glimpsed a dome inlaid with rubies of many sizes, a battlement adorned with sculpted figures, a theatre whose tiered seats cascaded down the stands, and above it all, a soaring tower topped with a monument shaped like a lyre, the only golden object in a sea of silver-flecked stone. My whole body yearned to touch it.

'It is not gold that our gryphons guard,' Calliope said, and I heard the hard edge in her voice, beneath the ecstasy of its melodies. 'No riches on earth compare to the arts. Tell me – what is it to feel, to express, to take delight, to see oneself reflected, to experience the stories of others?'

'Surely,' I said, 'that is to be alive.'

Calliope nodded. 'Life, in all its tumult. That is what we nourish, here, through art.'

I watched the way that her lips moved, marking their firm rhythm.

The wall that girdled the city loomed. We plummeted, and my stomach jolted as we swooped between two buildings, just clearing their eaves. Fury landed next to the pillared rectangular building that sat in the centre, her talons scraping the stones of a square.

Astonishment rose inside me. Fighting to keep my composure, I stared across at pillars shaped like women, sculpted of marble, propping up a vast roof. A scroll adorned one statue's hand, and another clutched a comic mask. I distinguished my mother's features on one of the sculptures before me, and realised that all of these pillars showed Muses, the folds of their chitons captured in white stone.

'You may speak, you know.' Euterpe dismounted with the same ease she had shown in mounting. 'No entitled men with faces like axe-blades will chop up your opinion here.'

I blushed, and Euterpe did not press me further.

While a pair of nymphs came out of the building and took the gryphons, handling the animals briskly, questions reared inside me. Before I could ask them, a woman strode out of the pillared building and clasped Calliope's arm.

'Let me check that no god has done any damage to those exquisite biceps.' She trailed her fingers up Calliope's arm, and the movement was like a lizard darting over stone. Calliope laughed. The stranger turned her gaze to me. 'A girl? You lied, Calliope, my dear. I would call her something more than that. She looks old enough for a wrestle in the water-garden. I should warn you, Orphia: I have a firm grip. Some decide not to disentangle themselves after they have begun.'

'Pay no attention to Erato. She never met an athlete she did not like.' Calliope's voice carried to all of us.

Muse of Love Poetry. I heard Erato's title in the voice of my tutor, high and stilted. How I wished that I had paid attention to every detail in his lesson on the Muses.

'Come now,' Erato said, still looking at me, 'you need to see our palace. Though I should be happy to show you to my tower later, if you like.'

'Two steps backward, Erato,' Euterpe said. 'And no stroking her.'

I ventured a small smile. 'It is an impressive Muse who has a tower of her own.'

'Oh, we all have those. But mine is far prettier than Euterpe's – and I shall not speak of that monstrosity that Clio keeps up the back, strangled by vines,' Erato said. 'Come, Orphia.' She offered me her arm, and at Calliope's nod I accepted it, smiling. Like her talk, Erato moved quickly, and I was steered beneath the frontispiece without the chance to look at the pillars again. Once in the foyer, I quickened my steps.

'Now, my dear, try not to let your mouth hang open,' Erato said.

Wine leapt and arced in streams of burgundy, pouring from spouts on all sides of a fountain, splashing into its broad bowl. I wanted to cup my hands and drink, but thoughts of poisoned chalices gifted by immortals stopped me. I examined the fountain while Erato pointed out the shape of each spout – a cluster of grapes here, a sword there, an aulos and a writing tablet, and halfway up one side, a cithara with many strings. 'By far the finest, an instrument to please,' she declared.

'That would not be the finest spout because it is yours, would it?' Euterpe said. 'How many women have you seduced by plucking away at those strings?'

Erato grinned, snatched my hand and kissed it, and strode off down the corridor. My cheeks warmed again. I watched her go, noting how her feet slipped over stones with a quick rhythm, as if she were an instrument that could slip between notes.

There had been a woman, three years ago. My thoughts swam back to her: the daughter of a trader. She had lingered with me in the steam baths on the island, talking of ships and salt water, of mist and heat and skin. We had lain on my bed in the light from the window, while the moon silvered the sky, and continued our dialogue in broken moans, muffling our noises in each other's hair. Afterwards, I had touched her slowly, tracing the lines of her cheekbones and the curvature of her calves. Two summers had passed before I found another who roused my interest: an actor in a troupe who had visited the Whispering Isle. When he had removed his hero's mask in the shade of the orchard and begun to untie his thin robe, ripples had spread within me, awakened by the way the moon painted his ankles. I remembered the way his eyes had closed as my hands found his waist, and the warming of his thighs beneath my fingers.

The man had spoken softly; the woman boldly. They could not have seemed more different. And yet in each case, I had recognised something different from the roles we were supposed to play: something different from the domineering men and dominated women we were expected to be. I had wondered if there was no pattern to my desire across the sexes. Perhaps this was the pattern.

Perhaps I desired those who stepped outside their roles.

The same desire swirled through me now as I watched Erato walk away. Yet something else moved in me, too. A suspicion, perhaps, that a feeling I had experienced with another had delved below flesh, making ripples far beneath the surface.

My mother took my hand, and we ascended three flights in silence. Portraits of female figures enlivened the walls of the stairwell: red-robed nymphs appeared on mountaintops, blue-robed nymphs rose from streams, green-robed nymphs perched on tree branches, and white-robed nymphs swam amongst the waves, all of them painted in fine strokes. A chant from my childhood echoed in my ears: *oreads of the mountains, naiads of fresh water, dryads of the trees, nereids of the sea.* It was short and simple, like all the lessons my tutor had given about women.

When Calliope guided me out of the stairwell, I thought I must have spoken the words aloud: for there before me, as if summoned by a spell, were nymphs clad in all four colours, sitting at tables with chisels and tablets, mixing liquids, stringing instruments and tending a garden in the centre of the hall, where trees, rocks and water blended in the light from open windows. My mother nodded to those who approached her, checking their work and answering their questions, all the while leading me to the door at the far end. We entered an empty corridor. In the quietude of cool stone, the harmonies of Calliope's voice reverberated.

'You want to ask why they are here.'

'How can you know that?' I said.

'Call it the knowledge of blood.' She shot me a glance. 'Many wish for the Muses to aid them. Only nymphs wish to serve us in return, however. They work, and we help to mould their wisdom, until they can set and harden of their own accord. They have beauty, and beautiful things need strength if they are not to be shattered.'

'I see.'

'You do not. But that is only natural, at twenty-three.'

'Twenty-three,' I said. 'Old, for a woman.'

'Young, for an artist.'

She led me onto a staircase, this one twisting up, its narrow width only permitting us to walk one behind the other. The gold flecks in her chiton reminded me of constellations, and

I thought of the ceiling in the Hall of Starlight. I wondered if it had been a dream. This new realm on Mt Parnassus, too, felt so exquisite that it seemed unreal, with its towers and pillared buildings and the women who lived amongst them, unrestricted.

I had scarcely time to glimpse the busts that we passed before Calliope led me onto the final floor of the building. She stopped outside a door and raised her hand. The wood melted away.

'If we are to speak candidly, we should do it in the hidden wing. Truth grows in the quietest soil.'

For all that I wished to look nonchalant, I am not sure that I managed it. Calliope led me through and halted at the end of the next chamber, where the floor became a platform, and I looked ahead into the vast space where a wall should have been. A series of stones floated in the air, like a ladder.

Calliope squeezed my hand and vanished. I repressed a shout. She reappeared instantly on the first stone, in mid-air.

It was one thing to feel myself suddenly transported. Seeing my mother do it was another thing entirely. I shivered – Calliope did not even look strained; indeed, she did not look as if she had made any effort at all.

'How?' I managed.

'You would be surprised what your imagination can do, when it is not encumbered by the ropes of rules.' She looked closely at me. 'Try. Picture yourself where you want to be.'

Closing my eyes, I pictured myself beside her. A snap; I opened my eyes, and I was standing at her side, my hand in hers. A new power throbbed in my veins.

For the sake of my own sanity, I did not question it.

One by one, we climbed the rest of the floating steps, leaping through space, until we stood upon the last stone and Calliope touched her crown. Another shimmering door appeared in the air before us, and I knew, through that deep certainty that poets call instinct, that the room we entered vibrated with a magic beyond any I had yet experienced on Mt Parnassus. Excitement chased fear from my mind.

'Sit,' my mother said.

As we took our seats on either side of a low table, the symmetry of our positions felt intimate. I looked up and drank in two portraits of great length, framing a window. The frowning woman on the left held a lamp in her open palm, while the one on the right floated amongst stars, roots twisting from her head, her face untroubled. I felt the vibration coming from each of the figures. It was not the painter's technique, nor the scale of the portraits that set my skin tingling: it was the spirit of the women in the paintings. I felt sure that they were alive.

I shifted in my chair. 'I suppose I am looking at two of the Muses.'

'You will meet all my sisters soon enough.' My mother's smile had turned to a flat line. 'No, it is those who came before me that I honour here. I cannot meet them anywhere but in paint.'

The eyes of the woman holding the lamp seemed to lock on to my own. A tremor passed through me. This woman knew my feelings about Eurydicius, along with the love I nourished for the rhythm of words and the awe I felt for my own mother. I was certain of it.

'My mother, Mnemosyne, goddess of memory, was deceived by Zeus when he took the guise of a mortal shepherd,' Calliope said, gesturing to the woman with the lamp. 'He seduced her and lay with her for nine nights, and once the nine Muses were conceived, he banished her to the Underworld, where his brother Hades holds sway. Now, in that dark place, she helps souls who do not wish to forget their lives, leading them to drink from her pool and retain their memories. She carries her lamp always. And not only for the dead.' She tapped the side of her head. 'Through her secret work, moments of your life are polished like gems. Anything that you turn over in the lamplight of your thoughts is thanks to her.'

Staring at the goddess, I took in the lines that sliced her forehead, tracing them with my gaze. As I drank in her visage, I felt the weight of the fact that this goddess had given birth to my mother: that her power coursed in my own blood. Something firmed and took shape inside of me.

Matrilineal. The word popped into my head, like an iris stalk pushing above soil. *The granting of kinship through the female line.*

'And the other woman?' I said.

'That is Gaia. Mother of the world. The first creator and the titan from whom everything springs. She created the sky and loved it with all her passion.' The titan's lips were curved slightly upwards in the painting. 'From their union came Mnemosyne, so you can thank her for your grandmother,' Calliope added. 'Great Gaia did more than give birth to Mnemosyne, however. She raised her, educated her, showed her how to channel her powers.' Her voice smoked with ember and ash. I could sense the fragments smouldering inside it.

We settled into a silence. There was more to be said, yet I soaked up the magic thrumming through these portraits, through the invisible lines that bound titan to goddess, goddess to Muse, and Muse to myself.

That thing firming inside me, I realised, was hope.

When I glanced at my mother again, I saw that she was watching me. Rising, I walked to the portrait of my grandmother and touched her lamp softly with my forefinger. I tried to imagine her holding it aloft in the caves of the Underworld.

Mnemosyne – I sounded her name in my head – goddess of memory. *Gaia*, creator of the world. How was it that my tutor had never mentioned either name?

'Listen to me carefully, Orphia, and only reply once you have heard my offer.'

My mother did not need to rise. It was as if she towered higher with every word.

'You were made by a god and a Muse. Such a combination was … new. When Apollo and I were lovers, I assumed that any child of ours would be immortal. But Apollo did not worry himself by thinking of children at all. Gods rarely do.' She smiled sharply. 'They say a dragon can tell if its offspring will be powerful by looking upon the hatchling's face, as soon as it has pushed through the shell. When I held you, the first time, I knew what you were. And I knew what you could become.'

The air felt thicker; or perhaps it was the weight of my concentration.

'Hybridity is a beautiful trick: a miracle that we do not see coming. There you were, a mortal child with divine powers, crying so melodiously in my arms. I sensed everything that glinted in you. I felt the rise of your every breath. When Apollo took you from me, I did not know of the prophecy he had received; I only knew that I had lost something more potent than gryphons' tears, finer than a unicorn's skin.'

She stood and waved her palm across the open window, and the landscape before us shimmered. The ancient majesty of the pools and crags transformed into a tapestry of different hues – grey limestone, striated with orange where it had been eroded, then the varied greens of firs, laurels and pines, and below them, stretching all the way to the gulf, so many dots of olive trees that it hurt my eyes to behold them all. Amongst the grove, a handful of farmers moved.

'After I learned that Apollo meant to steal you from me, I fled with you and hid in a cave,' Calliope said, coming to my side. 'I thought that I had protected us perfectly.'

I remembered my vision when she had first touched me. In the blink of an eye, I was back in the dim cavern, gazing around at hundreds of crystals. I felt Calliope's sense of relief, of a crisis averted, and this time I knew the cause.

'Such was my relief at escaping him, I believed so quickly in my own skill. Never believe too quickly.' She gazed at me for a moment. 'This time, when I came for you on Mt Olympus, I made sure of my work – because it was not only my work, but a community's. We are hidden here by an enchantment of the Muses' weaving, supported by the nymphs' magic. What you cannot comprehend, you cannot undo. Zeus and Apollo have never taken the time to learn the subtleties of our work.'

Below us, a farmer wiped his brow. He stood for a moment, looking down at his basket. 'Which is the real Mt Parnassus?' I said. 'The city, or the grove?'

'I told you, a moment before, that hybridity is a beautiful trick.'

I watched the farmer begin moving between rows of trees once more. 'They are both real,' I said, slowly. 'The farmers sell to you, but you remain hidden in this realm.'

Calliope smiled. 'Even Muses need to eat.'

My eyes picked out a spot in the midst of the slope; why, I could not tell, but my gaze followed a path from the summit to just above the olive trees. I sought out a small cluster of marble buildings encircling a pillared temple. 'Whose shrine is that?'

'They call her Pythia. Some say she raves, but others know better. She is no more mad than I am.' Calliope's finger traced the length of a pillar. 'You see, I was the one to suggest the name of Oracle. The seer of Delphi earned my blessing.' She paused, and I felt the force of her thoughts. 'That is where the prophecy about you was made.'

Calliope walked back across the chamber and took a chair again. It was hard to resist looking at the temple, as if a rope yanked my gaze towards it. I wanted to search for some sign of the Oracle, and yet the longer I looked, the more unease swelled in my stomach. I pulled myself away from the window at last.

'It was a temple of Gaia back then,' Calliope said. 'Steam hissed up through the ground. No pillared buildings towered, but pine trees and maples gave shade and water flowed from the mountain. Women gathered there to hear your great-grandmother's messages: Gaia's belief in generosity, her love for creation. Each day, they worked together, interpreting the poems they heard in the soil and springs. The thoughtful work of these women earned them fame, so I suggested that they establish a single mouthpiece: an Oracle, to pass on their learnings by responding to questions.' I heard a tremor of anger in her voice. 'Your father did not like it when the Oracle predicted your death. He did not kill her, though. Nothing so kind.' Calliope's face tightened. 'He turned her holy shrine to the mother goddess into a Temple of Apollo. Treasuries line a path to its doors, stuffed with the spoils of war. Men rule that temple and speak on behalf of the Oracle, now – they call themselves her priests.'

For a long time, neither of us spoke.

'I have considered the prophecy since Euterpe learned of it, over a year ago,' Calliope said. She paused, and her gaze fell upon my face. 'Understand, Orphia, that words of prediction are veiled in many layers.'

Could I choose to ignore that prophecy of blood and death – defy my father's order to remain a warrior? When I thought of my body being torn limb from limb, fame paled and dwindled to a wisp. Yet it was not fame itself I wanted.

I wanted to tell stories of men who were soft when they were supposed to be hard; of women who were loud when they were supposed to be docile; of people of every nature who felt scarcely visible, and wished to make themselves whole through my stories. Fame was how a poet earned the right to be heard. I knew that I needed to reach beyond one dusty corner of the world and across the glinting firmament – though I would rather not have known it.

'If your death will be, then it will be.' Calliope's remark broke through my musings. 'But if there is a chance to challenge it, it is best to use the talents which once lay dormant in you. What did Zeus say? *A woman's weapon.* The dance of words is not only for women, but any woman should be proud to master it.'

'My father sought to train me, too,' I said.

'Unlike Apollo, I do not believe a common spear is your best defence. And I do not imprison you. You are free to leave, or to stay under the Muses' protection.'

Her voice's music reached me. The notes still smoked, a pyre that endured.

'I will be casting another spell, soon,' Calliope said, interlacing her fingers. 'Once I am done, Mt Parnassus will be burnished with a new glow, and the skin of our world will harden further against those who seek to find you. Then the Muses will begin your training.' She regarded me down the length of her nose. 'That is, if you desire to stay.'

I drew a deep breath. What I needed to say was hard, not only because I had to face my mother, but because I had to admit it to myself.

'You have offered me what no one has,' I said. 'I feel the kindness of it in my core. But now that I have escaped the Whispering Isle, I would not trade one sanctuary for another. I would walk in the world.'

Her smile surprised me. I had expected a flinty stare.

'I did not bring you here to offer you an eternity in isolation, Orphia. I know too well that life is water. Over the years, I have come to understand that you will leave us in time, to win the kind of fame that echoes down centuries.' She extended a hand across the table. 'But you must be equipped to choose that path. Fame is not gifted, but carved out slowly, stroke by stroke. Think carefully on what I offer, and decide if you would learn how to write your name across the sky.'

Her words flamed at the edges in my mind, leaving an afterglow. *Fame.* Had I not mused on the concept, just moments ago?

Yet no one had ever dangled fame before me like this. Glory was a vessel, I reminded myself: I needed to win renown so that I could speak. Not once, either. I needed to earn the skill to make sure I could *continue* to weave words, and reach all those hungry ears year after year. How else could I help my listeners?

Words could fly like spears. They could soften blows like shields, too.

Yet a hint of doubt pricked at me.

'I do not know that I possess such talent,' I said.

'Talent is but dust without discipline and honing.' Her eyes met mine. 'If you work, and fashion wisdom out of minutes and hours, you will truly enter the birthline of Gaia and Mnemosyne.'

Holding her gaze, I weighed the thought that was upmost in my mind.

'Mortal tongues do not speak of Gaia and Mnemosyne.'

The moment I released the words, I felt their sharp points. Calliope's frown twisted.

'You would not be another forgotten woman,' she said.

Slowly, I shook my head.

'I have known what you would want from me since I listened to you on Mt Olympus.' She placed a hand over mine. 'Our agreement will be a pact. I will train you with the skills, the knowledge, and most of all, the discipline that you need, so that when your time comes, you will be ready to do as your heart compels you. You can sail far beyond the fame of a skilled mortal, Orphia; far beyond the fame of even the most glory-decked heroes.' The words touched a recent memory, and I felt it stir within me. It must have shown on my face, for my mother frowned again. 'What is it?'

'Queen Hera spoke such a thing,' I said. 'That is, she spoke to me in my head. *You will be happier than all heroes, and yet not happy*, she told me. I have turned her words over and over.'

'I am afraid I cannot lay their meaning bare.'

She turned her face away. The question rose in my throat again, and I swallowed it.

'I will preside over your program of education.' Calliope's voice brimmed with harmonies once more. 'You will need to commit to your lessons, however. The Muses will be your teachers, and our realm will be yours to enjoy, but it will be steady work.'

Through the window frame, the temple and olive grove had disappeared, revealing the domain of green slopes and sunlit water once more. Gaia gazed down at me from the wall. Mnemosyne cast her lamp's light towards me. The whole room vibrated with magic, its force reverberating inside me, and this time, I allowed myself to absorb its waves, to let the power sink into my flesh instead of passing through me.

My father's words seemed weaker and smaller in my memory. *All your life, I have acted to protect you.*

I wanted to dare. To fail. To labour like a craftsman and improve. I wanted to fashion poems like mirrors, in which others could finally see themselves. Perhaps the only thing I did not want was to be protected.

At least, not when that protection was bought with my silence.

I inhaled, feeling myself drawn into the golden strands of the web of my ancestors. The harmonies of my mother's voice echoed in my ears.

'I accept,' I said.

No gryphons flapped down to meet me, this time. A dryad led me down a path to the east of the palace, chattering as she walked. The weight of my discussion with Calliope rested upon my shoulders and I breathed into the warm air, letting my mind settle.

The palace was a place for work, not rest, the nymph informed me. She introduced herself as Melia, and hastened to describe the plants she grew for the Muses' gardens – 'leaves that can heal and stems that can kill. I work with aconite, wolf-slayer, and hellebore, curer of madness.' Her voice rose and fell like a nightingale's song.

I glimpsed the theatre to our right, and then a large, square building, overshadowing a thick copse that Melia proclaimed to be a dangerous place. We skirted the flower-fringed walls of the nymphs' quarters, stopping at last outside a tower.

It was handsome enough, with a roof tapering into a point, yet something about the sight of it made me hesitate: a cold vine unfurling inside me.

'You have been honoured with a chamber in Melpomene's domain.' Melia drew a key from a pouch on her belt. 'Muse of ... well ... it is not my place to say.'

Lights guided us into the lower level, ringing the round chamber, marking the doorways. The gloom pervaded, but the multitude of candles lent a queer beauty to the dark stone as we mounted the stairwell. I prepared myself for a dim chamber, and felt joy leap in my chest when I entered a room that was half-open to the sky, the bed draped in white silks.

Strolling to the vast window and looking down into a rose garden, I tried not to grin. A room in the Muses' palace. *My* room. With the training of my hosts and a room of my own, who knew what I might create?

'Dinner will be at sundown,' Melia said. 'I will find you, if you wish for company.'

'It would please me very much.'

Melia gave me a warm smile and strode out.

The room was elegantly simple: a bed and pillows, jugs upon a tripod, a small hearth, and a table beside the window. The view drew my attention for such a time that I almost forgot about the furnishings, so occupied was I with the waves of red petals that spread out beneath my chamber. Only when I turned away from the window did I notice the lyre on the table.

In the path of the fading sunlight, the curve of tortoise shell invited me. It glistened with a new sheen, the result of four pearls on the crossbar: in my gut, I knew that there was one each for Gaia, Mnemosyne, Calliope and myself. An inscription gleamed on the instrument's side. I lifted it and read my name, carved into the lyre. With the same innate clarity, I recognised that Calliope had left me this gift.

Something pricked at my vision. I turned my face towards the wall and forced myself to exhale. A gift, I told myself; it was nothing more. Yet to see the instrument set up there, not stolen, not hidden, but waiting for me … named for me … a droplet fell onto the table, then another. Salt slicked my eyes.

'I am a poet, it seems,' I said, to the air. 'By the grace of Queen Hera, I promise not to waste my days.' My thoughts returned to Hera's descent into the Hall of Starlight, and the way she had stilled the immortals. 'Great Queen of Heaven,

I promise that I will hone my poems for you, so that my words may resound across the plains and valleys of the world for all the years to come. I will sing of goddesses who stand tall, with flashing eyes and souls like lionesses' teeth; of lovers who save each other again and again, even when the world believes they have entered the dark earth; of men who raise women up, defying their peers. I will sing of women who raise themselves.'

A single petal floated through the window and landed on the lyre's crossbar. I picked it up and rubbed it between my thumb and forefinger, relishing it, taking care not to crush what remained of the bloom.

The day before my first lesson arrived with a flood of sun. While I ate my bread and figs beside Melia in the nymphs' hall, whispers drew my attention, and I looked up to see Erato standing at the end of the dining table, framed by the light pouring through the open doors. Next to her, Euterpe tickled the feathers of a gryphon.

Erato beckoned to me. Dozens of nymphs stared at me as I made my way over to the pair of Muses, and fresh whispers broke out when Erato embraced me, her hands wrapping around my waist. She held me long enough for heat to rise in my cheeks. 'I hope you've finished those figs, Orphia.'

The grass of the slope was even more lush than I remembered, the stony outcrops scattered below me, the pools a glittering silver. I drank it all in while we flew over the peak, squeezed onto the gryphon's back. We landed on the far side of the lake; Erato waved a hand and conjured another shimmering doorway.

I did not recognise the place where we emerged, a slope bare of all but the most stubbly trees, the earth baked in the midmorning sun. A black woodpecker eyed us balefully from a tree stump. We walked in single file, a thin path carrying us down the sheer side to a gentler part of the incline, where the red fruit of pomegranate trees jewelled the mountainside.

Through the farmland we wove our path, between barley fields and clusters of olive trees, the air growing hazy as we descended. By the time we reached a plateau at the beginning of the southern slope, Erato and Euterpe were singing a song about a youth who had fetched a cup of wine from an Egyptian pharaoh to win the Muses' favour. I was smiling, a little surprised by the ease of their company, but my grin faded as I looked down upon the plateau. My fingers clenched into a fist.

Marble treasuries and sculptures of men and horses snaked alongside the path to the temple. Now that I was within a field's distance of her dwelling, I felt the weight of the Oracle's prediction settle upon my shoulders, as heavy as all that marble.

A hot gust of wind blew up from the temple site. It seemed to buffet me.

Euterpe shot me a penetrating glance. 'Calliope thought you might like to see Delphi up close.'

I looked upon the pillared temple, framed against the sky, and tried to admire its breadth. I studied the vast ramp that led into the temple, and before it, the altar where men slit the throats of cows and goats, watching the blood gush forth before entering. My thoughts slipped swiftly to the screams and shouts of a mob, to the ripping of my tendons, to soil drenched in the torrent of my own blood. I could smell the mud, the metallic tang of my insides. I could feel it all as if it were already happening.

This time, my thoughts were tinged with the possibilities that Calliope had raised in the hidden wing. My guts churned, but not only with fear, and while I looked down upon those tall pillars, I thought of how I had defended my decision to my father. *If I must die, I would live, first.*

'I think,' I said, softly, 'I have no need to dwell here.'

The wind stole my words and threw birdsong back at me.

Words trickled from my mind and pooled in the corners of my chamber as I made my way to my bed. Perhaps hours of reciting history and revising equations were to thank for the speed with which I slid into sleep. I could not say how long I swam in that rich darkness; I floated on my back, breathing quietly, until something transported me.

I noticed the grass first. It was longer than the grass in the gardens around Dorus' palace, or any grass I had glimpsed on Mt Olympus. The soft blades began to tickle my calves. A perfume wafted on the same breeze that made the plants dance, and though I did not recognise the scent, it coated the skin of my forearms, the bronze of my armour, even the bark of the trees that shielded us. The fragrance sang to me without words.

I saw him waiting at the end of the copse, where roses massed between a pair of trunks. A single ray of sun blessed his forehead. I followed the lines of his torso to where they ended, and a shudder of something unnamed passed through me. I put one foot on the grass in front of me, then the other. In the perfect stillness of the moment, we might have been priests, meeting in a sacred bower on a mountaintop.

Petals twined amongst the strands of his blonde hair. Why the wind had scattered them through his locks, I did not know. I thanked it all the same. Eurydicius had not lifted his stare from my person since I began to walk towards him, and his gaze blended awe and respect – a combination that I had never seen in any man's look.

The dark centres of his eyes widened as I stopped, a finger's length from him. My breath whispered against his cheek and I felt the warmth of his chest against my own, as if it had seared through my breastplate.

A sunbeam fell on my armour, bronze sparks rebounding on his skin.

'Can I touch you?' I said.

Fear hit me a moment later. Eurydicius did not frown, nor clench his fists. A gentle surprise eddied in his gaze, and his lips curved into the kind of smile that I could not misunderstand.

'I was hoping you would ask me that.'

When I wrapped my hands around his neck, he smelled of elm leaves. Lines of poetry bloomed in my fingertips. I mapped the contours of his torso, sketched the shape of his hip-bones, and pulled him closer. Not once did I question why he was naked.

'We could make the most of our time,' I said.

He touched my armour with a tentative palm. 'I think you have a true power, to read my thoughts with such ease.'

Something sharp and sweet cut through my body. The path it left felt raw, yet despite the pain, I craved more of the sensation, and I held Eurydicius' jaw so that I might study his face. Wedging my knee between his thighs, I pulled him to me, until his body fit against mine. I could see each one of his eyelashes in the filtered sunlight.

Now, as we looked at each other, his admiration hit me with a force that I absorbed, a ball of heat swelling and filling my chest. The same interest that every woman experienced from men, I had known. It had sapped me. The heat Eurydicius transferred to me charged me with energy: I could do anything, I could be anything. I could pluck a star from a constellation and set it down amongst the blades of grass. *I believe in every particle of you*, Eurydicius seemed to vow, and from another man I would have thought it a ploy. Yet I had gazed upon him first and my eyes had asked dozens of questions of him. This was the reply.

I woke, sweating, in the first blush of dawn. With an inhalation I climbed out of bed. The water from the amphora felt cool on my mouth, and I drank until my breathing slowed.

It was only a dream, I told myself: a vision born of the moon's slyness. It would do no good to dwell on it. The copse with its tall, swaying grass, its scent that serenaded, and its clusters of roses – that place did not exist. I climbed back into my bed and stared at the ceiling. Even if Eurydicius had swum to some far-flung crag, it would be best for me to put all thoughts of him aside, for there was little probability that I would ever see him again.

8

'Before, you were unconscious of the music, focusing only on the words,' Euterpe said. 'Now, you are too conscious of the lyre. You will not find the right notes when your mind is occluded. Every time you hesitate, you add another rock to that wall.'

All sorts of intricacies sprang up to challenge me, my lyre sounding too loud or too soft, the strings vibrating a little too long after I placed my hand over them. For two months, I worked on producing better music, composing in Euterpe's domed building and practising in my own quarters. On some mornings, the rhythm fell out of step with my words. On others, the melody was at fault. I nearly threw the lyre across my chamber after I ruined the end of a poem for the third time in the same night, and climbing into bed, I resolved to spend a week without playing at all.

'This must be paradise,' I told Melia and her friend Balanos as we strolled around the Muses' city.

'Paradise needs a little more magic,' Melia said quickly, setting the branches dancing on a nearby beech, while Balanos charmed butterflies from an oak hollow. The dryads could only do humble tree-magic, Melia explained with a brusque wave, but I delighted in every wonder they shared with me. Balanos summoned acorns out of clusters of oak leaves, though when Melia kissed her on the cheek, she grew flustered and stopped, leaving one acorn half-grown. When Mclia spoke to the flowering ash, she adopted the language of the branches, conversing in a thin and creaking tune. Balanos watched her as if there were no other nymph in the world.

My throat tightened. After a moment, the emotion nearly choked me. I had never seen two women show their adoration for each other – smiling, kissing and touching, without fear of repercussions. It felt painfully tender.

On my fifth day without work, I rose at dawn, making my way quietly down the stairs of the tower. I found the water-garden in the centre of the city empty, and followed the sound of bubbling, weaving through the fountains to the smallest pool in the centre of the gardens where a current moved in a circle, splitting into waves and looping them around.

The door swung shut with a bang as I entered Euterpe's hall.

'Flow,' I said.

She looked up, one hand curled around her aulos.

'Poetry flows into music. And music flows into poetry. Each gives power to the other in an exchange.' I made my way over the stone floor towards her. 'The trick is not to ignore music, nor to labour over every note. The poet must find the heart of the story; feel it; let it flow into the hand that strums the lyre, and the rhythm will take shape, as water is shaped by wind: formless, yet full of a thousand forms.'

'I see you have been studying.'

I was halfway to replying that I had avoided study, but I saw the brightness in her eyes and reconsidered.

'Yes,' I said. 'In a manner of speaking.'

'Good. You will need to think deeply and guard your patience, if you are to satisfy all your remaining teachers. Have I spoken harshly?' Her gaze skipped to my wrinkling brow.

'Well ...'

'We are not strangers any more, Orphia.'

I swallowed. 'No one can tell how long I have left to live. I wish to learn from the Muses, yet I imagine finishing my lessons and meeting the violent death that I was prophesied – without the chance to walk in the world.'

'Ah, yes. You are your mother's daughter. Fame must always be the goal, then?'

'Euterpe, I do not wish for a kingdom. I do not wish for a hoard of gold. Calliope showed me that I come from a line of powerful women, but my grandmother Mnemosyne and my great-grandmother Gaia are never seen or heard. I *will* be heard. If I am known for one thing, I will make sure it is my voice.'

And what it can do for others, I thought.

Euterpe studied me for a few moments. 'Would you like my advice on how to make your training hasten?'

'I would like nothing more.'

Her lips curved upward slightly, stopping short of her usual smile. 'Work harder. Analyse, criticise, and question what you have learned. Put aside all thoughts of men until you are done.'

I nodded, and as I walked away, I determined to follow her advice. It was not easy, but that night, I pushed away all thoughts of Eurydicius and Jason. If I focused on Euterpe's wisdom, I told myself, one day I would speak my poems all over the world.

Weeks slipped by, rather than inching along. The lines I recited came out clearly, but beneath my words there was a quickening of footsteps, a lapping of waves against a shore. Euterpe let me channel stories into the music, only guiding me when I sought her advice, and in each performance, I burned myself to the embers.

One month after I had watched the wind on the pool, I entered her hall to find her waiting in the centre.

'Tomorrow, Clio will be waiting for you.'

This was it. No more hours soaking up Euterpe's wisdom. I had not thought it would be over so soon.

'You should be proud of yourself. One step along the path to fame. It is no small step.' She hugged me. Her eyes seemed to glisten in the half-light.

News of my progress raced around the dining table that night. The nymphs soon took up the task of speculating on what my lesson with the Muse of History might involve. 'Balanos thinks you will be fighting a chimera,' Melia said, over the top of her cup.

'I do not,' Balanos huffed. 'I only said that her task might have many different parts, *like* a chimera.'

I trod carefully along the pebbled path towards Clio's domain in the north-west corner just after dawn. The stones became more jagged as I progressed, the insects more persistent. The narrow tower that rose before me offered a chipped façade overgrown with vines, and a naiad eyed me down the length of her nose before leading me up the stairs.

'Your arms are thicker than I expected.'

The words reached me before I entered the topmost room. The speaker's hair glittered with austere light, not at all like the gentle glow of the morning. Her silver strands remained brilliant even after she stepped away from the window. She watched me as I knelt. I had the impression of a goddess who had sprung from the stones of her tower – or grown into them – and I half-expected to see vines twisting out of those hard cheeks.

'Indeed, stronger than I imagined ... and yet your mind has not yet reached its utmost strength. You must be Lady Orphia.'

'Pleasant to meet you,' I said.

'You are a poet, are you not?'

'I aspire to be.'

'Give me a poem, then. An exceptional poem about the Phoenician alphabet and the sarcophagus of Ahiram,' Clio said.

I stared at my host. Clio stared back at me, undeterred.

I rose, trying to remember everything my tutor had told me about the sarcophagus of Ahiram and the strange Phoenician letters inscribed upon it. I knew that the alphabet's creators had drawn upon Egyptian writing and blended it with their own strokes, but as I tried to shape this into a story, the letters crumbled between my fingertips.

I cleared my throat, while Clio settled into the chair by the window. Glancing quickly at my lyre, I hoped for a rush of inspiration from Hera.

The only good thing I can say of my poem is that it was curtailed from its intended length. My recitation had all the vigour of a full-bellied snake; in dynamism, it was only slightly ahead of a bedtime hymn, and after some minutes trying to describe the sarcophagus, I cut myself off. Clio let the last line echo off the walls.

'I have failed you,' I said, lowering my gaze.

'On the contrary. You have just begun to learn. Describe your preparation to me.'

I thought back through the mental process of composition. 'The words seemed to slip through my fingers. The facts were all there, and yet … I could not bind them.'

'Good.' She rose. 'This way.'

We descended to the first floor, where Clio led me into a closet-like room. Each shelf teemed with artefacts: a long and curving sword, a tiger's tooth, a brooch that whispered of the feats of dead queens. Clio lifted a slab of limestone from between two cups and handed it to me. I examined the carvings of men and lions.

Letters ran along the upper edge of the stone. I imagined a hand pulling a slender chisel through rock to make each stroke.

'Sarcophagus, they call it, as you well know. The word means flesh-eating stone. A case designed to devour the corpse inside through the slow bite of erosion.' She looked at me over the slab. 'This piece entombed a man from the city of Byblos. I think you already know who he was.'

I had been running my thumb over one of the letters. I met Clio's stare and felt the presence of something hardened, like baked clay, and I wondered if each of the Muses came to resemble the knowledge that they presided over.

The Phoenician inscription along the top of the slab had worn away a little, but it did not seem to matter; the alphabet I had read so much about was finally real.

'Some man with authority told you about the alphabet on this sarcophagus, no doubt. Did he ever take the time to tell you what the message said? Did he explain how the author expressed himself – his language, his style?'

Slowly, I shook my head.

'Tell me what you read,' Clio said.

I took my time, peering at the markings. 'Here I see ... that the son of this Ahiram made this inscription. He entombed his father. He warns ...'

'Ah.' Clio smiled. 'You have come to the best part.'

'He warns that if a powerful king should make war on Byblos and uncover this sarcophagus, the throne of the kingdom may be overturned, and peace and quiet may flee from Byblos.' I stared at the letters, carved so deep into the stone that I could still see them.

'Tomorrow, you will give me a new poem, telling the story of this Phoenician message in your own words,' Clio said.

Magic flowed through me again that night. The lines of the symbols on the slab snaked around in my head, bringing the Phoenicians closer and closer, and I spoke verses to the air. Morning found me composing, pacing in my chamber, adding new phrases. I could not fail this lesson. Who knew how long it would take me to finish the next one?

'Tell me, Muse, of the marks that sealed a man's life and death in stone,' I said, walking into Clio's abode.

The invention was no longer a list of facts. It had a face, a body, and hands. Someone had made stroke after stroke, carving out an alphabet with which their departed could be remembered. The wheel, the serpent, the eye, the ox and the hook: I knew all those strange Phoenician symbols, ever since I had held that piece of sarcophagus.

'Tell me, Muse, of the letters that warned against deaths to come – mutilation and hot smoke and charred bones – the soft sound of iron spear-heads piercing flesh, the whistle of javelins through the air, the patter of horses' hooves over the shore, and the grinding of chariot wheels. The legacy of war, for those who do not heed this warning.'

I guided the rivers of words out of my mouth, pouring them over Clio, my poetry carrying the smell of tombs and the deep grooves of stone carvings. Ahiram's son had left a piece of advice, not just a memorial, I explained in throbbing phrases. Clio's lips gave a twitch upwards. I took that as my reward.

The lesson had been hard, but its fruits immediately grasped, I told Melia over the evening's bread. If the listener could not touch, smell, taste, hear and see history through your words, then the past remained buried, no matter how many lines you composed about it.

'They must be rubbing your mind raw, with all this work.' Melia waved her cup at me. 'You know, we are in need of a third woman to practise with spear and shield. I have beaten Balanos too many times, lately.'

'You have not! It does not count as a victory if you stroke my cheek to distract me!'

We set off for the garden beside the nymphs' quarters, where I found the gryphons sleeping under cypresses. The sun flashed upon the pond beside the clearing. We circled and jabbed: Melia fought best with the spear, and Balanos moved swiftly with her borrowed sword, but I could see the weaknesses in each nymph's style, and I took the opportunity to use my muscle against them, employing my body weight to test their strength.

It still tightened my throat to see Melia kiss Balanos. I might have often felt like kissing women, and even done more, once, under the protection of closed doors and moonlight, but until now I had not realised how much it meant to see others love, unhampered by fear.

I did not have the luxury of training often. Clio gave me object after object to study, and I wrote poems that made the dead walk once more. My teacher's sharp face never softened, but she nodded her approval and allowed me to glimpse the occasional tug of her lips upwards. *If only I could work faster*, I thought. Then I could learn to tell the kind of stories that would stun the world – stories of fearless women and men with gentle souls – and perhaps live long enough to share them.

I tried not to think of the prophecy. Most of the time, I succeeded, but it was like forcing yourself to forget that a lion was stalking your village – even if you did not turn your mind to it, you knew that it was circling.

After a few months, I walked into Clio's room and found a dish lying on the table. A pungent smell reached me even before I glimpsed the chopped herbs.

'Just one pinch.' Clio stepped out from the dimmest corner of the room.

I managed not to jump.

'Eat just one pinch of those green and purple leaves. No more.'

'Some teachers would explain why they were asking a student to munch on a blend of unknown herbs,' I said.

'I am sure that some would.'

I sighed. Taking a pinch of the strong-smelling herbs between my thumb and forefinger, I examined the tiny pieces of leaf, then dropped them into my mouth.

A force hit me in the stomach and I bent over, clutching my arms. When I had gathered the strength to stand, I looked up and found myself in a palatial hall, in the midst of a crowd. All traces of Clio's room had disappeared. Panic washed through me for a moment, but I reminded myself that Clio had asked me to do this – surely, I would not melt away.

Before the crowd, a woman ran her hand over the head of a panther, tickling it behind the ears. The gold-and-blue-striped glory of a headdress framed her strong features. I stared at her, letting my gaze travel down, for not only did she wear a pharaoh's Nemes, but she carried the sceptre of that office too. As I gaped, she nodded to the panther's handler, who led the animal away and brought an ape forward for her perusal.

The crowd whispered, their eyes wide. The woman inspected the ape, then a baby giraffe, then several trees in pots, and finally, a vast amount of gold. The people around me cheered when they saw the plates of bright metal.

'Hatshepsut!' they chanted, 'Hatshepsut! Hatshepsut! Daughter of divine Amun!'

The same force pummelled my stomach again and I winced, closing my eyes. When I opened them, I was standing on a hilltop, looking down at a pillared building surrounded on three sides by a bright blue lake. A gust of wind picked me up and carried me to the front of the building. I tottered, just managing to right myself, and stared at the structure before me.

This was a temple, I realised, for the Egyptian men working in the first room were setting a statue in place, and the calm eyes and slight smile on the stone figure made me certain that she was a goddess. I drew closer to her. The men did not seem to see me, just as the crowd in the palace had not. Footsteps sounded behind me, and I turned to find the woman in the pharaoh's headdress striding across the floor.

She walked straight past me and circled the statue, and when she returned to the front of the figure, she beamed.

The workmen knelt before her. She gazed down at them with a firm but kindly expression, like a mother surveying a brood of children.

'Our sculptor has shown great Mut reverence,' she said, and her voice shone with slivers of lapis lazuli and carnelian. 'But more than that. He has done her justice, and you have finished the job, transporting her with care. I declare that you will be paid twice the amount we agreed, for your peerless work.'

'Great Pharaoh, you honour us,' one of the men cried out.

'Hatshepsut is proud to reward those who restore the divine mother's precinct. You are not only men, now, but blessed devotees!'

I did not hear the men's reply, only glimpsed their elated faces. A third blast of the powerful force struck me, and I winced, clutching at my arms again, until I felt myself being yanked from the temple and up, and then I was flying – speeding upwards through a dark tunnel – and landing on the floor of Clio's chamber.

I gasped. Clio peered down at me. After a few breaths, I hauled myself to my feet.

'She looked like a pharaoh.' I tried to calm my voice. 'That woman. But of course, she could not be—'

'I must stop you before you finish that sentence. Be very certain that you have good reason to decide whether a woman *could not* be something.' Clio gestured to a chair. 'Sit, and tell me what you saw.'

'A woman in a pharaoh's Nemes, receiving gifts in a palace. Panthers and apes came meekly before her, and she examined giraffes and strange trees, and loads and loads of gold. A crowd cheered her. Then I saw a temple, enclosed by a great lake, and I walked inside. This same woman – they called her Hatshepsut – entered and remarked on a statue there, and increased the workmen's pay. And when she spoke, I felt …'

'Go on,' Clio said.

'I felt as though I were watching precious stones tumble from her mouth. I felt wealthy, but not as myself. It was as if I had become Egypt, and she was enriching me with every word she spoke about her goddess, watering my soil and warming my trees.'

Clio was silent for a moment. Thin sunbeams danced along the hard lines of her face. 'History is the process of remembering,' she said, lowering herself into the chair beside me. 'Hatshepsut could not serve as the head of Egypt's armies, being a female pharaoh. Yet she sent her men off on a trade expedition to the Land of Punt. They returned with a wealth of animals, plants, and more gold than anyone had hoped for, as you saw.'

'She should be famous the world over. Her name should fly from every tutor's lips!'

'Not content with this alone,' Clio continued, 'she made a special effort to restore the precinct of the goddess Mut, creator of the world in their lore; the mother goddess who had fallen out of worship. By enshrining Mut's power, she reminded all women of their own power.' Her smile became a crooked line. 'Of course, Hatshepsut was not all righteousness. She usurped her stepson to take the throne. But because she was not born a boy, she would have been passed over as an heir … nothing is simple, when a woman reaches for fame.' Her eyes fixed on mine. 'History is the process of remembering, as I told you. And no one should forget a woman like Hatshepsut.'

A raw and potent feeling surged through me. Was this not exactly the kind of story I had yearned to tell? Was this not precisely the kind of woman who had shown the world what all women could someday do – one who might inspire ordinary people?

'No one *could* forget a woman like Hatshepsut,' I said, slowly.

'I am afraid you are wrong. After she lost power, Hatshepsut disappeared. So did her name. It was erased from stones and monuments, and her stepson's name was written instead. Hatshepsut has been written out of history: scraped away.' Clio drew a deep breath. 'It is for Egyptian poets to restore her name to the world. Your task is to carve out her story here. You will restore her name for the Muses – for your last performance, give me a poem that makes Hatshepsut stride proudly before me.'

'I have scarcely had a glimpse of her!'

'And did you learn nothing from that glimpse?' Clio leaned closer. 'What impression did she leave in the bright halls of your mind?'

I heard the lapis lazuli and carnelian of her voice. I saw her smiling at the statue of Mut, her gaze resting on those calm eyes. I imagined her name being scraped away from all the monuments she had built, all the pillared buildings and obelisks she had constructed, and from the temple of Mut that she had restored, where the mother goddess stood serenely.

That afternoon, I began to work.

The more my poetry consumed me, the more I determined not to waste my spare hours. I fought with Melia and Balanos and walked in the forest with them, peering at the overhanging branches and laughing at the thrushes that landed on my shoulders without fear. I drank from the brook that ran through the eastern garden. I found the gate in the wall where the farmers brought their deliveries, guarded always by two oreads with bows. I breathed in the scent of the roses below my window at dusk, and each morning, I came to my task with my mind replenished.

As I came to know the orchards and grottoes and ponds, I walked everywhere except to the north-east corner. Melia told me in a hushed tone that the tower with the golden lyre was my mother's. Although I glimpsed her vast swathe of greenery when Erato and Euterpe took me for a long ride over Mt Parnassus on my birthday, I could not imagine intruding there.

I wanted what Calliope had, yet it was not the size of the garden that mattered. The thought of finding a secret spot within the Muses' grounds took root in my head. I reminded myself that I had never had more than a chamber to myself; every garden I passed belonged to someone, so why could I not claim a patch for myself? I searched the city without result, until one afternoon, when the light was fading, I found myself next to the copse again.

Branches knitted above my head. Their black threads had twined together long ago, and a shiver of something unnamed ran through me. Had Melia not said that this place was dangerous?

My feet propelled me into the centre of the copse. Warm air enfolded my person. I knelt, trailing my fingers through the grass, feeling the heavy stillness of every blade.

'Hear me, Queen Hera. Seal this place with your sceptre and bless it as mine alone. I shall give you verses that brim with gold, silver and things more precious. I shall lay the lives of women at your feet in glittering words.'

The grass rustled. A single rose danced on my right. Behind the swaying of its petals, I felt the same force that had made the Hall of Starlight quake, softened, but present. Slowly, I began to memorise every detail of this place.

When I returned in the weeks that followed, I listened to the spiders spinning their silken threads, taking in their high-pitched nattering. I absorbed the singing of the wet soil. There was something about the density of the air here, some richness of magic and memory that permeated the grass and the bark, but I was not sure that the memories I sensed had been formed yet. I seemed to be looking backwards and forwards at once.

Even though I could take liberties with Euterpe and Erato, I did not ask to visit the outside world with them again. I was protected, here. My mother had laboured over her spell for a purpose. Despite all this, I felt the pull of the southern slope of the mountain; I wanted to look at the temple, and I did not want to look at it. My father's voice echoed in my mind, carrying the bitter song of prophecy.

The thought of my death overwhelmed me, yet I remembered the kinds of stories I wanted to tell. When I rejected that vast terror and reached out for the small pieces of my work instead, I found that joy crept into my waking hours: a pleasant intruder. I composed verses about Hatshepsut, I revised the weakest lines, and I practised with the spear and shield. Between my work for Clio and my time with the dryads, I allowed myself to think of Eurydicius and Jason, picturing them journeying across a deserted plain or a valley, trying to imagine them as they would look now. I could see Eurydicius' golden irises and the queer light they cast. I imprinted his features into my mind, returning to them over and over.

Whenever I doubted my skill, the respect and awe that he had shown me returned, strengthened anew in my memory. I knew Euterpe's advice. *Put aside all thoughts of men until you are done.* Yet I wanted to sun myself in the rays of his admiration; to feel the afterglow of his gentle words.

Before I climbed into bed each night, I silently hoped for a dream like the one that had caused me to wake in thirst.

Something blocked my mind's path, and a black tide rolled over me, pushing me into sleep.

My last morning with Clio dawned flame-bright, the sun rising angrily above Mt Parnassus. In the top room of the vine-wrapped tower, I stood, my hands folded over my stomach. Images flew thick and fast from my lips: Hatshepsut donned her pharaoh's headdress for the first time, standing before a window, taking in the ever-unfolding scroll of mud-brick houses and towering palms that was now hers. She held her back straight before a group of male officials, ordering the trade expedition to the Land of Punt. The verses I had prepared for weeks surged, and I concentrated, calling up the scenes, picturing Hatshepsut's strong features, recalling her easy stride, and most of all, trying to convey the multitude of wonders in her voice: the beauty of raw gemstones that I had heard in each syllable.

Near the end of my poem, I added descriptions of women from familiar tales, passed over quickly in those stories but imagined anew in my verses: Penelope, weaving and fending off a whole pack of suitors; Hector's wife, Andromache, struggling against her captors at Troy, crying out her contempt for conflict; the priestess Cassandra, uttering her prophecies of great and terrible deeds, unheard. Woman after woman, scene after scene. I would not forget them, I told Clio with my final line: not if their names were scraped from every tablet and stone, for no one could scrape them from the stone of my mind.

'Congratulations.' Clio's voice was still as sharp as the rest of her. I glanced down and saw the vines that had pushed their way through the window, reaching towards me, carpeting the floor with leaves. Somehow, I had not heard their dance.

Clio walked to my side. 'Remember what it is that brings history alive. And remember all the women you have to thank.'

The door closed behind me before I could ask who my next teacher would be.

In the nymphs' dining hall, we drained every cup that night, celebrating another lesson's end. My head was heavy when I woke. I stumbled down the tower steps.

'It matters not that you are drunk.'

With one foot on the floor, I stopped.

A woman faced me from the centre of the chamber. Her voice floated easily through the air.

'You are still most welcome in my tower. But a conversation may not portend well.'

'Melpomene.' I made to kneel, but she waved a hand, dismissing the movement. Shadows around her eyes spoke of stone hollows, of caves and sea-beds. 'Are you supposed to give my next lesson?'

'Calliope is too hopeful. There is nothing I can tell you that will be of any use.'

She crossed the floor and made for the stairwell. 'Will you at least tell me what your domain of wisdom is?' I blurted out.

A gust of cool air brushed my cheek.

'You are speaking to the Muse of Tragedy.'

The door closed on her silver chiton.

9

I slept in fitful bursts, dreaming of a newly dug grave and then of a ship bobbing over choppy seas, wending its way towards lumps of glittering rock. When I woke, a shadow crossed my bed. Melpomene gripped a sword in her left hand, a club in her right.

'Your mother insists that we begin now.'

The shadows around her eyes had darkened.

'Should we not eat lunch, with the day half-spent?' I said.

'The hour is immaterial. I will speak, and you will listen. You will absorb what I say, or you will not.'

I looked down the honed length of the sword, and nodded.

The sky's brightness welcomed us to the garden, and we walked deep into Melpomene's domain, to where a path carved through the roses. The sunlight faded as we moved further in, giving way to a dim haven. Balls of orange light led us onward. I absorbed the tinge of the magical glow on red petals.

'This is your first lesson.'

A chill permeated the air. Somehow, I knew it was not a coincidence.

'A poet cannot write tragedy until she has lived it,' Melpomene said.

'What if—?' I began.

'Perhaps you are thinking of the prophecy of your death.' Melpomene cut me off. 'And perhaps you wonder if the knowledge of that death will enrich your verses with the wisdom of tragedy. Understand this: death is not tragedy. Death removes us from pain. You see, pain abides in life. It lies in putting one foot after the other when every step brings the torment of loss.'

'I wish I understood.'

'You would not wish that if you truly did.' Her brow wrinkled, and I glimpsed lines that had been formed long ago. 'I have warned you that I can teach you nothing. So let us prepare for nothing to commence.' She beckoned to me and I moved to her side. 'Bring a single rose from this garden to the lake outside the city. Pull the flower out slowly.'

I could not forget those words. All through my task, they hounded me. As soon as Melpomene had departed, I perused the garden's offerings and selected the slenderest rose, a flower that shone in the sunlight. It refused my efforts when I pulled at the stem, trying to inch it upwards.

Soil sprayed around the base of the rose as I yanked it free at last. I looked down on a wound in the earth. Where the stem had stood, only dark space remained.

I regretted pulling it, now. In cupped hands, I carried the flower out of the front gate, staring at the deep crimson bloom.

Melpomene raised her head and called my name from the edge of the lake. Beams of afternoon light glanced off the sword beside her.

'Smell your rose. Touch its petals,' she said.

I ran my finger over the velvet, feeling the distinct shape of each petal: those around the outside were wider and easy to stroke, while those near the centre were smaller, more densely packed. Bringing the flower to my nose, I inhaled for a long time.

'Speak to it,' Melpomene said.

I knew that she did not mean aloud. I conversed with the rose, telling it how its beauty had reached me not only through sight but through my other senses. Silently, I apologised for plucking a being so rich in character from the earth.

'Now drop it,' Melpomene said.

I made to let go of the rose. She gripped my arm. 'Not onto the grass.'

I watched the stem break the gold-flecked surface of the lake and saw the flower plummet down, down. I waited for it to float up again. When it did not, I looked across to Melpomene. Her eyes were closed and her lips moving.

The rose had disappeared, as if weighted by a stone.

'You could bring it back,' I said.

She finished her incantation and turned towards me. I smelled salt and smoke, crushed aconite petals, seared bone.

'I could,' she said, fingering the end of her sword. 'But you are here to learn.'

My chamber door opened with a bang a week later, on the afternoon of my twenty-fifth birthday. I put my lyre down with a sigh, thinking to tell Balanos that she was early for our stroll in the water-garden.

My mother swept across the floor and grasped my hand.

We left the tower at speed, a speed she maintained through the grounds and into the Muses' palace. I waited until I was seated in the high chamber opposite the portraits of Gaia and Mnemosyne before catching my breath.

'Twenty-five,' Calliope said.

Her hand stroked my cheek for a moment, as if she were examining my face for the first time.

'I can scarcely believe it myself,' I replied.

'And now you have learned music, history, and something of tragic poetry. You are no longer the girl who knew only the spear and shield. Certainly, more remains to be done, but one should not wait until all the races are run before one celebrates a victory.' Eyeing me over the table, she leaned in. 'It is time to show the Muses what you can do.'

'Is this a test?' I said.

'If it was,' Calliope said, 'I would not tell you.'

I was to compose a poem that combined the lessons of my first three teachers. The performance would take place in the greatest hall of the palace, Calliope explained: the nymphs would lay out grapes and honey, cheese and olives, quail eggs, and bread stuffed with currants. Whether the feast would be a reward to me for reciting three poems, or to my listeners for enduring my efforts, it was hard to tell.

There was no chance of leaving this to luck. I worked through my leisure hours and into the night. Euterpe offered me her lyre and invited me to practise in her domed hall, and I seized the opportunity to play with a myriad of echoes trailing my notes. Between practice, I often thought of that day by the lake, picturing the rose sinking into the bright water.

Sometimes I stood in the garden and looked at the place where the stem had been. A hole remained in the soil, dark and narrow.

The night before my performance I selected the most vibrant of the four poems I had revised, and climbed into bed before moonrise. The morning found me sweating. It took a while for snatches of my dream to return.

He had stopped before me, again, and I had pulled him to me. The scent of elm leaves had lingered on his skin. Now, I remembered where I had stood, and recognised the copse in the Muses' grounds, the place I had made my own.

In my dream, roses had bloomed between the trunks; the grass had been longer, more lush. Yet his respect for my poetry had resonated in every word he spoke, as real as if he had been standing before me, and his belief in me gave me new courage. I thought back to our first meeting, and his remarks after I performed for him. *You weave words so audaciously that they echo and reverberate, like a song made of gold.*

I remembered how he had stayed still when I made to kiss his hand, not only letting me lead, but welcoming my advance. It formed a smooth mirror in my mind, reflecting not only his desire, but my own.

With more effort than I liked, I cleared my mind, and began to fasten my chiton.

Soon I stood at the end of the largest hall in the palace and faced the nymphs and Muses. Sunbeams showered over me through a high window, and I offered a quick prayer to Hera. Now that I had met her, in all her dangerous glory, I felt more confident that she could hear me.

The crowd chattered and pointed. Calliope walked towards me, holding a great sack that tied at the top.

'Your task,' she said, 'is to defend yourself with the splendour of your imagery, the power of your rhythm, and the sun-drenched beauty of your tale.'

'Defend myself,' I said, 'against what?'

I saw that the sack was twisting and changing shape, as if something inside were pushing to get out.

'The very antithesis of poetry.' Calliope set down the bag, untied the rope at the top, and strode back to her place amongst the Muses.

For a moment, the bag writhed. Then a shriek rent the air, a cry of splintered stone and rotting wood, a sound born of decayed and despairing things. The creature that had made it flapped free of the bag and rose above me. Its feathered wings spread in black plumes and its talons glinted diamond-bright, slashing at the empty air, while its beady eyes stared at me from a face that had once been a man's but had transformed into something neither human nor beast.

That face rang a chime in my mind. I remembered a statue that Dorus had kept in his hall, with the same brutish, ireful features.

'Harpy,' I breathed.

My opponent shrieked again and swooped, plummeting towards my lyre.

I ran my hand across the strings and launched into the poem, letting music and words flow together and aiming them at the monster. The moment I had pulled the rose from the soil: that, I knew, was the story I needed to tell. I worried it would not be enough. Gazing into the harpy's scowling face, I forced myself to keep going.

The creature's talons snatched at my lyre. I yanked the instrument to the side and spun around, and as I faced my attacker again, I saw a ravenous jealousy in its eyes – a hunger to steal that curve of tortoiseshell and rip out those delicate strings.

I redoubled my effort. Euterpe's lesson on flow; Clio's lesson on bringing history to life; I poured them into my language, until my words were strong enough to hurl at the harpy. The creature flapped above me, trapped in place by my description of the rose in Melpomene's garden, working hard to break its suspension and slash at me. Its furious glare made me tremble for a second. I drew a breath, and turned my gaze away. Looking along the Muses' table and the rows of watching nymphs, I began to speak again.

I wanted them to smell the flower's perfume; to feel the petals beneath their fingertips. I wanted them to see all that velvet beauty falling, breaking the skin of the water, sinking and sinking. I wanted them to stand on the shore of the lake, watching the rose drop away. Most of all, I wanted them to return to the garden and gaze upon the hole in the soil, where the stem would not regrow. If they could hear me, and understand what I had learned, the harpy would, too – for despite the fearsome look on the creature's face, I knew that it was harder to impress a Muse than to defeat a monster.

Images streamed from my lips, and the harpy flapped further back, shrieking and wailing as it retreated, flinging a cacophony at my ears. 'Do not seek to pluck, nor to steal, as I did when I pulled that rose from the soil,' I said, facing it down. 'For what you leave behind will be more than a moment's theft. The impact of loss lingers beyond the plucking of a beautiful thing: it leaves a legacy of sorrow and regret. Do you really want to inflict such a toll, for a moment's thoughtless cruelty?'

That brutal face looked down at my own for a long moment. The half-man, half-bird horror above me flapped once, and then it stopped screeching, its body dropping slowly through the air, landing on the floor beside the sack.

I was suddenly glad that I had cast aside my poems about epic journeys and wars. I was shivering, but not from the harpy's last glare. It was the thought of that soft rose, and the black hole in the earth to which it could not be returned, that made me tremble now.

'Treasure your roses,' I whispered. 'Treasure them, even though their lives pass like sunlight over a lake.'

The words arrived with a reverberation. Feeling the last line hovering in the air, I looked around, wondering if the crowd was still listening; if my mother had deemed me worthy, or if she had decided that her daughter was a mediocre poet.

Applause struck me from both sides. I let my gaze rove around the right of the hall, where red, blue, green and white robes mingled; some of the nymphs smiled, and others stared.

I caught sight of Melia and Balanos, grinning. The pair of dryads held hands as they drew closer to me. 'We knew you could defeat it,' Balanos said. 'We knew it all along.'

Before me, Calliope was bundling the harpy into the sack and retying it. A hand closed around my arm.

'Impressive.' Erato's fingers lit fires on my skin. 'I look forward to our lesson.'

Her smile stayed with me even after she strode away, leaving me dazed.

'You have earned this lyre,' Euterpe said, joining me and stroking one of the pearls set into the crossbar. 'But do not mistake one great performance for the end of your work.'

She left me there, holding the instrument.

I did not have to greet Clio, for she appeared at my side and nodded – 'well done' – before returning to the Muses' table. There had been longer congratulations in the torture pits of Tartarus, I suspected. I felt her approval, all the same.

Her companions chatted – I saw one Muse put down her silver lyre, while another of the goddesses spun a globe upon the table. A third held a bunch of grapes, her expression pensive. I saw a Muse at the end of the table brush against Melpomene, whispering into her ear, lips pressed to her skin. Melpomene inclined her head towards her, and their mouths found each other with the ease of breaking waves.

'A perfect union, one might say. Thalia and Melpomene. The simple fusion of comedy and tragedy.' My mother had joined me quietly. 'They make it look easy. As if finding one's complement was a matter of tossing knucklebones and watching them land aright, with no risk of violence to one's person.'

She was looking ahead, and I had the impression that she was not really watching the pair at all.

'You wish to reproach me,' she added, and her voice was free of mesmeric power.

'Should I be grateful that you set a harpy upon me with no warning, and no defence but my own words?'

'It was never your equal.'

'It was a bird with razor-sharp talons and a paralysing screech.' I saw some of the nymphs glance at me and realised that I had raised my voice, and my breathing was ragged.

'A personification of discord. A crude, senseless thing,' Calliope said quietly. 'There are worse birds than those.'

In the silence that stretched, I wondered what she was thinking.

'Do I merit your advice, mother?' I said, low enough for only her to hear.

Calliope glanced at me. 'An impressive performance. That was Erato's judgement. You dangled the fruits of each lesson before us, one by one.'

'But?'

'Would you search for ways to make the taste sweeter?' Calliope said.

There was no use in pretending that I had the answers to my problems. I wanted to speak with power – not in beautiful words that dissolved in an instant, but in phrases that reached people, resonating for years. I wanted that more than anything.

'Sweeter, and richer, and beyond forgetting,' I replied.

'Then remember that a scholar may take her lessons and recite them piece by piece to win applause. But an artist must find a way to make them work together. She must weave every thread of knowledge to create something entirely new. Then, she may take on more terrible challenges.'

I felt the truth of it, and saw what I had missed. I had been so focused on succeeding within the task's limits that I had forgotten I could make something that spread out beyond the borders of my lessons. Horses made of water, racing towards me on the beach; branches splitting rainbow stone to push towards me; Hera's voice sounding clearly in my head; the force of the rivers I felt inside me, coursing and surging: these were the paints I could mix. My life had given me the brush to tell stories of people who stepped outside their roles and transformed the world. I only had to grip it.

Turning to thank Calliope, I faced empty air.

I drew a breath. Voices played in the hall, layering over one another. The harpy had been transported – or possibly magicked away, for I had not seen the sack go. Every woman seemed to be looking at me as I slipped out onto the balcony, leaning on the railing between busts of Athena and Pallas. After a moment, footfalls sounded behind me.

'You did well to speak of what you know.' Melpomene folded her hands and leaned on the rail. 'That is the only way to give voice to tragedy.'

'I fear I do not know enough.'

'I fear that some day, you will.'

We regarded each other.

'There is something I wish to ask you. Melpomene, I do not know if you can help me, but the prophecy about my death ...'

Perhaps I would have finished the question, if the voices in the hall had not swelled so quickly, cries mingling. We moved as one, Melpomene sweeping a path before me.

'Orphia, have you heard?' Balanos took me by one arm. 'Calliope has gone out. The oreads say that she rode her gryphon onto the mountaintop to meet somebody.'

No one seemed to agree on why my mother had summoned Fury and flown off. The general feeling amongst the nymphs was that something exciting was sure to happen, or something quite terrible. We did not have to wait long, for my mother strode back within a quarter-hour, the harmonies of her voice filling the hall.

'Visitors,' she announced. 'Two men, with a spear and shield.'

'How did they know the exact spot to summon an oread?' Thalia cried.

'The answer can bring no good.' Clio's expression looked even harder than usual, a feat I had not thought possible. 'I say we banish them to the far side of the world.'

'To have journeyed here and reached the summit, they might have some Olympian's protection,' Euterpe put in.

'But does that immortal wish us harm?' Clio returned. 'A snake may be lying on our path.'

'It matters not,' another Muse said. 'Since they have discovered our location, we should find out how they did so. At swordpoint, if need be.'

After a long pause, Calliope surveyed the group of Muses. 'Tell the oread to restrain and blindfold them. Take their spear and shield away, then bring them to me. I intend to question them in full view of you all. Orphia!' She turned so suddenly that I jumped. 'You must hide from their view.'

I knew better than to question a statement pronounced with such clarity. Melia and Balanos accompanied me to the balcony, where my mother waved a hand across the width of the archway. A gasp from the crowd of nymphs told us that the balcony had disappeared.

Teetering a foot's length away from the archway, we watched two oreads march a man into the hall and shove him to his knees. He struggled with his bonds. I knew the lines of his mouth, which had smiled so often that it was strange to see them turned down.

One of the oreads pulled off his blindfold. I looked into Jason's eyes.

'Unbind me.' He tilted his chin towards Calliope.

The fine brocade on his cloak seemed at odds with the grime that slicked his hands and feet. He held his wrists straight, thrusting out the knotted rope that tied them. A wave of disbelief washed over me. It was as if a piece of my old life had floated halfway across the world, chipped and battered, yet identifiable at once.

My mother stood before Jason, unmoving. 'Bring in the next one.'

I wondered if I should step off the balcony and greet him, but my mind slipped on to the next thought, and I guessed who might accompany Jason. I clutched the railing of the balcony, trying to come to terms with the emotions running through me – hot desire, and at the same time, a fear that cracked like ice. What if I seemed different now? What if he did not wish to see me at all?

A breeze blew through the palace. It wafted beneath the arch to where I stood. The scent of elm leaves brushed against me, sweetness enveloping my body.

Eurydicius knelt silently, lowering his head. The blindfold looked very well on him, I thought, trying to breathe, feeling as if I could not draw enough air into my lungs.

'This one did not struggle,' the oread behind him said.

Euterpe spoke, standing at my mother's side. 'You are blessed to be in the presence of the chief of the Muses, Calliope, Muse of Epic Poetry and goddess of inspiration, she of the tablet and the gold lyre. Prepare to make your obeisance.'

The words washed over me, heard yet unheard. All I could feel was him – the gossamer of him – clinging to my skin with weightless power.

'Take his blindfold off,' Calliope said.

The nymph pulled the black cloth from around Eurydicius' face. I took in those queer golden orbs that I had only seen in dreams for some time, and felt fear rising within my chest: fear of something vast, like the beginning of a story.

His soft hair trailed over the shoulders of his robe. It bore the rufflings of wind and rain. He looked at Calliope and then glanced from side to side; only for a second did his gaze pass over the archway, but our eyes locked.

It was as if my mother's spell dissolved beneath our gazes; as if it had never been made.

'This is Eurydicius,' Jason said. 'I am Jason. And we have come over land and sea, through valleys of chalk and blood, to seek eternity.'

The laughter twined with the notes of the harp, the breeze curling around the table. Before me, the sun baked olives and fattened grapes, but under a trellis dripping with vines, the conversation moved in cool waves. I watched Erato engage Eurydicius with a question, leaning in and touching his forearm, and I felt something stir inside my chest.

A finger tapped my arm.

'Did you know I met Heracles, last month?' Jason's voice came out dangerously bright. 'A true hero. We spoke of desire, and he told me that appetite lies not in the stomach but in the eyes.'

I lifted my gaze from Eurydicius and tried to assume an air of dignity. Jason smirked and held up a bunch of grapes, selecting the largest. After a moment, I sneaked another glance across the table, to where Erato had touched one of Eurydicius' locks.

He shifted slightly away from her, toying with his cup.

I glowered, unsure whether I was frustrated with him or with myself. For months, I had tried not to think of him; I had forced myself to concentrate on work when I wanted nothing more than to dwell on the memory of him. Now he appeared at the home of the Muses, blindfolded and kneeling, like a gift. As he glanced across, our gazes met, and a flush suffused his cheeks; I could scarcely look at him without staring, yet the gentle admiration in his eyes made me feel stronger. I was tightly woven wool.

When Calliope clapped her hands, a hush spread.

'We do not offer you this meal like mortal hosts. As chief of the Muses, I shall name our price. Do not look so tense, Jason.' The Muses laughed, except for Melpomene. 'I demand your story. You must tell us the tale of your journey since Apollo burned the island.'

A few of the nymphs who were serving us water and wine stared at Jason as he rose. They seemed to have forgotten that they were holding amphorae. I noticed that a determination filled Eurydicius' gaze, as if he strained to keep it fixed on his friend.

The story rolled quickly off Jason's tongue. The two men swam away from the Whispering Isle, navigating chunks of burning rock, until they reached the nearest shore. They searched the hills surrounding the beach but found no other survivors. (The washer-women and wives, I guessed, had safely reached another shore; I thanked Hera's daring.) Setting off for Eurydicius' home, the pair took what work they could along the way, ploughing fields and chopping wood, earning themselves bread and even a spear from a wealthy landowner. Eurydicius had refused a second spear, asking for a shield instead, which he had fashioned 'into something quite extraordinary'.

I was very aware of the hint of cherry that suffused Eurydicius' cheeks.

'I wish I could say our journey stopped there,' Jason continued. 'We found Eurydicius' farmland burned, his family's cows slain and their fields scorched on every side. No one knew where his father and mother could be found – we searched the nearest town, but we could not track them.'

Out of the corner of my eye, I saw Calliope shoot a meaningful look at Euterpe.

'What then?' Erato said. 'Do not leave us unsatisfied.'

'We set out on the long journey to Iolcus, my home city in Thessaly. I was not easy about it. You see, my mother sent me away to the Whispering Isle when I was a child because my uncle Pelias plotted against my father and locked him up. She feared Pelias would kill me. I had no way of knowing what welcome awaited me after all those years, or if my parents were even alive.' He looked down, and I admired the artistry of the glance, almost sorrowful in its concern. 'I would like to say that our travels were easy, but we crossed valleys of chalk where corpses lay in piles. We fled from ghosts who haunted the hills. We fought off beggars who accosted us. Wolves circled our tent while we slept, howling through the night, yet somehow, we survived. Our last task was to cross the river Anauros, whose water was cruel as winter. Eurydicius saw an old woman trying to wade in, so we ran to help her across, and as we did, one of my sandals came loose and floated away.'

He paused, and his next breath was sharp.

'Arriving in Iolcus, we sought my father, only to learn that he had been exiled. My uncle Pelias had usurped the throne and vowed to persecute all pretenders. We followed a procession to the marketplace, where Pelias stood before a crowd, presenting prizes to athletes. People shouted as we walked through: "It is he!"'

'If you stop there, I shall come down on you with the wrath of Athena,' Erato said.

'You like my tale?' Jason raised an eyebrow.

'I refuse to be left waiting for a climax.'

'Ah.' Jason smirked. 'Then you will be pleased to hear that all the city knew of a prophecy that the true heir to the throne would return wearing one sandal. At once, they fell upon me, strewing me with petals and oils. Eurydicius was half-covered in oil by the end of it.' This image distracted me for long enough that I had to make an effort to listen. 'Of course, Pelias could not kill us, not with half of Iolcus celebrating our arrival. He told the crowd that he would offer me a noble quest: in order to claim my throne, I must fetch the Golden Fleece.'

Gasps sounded. Clio raised an eyebrow, which I felt was equivalent to a gasp.

'As I am sure you know, great Muses, he who seizes the Golden Fleece holds the power of true royalty. King Aeëtes, son of the titan Helios, keeps the fleece in a sacred grove in Colchis. It is guarded by fire-breathing bulls and beside it sits a dragon that never sleeps. It should be a pleasant task.' Jason smiled.

'Do you mean to say that you have accepted such an unjust condition?' Clio said.

'Readily.'

Whispers broke out all along the table. Jason kept smiling, his jaw set. I had seen the same look on my father's face when he spoke to Zeus: formal, yet unwilling to cede an inch of his own soil. I considered the difficulties that a returning heir might face – a lack of connection to both the minor nobles and the people – and I imagined what fame and triumph a quest might bring.

In his first training session on the Whispering Isle, Jason had challenged Zeno. Though he had lost, all the men who witnessed the fight had talked of his audacity, and within a week, everyone on the island had known Jason's name.

'I should bring a bunch of fine soldiers and sailors with me on such a quest,' Erato said. 'Strong, handsome men.'

'Indeed, great Muse. We are assembling a crew of heroes that even a flame-huffing serpent might cower to look upon.'

We. One little word. I darted another glance at Eurydicius, and had the impression that he had quickly turned his gaze back to Jason again.

'We took armour, sturdy cloaks, and weapons from the palace – no oil or petals.' Jason allowed his listeners a moment to grin. 'I am pleased to tell you that we have recruited Castor and Pollux, the twins fathered by Zeus. We have also received a promise from the famous King Peleus, ruler of Aegina. Our latest recruit is a man called Heracles ... did you ever hear the story of how he tamed vipers in his boyhood, flinging them around like toys?'

The attention of the company was fixed on Jason, and only Calliope spoke.

'"We have come over land and sea, through valleys of chalk and blood, to seek eternity." Bold words.' Nymphs and Muses alike switched their gaze to Calliope. 'So you cobble together your crew of extraordinary men. Eternity will be found in the soft fur of the Golden Fleece, I take it?'

Jason nodded.

'And how did you find us, on Mt Parnassus?' Her voice swelled with the question.

'That is the strangest part of our tale, great Calliope. After I persuaded Heracles to join our quest, we set out towards Aetolia. Within hours, a gang of thieves attacked us. Let me tell you, it takes a pitiful sort of man to live out his days by robbery on the road, but when a dozen such men descend on you with knives, you must wield your spear swiftly. I would not have had the opportunity, however, if Eurydicius had not blocked them – he had strengthened his shield over the course of our journey, using his craft. Without his aid, I might never have killed a single man.'

'It was nothing.' Eurydicius reddened further. 'I only did what anyone would have done.'

'It was a lot more than nothing.' Jason looked around the table. 'That is why I offered my friend here a reward. He said that there was only one thing he desired in the world.'

'Revenge,' Calliope guessed.

'Gold,' Euterpe said.

'Immortality, or immortal fame,' Clio posited.

'Wise thoughts, from the wise Muses.' Jason bowed his head. 'But Eurydicius asked only that I take him to Orphia, the warrior-poet he had spoken with on the Whispering Isle.'

Giggles drowned out the Muses' replies: the nymphs could no longer contain themselves. Jason laughed heartily along with them, while I tried to catch the thoughts that were rushing through my head. Had Eurydicius really been thinking of me since the island, just as I had been thinking of him? Why? When we had met so briefly, what could possibly motivate him to seek me out?

I ignored the gigglers, trying to catch Eurydicius' eye. He glanced away from me.

'Now I come to the end of my tale, and I think it will astonish you most.' Jason clapped his hands, basking in the delight of the nymphs. 'I was pondering how to find Lady Orphia, and it occurred to me that I might pray to her father, Apollo. Before I could kneel and prepare an offering, a voice called out a greeting. It was the same old woman we had helped across the river Anauros. She thanked us for our aid and asked if she could help us in return. I joked that she could only help us if she knew how to find Orphia, daughter of the god Apollo. And ...'

'You don't mean to say that she *did*?' Euterpe interrupted.

'Indeed, great Muse. She replied that Orphia was on Mt Parnassus, and it may sound strange, but the two of us believed her at once. The woman offered to take us there, and I agreed, though in truth I doubted that she could help us to such a lofty place. That night we shared our food with her, and she gave us some of her wine. What wine! It tasted like ... help me, Eurydicius?'

'Like the juice of a fig when it is opened and the hidden sweetness flows.'

'Just so.'

My breathing quickened. Eurydicius looked across the table for less than a second, then swiftly turned his gaze down.

'Do reveal everything,' Erato said.

'For you, I shall,' Jason said. 'We lay down, and the grass began to feel soft. Eurydicius and I talked of the strange day that had passed, but we soon became drowsy, and fell asleep in each other's arms, not making it to our tent.' Giggles issued from a group of dryads, and Jason winked at them. 'You will never believe where we woke up!'

'Do not delay my gratification,' Erato said. 'Give it to me directly.'

'Why, we were lying on Mt Parnassus! Or so the old woman told us. She helped us up, and we saw the slope of the mountain below us, while a vast white cloud hung above us. Our tent and cloaks were gone, and much finer clothes and a sack of gold had replaced them. My spear remained, and Eurydicius' shield lay beside it. The old woman claimed to know nothing of how we had arrived here, but she walked around the mountaintop as though she knew it, and guided us to a tall stone to summon an oread. She instructed us to ask the nymph for an audience with the chief of the Muses, great Calliope.' He grinned. 'And that, you see, is how we came to be here.'

Suspicions had swirled in my consciousness when Jason spoke of his arrival in Iolcus, and the happy recognition of the heir with one sandal. I could ignore them no longer. 'Did this old woman tell you who she was?'

'Eurydicius thought to ask. She said that she was "one who had saved us". When I pressed her for an explanation, she would only say that Lady Orphia would understand what she meant.'

It was not easy to keep from speaking again. *Mother*, I thought. *Euterpe. Shall we take a walk about the vines?*

Calliope sent the nymphs over with more food and left Thalia – the Muse of Comedy – entertaining the party with a song about an orator who lost his voice. Once the guests and Muses were guffawing, we met where the eastern garden stretched before us, and walked slowly between two long rows of vines.

'It seems simple,' Calliope said, when I had shared my suspicions. 'Let us assume that Hera was the old woman in the river, as you have guessed. She gave Jason his kingdom back. She brought these two young men to Mt Parnassus. Why?'

'To help them, of course,' I replied.

'An Olympian's help is a spear that returns,' Euterpe said. 'It may pierce you after your enemies.'

I lapsed into silence. We walked between bunches of grapes, the purple fruit dangling towards the ground.

'Calliope,' Euterpe said. 'I think another Olympian may be on your mind. It is not a coincidence that those fields were scorched, is it?'

The two women exchanged a glance.

It took me a moment to turn over the words and pick out *scorched*, and make a connection. Calliope's stare met mine. In it I read such clear confirmation that I did not need to ask another question.

If Apollo was angry at Eurydicius, then he might pursue him here. The memory of my father sending Ixion shooting into the sky returned with new force. I knew that when a god performed a deed out of spite – say, melted an island – he would not enjoy having his action thwarted, even by a solitary survivor. It did not matter if Hera had been the one to save Eurydicius. A goddess was a deep-rooted tree. Mortals were merely twigs to be snapped.

I did not want this gentle shield-maker to be snapped. As I mused on the danger, I was struck by the depth of my fear for him. Who was Eurydicius, that he could walk naked into my dreams? How had this man managed to strip my emotions until they, too, were bare, and I was aching to be near him?

I saw Calliope glance towards the table.

'If you turn them away, they may not be so lucky on the road this time,' Euterpe said.

'Mother, will you consider letting them stay a little while?'

'This quest may be worthy of a poem.' Calliope paused. 'There are some things that need time to rise to the surface, and some that must settle. In the meantime, your friends will stay the night.' She weighted the word *stay* like a boulder.

I could not read the second look that passed between she and Euterpe, but I knew that there was something I was not being told. Calliope's interest in the quest was genuine, of that I was sure. Yet I had determined some time ago that heroics held no appeal for my mother.

Jason stood up as soon as the news was announced. Cheers from several of the nymphs obscured his thanks, so he raised his cup to toast Calliope.

Around me, the talk increased; I saw Melia and Balanos pouring more wine, brushing against each other in the process; I saw them, and I did not see them. For the first time since the beginning of the banquet, Eurydicius' eyes had flicked to me.

Some kind of magic raced through the air, setting my skin tingling.

I pushed back my chair and walked around the table. The afternoon sun filtered through the overhanging trellis, and it warmed my back as I took the seat beside him.

'I was beginning to think that you were afraid of my gaze,' I said.

'Only of what it might make me do.'

'Does it entice you?'

'I fear it will entrap me in a net that I do not wish to escape.'

I fought to keep pleasure from bursting across my face like a sunrise.

'How long has it been? More than two years?' I asked.

'I am afraid so.' Eurydicius met my eyes, now. 'It is not time passing that makes a difference, I find, but experience. Anyone can stay at home for two years. But after this journey I have been on ... I feel as if I have lived ten years, Lady Orphia. I lay down under the stars many times, and beneath the strange lights of the firmament, I had much time to reflect. Amongst all the scuffles, the long days on the road, my mind always came back to creating.' A flame shone in his eyes. 'Crafting wood, bronze and leather. Decorating. Examining mobility and testing weight. Making shields: such gentle devices as keep a few inches between death and skin. A paltry thing, next to your poetry, I think.'

'Most poets could not use their verses to fend off a gang of thieves,' I said.

'I believe you could.'

I smiled, despite myself. 'The two years since we met have gifted me with more experience than I could ever have expected, in truth. Its worth is beginning to settle upon my shoulders.'

'I can see that.'

'How so?'

'You have a shine about you. A radiance. Not physical, but I can see it all the same. It is in the way you talk, as if your words surged upon a river of stars.'

I summoned the courage to reply.

'Sometimes, my poems seem pale and thin. But when you say things like that, you make me believe in their strength,' I managed. 'Back on the island, the way you spoke to me ...

it stayed with me, like a lump of gold in my throat. I wish I could give you something in return.'

'You give my days a spectrum of colour. Since I first heard you speak, I have come to believe in wonders, magic and heroic stories ... the things I was raised to believe in, but never could.' He looked down at the table, and his voice dropped. 'The heroes seemed so cruel, killing and maiming, raping innocent women, or letting their men do it; and the gods often punished people for no reason. But when I heard you weave the story of Pandora, I knew I was listening to a hero, and her magic was not cruelty but poetry. You asked to give me something. Lady Orphia, you've given me something to believe in – *someone* to believe in. I see a poet who can bring stories to life and inspire the weakest of us. Why you grace me with your words, I don't know, but every second near you makes me more alive.' He drew a soft breath. 'Before you, I lived in greyness.'

This time, my silence came from pure shock.

What could I say? It seemed that in praising my speech, he had rendered me mute. Gratitude and desire danced inside me, and instead of replying, I passed him a grape. I had seized it without thinking, but now I imagined placing it on his tongue, pushing it into his mouth.

He took it, and his thumb brushed mine. Heat travelled through me, though not as with Erato, where tiny fires had bloomed under my skin; this warmth came from somewhere deeper, and did not expire so easily.

'I expect they will invite you to take breakfast in the nymphs' dining hall,' I said. 'This garden might be a more pleasant prospect.'

His brow wrinkled. 'Will there be food here?'

'No. But we will be alone.'

Cherry stained his cheeks again. This time, the red did not fade but deepened, spreading the longer I looked at him.

The gentle breeze had given way to a gust by morning, and leaves stirred in the eastern garden, their rustle swallowing my footsteps. I watched from behind an oak tree. Four gryphons gathered around Eurydicius' shield while he stroked the bronze on the outer side.

'It must be a very good shield, to pique their interest,' I said, stepping forward.

The wind threw his locks into his eyes as he looked up, and he tucked the strands hastily behind his ears. One of the gryphons snuffled at his toes. He reached down and tickled its feathers. 'In her wisdom, Calliope permits me to continue my work. Am I to be blamed for starting early, when I have such an encouraging audience?'

As if in response, the gryphons cawed. 'Not at all,' I said.

The bronze of the shield glinted between us.

'Will you try it out?' Eurydicius said.

He picked up a spear lying on the ground, offering it to me, and I grasped its middle.

We circled each other, the gryphons retreating. He waited, a smile ghosting over his lips. I thrust. The iron spear-head struck the shield and the thrum of the impact echoed across the garden, and whirling, I struck again, moving without a pause, to meet the same resistance.

Harder and harder, I attacked, but every time he raised the circle of bronze.

'Some men swing at me,' I said. 'I have never fought one who wanted only to receive my strokes.'

'A wooden shield is best for fighting. Bronze for absorbing blows.'

I struck again. The metal repelled my force. I stepped back and pushed forward again and again, until at last I put down my spear and inhaled deeply. 'Give me that.'

'You will have to take it from me.' He raised the shield.

I strode over, leaning across him to touch the bronze, our bodies pressing together as I studied the device. At once, I saw what I had missed. Not only was the bronze thicker, but it had been beaten and shaped in a way that allowed it to mould to the wood with greater concentration in certain areas, repelling the spear-head where it landed. In other places, the iron of the spear could be trapped by small bumps. Like a map of terrain, the shield revealed its intricacies up close.

'Amazing,' I breathed. 'How many years did you train in smithing?'

'I like to teach myself, bit by bit, whenever I have time.'

Running my finger around the rim of bronze, I felt the perfect design of it. 'Another craftsman might have added a honed edge, or a spike in the centre,' I said.

He gave a small nod.

'This shield has been made to stop an attacker, and only to do so.'

'At a certain point, I began to wonder if living is more useful than winning glory.' He gazed out at the oak tree.

I had opened my mouth to say more when Jason arrived. 'I might have guessed I would find you two together.' There was a disgruntled note in his voice.

Eurydicius held out his shield. 'Returned to me for a few hours.'

'And my spear, too, I see.' Jason snatched it from my hands and gave Eurydicius a pointed look. The men seemed to hold a silent conversation, then Eurydicius bowed to me and walked back towards the garden's entrance.

Jason waved his spear at the gryphons. They shrank back from him.

'You know why I wish to speak to you, I think,' he said.

In that instant, I realised that I did know. I had known it ever since he told us of the quest for the Golden Fleece, but I had not wanted to admit it to myself. Looking to the end of the garden, I caught sight of Eurydicius kneeling next to a clump of anemone poppies. He was smelling one of the red blooms.

Jason had never been good at waiting. He tugged my arm and I followed him through the trees to the pond in the middle of the garden. On all sides, branches covered us from view.

'You need my skill,' I said.

'A unique power. Some would call it greatness.'

'Power implies that there is no work involved.'

'I saw what you did to Ixion. Work or no work, your power could save lives on our quest, and win us glory,' Jason said.

I looked out at the pond. The wind rippled the surface, silver diamonds shimmering and dissolving.

'Life seems long, when you hide from the world. Once you are living in it, the time to carve your name dwindles. So many people chip away with a feeble arm. I have never claimed to be Heracles,' Jason said, 'nor the son of some Olympian. But I will bind the heroes of our age together and carve a mark so deep that a thousand years from now, children shall bear our names.'

A team of heroes. Had any Greek attempted such a thing? I pictured rows of fractious men, fighting side by side.

'Who will hear of the strange seas we shall brave, the kings we shall meet, and the dragon we shall fight, and not wish that they had sailed on the *Argo*?' Jason said.

Ah, I thought. *Some wealthy man has already gifted him a ship. Even before sailing, he would set his name afloat.*

'Once,' I said, 'I would have jumped at the idea of sailing very far away.'

'But now, you have something to give up?' Jason waved his hand at the Muses' city. 'Perhaps fame is not your calling after all.'

Even though I knew what he was doing, I felt the words pierce me. A team of heroes might still fail; they might fall to squabbling before they ever reached the open sea ... yet I thought of dragons, of fire-breathing bulls. I thought of the harpy I had just defeated.

'I shall not rush you to choose, for I will be drinking wine with Euphemus, son of Poseidon, and shooting arrows with Philoctetes.' He did not add that the latter was the most famous archer in the land. Some boasts were all the louder for being unsaid. 'When I have won them to my cause, I shall return and ask you again.'

'You are determined, then, to win the Fleece.'

'No matter what.' His voice rang over the mountainside. 'Mortals live by different laws to gods, you know. We must fashion our own glory.'

He offered his arm, but I swept ahead of him. All the way back to the Muses' palace, I held up the pieces of his offer, considering them one by one like beads on a chain, conscious that my life too was composed of many beads: Eurydicius, Delphi, and my poetry, strung next to one another, separate and glinting.

'You would leave the realm of the nine Muses?'

Calliope crossed the floor of the foyer, the others flanking her. She stopped just beside the fountain.

'I hope to visit again, with your permission, great Calliope.' Jason bowed his head.

A thoughtful look passed over Calliope's face. I had learned that a silence could be as effective as a speech. After a moment, she turned her gaze to Eurydicius.

'I would stay on Mt Parnassus, if it pleases the chief of the Muses.' Eurydicius drew a shuddering breath.

Questions burst from all around, a dozen people speaking at once, some gesturing as they spoke. Eurydicius waited for silence.

'In return for my lodging, I can make shields which will withstand blows from the most determined warriors – for I think the farmers who supply your city lack a defence that they can employ themselves. If you will do me the kindness of keeping me here, my craft may protect them.'

He looked across as he finished his statement, catching my eye.

The soft fragrance of elm leaves seemed to swirl around me. The flurry of talk seemed far away, even as the others began to mutter anew. I could smell him as if my face were pressed to the crook of his elbow, his scent filling every one of my senses.

Calliope clapped her hands. Both Eurydicius and Jason jumped.

'You will not eat the fruit of our trees. You will not lay a hand on any nymph. You will not spend a night in my daughter's company, until her lessons are done, and you will never enter her presence unless she invites you to,' Calliope said, looking at Eurydicius.

He bowed his head, and Calliope nodded. She laid a hand on Jason's shoulder, looking at him meaningfully, then swept from the foyer.

The stones echoed with voices, nymphs and Muses talking at once, while Jason pulled Eurydicius aside. I stood, my limbs heavy, still taking in what had occurred. There was no getting near the men, and I watched the naiads and nereids thronging around them, until Erato took Jason by the arm. He looked up quickly and did not protest as she steered him away.

'Now,' I heard her say, 'we have so little time before you leave, and I promised to show you …'

Eurydicius excused himself from the nymph who had begun to question him. I pretended not to notice as he passed the fountain and moved towards me. His smile spread upon reaching me, as a rainbow arcs across an expanse of blue, and I grinned back. Behind him, the Muses were leaving the foyer, walking in pairs down the corridor. We were conspirators in our segregation.

'I dreamed of you.'

Had I heard him correctly?

'I could have sworn it was real. I was standing still, and you were walking towards me under the shade of the leaves—'

'—in a copse,' I said.

He stared at me, seeming to wrangle with his next words. 'And I was – I was naked, and you—'

'I pulled you to me.'

He looked as shaken as I felt. I scrabbled for an explanation, trying to find something we could both hold on to.

'Only witches and Oracles can share dreams,' he said. 'Am I a witch, then?'

'Can you crush herbs and charm men to sleep forever?'

'I don't think so.' He smiled. It softened the moment, but discomfort lingered around us. After a few seconds, Euterpe called me to follow her, and I forced myself to move, unable to drag my mind away.

I watched as Jason made his farewells outside the city wall, standing beside a shining pool, and Erato handed him his spear, the emerald grass and the pale pink outcrops extending behind him. She whispered something into his ear and the two of them shared a smirk until they were broken apart by Euterpe, who gave Jason a wry 'good luck'.

Eurydicius embraced his friend. The brightness of the midmorning light lent a sheen to the spear in Jason's hand and the shield in Eurydicius'; for a few seconds, they transformed into golden figures on a vase, one ready to attack and the other to defend. Then a cloud passed over the sun, and they were men again.

Stepping forward, Calliope tapped a small rock to the left of the pool. I felt a familiar jolt when the oread appeared before us with one hand gripping the dagger in her belt.

'Who sends this guest out?'

'Calliope, chief of the Muses.'

'And from whom do you conceal him?' the nymph demanded.

Calliope's eyes smoked. 'My daughter's father.'

The doorway shimmered into being before us. I watched while Jason climbed through, and felt my heart catch in my throat as the door disappeared.

He would be climbing down Mt Parnassus alone. Perhaps he would be sleeping amongst wolves tonight, under a starlit sky. I noticed my mother's smile, a sharpening line.

'If I had a daughter,' someone said, beside me, 'I do not think I would be pleased if she was offered a place on a ship sailing to fight a dragon. A harpy is nothing compared to that creature King Aeëtes keeps. Have you ever smelled bones when they are charred to a crisp?'

'My mother may not be thinking of dragons.' I did not need to look up to know who I was replying to. 'She may simply be smelling the flowers on the summer air.'

'Calliope has a good nose for fame,' Melpomene said.

I turned to face her. 'If my mother is ambitious, she has passed down her blood perfectly. We cannot all live in the shadow of tragedy.'

'We all do, whether we choose to admit it or not.'

Melpomene dipped her chin. I noticed the sadness in her expression, nestled beneath the sternness.

'You may as well say it,' I returned.

'Say what?'

'That you wish me to wait out my days in the shade, rather than hasten to die in the sun at Colchis.'

Sympathy tinged her look as she regarded me.

'That is not why I am sad, Orphia.'

We stood side by side, watching Eurydicius make his way towards us.

I did not need to explain anything to him, I reminded myself. If he had chosen to live here and make shields until Jason returned, it was not my fault. I had not lied, after all. We might never speak of prophecies or Delphi in all our time together; I might talk only of history and verse. In all the days to come, in all the discussions we might have as I explored his inner world, the subject of my violent death might never arise.

I might make sure that it never could.

He reached me. Taking his hand, I kissed it as quickly as I had done the first time, and ignoring Melpomene's look, I led him down the slope towards the city.

I could not decide on exactly what it was that kept him from me. The early start to my lessons? Or the way I was bustled from astronomy classes to dance instruction? When I arrived at dinner each night, I found no sign of Eurydicius; he had eaten before me, or been taken to dine elsewhere, and although I had no firm proof, I suspected that my mother's rules shaped my days.

You will not spend a night in my daughter's company, until her lessons are done, and you will never enter her presence unless she invites you to.

With each passing week, a sharp and strange feeling rose inside me. I bargained with myself: I would chart the paths of the planets for Urania, the Muse of Astronomy, and then I would seek out Calliope and ask if it would be wise or foolish to speak with him.

That night, I slept better. I did not wake, sweating, from a dream that I remembered in all-too-perfect detail.

Yet as I ate my bread and honey the next morning, Euterpe's words haunted me: *Work harder. Analyse, criticise, and question what you have learned. Put aside all thoughts of men until you are done.* If I ignored that advice, would I not be doing what all women were forced to do – giving up fame for the rutting of a husband, for child-rearing, for a diminished place in the world? I yearned to touch Eurydicius as a fisherman yearns to run his fingers over a pearl, yet even the rarest pearl was not worth throwing away my art for. I might as well throw away my lungs, my tongue, my voice.

I had scarcely finished my bread when I heard the sound of laughter, soft and yet unmistakeable. Following the path past the nymphs' dining hall, I stopped at a clearing.

The nymphs were giggling, but he did not seem to hear them. He was watching the shield that they held, following their hands as they moved across the bronze. The sun shone on the cluster of dryads.

He appeared in relief, dappled by shadow. The tree above him protected him from the violence of the sun. Around his feet, the grass offered flowers, wreathing his toes in white.

'She asked if you would have anything as a reward,' a woman said.

'Calliope has granted me lodging,' Eurydicius said. 'If she offers more ...'

'This is not a trick.' I saw Melia shift on the grass beside him.

A dove landed on his arm. He stroked the bird's head. It cooed, snuggling into his elbow, and everything that I had been holding back surged through me.

'There is only one thing I would like,' Eurydicius said.

'You know I cannot help you, Eurydicius. Orphia must decide to speak with you of her own accord.'

'Perhaps she has,' I said, stepping into the clearing.

They both scrambled to their feet. Melia smiled and retreated, taking the nymphs with her, the shield laid flat on the ground.

We closed the space between us. I looked quickly at the dove, then the grass, then the shield ... at anything but his bare ankles.

'You have done well with your shields, I take it,' I said.

'Your mother has been gracious.'

'How long has it been since that banquet?'

'Since the day Jason left? Twenty-three sunrises and halfway to the twenty-fourth.' He blushed, and we shared a silence. The grass looked soft, and I had no qualms about sitting down. He joined me. I pictured myself gripping his neck and leaning over to trace his lips.

'I think your work pleases my mother more than she lets on,' I said.

'Because she offers me a reward?'

'No.' I looked him in the eye. 'Because you are still alive.'

Comprehension settled on him. The heat in his cheeks was only just fading. I took in every bit of redness, knowing that Jason would have chuckled at the hunger in my gaze. *Do it*, I instructed myself. *Reach out and claim his mouth; run your tongue over the skin of his upper lip.*

My hand was halfway towards him when somebody called my name.

I looked up into Melia's apologetic countenance. 'Your mother, Orphia. She would see you both.'

It did not take long to run to the Muses' palace and reach the fountain.

'It gives me no pleasure to tell you this.' Calliope glanced around the foyer, and only then did I notice the ring of oreads with daggers, watching us. 'We must bear what we are given with strength, or else buckle beneath it. Eurydicius, the townspeople found this on your parents' land.' She handed him a ring. 'After the burning was done, there was nothing else to retrieve.'

He hesitated for a moment, then took it quickly. Not so quickly, however, that I missed the look that passed over his face, dark water pooling in his eyes. He stroked the ring.

'My mother would never have given it up; not even with her dying breath. She loved her only heirloom.'

'We all grieve with you, shield-maker,' Calliope said.

'How did you find it?'

'Euterpe scouted for me, to make sure your parents were not simply hiding.' She began to walk away, then turned. 'There are some questions that cannot be left open. Imagination makes the cruellest wounds. I choose to give you this news, so that you may bid her farewell.'

I wanted to touch him; to tell him that I was sorry. He gazed down at the ring and did not speak.

Did it take a long time to scorch fields, burn houses to the ground, and melt the flesh from bones? Or had my father simply blinked his eyes and killed all who lived there?

A soft sob came from his lips. My hand found his shoulder, and he nestled into me, like the dove. My conscience pushed its way towards him.

If it had not been for me, your home would be safe and your parents alive, I thought.

It was then that I decided I could not allow myself to be near him.

Time bubbled, and for the next month there were only two speeds: sprinting, in the work hours, and crawling, in my moments of rest. In the Muses' theatre I practised the movements I had been ordered to learn for Terpsichore, raising my chin here, stretching out my hands there, while the Muse of Dance kept her eye on me. I laboured over songs of praise for Polyhymnia, the Muse of Sacred Poetry, who towered over me, broad-shouldered. Her pensive face was not unkind, but she tutted at my efforts.

'I do not mind whether you wish to praise the gods,' she said. 'Convince me, or fail.'

So it was that I wrote false thoughts in true phrases, praising wine in my head if I could not praise the god of wine, celebrating lightning if I could not rejoice at its maker; yet all the hymns in the world would not keep my thoughts from *him*.

It was futile, I told myself. I had done him enough harm already, simply by desiring him. Because of me, Apollo had burned the island while he was on it. Because of me, Hera had stepped in to save him – and Apollo had responded by burning his parents alive. Only a silver ring remained to whisper of my guilt.

Perhaps my hunger, my strange, selfish desire, would have driven me to seek him out all the same, had it not been for my mother's news.

I climbed the steps to her chamber, drinking in the paintings of Gaia and Mnemosyne, absorbing my ancestors' gazes.

'Jason shares some rubies with me – out of the sweetness of his heart, I presume.' Calliope plucked a stone from the pile before her.

'Pretty, as bribes go.' I held the red jewel up to the light.

'He will return in two months. You would do well to think. In a fortnight, we will talk again, and then you will decide whether to sail on his quest.' Calliope folded my fingers over the ruby. Its hard edge dug into my skin.

Two months.

I had already avoided Eurydicius for that long. I only had to write, and read, and keep my thoughts on the Golden Fleece, instead of the swirling that his words set off in my most concealed places. Yet though I tried not to focus on his remarks, one of them came floating back, like a petal in a river. *I knew I was listening to a hero, and her magic was not cruelty but poetry.*

Outside the door of Melpomene's tower that night, the scent of elm leaves wafted to my nostrils, the fragrance clearer than the scents of roses and earth. I stood for a long moment, breathing it in.

My host came to greet me as I entered, her eyes full of hollow places again, her hands gripping the sword and club.

'He asks to see you,' she said.

I could still smell the elm leaves.

'He knows it is your choice to admit him or not.'

'I may have very little time to attain fame. I would not waste it chasing a pair of pretty ankles,' I said.

Melpomene smiled. I walked past her, trying to prise my thoughts from his person.

A break of two days between lessons arrived unexpectedly, gifted to me by my mother. Balanos and Melia met me in the eastern garden and we fought for hours, jumping and striking until our arms wearied. Melia lifted Balanos when she sagged at the knees and carried her back to the palace, like a prince carrying a bride who has danced too long. I saw Balanos' robe slip, exposing her shoulder, and Melia planted a kiss on her bare skin. I felt a familiar tightness in my throat at the sight of them, so openly draped in love.

At breakfast, I found the table awash with whispers, and looked up to see a woman in a thick peasant's skirt beside Euterpe.

'We owe you our thanks.' The woman held up a shield, grinning. 'My daughters and I saw them off soundly. Who would have thought three shields would be a match for six thieving scoundrels?'

I looked closely at the object she held. The bronze was finely beaten, moulded to the wood, with small bumps of bronze dotted here and there across the shield's surface. It was not hard to recognise the craftwork – or the craftsman.

'I am glad to hear it, Eudokia,' Euterpe said.

'Would you do me the kindness of passing on my thanks to your friend, the shield-maker?' Eudokia looked at the bronze of the shield with a deep fondness. 'I would sooner have three of his shields than a dozen men with spears about the place.'

Eudokia's daughters handed over a bag of olives from the vast grove at the foot of Mt Parnassus, and by the time the peasant women left, the nymphs carried plums, eggs and grain, holding up their gifts. As I watched them, I found myself thinking on how defence could replace attack, not only in a skirmish but as a way of thinking – a way of being.

Did thought always shape action? Or could action shape thought? Eurydicius seemed to weave the two things together as if his fingers worked a loom.

When we had farewelled the contented women, I caught Euterpe's smile.

'I could tell you that your friend is unique, but you already know it,' she said.

I looked down. It seemed strange to describe him as a 'friend'. But if not friends, what were we to each other, a poet and a shield-maker?

'He will supply the priests at Delphi, next. It is my happy task to tell them so.'

Had she noticed that I blanched, and that my feet faltered on the stones as I moved towards her? I forced my shallow breaths to lengthen, concentrating on the table, on the food, on anything but the name of the temple.

'Yes,' Euterpe added, gently, 'I shall manage that one on my own, I think.'

I could feel my lyre calling me that night, my whole being hurrying towards the taut strings. I had scarcely reached the door of the tower when my senses diverted my attention.

This time, the scent sank deeper into my pores, the sweet fragrance of his skin stirring me. I froze.

But it was the ghost of his presence that called me, only the trail of his body on the air. I cursed my own weakness. Hot phrases poured from my lips as soon as I was safely inside my chamber, and no matter how many poems I spoke to the air, my thirst would not abate.

I lay in bed while the moon washed over me. The longer I lay there, the more my thoughts turned to his bare skin beneath my fingertips, in the copse, just as I had imagined it in my dream; to the pressing of my knee between his thighs; to the grip of my hands around his jaw and the warm beating of his pulse. I thought of the bronze sparks from my armour that had reflected on his torso.

My gaze travelled lower, in my imagination, to pass over all of him, and as my eyes moved, so did my hands move over my own skin.

Sleep eluded me, that night. In my sweating wakefulness, I wondered if he was picturing the same thing.

'I hope I am not too early for our lesson.' Erato's voice drifted through my door as light began to spread through my chamber. 'I will happily carry you in my arms if you are tired.'

I dressed in a flurry of cloth. Erato marched me through the grounds, teasing me with compliments on my muscles. At one point she ran her free hand along my arm and I nearly walked under a fountain's spray.

At last, we stopped, where streams gave way to beams of scarlet light. Above me lay its source. I stared – and would not anyone stare at hundreds and hundreds of rubies, some winking, some sparkling, some blazing like mirrors in the light of the half-risen sun? The building they encrusted seemed a light-filled jewel itself.

Deep red silks draped the couches that filled the hall before us, while silvery fur softened the walk. A jug and two cups rested on a table, and Erato poured us some wine. We drank in silence, for she seemed in no rush to speak.

At last, she snapped her fingers, and two dryads carried citharas into the hall and began strumming.

'Soon, I hear, you will decide whether to face dragons and bulls that huff flame.'

'It is no small decision,' I said.

'Have you considered how ill-equipped you are for a great quest?'

The question buffeted me. Had Erato not been pleased with my performance?

'You think you have worked hard, and mastered every skill, no doubt. Without the art of love, these skills are but paltry tricks. If a hero is driven by gold, or land, or a prize, they may give up the quest when the odds seem to turn against them, for they cannot claim their prize if they perish, can they? But if a hero is driven by love, they need not fear death. Love endures beyond the limits of the mere mortal frame.'

She seemed to become taller as she spoke, and a cloud of gold dust floated around her. I waited, trying and failing to find a reply. The cloud slowly dissipated, and she regarded me once more with a lively eye.

'When you find the person you love, you will fit with each other like a key and a lock,' Erato said, and I heard the knowledge of it in her voice. 'Your task for tomorrow is to think on what I have told you and pick out the word that is most important.'

All day, I thought of her remarks, polishing them in my mind and examining each word's surface, as if looking for the one that would shine the brightest. I stood in the copse for a long time, listening to the trees. In the morning I walked slowly to the ruby tower.

'Find,' I said.

Erato looked up from her seat.

'The trick is to *find* someone you love. That is the word that matters most.'

She waited. Like Calliope, she could use her silence.

'As women, I think, we are taught to receive the suits of men. In every story, a bride is swept away by the man who falls in love with her. She gives herself up to his authority. But what if we, ourselves, were to pursue? To search? That is what you mean when you say *find* someone, is it not?'

I had not seen her smile so broadly since I first walked into the foyer of the Muses' palace. 'No wonder Euterpe likes you,' she murmured. 'I did not really expect you to solve it in one day.' I joined her on the long seat. She reached out and stroked a lock of my hair, studying my face.

'You may conceive of love as a matter of grammar. One lover performs the action – the kiss, the touch, the speech – and the other receives it. Our philosophers see men as the active party, but there is no such law of nature. A woman can act, and a man receive.'

I was quiet, musing.

From that day, I worked swiftly in composition, playing new songs for Erato about wooing, touching, kissing, and many more things that I had never been encouraged to speak of. Throughout the process of composing, I came to see myself as the lover more often than the beloved. Perhaps I had always had it in my nature, but never known how to articulate it until now. I remembered how I had kissed Eurydicius' hand, the first time I met him. Possibilities bloomed before me, tangling as they grew.

I walked to each lesson while the sun was still a pale yellow egg in the distance. After I wrote and performed, Erato read poems to me, and I memorised them, letting the words drip from my ears into the recesses of my mind.

Yet a darkness hung over me. I knew that I was training for a journey, one that could make my life greater and more terrible, and every day I felt the pain of avoiding Eurydicius.

Many women had given their lives for love. Few had ever been allowed to grasp at fame. I knew how rare my opportunity was, to train and to pursue a life of talent – and I could not ignore the weight of all those half-fulfilled lives that I carried on my shoulders.

I wanted to show the world that women were not merely objects to be desired. I wanted men in every corner of the land to learn that *we* desired, too. How could I do that if I pushed down my own yearning, like a farmer burying a seed in unwatered earth?

'A vast improvement,' Erato said, as she finished a bunch of purple grapes, having listened to my ode on the subject of inspiration for a quarter-hour. 'You laboured over each line. The even rhythm betrays it. I see that you have learned about the kind of love that can sustain a quest.'

I dared not ask if I were to be the hero.

'Orphia, I have a final question. When a shimmering fish is before you, few can resist leaning over the water and peering at the scales as they gleam. Yet the catch must be worthy of your glorious verses. Have you thought of widening your pool?'

'Perhaps I have already found the right fish,' I said, hearing a boldness in my voice.

'Well, then.' Erato smiled. 'Be very sure of your choice. You will find your way to all kinds of places, and there may come a time when love is the only thing you grasp in the darkness.'

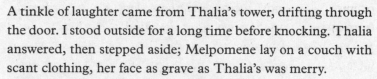

A tinkle of laughter came from Thalia's tower, drifting through the door. I stood outside for a long time before knocking. Thalia answered, then stepped aside; Melpomene lay on a couch with scant clothing, her face as grave as Thalia's was merry.

Neither of them looked surprised to see me.

'He is in his chamber,' Thalia said. 'Reading.'

My footsteps sounded louder than ever. Each stair of the two flights brought a new echo.

I had not expected to find the door ajar. Eurydicius lay on the bed, his legs tangled in the blanket, a swathe of smooth skin visible where one foot dangled over the edge of the bed. The coming and going of his breath made the strands of his long hair flutter across his cheek. His eyes were closed, and even a less keen observer would have noticed that he was naked beneath the cloth.

It would be graceless to cough, but if I did not wake him, I would be watching him uninvited. As I was deliberating and taking in the sight of his splayed hair, his eyes blinked open.

'Eurydicius, I did not mean to—'

He reached out for my hand. I let him touch it gently, and he smiled. 'I thought I might still be dreaming.'

He did not look embarrassed that I had found him sleeping. It was not easy, to push away the response of my body and turn to the speech I had prepared, but I called up the words; yet even as I made to speak them, I hesitated. I looked at his face for a long time. Only when I had settled the thing that reared inside me did I begin.

As I stumbled through my apology, a frown transformed his face.

'If it was Apollo who sent down fire upon my family, no one can blame you. We are not our fathers,' he said. Pain leapt into his eyes, then faded. 'I have found my own way through it, and time will aid me in keeping their memory close.'

There was a stillness about him, a calm that had not been there before. He pointed to something on the table beside the bed, and I reached out and picked up two clay figures, a man and a woman, shaped in curving forms and painted with black stripes. Each bore the beak of a nose, framed by the small, black dots of eyes. It was not only the expressive craftsmanship of these pieces that struck me, but their poses: each figure extended its arms upwards, revelling in the full-throated song of life.

'That is how I imagine them. I think they are together and happy, my mother and father. My mother would be dancing. She always danced when she saw the sun rise. At the fall of the day, she would sing, and my father would drum his fingers on the table.'

'I can feel their joy. You have done well not to idealise them in sculpture, for they come alive in this style.'

I pretended not to feel the warmth of his smile as I put the figures back down. As I faced him, I hesitated, and he touched my hand once more, a light brush of his fingertips against my knuckles. 'Will you let me say one thing to you, before you decide whether to stay?'

I nodded, my heart swelling in my throat.

'Perhaps you will leave me, and ignore me as you go about your lessons again. I cannot ask you not to; I have no right to your attendance. But if you would consider my choice in the matter, then know that I would choose to be near you.' He drew a long breath, like a parched traveller drawing water. 'In the fevered dreams of my nights here, I have imagined being in your presence. I have imagined the two of us on this bed.'

The hard lump lodged in my throat. I could barely squeeze out my reply.

'You do not know what future grief I may bring you.'

'And what if I am the one to bring you grief? It is a tough game to guess at the gods' plans.'

'No.' I could not let him remain innocent. 'I am afraid I carry a fate on my head that you must know, before you promise me anything.'

He listened, neither moving nor interrupting as I laid out the whole story, lingering on the moment when Apollo had pleaded with Zeus to keep me hidden. My voice trembled as I outlined the prophecy, for I could hardly believe it myself – it took great effort to force my lips to announce that I would be violently torn apart by a crowd. I had done so well at pushing it from my thoughts. That was precisely why it hit me with such force, now. I watched Eurydicius' face as I spoke. I could read no anger there, nor scorn; could he forgive me for the coldness I had shown him in recent weeks? I dared not hope so, but perhaps he might understand my choice to withdraw.

'You see,' I finished, 'I am a ship that surges on a tide of black water. Some day, my mast will crack and I will plunge down.'

'Until that day, I will happily sail in your wake.'

I stared at him. A determined expression had transformed his face.

'Kings misinterpret prophecies all the time. Warriors mistake omens. Who is to say that the Sun God cannot? Your death may arrive thirty years from now, or never,' he said.

His eyes held mine. I tried, with every particle of strength in my marrow, to believe him; and I almost succeeded.

'Have you always yearned for glory?' he said.

I knew, then, that I wanted to be honest with him about this, too.

'I will speak clear as a sunrise. Glory, to me, is not a throne, nor a gold tripod. It is not a fleet of ships, nor the fealty of men. Glory is knowing that people across the world will take my songs into their hearts and make chambers for them – that they will see ways to feel differently, to speak differently, to *live* differently because of my words.' I drew a breath. 'I yearn to help them, as stories help me.'

Eurydicius looked at me for a long moment.

'You labour and sweat for this sort of glory,' he said, at last. 'I see it in your efforts to hone your art. I recognise it at once, for I know it in my own work, when I tap and shape shields. That is how I know you will succeed.'

Tears pricked at my eyes, and I struggled to hold them back.

He leaned upward, and his cloth slipped slightly to the left, exposing a few more inches of his hip-bone. With all my concentration, I focused on his face. His lips looked redder than before, though perhaps it was my mind painting them with the juice of a pomegranate.

'You would be near me, despite everything?' I whispered.

'You are the most remarkable person I have ever known. Every detail of the moment you first spoke to me in that courtyard is carved in my mind, as if you had scored it there with a blade.' The image made my breath stutter. 'And it lingers with me. The sky brightens. I dream bigger, since hearing the magic of your words. I would be near you, yes. And if you would permit it, I—' He broke off and looked down, spots of red widening on his cheeks.

'Yes?'

'I would crawl on my knees to you, through burning coals. I would serve you while shards of ice pierced me, and even then, I would kiss your feet. I would give up my last breath for you at the end of the world.'

Instinct worked through me. I lowered myself onto the bed, grabbed the back of his neck, and dug in my nails with such force that a breath escaped his lips in a small, surprised huff; then I pushed my hand up into his hair, seizing the soft strands. The harder we kissed, the more I twined my fingers through his locks, weaving his hair and my flesh into a single cloth. He gasped into my mouth. I pushed him down, blood galloping at my temples and in my veins. There was not enough of him to consume.

'Orphia.'

The sound of my name seemed to come from far away.

'There is wine, if the two of you would like it.'

Thalia's laugh tinkled, followed by the sound of whispering, and I recognised Melpomene's voice, too soft for me to make out her words.

I drew back from Eurydicius and gazed at him. Strands of hair had fallen into his eyes and the edge of his lower lip gleamed with blood. At some point, I must have bitten it. I did not feel guilty, for Eurydicius leaned towards me, undaunted.

'My whole life,' he whispered, 'I dreamed of a woman who would seize me hard and kiss me. I could not discern her face. But now I see her before me, and I realise it could only have been you.'

My heart rattled in my chest. 'Stay here and sleep. We will meet again tomorrow.'

'Where should I wait for you?'

He would wait for me. Of course he would. Was it not the sweetness of his manner and his gentle patience that had made me fall in love with him?

The realisation stunned me. I had never used the word *love* in this way.

'Come to the eastern garden at dusk.' I ran my finger along his jaw, down to his chin. 'Do not worry if you become lost amidst the trees. I will seek you out. Even if you languish in pure darkness, I will find you.'

Her face shimmered as she ran, panting, her feet leaping over rotten logs and snapped branches. Fear passed across her countenance in waves as she glanced over her shoulder, and her skin flowed like sunlit water. The steady rhythm of her running gave way to a frenzied sprint, her soles striking rocks, her hands flailing.

Dirt smeared the blue cloth of her naiad's robe as she stumbled over a root, and my breath rose sharply in my throat. I glimpsed the god descending on her – and saw the savage grin spreading on Apollo's face as he lunged.

Gasping, I yanked myself backward. Water trickled from my hands.

'It is always alarming, to glimpse her right before the transformation,' Calliope said.

'Mother, I saw …'

'I am not surprised that the vision offered itself to you.' Calliope gestured to the stream of water in which I had dipped my palms. 'Gaia knows why you are here. Your great-grandmother wishes you to see this piece of history.'

My eyes must have spoken the question that my lips could not.

'Did the naiad die, you wonder?' Calliope did not look perturbed. 'Far better than that. Her skin burst and her blood turned to water and flowed downhill, and she became this spring, long before your father built his temple above her.'

A chill ran over my shoulders and down my spine. The early morning sunlight left some parts of the Parnassus range brilliant and some in shadow, some parts burnished and some almost pastel, layering down to the mirror of white where the gulf extended ... it had given me an exquisite delight as we walked here, with the scent of pines and firs rising in the cool air. But now, having seen what my father had tried to do to that nymph, I could no longer look out at all that beauty.

'That is one way to escape Apollo,' Calliope said. 'Dissolve.'

We stood without speaking for a moment, while birds trilled to each other in the boughs above us. It was one thing to know that my father could take women as he pleased. It was quite another to see him mid-pursuit, closing in for a rape.

'What was her name?' I said.

'Castalia. A lyrical name. I have heard she was the first nymph to become a poet.' Calliope clasped my hands and looked into my eyes. 'Poetry calls you here. I know how sorely you wish to make a decision about your art and this quest. Those who decide well must consider all facets of the issue first, however, and they must do so with their ears pricked. You must remember who you are, as you walk to the Oracle. And remember, I will be waiting for your signal. You are not alone. Castalia and Gaia and the Muses go with you.'

I felt alone, all the same, as I walked from Castalia's spring to the Delphi temple site. Wisps of cloud drifted across the mountain range and nestled in the folds of the peaks, as if they were watching me. I reminded myself that I had come here for answers, before Jason forced me to look his quest in the face, and all my father's guards could not deter me – not when I had determined to know my future, be it bitter as a snake's gall.

Calliope might have advised me to come here. I had my own reasons.

'Do you know why the Oracle is always right?' Calliope had said, before we left.

I had turned to her. 'Why?'

'Because she leaves holes, chiselled out in every sentence, waiting for the listener to fill.' Her voice had reverberated. 'Last year, a king came to her and asked if he should make war on a land across the sea.'

'A risky question for a woman to answer.'

'The Oracle replied that if he launched his expedition, a great kingdom would fall. He set out joyfully across the water, only to see his men die by the hundreds, and to limp back home with a few dozen. He rushed to the Oracle and asked her why she had lied to him.

'"I never lied," she replied. "You failed to ask a second question: *which* kingdom will fall?"'

I smiled, though I was sure my gaze was uneasy. 'Perhaps I should sooner seek help from a market seller.'

'Ah, but you are forgetting the skill of the one and only Pythia, Oracle of Delphi. She finds the precise words to spark a flame inside you. You will no longer hesitate, nor waver. And if you only listen, you will hear the truth.'

That was it, above all else, I told myself. Whatever the pain, I wanted to know the truth, for Eurydicius' sake and my own.

A small patch of ground teemed with stalls at the beginning of Apollo's sanctuary. I recognised votive offerings of spearheads and miniature javelins – here was a myriad of tiny monuments to brutality. Winding up from the marketplace, the gleaming façades of treasuries fringed a walkway along the side of the mountain.

I looked into the scornful face of the soldier who barred the Sacred Way.

'My father is taking no chances, I see.' My words rang out, bolder than my feelings.

'State your name.'

'Orphia, daughter of Calliope.'

'Daughter of Apollo,' he replied. His gaze flowed over my body, slowly traversing my breastplate and the skirt of my armour.

'The Oracle awaits you,' he said. By his smirk, I knew that the staring had not been a necessity.

Pillars jutted up before me: pillars of white Parian marble, behind which statues and tripods jostled for place and gold and jewels lay heaped in cauldrons. I faltered, looking at the spoils of war, and reminded myself why I was here. This had once been my great-grandmother's place for creation, a site for women to think and work. *Gaia*, I thought, stopping in the middle of the first step, bending my head.

When I looked up again, the stone of the next step glowed.

The purity of gold light drew me onward, step by step, past the replica of the Trojan Horse that marked a military conquest, past the pillared Athenian treasury stuffed with the spoils of pillage and murder and rape, past numerous other monuments that I knew had been bought with the deaths of the powerless and the unprotected. If I had not felt the benevolence of Gaia's glow, I might have turned back.

The steepness of the path reminded me that I was supposed to grovel and bend before my father's might. Ever since I had begun learning amongst the Muses, I was less and less inclined to grovel. I rounded the wall that separated the Sacred Way from the temple, noticing the breadth of the heavy stones, a reminder that I was nearing the sanctuary of a god.

Another soldier stood at the top of the stairs. He reached for my spear, and I handed it over wordlessly. Four robed priests stared at me from beside the temple.

'Offer a sacrifice, Lady Orphia, or become the sacrifice yourself.' The nearest man's eyes met mine.

Mother, I thought, *the animals*. A blink of my eyes, and two goats and a cow stood before me. The cow's hide glistened, its body flecked with radiance from the shoulders to the hindquarters, and the priests smiled as they gazed upon it. I stood back as the soldier drew a sword, carrying the animals to the altar, slitting their necks and stepping back. Blood ran over the stone in thickening rivers. The cow made a lowing noise as its throat gushed.

'Do not keep her waiting,' the priest nearest the ramp said.

Anger surged through me, fresh as goat's blood. They knew I had Calliope's authority to be here, yet they had demanded the death of three innocent things.

I strode past the ramp and around the side of the temple, down the walkway that bordered the pillared building. I would take my time, even if a slight delay maddened them. The white marble of the exterior looked the same as that of the treasuries I had passed. Sculpted pediments decorated the façade on every side, showing scenes of gods and goddesses. Unsurprisingly, there was no image of Hera amongst them.

Fury surged anew. Apollo could rape nymphs. He could banish his daughter to an island for twenty-three years, he could disrespect his wife's talents, and he could demand that pilgrims make tributes to slaughter. Yet for all that, he could not acknowledge the Queen of Heaven. My insides writhed.

My gaze passed over a detailed pediment, and I gasped at the audacity of it. There sat the Muses, sculpted in long gowns, placid and docile, with the god Apollo seated highest amidst their group.

I strode back to the front of the building and up the vast ramp, into the Temple of Apollo. Blackness enveloped me. I waited inside the doorway. Nobody emerged, and it seemed that I might stand there for a long time, but then something slithered past my ankles. In the dim light, I saw a snake gliding over the stones. Its long, cinder-black body stopped a little way into the temple, and it turned its head to stare at me.

The snake began to move again, and I knew, in the pit of my stomach, that it wanted me to follow. I pursued it through a round antechamber lit with a single torch, then through a doorway into a deeper darkness, where my legs seemed to disappear below the knee. The scales of my guide vanished into the blackness.

The carved entrance to a much bigger room emerged from flickering light. I moved past dozens of torches, their glow illuminating a series of steps, flanked by two priests. The men's robes shone like blood. My attention focused on the platform at the top of the stairs, where a light blazed, obscuring all but the outline of a tripod, and I felt a shiver pass through me.

'Kneel before the navel of the world.'

The voice sliced through the air. I knelt hastily, my knees knocking stone. The priest on the left had spoken, and now he raised his finger to point at me. 'On the seventh day of the month, the seven attendants of Delphi admit only a few.'

'Those who humble themselves may be lucky,' the second priest added.

A smell of rotting flesh pervaded the room. While I struggled to ignore it, something brushed my side, and I looked across to see the black snake, now slithering up the steps. It stopped on the platform, coiling around a pair of feet, and I realised that someone was sitting on the tripod. A gargling noise rent the air.

With all my concentration, I kept my knees bent.

'You come late to Delphi, Orphia, daughter of Apollo,' the priest on the left said.

Light blazed from the figure on the tripod. Motes of dust seemed to swirl around her like floating constellations. I knew, without anyone telling me, that she was the one who had gargled at me, and that a word was buried within that sound.

'I offer you shields, in return for questions.' Eurydicius' labour had bought me this opportunity; I could not waste it. I rose. 'I would speak with the Oracle alone.'

'Speak *with* her?' Both priests laughed, but I held still, my feet planted on the temple stones. *Mother,* I thought. *Help me.*

A swirl of air preceded the arrival of something that glinted in the dimness, and shields clattered to the floor around me. How Calliope had transported them, I did not know – yet it had worked. The noise of bronze ringing on stone moved the priests to hurry forward and examine the shields, peering at the fine bumps on each curved surface. I thanked the moon and stars for Eurydicius' hard work.

'These are no small gifts.' The priest stared into my eyes. 'We interpret for the Oracle. But I fear her rants and raves will not pierce a woman's understanding.'

'Indeed?'

'To an untrained ear, she is like one of the maenads, those women who whirl and dance and tear men apart under Lord Dionysus' control. And like them, she is dangerous – unless you are more powerful than the god of wine, Lady Orphia?'

'That is my concern. I have seen your Sacred Way, fattened with the loot of war, so I know that you understand tribute. And I have paid you tribute with these shields. A poet's kindness only goes so far. Do not make me regret my benevolence.'

The priests retreated, casting me pitying looks as they left. Drawing a breath, I tried to gather my courage and wrap myself in it until I felt as bold as my mother, and I turned towards the platform at the top of the stairs.

The sitter beckoned, and the light around her began to diminish. By the time I had mounted the stairs, I could make out the tripod on which she sat, its gold legs gleaming. A stone pillar thrust up behind her, sculpted in the form of two intertwining snakes, the twin pythons meeting above her head.

The Oracle stared at me, unperturbed, her feet planted and her long purple gown unadorned. She sat with one hand draped on each chair-arm, her grey hair tumbling over her chest. The snake hissed, resting its chin on her feet. A chill struck me.

'Voice of truth and most famous seer,' I said, 'I come to you with a request.'

She closed her eyes and gargled, raising her hands and whirling them, her voice bubbling with words that seemed half-formed, strangled by her own spirit. Calliope's remarks, spoken in her chamber on Mt Parnassus, sounded in my head again: *They call her Pythia. Some say she raves, but others know better. She is no more mad than I am.*

'I know you are not witless, only voiceless,' I said. 'My mother will protect us on this mountain, long enough for us to converse.'

'I am surprised you can breathe well enough to speak.' Her clear reply made me hesitate, and she laughed. 'It is a lovely stench. Putrid, and powerful. Did your mother teach you that this temple was built on the rotting corpse of the snake Python, whom Apollo slew in his wrath?'

I hoped my start was not obvious.

'Do not be concerned. The Oracle of Delphi will be ruled by no one – threaten her with fire, and she welcomes the blaze.'

As she spoke, she clapped one hand to her chest and leaned forward, as if shards struck her with every word.

I glanced at the snake, which was pushing its forked tongue in and out of its mouth. 'If you would grant me your wisdom, I would learn of my future,' I said.

'I have already given a prophecy about you.'

'I would hear of my life, not my death.' I pressed one hand to my chest. 'It is not my end I seek to know, for I have heard it already, and I would learn only how to make the most of my days. A quest is placed before me, yet love springs in my garden, too. A small seed may grow into a sapling. I would know whether to water it, or whether to leave for a journey ... to nourish love, or to chase after fame.'

Love. The word tasted like a just-ripe orange, sweet and delicious and new, leaving a tart aftertaste on my tongue.

A cold silence seemed to fill the hall. The Oracle eyed me from her tripod. 'Then we must speak under the protection of a different deity.'

She made to rise. Hurrying back, I moved to the bottom stair and watched her descend. The swirl of dust motes around her reminded me of faraway stars.

Through the dim area behind the tripod and pillar, she led me, stopping at a spout in the temple wall and holding her hands out. I heard the splash of water and glimpsed a glitter in the half-dark. When I looked up again, the Oracle wore a small smile. 'I tell Apollo's priests that this is sacred water, which only I am permitted to use.'

I considered her words. 'That way, you need not lie.'

'Very good.' Her smile widened. 'It is divine water, but not your father's.'

She was still here, then. The knowledge rippled through my skin. My great-grandmother still blessed this place with her breath and her bounty – Gaia's presence endured, no matter how many walls Apollo built. The sound of the stream made me think of Castalia's spring – the nymph's body bursting and turning into sweet, clear water – and with a shock I spoke her name into the putrid air.

'Ah, yes. I was wondering how long it would take you.' The Oracle was looking at me. 'Castalia's spring, and this one ... they formed through Gaia's efforts. She needs no treasuries to maintain her presence. Her bounty is glory enough. And to me, Gaia gives more than blessed water.'

She moved past me, towards the middle of the floor, and stopped abruptly. A small patch of thinned torchlight illuminated her face, which was deeply lined with years of thought, and I studied her for a moment. 'Gaia,' she whispered, and I heard the hiss that replied, and felt the vapour that surged through the fissure next to her feet. The steam dissipated slowly.

She closed her eyes. The torchlight set the gold paint on her eyelids agleam. She spoke softly, and the words were not of any tongue I recognised; the sound grew, until she was almost shouting, her eyes rolling back in her head and her arms slackening. No half-choked gargling, now; no feigned theatrics. The words rose in a crescendo, subsiding at last, and something nameless passed through me as I watched her body grow calm.

'Your destiny is greatness.' Her eyes opened slowly.

All the teachings of my youth had warned me to be humble, as women were meant to be, and I could feel the desire to deflect – to deny her statement and offer some modest vision in its place. Yet I could feel something else, too. I thought of how Eurydicius had looked at me when I performed my poetry. I thought of everything I had told him: the words I knew to be true. *Glory is knowing that people across the world will take my songs into their hearts and make chambers for them – that they will see ways to feel differently, to speak differently, to* live *differently because of my words.*

'Must I throw away that which I love, in order to achieve greatness?' I said.

'And who is it you love?'

I swallowed. It felt right to name him, in this hall of steam and shadow. 'Eurydicius.'

She raised her head as she regarded me. Her unsmiling expression did not crack.

'It is he who will lead you to greatness. Love will help you pass into legend.'

I could scarcely believe it. I did not trust it. 'I do not need to let him go?'

'No.' She moved her bulk towards me, and her voice was raw and terrible. 'I will say this only once, and you will heed it. You must not allow yourself to be parted from him.'

Tongues of flame sprouted inside my chest and licked their way into my arms and legs and fingertips. Her words had been so sure. So firm. I felt a strange confidence, just in hearing them, as if my life suddenly meant something new.

I thanked her, knelt, and said a prayer to Gaia and another to Hera, yet my mind was already leaping over hills and dancing on mountaintops with Eurydicius. I saw myself taking his hand once more; kissing the soft skin of his palm.

Not allow yourself to be parted from him. What had she meant by that?

'My throat will not endure, today.' The Oracle's voice weakened.

I offered her my arm, taking care to support her as we returned to the first part of the temple hall. A hiss drew my eyes downward. The same snake that had led me in had come to my side, its tongue slipping in and out of its mouth.

Without warning, the Oracle gripped my wrist, and her voice came out in a rasp.

'Remember this. Most heroes thrust their way forward in this world, trampling over soft and breakable things on their way to a hard-edged fate ... but while most heroes face a choice between love and fame, you need never choose.'

She detached herself from me and jabbed her finger at the air. Shaken, I followed the route that she indicated, into the antechamber and back through the area of pure darkness, the snake keeping pace with me. The Oracle's last words rang through my mind.

The last thing I heard before I stepped into the warm air was a hiss, soft and lingering.

I had scarcely set foot on the mountainside when Calliope appeared at my side.

'I will not follow Jason after the Fleece,' I said.

She listened without interrupting. When I explained that the path to fame did not involve Jason, that my love of Eurydicius would instead lead me along it, she smiled, and the flint in her eyes told me she was considering more than what I said.

We walked a little way up the mountain to where Fury waited.

'It is good that you will not abandon fame,' Calliope said.

'And yet I hear a note of concern in your voice.'

'Concern?' She smiled wryly. 'I only distrust a solution where nothing is sacrificed. The Oracle's statements have been known to hide some things, even as they make others plain. Still, it is no small feat to face her and to truly hear her speak.'

I knew that she spoke gladly, and I should have been relieved, for the advice was to my liking. Yet a flurry began in my stomach.

'Come,' Calliope said. 'Let us look upon more joyful things.'

Higher still, she led me, the two of us climbing between pines and cypresses and laurels until we stopped side by side, looking out over the mountainside. From here, I could see beyond the temple to the other peaks of the range, with the wisps of cloud butting against the mountainsides, the luminous dappling of trees returning now that the dark clouds had cleared. Beyond the range, the gulf stretched, no longer a mirror but a clear, blue jewel. I glanced upwards. As Mt Parnassus rose above me, swathes of trees gave way to outcrops of pale grey limestone, scarred with raw orange lines here and there. The summit where I had made my home was shrouded in mist.

Nature had never left this place: it welcomed me here. I could feel the warmth of Gaia's presence in the soil.

My nostrils filled with the soft fragrance of pine needles: not a cloying smell but a tangy scent, full of promise. Spindly branches stuck out from the pine trunks, like a sea creature's tendrils.

'Do you see that?' Calliope pointed to one of the swathes of orange on the mountain, a little way above us. As I watched, the sunlight crept across it, and the orange transmuted to gold, leaving me with a feeling of joy. The rock had been chipped and scraped and pocked, but the scarred surface shone more brightly than the smooth limestone.

'It takes a while, to practise with sunbeams, but I have been working at it whenever I am on this spot, drawing on Gaia's love.' My mother's smile loosened. 'Those patches of orange you see are eroded rock. I discovered that when I aim the sunbeams at those spots, the rock turns gold, not like a crown but like a blessing. I have turned the stone's loss into an artwork. That is what women are expected to do: take our wounds and make them into something beautiful.' She placed a hand on my shoulder.

We both fell silent, staring at the bright orange-gold of the sunlit rock, feeling the flow of divinity from it to us. I sent back my own love to the rock, letting my words pour silently out.

My thoughts turned to Eurydicius. I stroked a leaf on the laurel tree beside me. The green surface was mottled with yellow. Lowering my nose to it, I breathed in a scent so sweet and fragrant, it seemed part of the mountain's divinity – a divinity you did not notice immediately, but which crept over you the longer you explored the slope.

I longed to tell Eurydicius about the power of this place.

'News,' Calliope said, and she closed her eyes, her face a mask of concentration. When she opened them again, she fixed me with her gaze. 'Tidings pursue you, it seems. For Euterpe sends word that Jason is less than a day's ride from Mt Parnassus. He will be at our doors, awaiting your answer tonight.'

All the languorous hours I had imagined before me – the carving of my joy in fresh-dewed phrases, the wandering between the water-fountains, the seeking out of Eurydicius in some private courtyard – evaporated like mist. My mind had been running ahead to delights, but now I could think only of how I would face Jason with the advice of the Oracle loud in my ears.

Calliope called Fury to her, and we both mounted. As we flew, I imagined what I might say to Jason. I pictured his face as I rejected his quest. Only when we were mid-air and Calliope had slowed the gryphon did I look down at the mountain again.

'Time passes quickly, when a meeting is expected. It would be a shame to lose your afternoon.'

She had nudged Fury to circle above a patch of treetops. At first, I could see nothing but branches and leaves, but then, in a gap between two cypresses, I spotted a blonde head bent over the shining bronze of a shield.

'Is this a test?' I said.

'Only a gift.'

I gazed down at Eurydicius. His chin was tilted down, his attention focused as his hands worked. 'I am not so rash as to forget that I am not protected here,' I said.

'Did you really think I would let you walk into Delphi without casting another spell?' Calliope replied. 'It took all my strength, but by dawn, it was finished. No immortal can touch you while you walk on the mountainside, nor any mortal with ill intent. I know you crave the freedom to walk abroad with him.' She nudged Fury again, with easy command. 'Amongst other things.'

We dipped lower. Eurydicius' hair came nearer by the second. The air smelled of honeysuckle and of the bright yellow flowers scattered over the grass – nicknamed khrysokome, the golden-haired. There was another name that they were known by, I knew, but it eluded me while my gaze passed over him ... and as we landed, I remembered it. *Amaranthos*. The everlasting.

It was a strange thing, and I almost suspected that some alchemy had taken place; the more we talked, the more we had to say. The longer I sat with Eurydicius, the more I found myself forgetting the Oracle's remarks and Jason's visit, slipping into discussion, laughter and debate. I sprawled on the grass beside him, and he abandoned his shield to prop himself on his elbow.

He fended off my questions and asked me about my poetry. I saw him nod and frown as I answered, sinking his attention into my replies, picking out something to delight in and something to inquire about. After we discussed rhythm, he asked to hear my poems about Hera and Aphrodite, and he cheered my description of Hera's peacock-driven chariot flying into the Hall of Starlight, telling me that he could imagine the floor trembling.

'I thought you would tire of my stories,' I said, when I had finished a poem about Clio's wisdom.

'How could I? They vibrate and hum like dragonflies from the heavens.'

'Well, I had an idea that you might wish to take up the story we began last night.'

He turned a dusky shade of pink. 'Only if you wish it.'

'I should wish for nothing more.' I looked down. 'But there is something I must tell you, first. Jason comes tonight, seeking to take me on his quest.'

We talked for a long time about the *Argo* and the voyage to claim the Golden Fleece, and about Jason's ambitions for his kingdom; about the fame that such a quest might bring, and about my decision. His eyes crinkled with pleasure when I told him that I would stay. I did not explain about the Oracle's advice. Some things were best kept for my ears and Calliope's alone.

The sun grew angry, and slowly, we found the will to get up. We sipped from Eurydicius' pouch. As we climbed towards the summit, I thought only of the entrance-stone.

'Listen,' Eurydicius said.

I stopped walking. At first, I could hear only the wind, but then a yowling drifted from behind a boulder.

Eurydicius detached his hand from mine and ran, before I could stop him, towards the sound. I hurried to join him. We peered around the granite to where two bodies tussled in the shade of the rock, clawing at each other. The smaller cat made a fearsome cry, but as we watched, its opponent took a strong swipe, slashing it across the eyes.

The wounded animal shrieked and rolled over. 'Leave her,' Eurydicius shouted.

I gripped his arm, for the big cat had turned to snarl at him.

'Find a cat your own size. There is no honour in an unmatched fight,' he cried.

He stood with perfect stillness, staring at the big cat, while the other continued to shriek. Man and animal seemed to hold conference for a moment, their stares locked, then the big cat backed away and ran, disappearing into an olive grove nearby.

Eurydicius knelt and stroked the wounded cat. A pink tongue shot out. The animal licked his fingers and rubbed its cheek against him before limping away.

'You have a gentle heart.' I must have poured all my astonishment into those words.

'It pains me to see injustice. My mother believed that no creature on the earth should hurt another.'

'Was it she who chose your name?'

He nodded, reddening a little.

'He whose justice extends widely.' I sounded out the phrase, as if I were reading it from a tablet in Clio's chamber.

He looked at me with startled eyes. Perhaps he was only then realising how much I had thought of him since we first met.

'My mother chose my name, too,' I said. 'She has never told me so, but I know it. "Orphia" comes from "orphanos".'

'Fatherless.'

'Yes.' It felt strange, to speak the meaning aloud. 'We should quicken our steps before the sun grows angrier.'

The yowls of the cats lingered in my ears as I walked. I did not attend the land as I should have, nor think on what the sound might have attracted. Between glare and shadow, the brown shape might have gone unnoticed, lumbering along until it was upon us, yet an unlucky stumble sent a rock tumbling down the mountainside, and I turned.

A ball of bristles careered towards us on four legs. Pale pink nostrils flared.

'Get back!' I cried.

The creature sprinted onward. White tusks jutted from lips flecked with spittle. A grunt echoed over the mountainside, and the boar charged, barrelling at Eurydicius.

I drew my knife, leaping, too quick for it to dodge the blade. A kick off the ground bore me over its back, my body twisting. I aimed my stroke and prayed for Hera's blessing, sinking the knife between the boar's shoulders, forcing it in deep. The animal writhed. I realised my mistake as soon as I landed on the ground: the underside of the neck, where the flesh was soft and tender, was the only place I could have pierced that hide.

I yanked out my knife. The boar stumbled to its feet and charged past me, lumbering towards its target. The dry brush in my chest ignited. I would not let it touch him.

'Get down!' I shouted.

Thought was not part of it, and nor was calculation. The instinct that drove my muscles came from somewhere beyond sense. I hurled myself at the boar and took the impact with my shoulder, knocking it down, holding its jaw shut with one hand and stabbing it with the other.

This time, my blow landed below its chin.

A squeal; a shudder. The sound of heavy, strained breaths. Then stillness. I checked the boar, feeling amongst the bristles for its heartbeat, and when I was certain it would not rise again, I ran to Eurydicius. Without thinking, I wrapped my arms around him. I took it all in: his long hair, askew, streaks of mud covering the back of his neck from where he had fallen, a tiny scrape on his arm. No blood in sight. I held him for a long time, until he began to wriggle, and I realised that my grip was almost crushing him.

The sun refused to sink. Hours slipped away, but the orb in the sky remained fiery as it had been since midday. The mountain sweltered.

It took me a long time to leave Eurydicius' chamber, even after I had settled him on the bed, stroked his cheek, and watched until his breathing was deep and even. I found Melia and Balanos waiting for me in the foyer. We walked eastward, the dryads leading me to a courtyard.

My mother stood, feeding Fury pieces of meat, while three guests waited on a stone bench.

I noticed the gold band resting in Jason's dark hair, the detail of a ship on his breastplate, and the square hunk of a blue gemstone on his ring.

He clapped me on the back and we embraced. His rough laugh, at least, had not changed. His soldiers rose to stand by him.

'A band of the most famous Greeks waits for my word to sail,' Jason said. 'Sharp swords. A fresh wind. Minds that know no fear – and only one place left on board. What do you say, Orphia?' His smile revealed bright teeth.

I thought of the moment when I had turned to face the boar and the animal had barrelled straight at me. I thought of the white tusks thrusting from its spit-mottled lips.

'My answer has not been formed hastily,' I said. 'I know your quality, and know that you will honour my choice. My destiny does not wind alongside yours.'

He was silent. I feared his reaction, for a moment. But slowly, he nodded. 'You strike our quest a blow. It is not fatal, however, and I should rather have a pack of eager singers on board than the finest poet in the land, if she resists me. I ask only one thing of you.'

Behind him, Fury snapped at the air. Calliope had stopped feeding the gryphon. I could feel her gaze upon me, and I motioned for Jason to continue.

'There is a service you could do me, if you could find the time and the generosity. My band of heroes assembles at the port of Iolcus tonight: wrestlers and runners, bowmen and rowers, navigators and augurers. With only one night before we depart, they have little time to grow familiar. And they are lodged at the same inn. I fear their tempers even as I rejoice at their skills.'

'I fail to see how my daughter can help.' Calliope's voice cut in.

'Her tongue could cool even the hottest temper, if she would speak poetry to the men.'

I exchanged a sharp glance with my mother. 'And how am I to travel to Iolcus in the blink of an eye?'

Jason pointed to something behind me.

We all turned towards the sound of chewing. Fury had snatched the last piece of meat from Calliope's fingers and was slobbering on the floor.

'Fury is no beast of burden,' Calliope said.

'And this is no ordinary request. I ask for the sake of my people, my kingdom, and the great men who risk their flesh and bones: allow your gryphon to bear us through the sky.'

Part of me was weighing the adventure he offered, checking it for risk and necessity, holding a torch up to see it clearer. And yet another part of me awakened at the thought of weaving through a band of heroes and conversing with them. I might see Heracles up close. I might trade words with Philoctetes, and admire his bow.

It did not matter that I would have to return. The Oracle had said that Eurydicius would lead me to greatness, that love would help me pass into legend, and so it must be that I could reach others by honing and practising my poetry with him. I did not need to sail with Jason to fulfil my destiny: this would be a simple excursion, for my own curiosity.

'I will do it,' I said. 'Then I will ride home to Mt Parnassus. You will not follow me, Jason.'

The wolflike smile disappeared. I saw only relief in his countenance as he clapped me on the shoulder.

I watched the dryads showing Jason and his men out, and I knew that Calliope was watching him, too. She did not say anything, but she did not need to; the cases for and against my going must have been apparent to her, just as my determination must have been written in every line of my face.

I found Eurydicius in the eastern garden, crouching beside the pond. A rainbow graced the surface, and in its colours his face shimmered; the pile of daffodils beside him told me he had been scooping them from the water for some time.

'You look like a painting on a vase,' I said.

He started. A flower fell from the pile.

'Forgive me,' he began. 'I could not work on my shields, today, not after ...'

'You should be resting. A charge from a boar like that is enough to wear one out.'

'I can never repay you for saving me, but I will find some way to try.' He reached for a metal object resting on a leaf, and handed it to me. Taking it, I curled my fingers around a necklace.

The metal was warm from resting in the sun. Two chains hung from a single clasp, fashioned so that they would fall in layers: on the top chain hung a finely fashioned star, boasting many points; the second chain bore two simple stars, one larger than the other, joined by their tips.

'Some symbology lies beneath a gift of such beauty,' I said.

'Indeed.' His smile blossomed.

'You do not wish to explain it?'

'I prefer to hear you explain things. It is like watching a sapling grow to an oak.'

I felt a pleasant burst of heat in my chest. 'The first part, I think, is the jewel of the finest constellation: the she-bear who guides us through the night sky. This is her brightest star, is it not? The star she keeps closest to her body. Guidance and safety.' He nodded, and I allowed myself to smile. Urania had always maintained that her lessons would be of use one day. 'As for the second pendant, its shape is plain enough, but its meaning is less obvious. Why two stars?'

'Two souls may touch and be joined, some philosophers claim.' His blush was familiar to me by now. 'I have reasoned that such a bond could withstand all physical hardship, like the firmness of stars when they set in constellations.'

I touched his cheek, running my fingers down to the base of his neck. With the smooth motion that Erato had helped me practise, I ran my hand down further, beneath the thin wool; the warmth of his chest rose and fell. I kissed him long enough to breathe his scent into my lungs.

'I will not be gone long,' I said. 'There will be much to enjoy when I return.'

A helmet, breastplate and greaves lay on my bed. The bronze gleamed even in the faint light from the torch, and I knew at once that it was finer than any armour I had worn.

Calliope's voice sounded in my head.

I hope that you will not need it, now or ever.

By the time I stood with Fury on the mountaintop, I was well attired, and I clutched my lyre to my side. Jason loomed in his own armour, his men flanking him. The farms, the temple of Delphi, and the bare patches of the slope receded as we rose, the air slapping our cheeks; the deep emerald tops of smaller peaks clustered around Mt Parnassus, yet I saw them for only a moment before Fury picked up her pace, speeding into the sky.

A pair of arms gripped my waist, but that was our only exchange; Jason was alone with his thoughts, and I with mine.

The buildings of Iolcus emerged from the darkening land below, sooner than I had thought possible. Fury landed softly outside an inn, and after I dismounted, I whispered to her to wait for me.

At the door of the inn, I blocked Jason's way.

'If my mother had refused to lend Fury, how would you have travelled here?'

He did not reply.

I looked at his face for a long moment, and saw only closed doors.

Many thoughts swirled in my head, and I wondered if Hera had helped Jason to Mt Parnassus once again, or if he had risked his luck with a different god or goddess.

I advanced to the door. 'The poet walks before the prince, I see,' Jason said.

'I did not notice a crown upon your curls.'

The door resisted me. I put my shoulder into the thrust until it gave a sudden swing; torches lent a glow to the room before us, and the smell of cheese, olives and bread rose through the air, while everywhere voices contended with each other. Men filled the seats and stooped over tables; some stood, laughing or debating, their swords strapped to their hips or resting against the table legs. I surveyed the inn, but did not hesitate.

Heads turned when we began to weave our way through the crowd, and Jason steered me towards a group laughing in a corner. They welcomed us to their circle, breaking off their mirth.

'I thought you might miss out on the wine,' a curly-haired man said.

'With you around, that is likely,' Jason replied. The group chuckled again. 'I bring you Orphia, fresh from the Muses' care. She will entertain us this evening.'

'I prefer the music of the grape,' the curly-haired man said.

'This wit who addresses us is Phlias, son of Dionysus,' Jason said to me. 'And beside him, you see Erytus, son of Hermes, skilled in trickery and silver-tongued.'

Erytus bowed. I stared openly at the both of them. It did not seem to matter, for the whole group was staring at me too.

Had I really been foolish enough to think that amidst a band of heroes, I would stand out in skill and divinity?

'This is Zetes,' Jason said, pointing to a swarthy man in a cloak, 'son of Boreas, the god of the North Wind. And his brother, stout-hearted Calais.' The pair bowed to me stiffly, grudging every inch they moved. 'And these two are Ergnius and Ancaeus, sons of Poseidon, each as skilful as the other.' The two bearded, broad-shouldered men did not bother to bow. I donned my best smile.

In this corner of the room alone, there was divine blood enough for the whole quest. This was not the crowd of mortals I had battled on the Whispering Isle. How would any of them be moved to listen to my songs?

While Jason and Phlias clinked their cups, my gaze fell on two men who had not been introduced. They leaned close together. The taller one could have lifted a boulder in each hand and still not strained his muscles, while the other looked as if he were painted in a delicate study on a vase, gifted with high cheekbones, long eyelashes, and soft copper hair falling around his face. The large man stroked his companion's neck.

'Before we go, Orphia,' Jason said, noting my gaze, 'you should meet Heracles.'

The big man nodded to me, his eyes twinkling. 'Honoured, Lady Orphia.'

'The honour is mine.' I bowed. 'But Jason, you have forgotten to introduce the eighth hero of this group.'

The others roared with laughter, and Heracles kissed his companion's cheek. 'This is Hylas,' he said. 'Some may think him no hero, but he is fine enough to share this hero's bed ... and I say he is a finer man than many of these ruffians.' He gestured at the others.

This set off fresh laughter, mingled with objections from Poseidon's sons and a call for more wine from Phlias, and while the group was busy debating the issue of Hylas' talents, Jason pulled me away and guided me through the inn.

As we moved, my mind moved faster still, a spark of anger setting off a quick-burning fire within me. How was it that men were allowed to lie with each other – to care for each other, to educate each other, to stroke and, reportedly, to penetrate each other – and yet women were supposed to remain virgins? Of course, the law only allowed for certain circumstances; young men who took up a mentorship, both physical and spiritual, were still expected to marry later on. But what were women allowed? A lifetime of obedience to a husband. No kisses with another woman, before marriage; no nights of leisure in the forest or lolling on couches, exploring each other's minds and bodies; no freedom to understand our desires and, by consequence, ourselves.

'Do you ever envy Heracles?' I muttered.

'It is not Heracles who concerns me,' Jason replied.

He jerked his head to the left, where a cluster of men gathered near the far wall. I did not like their stares. The man at the head of their table had an ill-favoured look; he watched Jason through the crowd, yet Jason made no move to confront him. Soon a pair of old men hurried over to request Jason's attention, calling on him to explain the route.

'Fame waits beyond deep gulfs, sharp islands, and the Clashing Rocks, it seems.'

The statement had been close to my ear, and I looked up to find a smooth-skinned man winking at me. 'We must be fools to chase it. Brave fools. What say you, Lady Orphia?'

'Fail or succeed, your names shall be carved amongst the brave,' I said.

'She speaks like a poet.' The man laughed, drawing closer to me. I noticed that he wore a fine gold ring, and his skin had a golden sheen, as if it had been burnished.

The detail made me uncomfortable. I could not say why.

'A lady must be fierce indeed, to venture into such company. Shall we ask Atalanta what she makes of our crew?' he said.

I had expected to meet warriors from the farthest corners of the land. If Achilles himself had come striding through the crowd to join us, I should not have been surprised. Yet the sight of a woman walking between the tables struck me speechless. She pushed her way through the centre of the room, nodding to the men, and her fingers grasped the hilt of her sword as she approached us.

'Well met, Idmon.' Her gaze swung to me. 'And you are?'

'Orphia, my lady.' I should have bowed, but I could not take my eyes off her.

'You are speaking with Atalanta, suckled by a she-bear, slayer of centaurs, and the huntress for great Artemis. I was first to draw blood on the Calydonian boar when it attacked Aetolia. But you will know that.' She looked me over from head to toe.

I thought about telling her that no one had breathed a word of her deeds to me, not even Jason. For a moment, I tried to imagine how many women's stories rested like pearls at the bottom of the ocean, darkly gleaming, waiting to be brought into the light.

'Have you come to the *Argo* unarmed, Orphia? What weapon do you use – the spear, the sword, the bow? Or do you grease your limbs and wrestle, like Heracles?'

'Alas, I have brought neither spear nor sword tonight. I wield only words.'

Idmon laughed again, so freely that I wondered if I had provided him with sport for the entire night. Atalanta only studied my face. Her gaze lingered there for some time.

'There are some who can do damage enough with those,' she said. 'It does my heart good to see another woman. Let us talk together, sister.'

She drew me apart from Idmon, who returned to Jason and the maps. We looked at each other again for a moment. Atalanta clapped her hand to my bicep. 'Time is short, so let our words be, too. I know that you are here to help Jason.'

'How?'

'Because there is much that Jason needs help with. And then you arrive.' She smiled wryly. 'I suppose he has told you some tale or other about the group.'

'Only that the men may become restless.'

'Oh, they are already restless. And it is thanks to Jason that they finger their swords. You are a bold speaker, I can tell, but if I were you, I would have something sharper than your tongue at the ready tonight.'

I gripped her arm, too. 'Tell me more.'

She made to speak again, then she let go of my bicep. 'Look around you.'

At first, I saw nothing but a crowded inn. But then I picked out an empty table near the wall and noticed the group of men who had risen from it, moving towards us with blades drawn, the man with the ill-favoured look walking in front. He marched up and pointed his sword at Jason's throat.

'Cede to the true leader,' he declared.

'You look upon your true leader, Idas. As you know well.' Jason's reply was like a pond on a winter morning, hardened with frost, ready to splinter into shards.

'Is this the man we elected?' Idas' voice had a mocking ring. He turned to face the crowd, who had all fallen silent.

'I say you look upon the man who leads your enterprise,' Jason said.

'It is strange. I seem to remember that Heracles won the vote. Do you remember that too, friends?'

The men with him made noises of assent. I looked to Jason, but before I could signal to him, a booming voice called: 'Enough!'

Heracles seemed to have grown even larger since I stood beside him. He moved through the room to where Idas stood, and no one ventured to stand in his way. 'Do you wish to fight it out, little man?'

'No. But I say Jason asked you to cede the power of leadership.'

Now I saw why I had been called. I only regretted that I had not realised sooner how Jason had cloaked his part in this.

'Sit down, Idas. You swell like a rotten peach: ugly on the outside, soft in the centre.' The accusation came from beside me. The man with the golden ring had stepped forward – Idmon, I recalled. He was standing boldly alone, and I saw his lips twitch into a smirk.

'Shut your mouth, Idmon.' Idas made a gesture that could not be misconstrued.

My gaze swept them all, and I saw Jason take a step back. I wondered if he was afraid or if he was calculating. I could imagine a sword or arrow being drawn at any moment, and then the quest would be over before it had begun, my songs unheard.

But I had not counted on the huntress who stood beside me.

'I will fight you all, if you are in need of sport.' Atalanta stepped up to Heracles and Idas. 'Come now. Who will be first? Let me strike you like I struck that boar, or let us get the oil and take to the floor. I wager Jason will not shy from a match.'

'Not if my life were part of the bargain.' Jason grinned, clapping as if at a comedy, and slowly, the others began to applaud, until the inn was ringing with noise. Only Idas and his men refused to clap. 'But I have a greater delight for us all,' Jason added. 'Friends, I have brought you a gift: Orphia, daughter of Lord Apollo and charmer of ears, the greatest poet in all of Greece! She has come to grace you with a song. Let the wine flow, and let us clear her a stage!'

Movement, the thrum of voices, and the scrape of chairs. My eyes locked on Jason's. I did not need to search for a topic, for I had used my time well on the ride over; my task might be to cool the tempers of men, but I could do more than that. I could give them the goddess that towered behind their existence.

Heracles joined Jason, the beautiful Hylas beside him, and the three of them stood without flinching, facing their opponents. Idas and his men moved to the back of the room but did not draw their swords. I felt a slap on my shoulder. Inches away, Atalanta regarded me.

'A bear in a cage dances to an aulos,' she said. 'Do not let them make you dance.'

We shared a longer look.

The men who surrounded me had fought and killed, but none of them could shoot lightning from their palms, nor turn islands to ash. I inhaled, and began to strum my lyre.

'Tell me, Muse, of the great nothingness, an infinity shuddering in the dark. Tell me of the quake, of the cracking and cracking and cracking. Tell me how the void splintered, nothing bursting into something, streams of jade and sapphire meeting and dancing. Tell me of the birth of the sky, of the jutting hills and the wide sea. Tell me of the deeds of Gaia.'

I had considered, as I soared through the air over the dark land, how I might bring together my lessons at last. Techniques for joining music, movement, history and praise: I had gone over them all, laying out a plan, but it was not the plan that poured into the inn now, stilling the tongues of Jason's crew. My study had provided the skeleton for my poem. Imagination provided the flesh and blood. I would show them Gaia as I saw her, the force of divine kindness who gave bounty to everyone who walked on the earth: I would make them kneel and pray to her endless creation.

They all knew of the father of the gods. Let them tremble before the mother of all things.

The unfurling of petals was so soft that I almost did not hear it, with my mind and soul focused on the poem. Yet when my eyes flicked to the opposite wall, I saw a silver flower swelling on a stalk that had thrust between two bricks, and knew that I had called it to me. Panic rose in my chest. I said a prayer to Hera, inside my head, even while I spoke the last lines of the poem.

The applause that broke over me came in waves, one starting as the last ended, groups of men standing as they clapped. They did not seem to have noticed the magic, but I waited until it was safe to sneak a glance at the silver flower.

'You have trained hard with that lyre.'

Atalanta's voice pierced my thoughts. I turned to her. She was sitting on the corner of a table, her legs dangling over the edge.

'If my poem pleases you, then I have struck one target worth reaching,' I said. 'If you were the only one, it should be enough.'

She grinned. 'I love a powerful tale.'

'From what I hear, you have featured in them.'

'Those centaurs asked for it.'

'I should like to hear how you slew them, another time.'

'And so you may. They tried to ravish me, and they met their end, not without blood. Do you fight, too, Orphia?'

'I was trained to fight with spear and shield,' I said.

'I hope dearly that you will change your mind and join us on this quest.' She looked wistful. 'Imagine the adventures we could have.'

I could imagine them well. We embraced, and I let her go with reluctance. Jason was moving towards me, and I fended off others and made my way to him.

'I should be a hard master indeed if I did not say how well you performed your duty,' he said.

'Your memory is weak, Jason. You forget that you are not my master.'

'I shall never outmatch you with words, at least.' Jason offered me his arm. 'There is nothing I could pledge that would make you change your mind about the quest?'

I shook my head. He sighed. 'Very well. Come this way.'

He guided me through a door, and we moved from the main room of the inn to a smaller chamber where only two torches burned. A square table filled the space, and two men were talking over a bottle of wine.

'Idmon and Butes,' Jason said, 'pour Lady Orphia a cup. And one for yourself, while you are at it.'

The men did as they were told. I recognised the smooth-skinned man who had spoken to me earlier.

Jason drank, and so did I. The wine tasted rich and good on my much-used tongue. He clapped me on the shoulder. 'I must see that the mood you have spread does not dissipate. Idmon here will lead you out the quiet way.'

Idmon smiled pleasantly, taking my cup. 'We are all grateful to you, Lady Orphia.'

At the sound of my name, something that had lurked at the back of my mind clicked into place. Idmon had been introduced to me now, and he had heard my song, but before that … before Jason had presented me to the room … how had he known to call me 'Lady Orphia'?

'These rooms are a little dim. Let me guide you,' Idmon said. He offered his arm, and up close, I noticed again how smooth and golden his skin looked. It remained the same colour even in the half-dark.

We passed the bracket in the next room, and under the glow of the torch, Idmon's hand entwined with mine. Light flickered over the gold band of his ring. In the centre of the metal, an engraving shone, tiny but unmistakeable in the sudden brightness.

Points jabbed out from a circle. The carved sun gleamed as if it were real.

'That is a very fine ring,' I said.

'I am glad you think so.' His smile was a little too pleasant. 'My father gave it to me.'

We reached a door. Idmon pushed it open with his free hand, gesturing to me to walk through.

Something flitted through my mind, like a horse bolting from its stable.

I twisted away from him, and in the same breath he drew his dagger and held it to my throat. We tussled, shoving. I yanked his dagger away and flung it to the floor, but even as I made to grab him, he pushed me hard into the next room; my toe caught on a stone and I stumbled, catching hold of Idmon's arm.

The two of us fell on our faces against the cold floor. Idmon jumped up and kicked me in the chest, digging his boot into my ribs. Wincing, I gulped down as much air as I could.

'I see you have met your brother,' a graceful voice said.

My stare swept to the right. I drew a lungful of air, gasping.

'You will not be running, now. Not unless you wish for that savage gryphon to burn ... or for your sweet shield-maker to wake engulfed by flames.'

The voice reached me as if through a wall of sunlight. I pushed Idmon away and clambered to my feet. An aura blazed around the figure that stood before us, and this time, it was cold and cruel, like a fire that ravaged a battlefield long after the fight was over.

The white light filled every corner of the room.

'No more hiding, my child,' Apollo said. 'No more ignoring my orders.'

The last thing I saw was the tip of my father's arrow, bearing down upon me.

It seemed an exceptionally painless wound. But then, I had not been shot in the face before. Perhaps the experience was always this pleasant.

My hands were clasped behind my back. I tried to pull them apart, but whatever force held me, I could not break it. I blinked until the white light no longer hurt, and my father's face came into view.

'You will bear no mark, feel no pain, and live.'

I waited until he was close enough to examine my expression. Then I spat in his face.

'That is not graceful.' He wiped his cheek. 'Not when I have only used my arrow to hold your limbs still.'

'Was it graceful to murder Eurydicius' parents?'

He had the sense to step back. I saw Idmon hovering in the shadows behind his aura. I wished I could spit far enough to strike him, too. Half-brother or not, he was a traitorous worm.

'You should be glad,' Apollo said. 'Though I do not approve of your defiance, my child, I have decided to allow your use of poetry. The greatest seer in the world has made it clear: you will help Jason.'

Throwing back my head, I laughed. If I had been able to move my hands, I would have clapped slowly. 'Pythia saved a different prophecy for me, father.'

I watched him frown. I had never been more proud of my mother for concealing my visit.

'Yes,' I said. 'You are not the only one to speak with the Oracle. She declares that my destiny lies with Eurydicius; that I must not allow myself to be parted from him. And as I do not wish to exchange happiness and glory for a death in some dusty field, the matter is settled.'

'Not parted from him ... at a certain time? Or forever? What does she mean by greatness? Did she make any other remarks during your visit, my child?' It was his turn to laugh. 'You need to ask many questions to reach the truth, and I know how to get it out of Pythia.'

Bitterness infused my saliva, as if I had tasted bad fruit. Had my mother not warned me about the Oracle – had she not given the example of the king who lost his army, precisely to advise me that I might hear what I desired instead of the truth? And yet the Oracle's words had been so firm. So confident. Her message for me had seemed perfectly clear.

A thought lengthened in my mind, and I followed it like a traveller down a path. 'You know something, don't you? You know that I will be very famous.'

'What makes you sure, child?'

'You always wanted me to stay safe on the island, so that I might live to be helpful to you. Do you really expect me to believe that you have changed your mind out of respect for a raving woman?' I laughed. 'Did the Oracle tell you that if I sail on Jason's quest, I may bring you some profit by association? You always use your children when they can give you something. Some of us are good for fame, and some are only good for sticking in a boot.'

Idmon took in my last words and lunged at me, hand raised. A blast of air pushed him back across the room.

'No,' Apollo said, giving him a withering glance. When he turned his gaze on me, it was more thoughtful. He moved around behind me. 'I command you to help Jason.'

'And I reject your order. I have the support of the Oracle.'

A sudden bite tore my flesh. My wrist sang; I could feel the wound's cruelty, even if I could not see it, and I imagined a slash of red where the dagger had struck. Something warm dripped over my palm.

'Blood makes the spell complete.' My father circled back to stand before me, re-sheathing his blade. 'When Jason calls you on his quest, you will come. I grant you the kindness of a little more time on Mt Parnassus, until you are needed.' He cupped my jaw in his hand, and I winced at the heat. 'Be grateful, my child. This magic I do for your eternal glory.'

There were so many words I wanted to hurl at him, but I could not get one out before Apollo spread his hands and sleep overcame me. As my eyes closed, I saw Eurydicius. He was sleeping in his bed on Mt Parnassus. The sight calmed me, something so delicate and peaceful still enduring.

No one was moving when I woke. The darkness of the inn accompanied the noiseless sleep of travellers, and I ran a finger over the scab on my wrist. I could move my limbs again, and I felt my way through the rooms to the front door.

A dark shape sat outside, staring up at the moon. Under Artemis' light, a square blue gemstone shone.

'Even when you climb high, your raggedness will lie exposed. A weed does not change its true nature,' I said.

Jason turned at the sound of my voice. 'Thank the gods! I had begun to wonder where you were.'

'Do not worry. I have a good memory. When someone betrays me perfectly, I do not only remember the result. I remember who brought me to it.' I clicked my fingers and whistled, and the sound of wings told me that Fury had arrived.

Jason was staring at me as if seeing me anew. 'I knew nothing of Lord Apollo's ambush.'

'Who mentioned Apollo?' I said.

I mounted Fury and nudged her with both knees, and we lifted off into the night.

From the sky, Jason diminished, a thread in a tapestry that was dark and still and wide. I ran my hand over the great star on my neck, then down to the two joined stars, feeling the point where their tips fused.

The bubbling of the fountain ceded to the rise and fall of voices, and after half an hour, there was still no lull in the debate. I slipped out of the foyer. Erato might be demanding an attack on Apollo, and Clio might be proposing a plan of vengeance, but I felt sure that Calliope's cooler wisdom would prevail.

I also felt a little guilty, as if it were my fault that I had no palate for argument. After a sleepless night, I nourished no desire for rancour.

I slipped to the front of the palace, peeping out at the sculpted pillars and the figure waiting beneath them.

The blue chlamys caught my eye first. The short cloak hung over him, unfairly covering half of what I wanted to see. Its fabric displayed the colour of the sea. Nereids' dye. It must have been Calliope's order to fashion him something to cover his chiton on the cooler mornings, yet I guessed that the rich dye and the fine weave were the maker's choices: I was not the only one to have noticed his beauty.

I called his name through the bright air.

Eurydicius rushed to me. Giving thanks for my health, he deplored Apollo's trickery, and I kissed his cheek. Holding out both hands, he offered me a small bowl containing a milky paste.

There were lotos roots in that mixture, and manna from the
ash tree. Even the palace healer on the Whispering Isle had not
been able to concoct such a potion. 'Where did you get this?'
I said.

'Wisdom enfolds me, in this place. The nymphs have been
teaching me the arts of healing.' He looked down. 'I have much
to learn, of course, but I could determine that these roots give
balm, while the manna restores strength. I plucked them from
the grounds.'

I dabbed a little onto my scab and sighed. The itch was
melting away. I kissed his lips, this time, and he struggled to
hide his surprise. Over the course of the day, my anger at the
night's events had metamorphosed, ending in determination; if
I could be yanked away at any moment, then I would make the
most of what I had.

'Let us take a walk,' I said, 'to a place you have seen, and
not seen.'

We moved side by side, walking so closely that our hands
brushed. I felt the heat of his fingers matching my own. Was
it just that the sun had baked his skin? As we turned a corner,
I moved close enough to rub our arms together, and sneaking
a glance over, I caught him looking back at me.

The trees knitted together at the front of the copse, and I
led him through them. He did not ask me why we were straying
from the path, though I knew he must be wondering. Branches
blocked the sun's rays; then it came: the waft of perfume that I
remembered from my dream, coating my forearms, my armour,
even the bark of the trees.

Yet the grass was not long enough to tickle my calves. A
single bloom pushed up between tree roots. No clusters of
roses sprouted from the rich soil. We were in the same place I
had come so many times to speak poetry and pray, not some
haven from a fantasy.

I wrapped my arms around his neck, and he leaned into my movement. When I kissed him, it was a question, expanding to a statement when he parted his lips to receive me, and he clung to my waist, the two of us scarcely able to let go.

A second kiss. A third. I stepped back and examined him, then unfastened his chlamys, flinging it to the ground.

He grinned. 'I like it.'

I knew that he meant my audacity, not the cloak.

'I desire you,' I said, my words clear, carried by everything Erato had taught. 'It is not in my nature to wait. Tell me what you feel.'

'If there were a thousand stars in the sky and you floated amongst them, I would see only you. The black infinity of night, and a single bright point.'

Slipping my hand under his chiton, I passed my palm over his chest, trailing my way down to his stomach and back up again. I seized one of his hands, examining it, feeling the warmth of the skin. Shield-maker's hands: no scars, no calluses, but skill written in each fingertip. I ran my tongue down the middle of his palm, tasting salt.

Sitting down, I extended a hand to him. The grass was soft beneath us. As he settled himself beside me, he dipped his head and kissed my foot. He pressed his lips there for a long time and looked up at me.

I had started it, with the kiss on his lips. But that had been playfulness. It had not conveyed this devotion. I was aware of silence cloaking me.

'Are you all right?' He spoke softly. 'I mean, really?'

'In body, yes. In spirit ...' The thought of being pulled away from him across land and sea had knotted and re-knotted inside me. How could I burden him with that tangle of desperation? 'I have had better nights, in truth.'

'If you wish to talk, I wish to listen.'

I had not known, until then, how much I wished to unburden my mind to someone who was not Calliope, Euterpe or Erato.

I did not leave out anything, from my arrival in the inn to Jason's deception, and Apollo's arrow, with all the consequences it had wrought. Amidst frustration, I found moments of joy: Atalanta's grin, directed at me. The silver flower, swelling on its stalk.

Eurydicius listened carefully. When I finished, his eyes brimmed with something stronger than sadness. 'I cannot – I scarcely – I am almost …'

I waited.

'I cannot tolerate losing you. Nor can I accept that we must simply wait for Jason to call you away. I would scream a litany of curses at your father.'

'Do not think of him. Think of the poem I performed. Think of how the strength of my words will carry me through Jason's tasks, and back to you.'

He sighed. 'What I would not give to hear those verses, and tremble like the others in that inn.'

I drew a deep lungful of air. As if Erato's voice called me to move first, I stood up, and strode a few paces to the end of the copse. 'I will give you the poem, if you will bestow a gift on me in return.'

'Anything,' he said.

'For each verse I speak, you must remove a part of your clothing.'

Our smiles met and sparked.

Later, I would think about what might have happened if I had put such a proposal to a man like Ixion, or even Jason. I would think about the revenge that men had taken on women who asked for anything boldly, in history and in legends, and indeed, on the Whispering Isle. But in that moment, all I knew was what I felt. The desire was too strong to be contained.

I called up the violence of the universe: the cracking of the void, the surging of sea and sky, the pushing and setting of peaks and hills, the deeds of Gaia spreading through the layered earth. The poetry flowed through me, gushing like molten rivers from the world's core. I was nothing and everything – I had merged with her, the creator of the land, the mistress of air and cloud and soil – and as I revealed her power, my own strength settled upon me in a golden cloak of words.

'Tell me, Muse, of the dance and sway of wheat in the mid-morning sun. Tell me of the rhythm of those ripening ears, bending and bowing as they offer themselves to wind-battered hands. Tell me of the gift of Gaia.'

Opposite me, I could see Eurydicius stooping to remove his sandals, then beginning to unfasten his chiton.

The rhythm of my lines built. An image of the never-ending expanse of the sky poured from my mouth, and the tremble of soil around my feet and the rustle of grass preceded a hiss of growth, as plants grew in time with my poetry. Crimson roses bloomed from the earth, pushing up in groups between trunks and roots, scattering flecks of colour. I built to the poem's conclusion – to Gaia giving birth to the titans, her chest heaving, her thighs glistening with sweat.

Petals flew into the air. Some landed on Eurydicius' head, the breeze twining them into his hair. I had created the magic of the copse, in my vision, I realised, at last: *my* words had done this.

He unwrapped his chiton and dropped it beside his chlamys. A ray of sun fell on his forehead, granting him a touch of gold. As the grass stopped rustling and the petals stopped falling, quietude enclosed us, veiling his nakedness and my bare emotions.

A carpet of grass stretched between us. I put one foot upon it, then another. He watched me, and I watched him, taking in his soft tresses and the steady admiration of his gaze.

Now I knew how it would go. We had both already dreamed it, but the ray of sun that rebounded off my armour and onto his chest was no less exquisite for being expected.

'Can I touch you?' I said.

Though I knew it was coming, my fear caught me off balance. I felt terrified by what I had started. Yet the surprise in Eurydicius' gaze swirled gently into something else, and his smile spread all the way to his eyes.

'I was hoping you would ask me that,' he said.

Mapping his body with my fingertips was easy. Holding myself back from gripping him was less simple.

'We could make the most of our time,' I said.

He brushed one palm against my armour, gingerly touching it. 'I think you have a true power, to read my thoughts with such ease.'

I had forgotten those words, until now. Perhaps they had been driven out of my mind by the sensation that I remembered so clearly, the mingling of sharpness and sweetness that sliced through me. I wanted more of this. I held his jaw and studied his face; I wedged my knee between his thighs and brought our bodies together.

His belief in me entered through touch, as it had in the dream, swelling inside my chest. Again, I absorbed its force. Nothing was impossible any more. This time, his vow might almost have been spoken: *I believe in every particle of you.*

I held my palm to his neck and felt the pulse beating through warm skin. 'From now on,' I said, 'I give myself to you, and I claim you.'

'I would be yours completely, if it pleases you.'

It took me a moment to realise what he was doing. He knelt on the grass and slid a hand along my thigh, slowly, moving from the top of my greaves upward, slipping beneath my armour. I caught his eye and saw that he was seeking my approval.

'It pleases me very much,' I said.

No man had ever offered this. Women gave pleasure, and men took it. Or so said the hundreds of poets who had visited the Whispering Isle.

Later, I would compose verses about the tickle of his hair against my inner thigh, the hot silk of his tongue. Now, there was only the song of flesh. I felt bursts of heat in my blood, stars burning and leaping and then flaring anew.

He did not stop when my breathing had slowed, but brought me back to the same state three times. No doubt there would have been more, but I desired to return the affection. I was hungry too. We spread out his chlamys and lay on it, and I rolled him onto his back, smothering him with my arms.

'You pin me down so easily,' he said, when I held his wrists above his head. 'As if you knew what I wished.'

'And you wish …?'

'To be at your mercy.'

I kissed him furiously, and reached down, hearing his gasp as I began to touch him.

'Is it strange? For a man to desire things to be this way?' he whispered.

'If it is,' I said, 'then I must be strange too.'

When there were no more melodies of sweat and breath, we lay propped on our sides, facing each other, our smiles matching in their felicity.

'I have no right to ask,' I said, 'but a question springs to my lips.'

'I promise I will answer.'

'Have you ever done that before? You know …' It was difficult to name. 'With another?'

He rubbed his cheek against the side of my hand. 'Not with a woman.'

He coloured slightly. I caressed a lock of his hair, trying to tell him without words that I did not mind in the slightest, running my fingers slowly over the soft length of those blonde strands. I looked up and saw him gazing at me from inches away.

'I have a question, too,' he said.

I hoped my smile was encouragement enough.

'Do you mind that I am not the kind of man who wishes to lead?'

'I call it good fortune,' I said. 'For I do not like to follow.'

A wave of perfume rolled over us, his elm-leaf scent blending into the notes of roses. 'I do not know how much time we will have before Jason calls me, nor what will happen on the quest,' I said. 'But this I vow: I shall be your protector, as long as I live. We will fit with each other like a key and a lock.'

When our fingers interlaced, I breathed in the whole universe, drawing light from all the constellations into me.

They were weeks, not years. Yet every week felt like a year, and each day contained more joy than I had known in all my years; in my breaks I would seek him out, and together we would slip out of the Muses' walls, rambling amongst the pools and the outcrops of pale pink limestone. Sometimes we took off our sandals and walked barefoot on the grass. We swam in the lake, splashing each other, diving beneath the skin of mirrored sunlight. At times, we sat in the shallows, touching each other until our breath quickened.

Sprawled on the shore, we poked at ideas, discussing and debating. Eurydicius' mind was always asking questions, and mine was always looking for patterns, and we turned over issues of philosophy, science and politics. Hours would slip by without my noticing the sun dropping in the sky.

'Do you believe that life is ultimately tragic?' His words quivered between us.

'Melpomene says so, but it stands to reason that the Muse of Tragedy would see things that way.' I allowed myself to ponder it for a moment. 'I cannot agree with her. As I see it, life teems with tragedies. But one may always choose how to respond to them.'

'And what of the gods and goddesses, knocking us down with the backs of their hands, sometimes on purpose, sometimes by chance?' he replied. 'What of the Oracle and the other seers who pierce the future with their gaze? Surely, you could say that your life and mine were determined long ago.'

'Look at Jason. The heir with one sandal, returning to challenge his uncle, just as the prophecy has it. Yet whether he proves himself to be the true heir will rely on more than just a sandal. How he treats his crew and the people he meets on his quest will matter more than a prediction, I think.'

'Do you truly believe our lives are our own to shape?' His brow wrinkled.

'I must believe it.' I did not want to add more, for I feared that I had betrayed my need to see my own life as a series of choices. With choice, I might carve out a glorious destiny – one that might lead others to raise their voices and hold their heads high in the face of the arrows of doubt. If all things were set in place, I knew where my road would end.

We exchanged views on morality: on the need to show kindness to strangers, and when it was right to use force against others. With a little coaxing, Eurydicius explained that his parents' farm had been raided and plundered when he was a young boy. His father had lacked the will to fight, while his mother had lacked the means. Eurydicius had watched his father carry on tending to his cattle and fields and his mother continue cooking and cleaning, and in time they had been robbed again. It was then that he had begun making shields.

'Another man would have sought to kill the thieves,' I said.

'If their raid inspired me to attack, then might not my attack inspire another raid? One vengeance for another. A wheel turning, and so many lives flattened beneath it.' The trenches in his brow deepened for a moment. 'I could not see the good in that.'

He was too precious for the company of noblemen. I could imagine what the lords of the Whispering Isle would have done to any returning raider.

'What you have fashioned with wood and bronze is more than an object. It is an idea,' I said.

'I hope so.'

'Your parents would be proud of you, if they were here.'

He smiled and cast his eyes down. A swallow chirped, somewhere above us in the branches. He pressed his lips to my knee, and the movement seemed to come easily, an extension of him.

I reflected on his hardships. He had kept his spirit despite all that had happened to him. He was gentle, and sweet; thoughtful, and quietly kind. They were not qualities that men prized, but I thought they were amongst the greatest qualities that a man could have.

I was risking his happiness by getting close to him, I knew, yet to be apart from him was impossible. I desired fame. I desired him, too. I would no longer try to put away the needs of my soul and tell myself that they were only greed – or that they were not connected – for as we nourished each other, so might I nourish the world.

We slipped away together most nights, after dinner, when the Muses were busy with their own affairs and the moon silvered the paths in their citadel. That first night, I brought him to my chamber. The silence of the tower made every step to my door a drumbeat. In the doorway, he waited for my kiss, smiling into my mouth when I walked him backwards.

Secretly, I had wondered if that moment in the copse had been planned, a gesture to prove his passion. But when he knelt, as I sat perched on the bed, I knew that he did so without design, for he moved naturally to kiss his way up my leg, beginning at my ankle and continuing over the hard muscle of my calf, my inner thigh, and then higher still, until I twined my fingers into those long locks.

The shifts in his breath stirred something in me. When his gasps quickened, a wind rattled through me. I touched him until his release sent him shuddering against my chest, his face blissful.

Sometimes I wrapped my body around him. Sometimes, I climbed on top of him, and felt myself a goddess.

One night, as we lay in my bed talking of medicine and astronomy, and whether they might be linked – amidst a dozen other questions of science and philosophy – a ray of moonlight fell across his face, illuminating his fine cheekbones. A memory came upon me, swift as a soaring swallow. I was back with the woman in the steam baths on the island, touching and talking, her sharp cheekbones standing out boldly in the silvery moonlight; my fingers trailed along her thigh and then upwards, moving inside her, until she moaned into my hair. It meant something, that memory. As I looked at Eurydicius again, I realised that I wanted no secrets between us.

'I have something to confess to you.' I met his gaze, and suddenly remembered what he had let slip, before. *Not with a woman.*

Perhaps this would not be so bad.

'I will happily hear it,' he said.

'I lay with a woman, once. Sometimes, I desire women still.'

A silence lingered between us, and his face told me that he was not concerned but searching for words. At last, he replied, 'I think that is natural.'

'You do?'

'I have sometimes wanted to kiss men. Or rather, to be kissed by them. To be touched by them in certain ways.' His eyes held mine. 'The first night after I reached the Whispering Isle, I stayed in Jason's chamber ...'

He did not need to finish. I already knew.

'Was he gentle with you?' I said.

He seemed to search for words. 'Not exactly. But it pleased me. I think it meant nothing to him, but it meant something to me.'

I reached out for a lock of his hair and trailed my fingers through it, trying to touch him as softly as possible.

'For a while, growing up, I thought that I could only love men ... because only they would be willing to lead me,' he added. 'Now, I am certain I love both kinds. All kinds.'

I smiled. 'What made you sure?'

He looked thoughtful again. 'One day, my father took me to sell my shields to the richest man in our area. While they talked, I was allowed to wander into the man's courtyard. A sculpture of Athena stood in the centre, her gold paint gleaming in the sun. The goddess wasn't wearing her usual chiton, though. She wore her helmet and clutched her spear, but not a scrap of clothing was sculpted on her. Looking up at her, I realised ... the angle made such a difference, for men are usually encouraged to look down at women. In every way.' He reached out and slid his palm beneath my own, letting my fingers lie on top of his. 'That day, I realised that I liked women too, but I did not wish to stand over them. I dreamed of finding a woman who could shake the world ... a woman whose voice made men tremble and rivers flow ... a woman I would happily kneel beneath.' A tiny smile curved his lips as he looked at me. 'I do not mean Athena.'

I kissed him, and as I pulled away, I kissed his hand, too. 'Perhaps we both seek the same thing, but from opposite paths.'

'What do you mean?'

'I have always liked women easily, but when it comes to men, I have only ever been drawn to softness. A gentle manner. A kind heart.' I smiled. 'I can only love one who defies the world's rules: a man who dares to be water when I am fire.'

We kissed again, and this time, he ran his fingers down my side as I clutched a handful of his hair. When we stopped, he whispered, 'I am glad that we share the same queer spirit.'

We lay in silence for a moment. A thoughtful look came over his countenance. 'What of people who are neither man nor woman? What of people who seem to change from one sex to the other, like melting gold that reforms? Do you find yourself drawn to them?'

'I do not know,' I said, feeling my own lack. 'I have never met one.'

'Ah.' He smiled.

'You seem wiser than me, in that province. What of your desires?'

'I open my mind to all things.' After a long silence, he added: 'But the wanderings of the mind are light-footed, and the tracks soon fade. It is the heart that knows most of desire. And my heart has never wandered from you, since I first heard you speak.'

I held him tightly. I was afraid that if I let go, something so precious would slip from my grasp.

The memory of my father's mirthful face cut through my mind, carving the moment like a spear-tip through soft leather. I heard his words ringing with new reverberation. *Not parted from him ... at a certain time? Or forever? What does she mean by greatness?*

A single rose petal fluttered through the window and landed on his neck. With it came the fragrance of the garden outside.

'I dropped a rose in the lake, once.' I was not sure why I was sharing this with him. 'I watched it fall towards the depths.'

'Is that poetry?'

I could still picture the hole in the earth. 'Perhaps.'

He nestled into my side and asked the same question that he asked every time, after we lay together: might he hear a poem? In speaking my verses to him, I felt the tapestry of my work coming together, thread by thread. Some of my own stories had lived in my head for too long. By sharing them, I firmed them into an existence I could finally believe in, their clay setting in the kiln of his joy.

His appetite for stories was never-ending, but the next day, as I began a tale about Atalanta fighting the centaurs, a knock sounded at my door.

Euterpe glided in, and a man in a red robe stepped out from behind her, his features recognisable at once. The last time I had seen this man, he had been standing on the slope at Delphi.

I bowed my head. The priest walked up to me, stopping close enough that his breath gusted in my face. 'The Oracle would share her vision with you. Out of kindness, daughter of Calliope, she wishes you to know that Jason will ask for you in two weeks.'

What can I say of hunting? Some warriors love to sink their spear-head or arrow-tip into the deep hide of a lion, grinning to their comrades when they know that they have penetrated it. They stand over the writhing animal and cheer when its throes end. Theirs is the glee of a warrior who has defeated an unarmed opponent, dripping smiles on a crowd who have gathered only to see them win.

My aunt Artemis, goddess of the hunt, was also the protector of wild animals. Most of the hunters in Greece had forgotten that.

Oh, I did not begrudge Atalanta her pride at slaying a centaur when the creature was bearing down upon her, slavering at the sight of her breasts; yet I felt that to kill a stag sleeping in the sun, a wolf encircled by men, or a leopard protecting its cubs ... that was another matter.

Every minute that we spent on the mountainside, I feared that with his soft gaze and his even softer heart, Eurydicius was still a cub.

Two weeks. The priest's voice rang in my ears.

I taught Eurydicius that listening was more important than striking. Keep your ears attuned for a crackle of leaves or a footfall on the mountainside, and if you can, slip away. If you must fight, protect your body at all times; and when the need arises, run without shame.

'I am not joking,' I added, when he gave a bashful smile. 'You must promise me that if an animal should come into your range, you will not seek glory, only to defend yourself.'

'My father never spoke of glory. His was a ploughing, harvesting, sweating life. There is no time to think about a grand hunt when you are working a farm ... and to my mother, animals were food and goods. Not prizes.'

'What are they to you?'

Surprise flared in his eyes, and I remembered that he was still not used to voicing his opinion. 'I think the wilder and more powerful they are, the more beautiful they are,' he replied.

Our hands twined, his resting beneath mine. We did not finish our lesson that day, though I returned to it soon enough.

I brought him to the eastern garden to train with the nymphs, as well as wrestling and shooting with him alone on the mountainside, until I was satisfied that he could fight off any lion or wolf. I taught him where to aim with his dagger in a boar's neck if another such beast should attack him. We grappled in bed, too, though he was not interested in fighting me, then, only grinning as I pushed him down.

It should have been hard to concentrate on my lessons. When Euterpe escorted me on gryphon-back to the lyre tower, however, I was a bow-string ready to be pulled.

Calliope embraced me.

'Come,' she said. 'Your destiny is too close for my liking.'

'One week and three days,' I said.

She pursed her lips. 'Counting will not lengthen it, I am afraid.'

My mother led me through nine levels, striding before me up the staircase and stopping just long enough for me to gape at what I saw. Baths sparkled in colours that should not have been possible, hues that existed between hues; shelves teemed with gemstones that seemed to call to me in echoing voices;

trees curled their branches over a banquet table, their leaves glistening with unearthly light. In the heart of the tower, a walkway carved a path through utter blackness, ending at a waterfall.

Something about the golden sheen of the water tugged at the fibres of my being, though I could not say why, and as I strayed towards it, Calliope called out:

'Unless you wish to trade your inspiration away, you should move along.'

We stopped at last in a hall where shelves lined the walls, jutting out at different heights, some layered like steps and some shadowed in corners, seeming to guard their secrets. I glimpsed a marble floor studded with mosaics. Streams of light ventured through windows high above us, bathing the cauldrons and tripods that clustered in the hall, and I tried not to gawk as Calliope strode over to a cauldron and stroked its rim.

'Ever since you arrived, you have been longing to enter my tower and prove yourself to me. But now you have a reason for it.' Rain mingled with stars in her voice, as it had when I first met her. 'If you really wish to keep both love and fame, do you think you can do so without enormous effort?'

I wanted to shy away from the task; to return to the world of Eurydicius' warm fingertips, his soft words of encouragement. But I remembered the priest's grave look. *Two weeks.*

I could not resist staring at the shelves. Tablets lay on all the lower ledges, and the letters engraved on a nearby slab gleamed. They told of a group of Athenians who had attempted to sail past a cluster of rocks, only to find themselves lured by the winged monsters who lived there – the sirens – bird-like creatures with human faces, who had swooped down to the deck and unleashed their magical song. The Athenians knew the risk of shipwreck, yet still they sailed onward, and the sirens steered them into a cliff wall. I could feel the characters jostling inside the stone, leaping against the smooth surface. 'Did you bring me here to read for days, mother?'

'The time for study has passed. You may read these tablets one day, but for now their presence alone matters. In this room lie shipwrecks, the labyrinth of Crete, the one-eyed Cyclopes, and the eternal sleep of Psyche. Here, too, are visions of the Underworld: from the shadowy fields of Asphodel to the gold-wreathed pastures of Elysium, and deeper, far deeper, the pits and pools where cries of pain echo for eternity. I speak of Tartarus.'

I shivered. I was not sure I wanted to read these stories after all.

'When a quest calls you to fleece and fire, every hour counts. Your task is simple.' My mother rose. 'In this room, every morning and afternoon, you will feel the souls of these tales. You will speak verses of your own making and strum your lyre, until you can create an epic worthy of their company.'

'How will I know if I have succeeded?'

'Know? That is impossible. But guess, maybe.' A tingle ran through me, and I suspected that Calliope read my excitement. 'Only when you have poured all your lessons with the Muses into a single poem should you come to me. Make it a tale that can serve you on the far side of the world. Jason does not seek the kind of fame that can be found in a local olive grove; nor does he bring you on his voyage to enjoy the views of the sapphire ocean.'

The flint in her gaze sparked a fire in my mind. I would do better than she could hope for, I vowed silently. Piece by piece, I would hammer my poem into armour.

I faced the tiers of the theatre and slowly bowed. The faces of
my teachers, stern and calm, appeared as if in a painted scene,
frozen for a second. Visages of nymphs mingled with them.
I drew a breath from the bottom of my lungs and squared my
shoulders to the crowd.

'When Poseidon pinned her
To the temple stones, her voice
Flared like pyre-wood,
Faded like smoke.

'As Perseus bore down upon her
She bestrode the pitted ground;
The snakes that writhed from her head
Cried mercy of the clouds.

'From her neck, Pegasus sprang –
The white horse spread his wings,
And bore her name through Greece
Swooping to Cretan shores.

'Her blood birthed the corals
Of the Red Sea – sharp as tongues.
O Hera, grant Medusa
Her legacy: woman, monster, might!'

I exhaled, and when the stasis broke and the applause hit me,
I did not hear it; I only saw the approval etched on Calliope's
countenance.

I left the stone circle at the bottom and began to climb.
Halfway up, my mother stopped me. 'I have never heard
Medusa so described.'

'The snakes that writhed from her head cried mercy of the clouds,' I said.

'Her blood birthed the corals of the Red Sea – sharp as tongues!' With a mingling of harmonies, she had made my words sound more powerful.

'I only hoped to tell her story,' I said.

'You did more than that. You sang of her power, even whilst you revealed her rape and murder. The way you mixed tragedy and triumph; the way you strummed your lyre to fit every emotion … Orphia, three years since you first graced this summit, you are ready.'

Something about the tone of her voice made me tense. A flash of crimson drew my attention to the tiers above her, and I watched a man in a familiar robe descend to us.

'The Oracle would share another vision. Out of respect for the great-granddaughter of Gaia, she wishes you to know that Jason will ask for you tomorrow morning.'

Not even a day. For the first time, I felt the difference between awaiting the summons and receiving it, my life withering into hours, each minute decked with jewels and glittering in a light that must soon pass into the west.

I thanked the priest and made my way out.

In the copse, I prayed to Hera, then sat and turned over the possibilities. How should I prepare for a parting of this magnitude? Fear swelled in my throat. I had taught Eurydicius how to hunt if he faced a wild animal, and I had seen the quality of his shields. Only now did I realise that there was something else to protect beyond his mortal frame.

While the sun grew angrier above, I breathed in the scent of roses and trailed my toes through the grass. The rhythms of love poems came back to me from one of my lessons: not the pulsating of the erotic verses that I had repeated, but the soft and steady thrumming of devotional lines. Suddenly, as if a stream of light poured over me, I knew what I should do.

'Are you sure?' Euterpe said.

I nodded.

'This is not a game, Orphia. Once you proceed, you cannot go back; this will last a lifetime. What if the outcome fails to satisfy you? Will you suffer the consequence?'

'Suffering may find me in time. But not through this.'

She sighed, and threw up her hands. 'Very well. If you see my headless body when you return, you will know that Calliope does not agree.' A familiar twinkle filled her eyes, and I kissed her quickly on the forehead before dashing from the foyer.

I knew exactly where Eurydicius would be. He had been working on a new shield all morning, and had missed lunch so that he could deliver it to my mother. The eastern garden looked empty when I arrived, except for a group of gryphons dozing, and the pond rippled in the faint breeze.

He was sleeping beside the water, a willow blocking the sun's anger and leaving remnants of softer light to play over his calves. Between the silver reflection of the water and the filtered gold of the sun, I spoke a poem to the air: one of the oldest poems I knew, about the birth of the almond tree.

The verses seeped into the earth and flowed. I concentrated, letting my mind become one with the story, and soil began to scatter, branches pushing up, leaves sprouting and spreading, until the tree I had raised covered him with shadow, its bright yellow-green leaves protecting us both. Finally, I pulled a silver flower up through the earth.

When I shook him awake, he smiled to see me leaning over him. It took all the restraint I had not to stroke his thigh as I told him the news.

'Of course, I dread the moment of our parting. But I am glad for you, all the same.' He took my hand in his. 'Through this you escape the lot of mortal women. Whatever you do amongst the Argonauts, you will be remembered, not for a punishment but for your deeds. As a hero, you will never be chained to a marriage bed, nor yoked to a loom.'

I wanted to laugh. He had managed to find the goodness in the very thing that threatened to tear us apart. 'You are right. Mine is a hero's life to claim,' I said. 'And with it, I think, a hero's doom.'

Leaves rustled above us. A zephyr touched my cheek and toyed with the hem of his chiton. Somehow, the nearness of the sun made the shade more precious to me.

'I am not to be bargained away to a husband for my father's contentment. My life is my own, to do with as I please until destiny catches up to me. If I could give every woman in this land the freedom to choose her husband, or to take no husband at all, I should do so. But I am only gifted the choice to be happy in my own life. For as long as I can, I choose happiness.' I drew a deep breath, holding the sweet air in my lungs. 'And I choose you.'

Sunlight striped his face, a single beam piercing the leaves above us. 'There is something weighty in those words. Yet I do not think you doubt my affection.'

He had not quite arrived at the place I was leading him to. I liked the concern that was written on his features. It showed me I had made the right choice. He joined me when I rose, the two of us concealed together beneath the tree that I had spoken into being.

Positioning myself with my back against the trunk, I gathered my courage. It was strange – ever since leaving Mt Olympus,

I had rarely knelt, and my spine had grown accustomed to remaining straight, yet many times, Eurydicius had bent to his knees before me. I could force myself to do it, this once.

I dropped to one knee. It was as if I were making an offering, yet my hands were empty. The rest of me was full, however – so full that I threatened to brim over my edge.

'No dowry. No veil. No ownership,' I said. 'Equals in life, as we are in love. In this lifetime and beyond, I would have you be mine, as I would be yours. Will you be my husband, Eurydicius?'

He stared. My whole body trembled; I hoped that it did not show.

His smile came like the dawn, gentle, and then engulfing everything. 'Yes! By Olympus, by Parnassus, by every sacred mountain in the world, yes!'

He reached out to me. I sprang to my feet and wrapped my arms around him, kissing him so hard that my lips hurt. I lifted him off the ground for a second and then lowered him, our mouths finding each other as easily as a river meets sand. In that moment, I did not feel the weight of my destiny. I was sediment and water, the gleam of grains and the flow of sparkling liquid; I was beyond striving, beyond spear-heads that could pierce me and nails that could tear me apart. I was movement and stillness in each breath.

18

It should have been quick, or so I had thought: a flash of light and a bang, and then I would be facing a dragon.

When Jason's call pulled me away from my chamber in the Muses' city, my eyes closed against my will. I opened them onto a colourless sky. Suddenly, I felt weightless. Each minute stretched on and on as I coasted on currents of air, and I became aware of a faint grey landscape unscrolling below me. The wind, when it came, took me by surprise, and I had no time to steady myself before I plummeted down into a world that was suddenly blazing with the impassioned force of the setting sun, a pink inferno.

My shoulder struck the ship's deck. I winced. When I had ascertained that there were no broken bones, I opened my eyes and took in a ring of peering faces: all of them familiar from the inn, yet transformed by astonishment.

Atalanta pulled me up, and I embraced her.

The *Argo*'s heroes erupted into a storm of talk, and I let their news wash over me as I gathered my fallen weapons, shield, and sack of belongings. Their voices rose steadily as they spoke of fighting six-armed giants, of setting up a shrine so that they could win back the winds, of trading punches with King Amycus of the gulf: each of them described part of the voyage, raring to tell a story that showed their own exploits.

I learned that Hylas had been abducted by a nymph as he fetched water, and Heracles had chased after his pretty companion until both men were lost. Looking around at the faces of the crew, I guessed that it would not be wise to compare the courage of Jason and Heracles.

In Colchis, Jason had strode into King Aeëtes' palace and asked for the right to win the Golden Fleece. Caught off-guard and surrounded by most of his court, King Aeëtes had been unable to refuse, but he had presented Jason with three tasks to win his precious Fleece.

'To plough a field with fire-breathing oxen, to sow it with dragon's teeth, and to seize the Fleece from behind its guardian – the beast of flame, the most fearsome serpent to glide over earth – the famous dragon of Colchis.' Zetes sounded pleased as he repeated the demands to me.

Jason, I gathered from the crew, had pondered on the tasks that night, trying to devise a way to complete a set of near-impossible challenges without dying, refusing all food and company. At last, soft-voiced Butes explained, he had been struck by an idea and climbed onto the prow. Straddling the wood, he had spoken with the chubby cupid Eros long past the fall of darkness.

They had spoken of Medea, King Aeëtes' daughter: princess of potions and dark arts: a priestess of the goddess Hecate who was said to spend more time gathering plants than any man of healing in the kingdom. It was rumoured that she had accrued all kinds of arcane knowledge – though men preferred to call it witchcraft, when a woman was involved. Jason seemed to find this very interesting indeed.

The comely god of desire had agreed to pierce Princess Medea with one of his invisible arrows and swell her heart with love for Jason. Our leader, it appeared, had done well by appealing to the most capricious god of all, the boy who thrived on mischief above all else.

'Jason did not need to wage war on Colchis,' Zetes bragged to me. 'Though he kidnapped the sons of Medea's sister, just for a little extra assurance.'

But then came a problem. Medea might refuse to see Jason at all: she might never step into Eros' sight.

'And then you fell from the sky, as if the Fates knew what Jason wanted,' Butes finished.

'Indeed?' I said.

I looked around the ring of warriors. Smugness mingled with genuine pleasure on their faces; only Atalanta frowned, and we locked eyes for a moment.

'Here she is.' Idmon pushed past her. My brother's lips pulled back into a rigid smile. 'No bruises, yet.'

'How good it is to see you, Lady Orphia.' Jason emerged from behind him before I could spit out a reply. 'We will be much more comfortable up near the prow. I have a pouch of wine waiting for you.'

I knew better than to protest. No sooner had I taken a sip than Jason was laying out his demands, in a pleasant tone, as if I had not just been yanked from Mt Parnassus after the most beautiful day of my life. The sound of Eurydicius' breath quickening as I laid him on a white fur returned to me. I tried not to think on the hours after the wedding, but I could feel my jaw clenching.

Jason broke off mid-sentence.

'Do you have better things to be thinking of, Lady Orphia?'

I realised that he was eyeing me.

'Perhaps you have torn me from them,' I said.

'You peck at the fact that I interrupted your married bliss?' He laughed. 'The god of love whispered your news so silkily into my ear. I only acted as a leader must.'

'What do they call a man who names himself leader?'

'Ah,' Jason said. 'I see, now. The songbird turns vicious. I understand, of course; you are angry that I lay with your husband first.'

I looked at him for a long moment, taking in his smile.

'We have both lain with him,' I said. 'But only one of us has loved him.'

I turned my back and walked away.

With Atalanta playing messenger, we agreed to depart at once for the temple of Hecate, and I kept my thoughts silent as we set off through the dark outskirts of the city, Idmon and Butes bringing up the rear, dragging the two kidnapped boys. Jason and I trudged steadily, ignoring the storm at our backs, coming to a stop outside a large temple.

Lightning cracked the sky but refused to strike the ground. The growl of thunder kept its distance. A little rain began to fall overhead, pattering against our cloaks, and I felt as if I was sitting inside a bowl, waiting for the baked clay to shatter.

Beside me, the hostages shivered. Jason shoved them to their knees, and I met his stare, trying to make out the friend with whom I once shared my figs.

I wanted to stand there and think on my wedding until everything seemed bearable, but it was not safe to dwell on such joy.

The sound of the rain disappeared as I reached the temple threshold, and the doorway yawned to greet me, its black silence a comfort after the crying of the hostages. The last time I had dared to glance at their wrists, the ropes had almost rubbed through the boys' skin.

A deeper silence welcomed me inside. In the glow of a few torches, I could just make out a table laden with bottles and jars, a pestle and a grinding bowl full of a green paste. I slipped into the dense centre of the hall. Nothing seemed to breathe in here.

As I drew near the last pair of torches, I could see the altar, and beside it, the statue of Hecate, holding a key in one hand and a dagger in another.

'Of course, I know why you have come.'

The voice seemed to issue from the statue. I almost jumped. A woman rose from the floor, gathering up her gown.

I had decided, on the long path to the temple, what I would say. I had expected a young woman – a woman who had grown into the silence of a priestess' life, who preferred the company of plants and herbs to that of people – and I had thought to soften my words. Yet I had not been ready for her hard poise.

'Is he a ruthless man?' Medea stepped further into the torchlight.

'Jason will not leave until he has the Golden Fleece,' I said.

Her face was composed, her posture stiff, but her eyes revealed a raw anger that I had not seen since I faced down Ixion beside the black rocks. She waved me forward to sit at a small table by the wall. 'Are you his messenger, then?'

'My name is Orphia, Princess Medea. I am a poet.'

'Ah. Then I should be wary, lest you persuade me with silver words.'

'Like you, I am not here of my own will. But I will make the best of the scene I am thrown into. So may you.'

She glanced over at the statue of Hecate for a moment. In that movement, I saw the priestess in her, looking to her deity as a natural reflex. And yet a priestess of the goddess of crossroads, entrance-ways and witchcraft should not move with the jerky manner of a foal leaving her mare, I thought. She reminded me of someone.

'The hostages are outside,' I said. 'But I suspect you know that Jason has a price.'

'My help.'

'As I thought ... you know how this game works.'

'It is a game to them. But what players must I face?

My father, Aeëtes. And this foreigner, Jason.' She looked into my eyes. 'On either side, deceptive men who care little for me.'

I could understand her displeasure. Jason held a knife to her sister's children, yet Aeëtes worked to cheat Jason of the Golden Fleece at any cost, and seemed more concerned with plotting from his palace than winning back his grandsons.

'They have their goals, and you have yours,' I said.

'I do?'

'You must.' There it was again – a jerking of her head, as if my reply might make her bolt. 'Princess Medea, if you could choose anything in life – not merely a husband, but a reward, what would you choose?'

'Power.'

No hesitation. Not even a second's pause. I smiled. 'Jason will promise you that. But you may only achieve it through your own deeds. He will speak of love and seek to use you.'

'So you counsel me not to aid him?'

'No. Seize this chance. If you would be free of King Aeëtes – free of a father who will bargain you off to some man of his own choosing – then go. Only make sure you are not bound at the wrists by another man, in another kingdom. Let Jason pledge and promise, but if a time comes when he seeks to betray you, take all that you have. Ascend.'

The heavy stillness of the temple settled in her eyes. She turned her face away.

An owl hooted somewhere outside – or perhaps inside, for it was difficult to tell what was close and what was far. After a while, Medea rose and walked to the large table, seizing the grinding bowl and pestle and pounding the herbs with such vigour that I could not resist following her over. I watched her grind the paste until it oozed.

Beware, a soft voice said.

I swivelled, staring around the temple.

A weaker potion would kill an ox, Eurydicius' voice said. *Protect yourself, for you are the most precious thing in this world.*

With the last word, his presence faded. He had spoken to me: of that, I was certain. I shuddered. The Fleece, the dragon, the chance to have my name echo in the Hall of Starlight and in the chambers of queens – none of it mattered. He existed. Perhaps we were two small people in the breadth of the world, but I would have given the black soil and the boundless sky to see him right now.

I could picture him tucking his hair behind his ear, the way he did when he was thinking. I could picture him eating a plum and holding up the stone, turning it in his fingers, smiling at its smoothness. I could picture his queer golden eyes brightening as we spoke of wars, and of ending them. 'A spear is always necessary,' I had told him as we sat beside Fury, watching midges dance over the pond. 'Ah, but imagine a world where it is not,' he had replied. 'Because if you cannot imagine it, it cannot happen.'

Will you focus, my love? The interruption came softly into my mind. *For a moment?*

His voice brought me back to the temple. Heeding his advice, I stepped back from Medea, yet something about the intensity of her gaze as she ground the herbs told me that I was not the subject of her anger.

The owl hooted again. Medea put down the bowl and pestle and exhaled.

'Healers call hellebore the curer of madness, do they not?' I said.

She raised an eyebrow. 'You know the medicine of plants?'

'I know two dryads who do.' How it hurt to think of Melia and Balanos, now that I might never see them again. But I had promised myself not to think that way. I vowed to Eurydicius that I would not despair. 'There is something else in that potion. Something that blends the mixture, adding a milkiness,' I said.

'Hemlock stems.'

'Ah.' My tone must have betrayed my thoughts, for her mouth curled in amusement.

'Ground in the right place and at the right hour, the plant has many uses. If we had time, I could show you the arts of Hecate.'

My eyes roved over the bottles, the jars, and the leaves and roots laid out in various stages of preparation. 'I should like to work with you.'

She sighed. For a moment, we looked at the grinding bowl together. 'I will help Jason,' she said. 'When I have finished my potions, I will come to where the *Argo* is moored.'

We shook hands. After some persuasion, she came to the temple doorway to look upon Jason. Rain struck my face as we walked out, and I felt the air lighten, the stillness of the temple leaving me. Jason stared like one transfixed. I saw Medea return his gaze with widening eyes. She clutched her arm, the pose shrinking her and yet ossifying her, as knots on an olive tree stiffen and harden after frost, and I wondered if in solving one problem, I had planted the seeds of another.

As we returned beneath a slowly lightening sky to the *Argo*, I dwelt on the voice that had spoken in my head, just minutes ago, as Medea mixed her herbs.

I miss you.

I projected the thought as loudly as I could. In the silence that followed, I compounded all my desires and fears into a ball and pushed it towards the horizon, sending it rolling.

I miss you painfully. The reply sounded in my head, so clearly that he seemed to appear before me. I could almost see those lips that I had kissed, only hours ago.

Let us not compete in affection. I will make sure that I win,
I replied.

He laughed. *Orphia, whatever they ask of you, you can do it.*
Even if you feel you may crumble and collapse, remember that you
made Zeus cry, and faced down Apollo. You can hold to your centre.

Do you truly think that?

I know it. Have faith in yourself. I do.

All my life, I had drawn my motivation from within. I had
relied on my own will, because it had seemed the only thing
that could carry me through the bruises that did not show on
the outside: the blows directed against the softest parts of me.
Yet now I felt the voice of another, guiding my spirit through
each challenge. His words were like hands that held my own.
For the first time, I felt the power of belief and support from
someone else, and knew that it was greater than my will. There
had been times when doubt closed in; when failure loomed in
my vision, and I felt myself a paltry and fragile thing; but in
Eurydicius' eyes, I was peerless bronze. Through his utterances
of faith, I began to believe in what I could do.

If your return takes longer than you hoped, I will set to planning
a gift for you. You are rich in imagination, so I need not explain …
there are all kinds of ways to give.

He was gone, then, smoke dissipating into the air, yet
lingering in my senses. The sunlight of his last remark heated
my ankles and reached to the base of my heels.

It was not a betrayal of all I had strived for, surely, to want
to be with him. I was not abandoning fame. Eurydicius would
lead me to greatness, the Oracle had declared, and I must not
allow myself to be parted from him; I still remembered the
rasp of her final whisper, as if she were straining with all her
remaining vigour to make me understand. *While most heroes*
face a choice between love and fame, you need never choose.

The words echoed again.

If I wanted to lift him into an embrace and never think of this quest again, I need never give up my chance of earning fame with poetry – of winning the right to keep performing – of raising my voice until I could show those like me how it felt to live fully, to walk in the sunlight exactly as they were. In him, I found the deepest core of my art.

The sooner this was over, the better. I focused on my surroundings, and on the back of Jason's head as we walked, the trees encroaching on either side.

A conclusion firmed in my mind. This was not my last task. For one thing, Jason had not sent me back home. And for another, I still remembered the way he had spoken of my skill as a power, one which would help him to win glory.

Salt carried on the wind, a sharp breeze cutting across the port. I braced myself and weathered the slap of the brine, clutching Eurydicius' words to my chest.

The crew slumbered on the deck. I picked my way between bodies to my spot and, ignoring Jason's whispered thanks, slipped into the honeyed silence of sleep, yet I had scarcely entered that state when an arm touched my shoulder. Shifting away from it, I mumbled, reluctant to cede my rest. There was no wind, no sun, no voices: I came to realise that I was dreaming, and as I looked down, warm skin brushed against me. Something tickled my thighs beneath the skirt of my armour.

Eurydicius' kiss felt as light as the gossamer strands of his hair, sending tiny stars shooting through me. He wriggled up to lie beside me. As he rolled into my touch, I stroked the curve of his back and breathed in the scent of elm leaves, inhaling deeply before he disappeared.

The boards of the deck felt warm against my side. As I woke, the name of that other scent came back to me: amaranthos, the everlasting.

'They say that this ship is made of magical wood, you know.' Atalanta was sitting up beside me, polishing her sword. 'I have heard that the ship-builder put a beam of oak in the keel from the sacred land of the Dodona, the second-greatest Oracle. Some of the men say it calls them to their destiny.'

'It sounds like the kind of thing a bunch of ambitious men would say.'

Atalanta laughed. I was still thinking on Eurydicius and on our communication, wondering how it was possible, for I knew already that I had not imagined his words but received their sound. Everywhere, the *Argo*'s crew were moving. Men tied on their cloaks, washed their faces, ate the food that had been brought from port, and chattered in a steady stream. I checked that my spear, knife and shield were still beside me, and opened my small sack. The lyre and aulos had not been thieved. Thank Hera.

'Have you seen her?' Atalanta said, pointing. I followed her finger to where Medea stood, holding up a small bottle and talking with Jason, the two of them standing close together by the prow.

As we watched, Jason smiled and took the bottle from her. They kissed on the lips, then deepened their touch to an open-mouthed kiss. Medea wrapped her hand tightly around his neck, and after a moment, Jason guided her down the middle of the deck, his gaze daring anyone to say a word.

'Ready the men,' I heard him tell Idmon. 'We are going to take the Golden Fleece.'

Medea did not speak. She was looking at Jason as if there was no other mortal beneath the sky. The trees by the port shivered, dropping their dried leaves onto the ground.

I had never seen so much gold. Not even in Dorus' palace had anyone worn sandals with golden studs and gold bracelets inlaid with ovular gems, and a few of our party muttered and pointed at the necklace draped around King Aeëtes' neck, dripping with golden ram-heads.

We climbed briskly onto the platform that stood on the grass. The people of Colchis perched on the hillside above us, pointing at the pair of oxen that waited at the end of the field. The beasts' horns curved skywards and their eyes glowed like coals while they stamped their feet, the wind exposing scars on their tawny hides, and every so often, one of them snorted a puff of flame, causing the Argonauts to murmur and point.

Despite the blazing whiteness of the ball in the sky, my arms and neck remained cool. I remembered the crew's account of Jason speaking with Eros, and wondered what Hera, the goddess of women and marriage, would do if she discovered that Jason had tricked Medea into helping him.

A smirk played about Jason's lips. Striding into the middle of the field, he was a moving sculpture, his arms and thighs shining in the light.

Everyone halted their talk. Even King Aeëtes ceased arguing with his advisors. I wove through the group on the platform, stopping next to one of the Colchian party.

'Curious,' I whispered. 'No heat in the day, and yet he glistens.'

Medea did not reply, her gaze fixed ahead.

'The ointment he wears … did you make it last night, while he was brooding? Or did you have it bottled in your temple storeroom long ago?'

'I am afraid I do not know what you mean.'

Before us, Jason marched up to the oxen and laid a hand upon the nearest animal. It belched fire. The flames touched the skin of Jason's forearm, turned blue, and died at once, while Jason remained unmoved. *No wonder he had been so eager to make use of Medea's skills*, I thought. *Only the most potent ointment for a man who already wore a crown in his mind.*

Jason patted the ox's side and moved around to stroke the other animal, before taking the yoke that was lying on the ground and fitting it over the pair. The crowd shouted, their expressions incensed.

'They feel they have been denied blood,' Medea said, answering my unspoken question. 'They will have it later; do not worry.'

She darted a glance at me. She was so quick that no one could have noticed. To King Aeëtes and his nobles, we must have seemed like any other spectators, focused on the field.

'He has promised to make me famous throughout all Greece.' Her lips quirked.

Now, I realised who she reminded me of. Before Ixion betrayed me to Dorus, before my father bound me to a chair, and before I was forced to fly through the air to help Jason on his quest, I too had trusted promises which seemed fairly sworn.

She held herself tightly, like a woman grown, yet she still seemed a foal to me; not in years, but in the ways that counted.

'You will need more than a private promise, if you wish for the glorious type of fame,' I said.

'You know much of fame, I suppose.'

'A little. I have won some renown on Mt Olympus and Mt Parnassus.'

Her glance came lightning-swift, again.

Before us, Jason bowed, and the Argonauts burst into rapturous applause. He had finished ploughing the field, I realised. Butes and Zetes led a cheer on my left, yet I paid more attention to the muttering that spread over the hillside. The Colchians bent their heads together as they whispered, glaring at this man who had tamed their oxen without spilling a drop of blood.

'At last,' I heard Atalanta bark. 'The teeth!'

Someone was running out to Jason with a sack. I wondered if dragon's teeth were plentiful in King Aeëtes' stores, or if a serpent had been slain for this single task. After a pair of fire-breathing oxen, sowing a bunch of teeth in the ground did not sound so bad, yet I felt a hum of unease over the simplicity of it. Next to us, the king and his nobles brayed at some joke that we foreigners would never hear, and Medea stiffened; I expected some kind of trick from her, some way to pass Jason a new potion or cast a spell on him, but she only nodded; her eyes fixed ahead. Clutching the bag, Jason nodded back.

He drew the teeth out and planted them in the ground, covering each with a little soil, checking each spot, then he ran back a distance from the disturbed earth. I noticed that his whole figure tensed when he stopped.

The crowd did not clap. The breezeless air weighed heavily upon us. A rumble ran through the ground, stones trembling and grass shivering, and I forced myself to stay fixed to the spot while heads pushed out of the soil. Bald pates sprang from where dragon's teeth had pocked the ground. Heads became bodies, and bodies became soldiers, brandishing spears.

The earth-warriors streaked across the field. This was different to a fight on the Whispering Isle, I knew: here, I could not raise my spear and thrust at the enemy. I was relegated to a spectator. The newly formed soldiers screamed a wordless battle-cry, and when they had covered half the distance, Jason drew something dark and shiny from his bag and flung it into their midst.

I had seen youths turn on each other at training. Never had I seen a change like this. A thump of the stone saw the warriors stop, pivot, and face each other with deadly silence, until at last, one warrior raised his spear.

A spear-tip protruded from his chest before he could attack.

Suddenly, the air teemed with weapons and blood watered the soil, red paint spattering with artistry, marking out the finality of each blow. Jason stood firm, forgotten by the warriors as they fell, one by one, the last two toppling onto the grass in unison, each pierced by the other's shaft.

Medea's smile lingered just long enough for me to notice. The crowd cheered and rejoiced over the broken bodies, and King Aeëtes screamed and gesticulated at his generals, scrambling to mount his chariot.

'Your stone, of course,' I said, looking over at Medea.

'I simply helped the generals put the teeth into the bag. That is all.' Her cheeks showed only the faintest sign of a flush.

'And the dragon?'

'No chance of that today. My father will save the third task until the morning. He will seize even the slightest chance of tricking Jason out of the Fleece.'

I followed her gaze to where Jason was approaching us, swaggering, the bag now crumpled in his hands.

'Will you try to remember my advice in the temple?' I said, softly.

'Jason will not betray me. He loves me. You cannot know what it is like to love someone to the very core of their soul, to the depths of their being, to see every wound in them and yet find only starlight shining from the cracked places.'

I did not reply. If I squinted into the distance, I might look as if I did not understand.

The stars pricked the black wool of the sky with their needle-points. Lying on my back and gazing upwards, I could make out the she-bear, her tail raised, and tracing the constellation with my gaze, I spotted the star closest to the tail, the brightest point amongst that gleaming cluster. I fingered the necklace beneath my armour, thinking of the hands that had fashioned that star, until the faint crunch of leaves disturbed me.

Near where the boots had trod, orange tongues flickered, half-blocked by a cloak. Jason stood beside the fire. I could not see who he was confiding in, but I saw him turn and stare in my direction. I slumped on my side and feigned sleep, trying to hear what they were discussing.

The exhaustion that had been with me ever since I arrived on the *Argo* took over, and I slipped into a deep rest, my thoughts returning to where I longed to be.

The scent of orange blossoms permeated the air. I followed the narrow path through Calliope's garden, passing between fruit trees and brambles to the clearing. Had it really been just yesterday morning that I had stood on the spot she had marked out, amongst the deep foliage?

My words flew upward as I spoke, describing Eurydicius, drawing red flowers from the bushes with my poetry, garlanding the ground with them and suspending strings of them from the trees. Nothing could have stemmed the wave of power that flowed through me as I drew upon my deepest reserves of love. I transformed my feelings into poetry, pulling stems and leaves and petals through the air with the strength of my gratitude for him – my yearning for him – my ever-increasing desire for his presence.

Then, ease. I was listening to the song that Polyhymnia had composed for the marriage ceremony, from the fluty voices of the dryads under the boughs. I was gasping as dozens of butterflies jewelled the sky above us, drawn by my poem, one of them landing upon my hair. Euterpe and Thalia cheered. The rest of the audience smiled and chatted, nymphs and Muses mingling.

I felt it, then, a quaking in the depths of my being, in the part where poetry grew. I turned on the spot. He walked towards me, his hair fluttering around his face, a crown of pink roses resting on his head while the hem of his sapphire-blue chiton swirled gently in the breeze. I felt his beauty as a swallow feels an early summer.

Euterpe held his left arm and Calliope his right, and together they steered him between the rows of chairs to where I stood, beneath the hanging waterfall of red flowers.

Compared to him, I was a paltry thing to look at, but the chiton I had donned, woven by Euterpe to display a symbol of each of the Muses, gave me strength. It bore the emblems of my family: the only family that mattered now.

I waited a minute before taking Eurydicius' hands in mine. There was only so long that I could tarry.

We had crafted the vows slowly in my chamber, but now they flew from our lips. To protect each other, to aid each other, to love each other: it was easy to say what we had already pledged with fingertips many weeks ago. When we had made our last promises, I wrapped one arm around his shoulders and devoured as much of his sweetness as I could, smiling into his mouth as he smiled into mine.

'I will love you beyond this life.' His whisper tickled my ear when we let go.

Whether he had planned those words or spoken them in the surge of the moment, I could not tell, but I felt their truth chime within me. I felt it still while the dryads danced in rings, while the oreads performed comic and tragic plays, and while Euterpe recited a poem about a pair of happy lovers from Thebes. The nereids and naiads poured the katachysmata over our heads, and Eurydicius took the shower of figs, dates, coins, nuts and dried fruits with a grin, while I picked pieces of walnut out of my hair.

I held up one of the figs and pressed it to Eurydicius' lips. He bit into it, juice running over his chin, and I smeared the stickiness over his lips until he stared at me, struck dumb. I kissed him again, and then again, ignoring the whoops and clapping of those around us, forgetting all about the fruit. This kiss, more than any other, braided his gentleness with my determination.

Shortly afterwards, Calliope drew me aside. 'A magical sound, is it not – the laughter of women?'

Her voice reverberated with a hard power.

'Even the many nymphs here who have cause to shake their heads at marriage can see that this one is different,' she added. 'I have never passed a husband over to a bride, before. I could become accustomed to it.'

'I wish you could share some part of my joy.'

'Sweet child.' She stroked my cheek. 'You have chosen well.'

I felt cool metal against my hand. A gleam dazzled me. It took a moment before I recognised the gift for what it was, and I clutched the golden lyre in my palm.

'Do not wait too long to strum it.'

She disappeared into the crowd of nymphs, to be replaced by Euterpe holding an aulos and Melpomene holding a sword.

I accepted the gifts, getting out as many thanks as I could, while Eurydicius delighted in his gifts of a harp and a finely woven cloak. My attention returned again and again to the golden lyre. Each time I looked at the instrument, it seemed to call to me, asking me to touch it. I had scarcely begun to run my finger across the strings when Erato came before us.

'My gift far exceeds the bounty of the others,' she said, smiling. 'I hope you are not too tired, Orphia; if you would have it, my entire dwelling is yours for the day. The water-gardens, the halls and the dome, and the beds … I turn them over to you.'

Eurydicius mumbled something half-woven. I had no sooner thanked Erato and attempted to imagine what we might do in the afternoon when a hush fell upon the clearing.

A pair of figures stepped out from beneath the last pair of trunks. Even protected from the sun, Clio's hair framed her sharp features with brilliant silver.

'I hope my son does not come too late,' Clio said.

The god who walked beside her unfolded his wings and stretched them to their full span. He floated a few inches above the ground, as if he trod on the very air. A glint of diamond-bright light blinded me, until the sun passed over those pinions, leaving them to cast shadows on the ground.

Everyone bowed to Hymen, except for Calliope. 'God of marriage, you come late indeed.' I discerned the hint of iron in her voice. 'I hope you come to bless, not merely to dance.'

Hymen knelt in front of Eurydicius. His gaze roved across our faces.

'This marriage needs no blessing from me. It is already blessed with every felicity on this earth, thanks to the virtues of an equal match, which need no voicing.'

Calliope's stare held his, and he added:

'But of course, I give the union of Orphia and Eurydicius my blessing!'

Fresh cheers broke out, and dancing began, more vigorous this time, the nymphs smiling at us as they passed in a ring. Some of the Muses joined them, and Euterpe and Polyhymnia played the aulos and flute. Only Calliope pressed closer to Hymen, and her stare seemed to ask a question. I had seen her stare down Zeus, and I was not at all surprised when Hymen rose to speak with her, drawing her aside. The sounds of the flute and clapping drowned out most of what he said.

'Perfection? Truly?' I heard Calliope say. I beckoned Eurydicius to me, and we edged towards my mother, trying not to look as if we were eavesdropping.

'Of all the matches I have blessed, I have not seen the like of it. Nothing is strived for. Nothing is expected, either from the man or the woman.' Hymen dropped his voice to a whisper. 'Of course, such perfection was not meant to last.'

The chill that reached me with those words cut deeper than a mountain wind, stealing into my flesh. It sank beneath marrow and bone, to reach a part where only spirit lived. I turned to Eurydicius. He was already studying my face, as if he hoped to engrave it in his mind, a phantom of a carving to be called up when no trace of the real remained.

The hand that shook me was not tender, its fingers not long and elegant like a shield-maker's.

'Hurry, dear sister. Jason wishes to speak with you.'

I sat up and stared into the rictus of Idmon's smile.

I picked my way through the camp, not bothering to reply, letting my eyes adjust slowly to the night. Beneath the shroud of the darkness, only a few torches flickered. Guards flanked Jason's tent. I might have been alert as I passed through the flaps, but my heart was still dancing with Eurydicius, under the waterfall of red flowers.

Jason looked up from an unfurled map. 'You will need your weapons.'

Medea crossed the tent floor. I looked from her to the map.

'Of course,' I said. 'You mean to steal the Fleece.'

'You must agree it is the best time. Hecate's protection lies upon us until the dawn,' Medea said.

I raised an eyebrow.

'As her priestess, I have read the signs. Darkness provides the most auspicious opportunity to seize a magical object.'

'And have you also read your father's intentions, and guessed that he has not had time to put a plan into place?'

Medea pursed her lips. 'Perhaps.'

I noticed that her right hand was clenching and unclenching. 'Very well,' I said, 'but if you need a warrior to defend you against the dragon, Atalanta would be a better choice. She seems to wake each morning raring to perform an impossible feat.'

Jason smiled, rolling up the map and pointing it at me. 'It is not a guard I seek, but a poet. You will bear witness to my deeds tonight. Someday, perhaps, you will speak of them.'

I let a pensive aspect steal over my countenance – or so I hoped. I had no intention of wasting verses on him, but it would be better if Jason remained ignorant of that. 'I will return with my spear and shield.'

I neared Medea, opening my arms wide. She allowed my embrace, and as I pressed my face close to her ear, I whispered: 'You should know that Jason asked the god of desire to make you fall in love with him, well before he reached the city.'

'What?'

'Oh yes. After landing in port, he persuaded Eros to give him your affection, like a necklace or a crown.'

The tent flaps swung shut behind me, sealing her inside.

I made swift work of gathering my spear and shield. In the darkness, I tied Euterpe's wedding gift onto my back with a rope, checking that the aulos was firmly fastened with a sailor's knot. The thought of watching my mother's gift burning in a dragon's flames made me leave the golden lyre behind, and I headed back through the camp before I could change my mind.

I nearly stumbled into Idmon and Butes as I entered the tent. They framed Jason and Medea, who were holding hands.

'Before these witnesses, I pledge to marry Medea, Princess of Colchis, and make her famous throughout all Greece. This I will do when I take my throne.'

Jason pressed his forehead to hers and closed his eyes. I caught a view of her face from the side, and saw the determination written upon it, visible to none but me.

The men clapped when the lovers broke apart, Idmon patting Jason on the back, and my eyes found Medea's. She smiled, this time without falsity, and I knew it was as close as I would get to her thanks.

When we made to depart, she walked beside me. Together we led the way down the path she indicated, heading along the edge of a small forest, the smell of pine needles thick around us. Her tread was firm, and I thought that there was something new in her bearing.

'Have you brought it, my love?' Jason whispered.

She reached beneath her cloak and pulled out a vial. A beam of moonlight unveiled the iridescent glass.

I fought the urge to ask what was inside it. Somehow, I knew that what we were about to attempt would only loom greater if I knew every detail.

We passed out of the cover of the trees and into the fields. The darkness swallowed us, hair and fingernails, teeth and calves; it was not a still dark but a creeping, slinking thing, and I felt the hunger of it, the blackness consuming even the sound of my feet. Part of me knew that this was the deepest hour of the night, when the moon dared not show her face, the goddess Artemis ensconced in her chamber with her hunting dogs until the depths of blackness passed. That was only natural.

Yet another part of me feared that without the delicate creature I had come to love, I was already eroding, my flesh chipping away where his love had held it firm: that piece by piece, I had begun to disappear into the wild night.

Imagine red dots that illuminate for only a second, leaving you to wonder if they were ever there. You search for them and find something else instead: a scale here, a tail-tip there, none of it shining long enough for you to trust your eyes. Your feet remain buried in blackness.

Now imagine that words are muttered and a dove flaps up above your head, its plumes glowing silver. It catches a current and soars. A blast of flame chars the feathers and a shriek emanates from mid-air. While the dragon is busy scorching the bird, you step forward from the darkness, and your companion makes her next move.

This time, it is no conjuring; no false dove. She whips her arm in a circle, churning the air, forcing it to move even though it resists her. Sweat slicks her neck. Her arms and shoulders strain, for Medea is pulling something out of the air – and as you watch, you feel the elements trembling and yielding to her, gold dust becoming visible all around you.

The dragon spots the three of you. The blast it sends widens enough to engulf you all, yet Medea rips more gold from the air. Greed swirls, transmuted and given form. At her whisper, the gold dust forms a wall, blocking the flames. The dragonfire dies, and you stand back while Medea raises her hands and transforms the dust into chains – long, gilded chains, which drop over the serpent's body.

It is no small beast. The sight of it alone would make you shiver, except that you have realised now what Medea can do. What you saw on the field earlier was but a trick.

The beast slumps to the ground, puffs of flame issuing from its nostrils as it snores. Jason lunges forward.

Imagine that he takes the Golden Fleece from where it is nailed on the tree behind the dragon, ignoring you and Medea, his whole being focused on removing that pelt. Imagine that he does not see the extent of Medea's power; that he does not really see her at all.

He clasps the Fleece in his hands, and after a moment's hesitation he runs back, forgetting to dart a glance at the dragon. A loud snore issues from the beast, twin streams of fire pouring from its nostrils, and one of them catches Jason's neck.

His scream rips through the night. Before the fire can spread to his chest, Medea runs forward with the vial and opens it, pouring a substance over the dragonfire – you see it glinting in the flickering light – and *of course*, you think, *of course the potion was not meant for the dragon*. You can tell by how Medea's hands shake that she needs this salve more than Jason, though she shakes the potion onto his skin until the last drop is gone.

Jason groans, winces, then looks at Medea. 'We need to leave.'

He does not look at her long enough to see those trembling hands.

Imagine that voices begin to clamour in the distance and bells peal through the darkness. Pinpricks of torchlight mark the city out at the end of the fields, a very long way from you, but not far enough for your liking. Has the dragonfire roused the city, or has some property of the pelt alerted King Aeëtes to its theft? It does not matter, now. While Jason rolls up the Fleece and ties it with a rope, you watch scales of the serpent's neck glisten in the sheen of the flames, illuminated for a moment, then gone.

'Orphia.' Jason takes you by the arm, his grip unrelenting. 'I will need your magic while we run.' He gestures to Medea. 'She is too weak to protect us now.'

You have known this since she pulled magic from the elements, not conjuring but using the air itself, drawing greed out of the serpent. A feat of such power must exact a price. But you did not know that Jason had planned for this.

'*You will bear witness to my deeds,*' you repeat. 'You must think me a fool.'

'I think you should save your moral stand for when we are back on the *Argo*.'

You laugh, the sound coming out too loud. 'Recite a poem while running – just like that? There is no way to be sure if the magic will flow while I am gasping for air.'

'Let us find out.' Jason shoulders the Fleece.

You look at the fur for a long moment. It shines with the same luminosity as the chains that bind the dragon; the whole pelt stands out, even in the darkness, thanks to its golden hue. But it is only a dead ram. No special power resides in that fleece, except, perhaps, that it is kingship to Jason, and that makes it more dangerous than a whetted sword.

You glance at the serpent over your shoulder, one last time. The scales on its head remain invisible, but then another snort reveals their dark mirrors, and you look down the body, down the length of that magical armour, and the word that sticks in your mind is *magnificent*. You can understand why the dragon keeps its distance from the city.

Imagine that you begin to run. Three pairs of feet pound the soil. Shouts in the distance splatter you with fear, and that is what you use: words stream from your mouth like hard pieces of onyx and ruby and sapphire, pouring forth even as your lungs work tirelessly. You allow the strength of your fear to come out, and you transform it into something of beauty. Trees bend on either side of you, reaching to seal your party from view, creating a tunnel down which you sprint, the sharp words of your poetry drawing trunks and leaves. The earth forms walls on either side of the trees, shielding you further.

'Keep that up,' Jason shouts. 'Whatever you do, keep speaking!'

Imagine that the fear begins to turn inward, those phrases targeting you, pieces of precious stone slicing into your skin. You feel yourself breaking even as the earth rises to protect you, and then something happens, something that you did not foresee. A message stops the destruction. You feel it rather than hear it, the love wrapping you in a warmth that the night cannot provide.

Even while you channel the terror of dying far from him, he returns to you, the vitality of his love encircling you.

I did not know how much I had changed, you tell him. *I thought I could strive in the darkness without you, watching fire race through the air. I thought I could flee without thinking of you. I thought I could rely on myself, as I always did. But you were already there, ingrained in my soul's walls, were you not? I am half of you, and you are half of me.*

When you feel him crying, you know that they are tears of joy.

Yes, you can imagine this. And you will do so when you float in darkness, later, much later, and it is time to remember yourself back to life.

I boarded the ship at a jump. There was no time to collect my emotions, after my poem had scattered them, for the crew brandished their spears and cheered our return. Jason carried

Medea onto the deck. He stroked her face and doted on her under the gazes of the men. I caught Atalanta's eye, and she shook her head, her smile as pointed as her sword.

Jason passed the Fleece around and the men broke into awestruck whispers, handling it one by one, affording Butes a chance to draw us aside. 'How far behind us do you think they are?'

'The Colchians?' Jason peered back to where the camp had been, as if the dark patch of ground might help him. 'Hard to say.'

'They should be here within a short ride, though that was before Orphia blocked their path with trunks and soil. She has bought us time, but my father will not part with his treasure until the sea thickens with our blood.' Medea propped herself against the side of the ship as she spoke.

In the silence, I watched a moth writhe in a slick of spilt water.

'Does King Aeëtes move his men quickly?' I said.

'Oh, it will not be my father who attacks first. He values his head too highly. I would expect Absyrtus – my half-brother, the prince of Colchis – to come first. And if you think he will hold back for love of me, you have not met my family.'

I held my tongue, my gaze shifting to my own half-brother. At a nod from Jason, Idmon and Butes dispersed and began calling to the oarsmen. I watched the moon catch the top of a wave for the first time and saw the foam shine with a hard glitter, like the memory of bronze.

The aulos was no sooner wrapped with my lyre and tucked against the side of the ship than I was feeling the length of my spear, testing its weight. The ship cut through the sea, moving towards the horizon. I was not fooled by the peacefulness of the half-dark, and when the cry came from the helmsman, it sliced through the night air.

'Attackers, within a few lengths!'

Those who speak of war never tell of the moment when death becomes real, when the prospect of an attack changes and is no longer a prospect. Who would want to speak of muttered prayers, of fingers clasping spears and arrows as if they were more precious than gems? Who would want to describe hunched shoulders and eyes that strain for a glimpse of the enemy? The sound of jeers grew from the ship speeding towards us. Around me, warriors held themselves still, but I could see that they were just holding back from shaking.

When the vessel pulled alongside us, a man in a fine cuirass climbed onto its edge. An eagle gleamed on his armour. Even if Medea had not called out to him, I would have recognised the confident movement of the king's son as he threw his spear, grabbed another from his men, and leapt onto our deck.

Absyrtus' war-cry sliced through the man who met him, a second before his iron did. The fear within the crew transformed to a furious energy. Shouts went up from Zetes and Calais, from Idmon and Idas, from Jason and Butes, and loudest of all came the roar of Atalanta, her teeth bared in a wolf-snarl. The attackers poured onto our deck, a whirl of metal and flesh.

There was rhythm in battle, just as there was rhythm in poetry. I could scarcely move on the packed deck, but I wielded my spear as best I could, seizing each opportunity to thrust at a neck; beat after beat after beat, my blows landed. After a few men tumbled into the water, the rhythms began to quicken, our warriors lashing out without using their shields, the attackers jabbing and slashing, pushing or kicking in the fray. Every now and then I glimpsed the eagle cuirass, but Absyrtus whirled from foe to foe, his sword spraying dark droplets wherever it swung, speaking the language of revenge. He had almost reached Jason when a war-cry pierced the air. A figure tackled

Absyrtus about the waist, slamming him to the deck – a figure that I recognised by its snarl.

Atalanta had her hands around Absyrtus' neck when others fell upon them, piling on from either side. Bodies jostled, smearing blood and sweat on each other. I had no time to calculate, as when I had faced down one opponent at a time on the island; within seconds, I spread my arms and let the dark throb of the battle move through me, the desperation of angry men filling my veins, flowing into lines that came out like spears.

My words struck the Colchian soldiers in pairs. Two, four, six: I felled enough men to clear the way to where Atalanta and Absyrtus still wrestled on the deck, arms and thighs locked, each struggling to squeeze the life from the other. I readied myself to launch a verse at the prince's back.

'Very beautiful, those poems,' a smooth voice said. 'Father has always favoured beautiful things.'

I whirled and raised my spear. *Too slow*, I told myself, as Idmon's hands closed around my arm.

'Oh, no. Not this time. You might have father's backing, but I will be taking some of the glory.'

The butt of his spear met bone. The crack my skull made must have been audible through the whole battle, though perhaps it only seemed that way to me: *everything is a matter of perspective*, I thought, as the deck rose to meet me.

Time passed slowly, in the clouds. They welcomed me into their bosom, cocooning me in softness, whispering that I could stay so long as I did not think. For a while my mind seemed to take solace in its own silence. It rested, slowly regrowing vines and branches that had been severed inside its garden; yet after a while, shoots burst forth, and I found myself thinking of Eurydicius.

A flash of light coloured the world silver, so bright that it almost burned. I closed my eyes. It did not alarm me that he sat before me when I opened them again. He leaned over a table, talking to a woman. She dandled a baby on her knee, while she examined a shield: a shield Eurydicius had made, I knew, from the bumps and the carefully moulded surface. Eurydicius smiled in that devastatingly sweet way that he did when he was focused on helping someone. I reached to him, touching him softly. He did not seem to feel my fingers on his forearm.

Another flash of bright silver, and I was standing on the slope of Mt Parnassus, a hot wind slapping my face, a mountain lion stalking through the grass towards Eurydicius. I saw them both as if observing a scene on a vase. The animal did not heed my cry, nor sense me as I sprinted towards it, only baring its teeth to snarl at Eurydicius. He raised his bow, aimed, and let go of the string.

The arrow found soft flesh. He had practised, then. Relief buckled my knees, but I scarcely had time to feel it before another burst of light transported me.

Dozens of stars jewelled the cloth of early evening above us. He did not seem to have noticed the darkening sky, his gaze directed solely at the shield he was working on. He examined it, turning it over and back again.

Watching him bend his head, I cherished the way that he became absorbed in his work, forgetting about time and place. It was like the moment when a poem was born, when I laboured over phrases and honed sounds, tested beats and rhythms, changed things and checked them. He saw wood and bronze and leather the way I saw words. Yet his goal went beyond expression, or even helping one person: one shield at a time, he hoped to change an entire system of warfare.

'Perhaps you can hear me,' I called.

He did not look up. Something stirred inside me.

'Or perhaps you cannot. But no matter what wall has been built between us, I hear the song of your fingers as they tap and dance, the rhythm of your hair as it flutters. I feel your music within me. I will not let it fade.'

The part of my mind that had withered regrew at speed now, nourishing itself on these thoughts. I no longer trusted purely the Oracle's directive, but my own, too.

'I refuse to die here,' I said. 'Do you hear me, gods?' It felt good to shout, to fling my anger at them. 'I refuse to leave him!'

A flash of silver light forced me to close my eyes. I saw the twitch of his head, first: the movement as he turned to search for the origin of my voice.

I awoke in softness. The clouds parted immediately. Air chilled me as I dropped, and I spread my arms like wings and straightened into a dive; somehow, I knew that I would come to a halt just above the *Argo*, where my body lay with its arms positioned stiffly by its sides, arranged to take up less space on the deck.

Medea crouched over me, rubbing something into the wound at my temple. She whispered as she worked. Pain screeched at me as I dropped into my body, gristle and blood and bone deafening me, threatening to tear me sinew from sinew, and I held on to the feeling of my flesh for as long as I could manage.

Then nothing. Or something, but the kind of something that did not take form. Time dissolved and pain shrank into a stunted thing, and the place where I rested cleansed me, its stillness finishing what the clouds had begun. It was impossible to tell how long it held me. Memories slid up through my consciousness and I seized them one by one, returning to the Fleece, to layers of blackness and puffs of flame, to the mirrors of scales, and the churning of the air as Medea whipped her arm around. Then: the taste of fear in my mouth, the fear of my life ending like a taper snuffed out by an early winter breeze; the fear of Eurydicius walking on Mt Parnassus alone, wrapped in a cloak, haunting our copse for the rest of his days ...

I woke to salt spray on my lips, and opened my eyes to a choppy sea, foam leaping beyond the rail.

Atalanta grabbed my shoulders as I made to sit up. My head weighed like a boulder.

'Friend,' Atalanta said, 'it is good to have you back. Medea may be skilled with potions, but she stoppers her mouth like one of her vials. And a voyage with no conversation is like a dinner with no wine.' Her gaze skipped to my head. 'You look less like a cracked egg, now.'

I grinned, despite myself. As I shifted on the deck-boards, I took in the scar that carved her cheek, and my smile faded.

'Absyrtus,' Atalanta said, before I could ask. 'I pinned him down in the end, and Jason tipped one of Medea's poisons over him, but not before he had taken a good slash at me. Still, I do not envy his ...'

She trailed off. Looking past her, I saw men sitting in groups and whispering, others silently staring out into the waves. Jason's cloak hung from his shoulders at the end of the boat.

'Atalanta,' I said, 'how did we win?'

'Blood and bone, entrails and skin, and magic. That is how. Medea healed my cheek and your head, plying her herbs and chanting like a witch.'

The skin over my temple felt smooth and unbroken. I ran my hand through my scalp and found no sticky patches, not even the hard surface of a scab.

Could Eurydicius see me now? Did he know that I had survived Idmon's blow?

I forced myself to focus. 'Blood and bone, entrails and skin?'

'King Aeëtes pursued us, after Absyrtus' ship did not return. It was horrible, Orphia. His vessel cut a silver line through the sea behind the *Argo*. Nothing we did would gain us any speed. Jason scrambled for an idea to head off Aeëtes, but no matter how hard he tried, he could not come up with a plan … that was when Medea came forward, picking her way between the men, knife in hand. She stood above her brother's corpse and whispered a few words.'

Her eyes met mine. I had never seen Atalanta look horrified before. 'What next?'

'Her hands trembled. She closed her eyes and inhaled like a goddess steeling herself, and suddenly, they stilled. Then she sliced through Absyrtus' arms and legs, cleaving flesh and bone smoothly, and she crouched and looked him in the eye. She severed his head last of all.' Atalanta shuddered. 'The thud it made on the deck, and the silence, after … I will never forget that silence.'

My stomach had dropped. Atalanta looked as if she might be sick.

'Jason gaped. None of us could look away. Medea took the limbs to the rail and shouted to Aeëtes that she was throwing her brother piece by piece into the sea, so that he would never reach the Underworld. She held up the head for a long moment before she threw it. Of course, the king ordered his men to cease rowing, and they stopped to gather the scraps of his son. Orphia, our second battle was won without a fight.'

I glanced around the deck once more, and wondered if all these silent men were thinking of the moment when Medea tossed her brother's head into the bruise-dark sea.

It would have been easy to claim that Medea was driven blindly by love for Jason, like a chariot whose horses have bolted. The strategy in her actions told me otherwise. I guessed that Eros' magic had worn off as soon as the *Argo* pushed out to sea, and Medea had understood her situation all too well.

Everyone looked at Medea and saw a foreigner and a woman. And if Jason should die … I had been around warriors from noble families long enough to know that an abandoned princess would be a prize.

A woman's protests did not inspire fear. A spectacle might.

I could not blame Medea. But I could never have sliced up my brother, I was sure – not even though he was Idmon.

A few of the men looked over at the sound of our voices. 'Atalanta, how long have I been asleep?' I whispered.

'Seven nights.'

I could not have concealed my shock, even if I had tried.

'Storms tossed the *Argo* for days. Some of the men accused Jason and Medea of angering Zeus, and so we stopped on the island where the witch-goddess Circe lived.'

'Tell me of her,' I said.

She shook her head. 'Another poet must tell of her. She is beyond my poor words. But she is wondrous, and worthy of an epic tale. I can only tell you that Jason pleaded for a blessing, and she refused him. Medea's voice carried the day.'

I was not surprised. I tried to imagine the scene, and thought of something Clio had once mentioned. 'I have heard that only a witch can cleanse blood guilt.'

'Whatever she did to them, Jason and Medea came out of her house smiling. Our ship set off into a calm sea, and we all cheered Circe from the deck.'

I looked around the *Argo* and, as I took in the men's expressions anew, something stirred in me. If we were out of danger, as Atalanta said, then why was the mood on board so dark? Were we not a triumphant crew, sailing home?

A shadow fell over our faces. Medea lowered herself to sit beside us and the wind flung her hair out, making dagger-points. Her hands did not tremble now, but lay folded in her lap. After examining me for a moment, she ran a finger over my temple. 'It looks as if there was never a wound.'

'Blood can be wiped away,' Atalanta said. 'From the surface, at least.'

'I owe you my thanks,' I said to Medea, touching my finger to hers.

'If it will provide any comfort, I can punish Idmon for what he did to you. His arrogance is an affront on us all.'

'That will not be necessary,' I said.

'You are quite right.' Her smile tightened. 'A vision came to me last night of Idmon at the mouth of a river, on our journey home. He lay bleeding. A boar stood over him, its tusks wet with blood.'

The beast that had nearly gutted Eurydicius appeared in my memory, frozen as it charged. The points of those bristles and tusks ...

I looked at Medea. Satisfaction lurked in the line of her mouth.

Something drew my eye to the island we were passing. Slabs of wood glinted in the sun, impaled upon the points of small rocks in the cliff-face that fringed the tiny outcrop. As we passed the smashed guts of a second vessel, I glanced over at the nearest group of men.

They did not look shocked.

'Tell me,' I said, quietly, 'and do not spare my feelings. What lives on those rocks?'

Medea's eyes glinted, and in that gleam, I saw the woman who had dismembered her brother.

'That is why I have come for you,' she said.

21

The wind whipped Jason's cloak, making him a giant, but when I stopped at his side and blocked the breeze with my body, the fur sagged, and he reduced to a man once more.

'At last. She wakes.'

'You sound pleased to see me. Danger must be very close,' I said.

'You know, from the first time we ever sparred together—'

'Spare me the false compliment. What is it you want from me this time?'

He gazed out at the rocks for a moment. The lumps on the horizon reminded me of the vertebrae of some ancient creature, scattered amongst the waves, the lower halves of the outcrops submerged. What remained above the surface glittered, turning gold as the sun struck it.

'Before I sailed on this quest, I consulted the centaur Chira,' Jason said. 'She met me on Mt Pelion, granting me leave to ask her one question. After agonising over it, I asked her what weapons I would need to get home alive. She fixed her deep gaze upon me and listed many things, from Medea's potions to Philoctetes' bow, but one weapon, she said, was greater than any other – the voice of the poet Orphia. I would need it to get the *Argo* safely past the sirens.'

I turned and stared behind me, taking in the shipwreck on the last rock, feeling the air leave my lungs.

Everything that I had heard about the monsters of these sea-rocks hurtled at me: winged horrors with the faces of people and the scaly feet of birds, they sang with magical beauty, luring sailors to their deaths and displaying the smashed ships on their cliffs as trophies. In all the centuries the sirens had lived, my tutor had informed me, no crew had resisted their song.

I thought of the story engraved on the tablet in Calliope's tower, about the Athenian sailors who had been lured by the voices of sirens. I imagined their ship sailing closer and closer to these brutal crags. I pictured the decoration I had glimpsed on a bronze cauldron in Dorus' palace – a sharp-featured head with wings spreading out behind it, silent and ominous, staring as if it were about to break free from the bronze and launch at me.

What was it that Calliope had said, after I defeated the harpy on Mt Parnassus? *There are worse birds than those.*

I shivered.

'Did you think that speaking one poem when we fled was enough?' Jason said, closing the space between us with a step. 'Are you not here to become a hero?'

I gazed out at the splinters of masts and hull again, feeling anger jabbing at me like those slabs of wood, raw-ended but held in place.

'Did you think I would not notice that any woman is a chattel to buy you a throne?'

His cheeks flushed.

'You were my friend, once,' I said. 'Leave me room by the prow.'

He did as he was told. The waves that had slapped the sides of the ship subsided. A cry came from the helmsman and the *Argo* slowed, the oarsmen ceasing their movement until the hull becalmed. I looked ahead, making out what I could of those crags, searching for a sign of movement atop the cliffs. Only the flapping of an egret answered my gaze, white wings arcing away from black rock.

Questions came upon me, thick and relentless. Was there anything in my life that would prove strong enough to block a magical song? Could I really create the kind of poem that would ward off the sirens' lyrical seduction? The epic about Medusa that I had performed for the Muses seemed distant now. My work might not be vast enough in scope, nor rich enough in imagery to protect the whole crew.

Even as doubt snaked through me, I reminded myself of the decision I had made when I floated between life and death, dripping my blood onto the deck.

I refuse to die here.

I loved him with every breath in my body. I would survive for him, and I would raise my voice. In doing so, I would win fame for all the women who had never had the chance to speak of their own lives ... the wives, market-sellers and washer-women ... that was, if I succeeded.

The *Argo* neared the half-sunk islands. I held a pick in one hand and my golden lyre in the other, and despite its weight, Calliope's gift felt light in my grip.

This might be over before the ship could clear the first pair of islands. I could do my best to make sure that it lasted longer than that, and perhaps if I reached out with every fibre of my being, I could grasp a way to succeed. I would simply refuse to leave Eurydicius for the Underworld.

That was all that mattered, between each breath and the next.

Silence blanketed the deck. I became aware of the crew watching me, and as I waited, I realised that this was why I had been respected. Men who might have tried to lie with me or strike me down had kept their distance, from the moment we set sail. I had been dealing with other things, but in the back of my mind, I had wondered at it. Now, I guessed that Jason had told them that Orphia, daughter of Apollo, would save them from sirens.

If I failed, of course, that reception might change.

'Do you hear that?' Atalanta said.

The skin on my wrists prickled even before I heard the singing. At first, the sound rippled through the air, passing quickly. The second wave came like a jug, pouring a trail of honeyed wine where it passed, leaving an elixir of song dripping from the clouds. Some of the men began to drag themselves towards the edge of the boat, and Medea and Jason forced them back. The air throbbed around me, promising me a sweetness even richer than this nectarous song, and I could feel possibilities opening that had never existed before, opportunities for fame and gold.

Orphia, I heard a voice say.

It almost worked. The timbre came close to his; the cadence was nearly as gentle.

This is your chance, Orphia.

It was nearly the same sound, but his reticence had been replaced with something smooth and sea-polished; there was no such note of smugness in Eurydicius' voice.

This is when you can seize rulership of the earth.

'I know who you are, and I name you siren, creature of wings and talons, singer of nightmares, shatterer of masts and men. I hear your true voice,' I called out. 'And I command you to appear before me as you are.'

I forced myself to believe it would work. Eurydicius had told me, once, that if you could not imagine something, it did not stand a chance of coming to pass.

Within seconds, the singing stopped, emptying the air of its sweetness. Grit and dust spiralled up and scattered over the deck-boards. The crew coughed and hacked. Something obscured the sun, swooping to land beside me and gripping the rail with its talons, and I gazed up.

Orphia, we know the talent you possess.

The face of a man looked back at me. Feathers the colour of charcoal fanned out behind him, the wingspan revealing itself as he stretched, displaying pinions almost as long as his body. The fine cheekbones and the soft, phlegmatic expression lured me into a sense of calm, but I fought against it, directing my gaze to the talons at the ends of those scaly feet.

Do you feel my voice? The rest of your ship's crew do not feel it. They hear only our song. But you are half a god, and half a Muse.

A shadow passed over me as a second shape swooped, white wings spreading, this siren's face contorted into a smile. *Join us*, she added, and, as with the male creature, I felt her voice in my body. *Think of untapped power. Others are but cracked copper vessels … so follow your golden ambitions. Picture a place where you answer to no one.*

I did not know how, but suddenly I found myself in a city square I had never seen before. The sweet tunes of sirens surrounded me, guiding me towards a plinth on which a laurel crown rested. The leaves felt cool in my palm. I raised the crown to my head, slipping it on, and cheering billowed, hundreds of men and women pouring into the square and shouting my name.

All this is yours, the female siren promised.

As naturally as soil dissolving in a storm, the square melted away. I sat on a chair, elevated before a white marble hall. Men in robes knelt before me while soldiers stood between pillars, clutching their spears and shields, their eyes fixed on me. One of the noblemen carried a sack to my feet. He opened it, spilling gold onto the tiles. Another man deposited sapphires before me; another held a peafowl with iridescent blue and green feathers; another opened a chest of spices.

Gripping the arms of my chair, I noticed their brilliance. I ran my finger over the shining surface.

You look comfortable on a throne.

The voice of the male siren sounded in my ear, its melody offering me wide gardens, arbours full of orange trees, pools where I could bathe alone for hours, rooms sweetened by the song of trained birds. It would be so easy to take these gifts. No more striving; no pain. I would want for nothing amidst piles of treasure.

Iolcus will be yours, if you come with us. Jason may believe he is the rightful king, but you have the power to charm the citizens better than he ever can. You will make a great queen.

I looked down at the gold and sapphires and spices, and the peafowl, now nestling on the gold. 'Where is the other throne?'

You only need one.

'I could not rule in a realm without Eurydicius by my side.' Reality began to slap me, leaving my cheeks stinging. 'And what of my mother, Calliope? And my friends on Mt Parnassus? What of Euterpe? Of Melia and Balanos?'

You are a poet queen, Orphia. No blunt tools should be allowed to shatter the foundations of your rule.

'No. The others would share my power, not shatter it. We would help more people that way.' The floor before me began to crack, tiny fissures crossing the marble, forcing the robed men to scamper to the sides of the room. I rose from my throne. 'Tell me, sirens, why do you wish to part me from everything I care for?'

I kicked the pile of treasure, sending gold pieces spraying across the floor and sapphires rolling into the widening cracks.

Dust fell from above as the pillars began to crumble, breaking into chunks, shattering the floor further. I stepped away from the throne and looked around the hall. Everywhere, the faces of the men disintegrated, crumbling inwards. Something wet made me slip. The throne now pooled in liquid gold on the floor; a scream shrilled through the hall, yet whose throat it came from, I could not tell.

The air before me ripped open. Light blazed through the tear. I held on to the thought of seeing the one person I cared for above all, chanting his name in my mind, and just as I was sucked through the fiery wound, the hall and the marble pillars erupted into a cloud of dust.

Very well. We will do this the difficult way.

I righted myself quickly. A cloak of densely woven magic enveloped the ship where I stood. I kept my feet planted on the *Argo*'s slippery deck and faced the sirens who had spoken to me, noticing that this time, they were not alone.

I counted eight winged creatures perched on the rail and another four on the mast and sail, all of them singing without moving their lips, their feathered bodies crouched, their smiles sickle-sharp. My cries went unheard. Every person on the *Argo* gazed at the creatures with a moonstruck grin. I wrenched my stare from Jason's dazed face and, at last, I glimpsed the wall of rock coming closer to us.

'Stop!' I shouted.

The nearest siren turned the full power of his voice upon me. I clapped my hands to my ears. How could I have been so stupid? It did not matter that I had fought my way out of the illusion – they had held me long enough to drag the *Argo* towards the nearest cliff.

I closed my eyes. I felt Eurydicius' soft, warm neck under my hands. I trailed my fingers up and ran them along the curve of his smile, drinking in his feelings of gratitude and joy, invigorated by his belief in my poetry.

A fire gathered under my skin. Love burned softly but tenaciously inside me, and I realised that it was the one thing I needed to overpower the sirens. The promises of their song would not yield to anything so ugly and unrefined as hate or even anger. I opened my eyes and let all the fire in my soul burst from me.

The pain. The thrusting spears of pain. How I withstood that first attack, I do not know. My organs threatened to burst as sirens attacked me from every side, flapping up into the air, directing their music at me, and the sound transformed to a screeching like metal against metal, rubbing my mind raw. I held my poetry as a shield, telling the sirens of my wedding day and of how I peeled the clothes from Eurydicius afterwards, in Erato's tower and in the water-gardens, the beats of our bodies becoming real verses now. I recounted our debates about destiny and choice, and our meanderings into the thickets of desire, where we discovered our shared natures: our feelings for women and men, and other possibilities still. My chest glowed hot with love. Every part of me threatened to break, and yet nothing did, the force of the sirens' anger bouncing off me.

At last I felt a shudder beneath my feet, and saw that the *Argo* was drifting away from the islands, back into open water. I allowed myself to draw a long breath. Then I launched a new poem at the winged creatures on the rail.

It was not a shield this time, nor a weapon, but a ball of light, knitted together with the smallest of details. I described the way Eurydicius had run across the eastern garden to fix my sandal after I broke the strap, kneeling in the wet grass while he retied it. I spoke of the way he had held me when I leaned against him, my breath coming quick and fast, while I recounted the prediction of my death a second time. He had listened at length to my description of the mob tearing my

limbs from my body, and he had held me, without promising
me that everything would be fine; without offering me a
solution. When at last he had ventured a piece of advice, it had
been gently spoken. *If you struggle to survive, do not be afraid to
use your art.*

I inhaled, now, into the depths of my lungs. I assured him
with a silent reply, passed to him in thought: *I am not afraid.*

As I shared more slivers of precious memory, the ship pulled
away and sped through the gap between the next pair of rocks.
Sirens hovered beyond the prow, forming one block of talons
and feathers and angry beauty, hurling their song at me. The
louder they grew, the more I knew I was succeeding. Something
moved at the edges of my vision and I wondered if Medea had
shaken off their magic, but then I saw Butes stumble towards
the front of the ship, his eyes clouded mirrors.

His legs propelled him to the prow. I saw him grip the wood
and look up at the siren with the charcoal wings, the one who
had first spoken to me, and man and creature locked gazes.

I had almost finished my verse, my body prickling with
pain where darts of siren-song had penetrated my poem's
shield. I could already feel my lines weakening. If I paused and
snatched my spear to aid Butes, the ship might be driven into a
cliff before I could regain my strength. But I should help him.
I should do as Eurydicius would.

The splash that sent droplets of salt water spraying over the
deck told me that it was too late.

Just a moment ago, Butes had been one of our warriors, one
of the few who spoke gently and never glared. Now, ripples
spread from where he had dived. I took a deep breath and
thought of the rest of the crew, helpless before their attackers.

I poured love at the monsters, and they replied with a tide of
fury, their voices threatening to wear me away until only bones
remained. Yet something in me withstood the terrible music.

It was Eurydicius, I realised, a jewel inside me that would not be broken, a piece of him that was also a piece of me.

The sirens shrieked and flapped away from the *Argo*. I watched their feathered wings spreading over the waves, their bodies soaring as they turned back towards their rocks, and my legs gave way before the creatures were out of sight.

I grabbed hold of the rail, breathing hard, hearing the shouts of the crew as they came to, willing myself to find the words to explain that we were safe. My name bounced around the deck, at first in tones of shock. Then, as our circumstances sank in, jubilation rang out from the men. I did not need their thanks, nor their promises of tributes and shrines. All that mattered was that we had survived. I would lie beside Eurydicius once more, and stroke his soft hair, and I would be glad I had endured this pain.

'Butes!' somebody cried.

We thronged as one to the rail. I could just see a figure swimming through the churning water, moving towards the sheer cliff-face. Butes cut a line through the waves. Jason looked as if he were about to call for the ship to be turned around, but Medea whispered something into his ear, and he nodded.

The helmsman took charge, steering us towards an ochre-red sunset. Behind the ship, the tiny swimming figure passed the cliff-face and kept swimming.

Through the mass of bodies on deck, I glimpsed a man descending from the sky and landing beside the mast. He looked like my father, except that he was smiling. The golden aura around him flared as he approached, and so did the smile, broadening on his face until I was sure I was imagining his presence.

'The time has come for us to talk alone, daughter.'

I let him join me beside the rail. No one came near us, so I stood there with the god who had brought me to the verge of death, watching the sun bleed into the sea.

'Poetry is your birthright.'

The words rattled around. I tilted my head slightly, then shook it, until I could be certain I had not misheard.

'Already, I am spreading news of your deeds. From the Thracian hills to Sparta, men will learn that Orphia, daughter of Apollo, defeated sirens with the power of her verses – a power she inherited from her father.'

I laughed, the sound like a snapping branch. When Apollo frowned, I laughed again. Even after a blow to the head, a flight from a dragon, and a siren attack, this was too much.

'So I am famous enough for you to justify throwing me into the service of treacherous men,' I said. 'Famous enough for you to take credit for my work, too?'

'You were born with a gift in those veins.'

A gift from my mother, as much as you, I thought. *And that gift was only a seed.* Apollo's gaze fixed on the water, focusing on something far from me.

'Death has not claimed you, my child,' he murmured. 'The gift is yours to inherit.'

I remembered my hands pinned behind my back, the sting of a blade on my wrist, and the drip of warm blood over my palm.

'You will need to accept my conditions.' It was as if he had rehearsed this speech and expected my silence. 'Note them carefully. You will not embark on any more quests. You will avoid heroes altogether. You will have no more contact with gods or goddesses. You will enjoy the reputation I fashion for you, keeping your poetry quietly to yourself on Mt Parnassus, seeking no other recognition. Do not fret; you will have fame enough.'

'Enough for who?' I said.

I turned my face away from him. The oars of the crew churned the water as the men focused on their rhythm. Exhaustion painted the faces of all my companions. Although I shared their fatigue, something bright and voracious surged through me.

If I went to Mt Parnassus, I went back to the other half of my soul. Let my father fail to guess that I would perform in cities and towns, while my love for Eurydicius flowed more potently into my poems with every day. Did he truly think that tales of our bond would not spread in the world? That people would not see themselves in our story?

Let my father watch as I twined love and fame and poetry together. Let him marvel.

'A few words sweeten parting's gall. You could give me a minute to make my farewells, father.'

'I could.'

That, I knew, was the closest I would get to permission.

Atalanta met my arms with a grip of equal force, wishing me well with a squeeze of my shoulder. I pressed my aulos into her palm and whispered that she should keep it. Further along, an arm thrust out to block my path, and I swerved into two other Argonauts. I pretended to ignore Idmon's smirk.

'May you receive the voyage home that you deserve, brother,' I said.

I did not mention Medea's vision of the boar.

Jason swaggered towards me, grinning, while I saw a different kind of confidence in Medea's unsmiling regard, and her stiff, upright posture. Before we parted, we locked eyes. I detected a new layer of determination in her gaze, ossifying and gleaming.

The surface of the prow heated my palm, still baked from the sun. When I pressed my lips to the wood, I felt a shiver run through the Dodonian oak; perhaps the keel below could hear me. I gave my thanks to Hera.

'Come, my child.'

My father's hand radiated gold as he extended it.

I had no time to steady myself before he pulled me into flight. As we rose, the *Argo* turned into a craftsman's model of a ship: instead of a slice of deck here or a stretch of sail there, the entire vessel presented itself for my pleasure. It was hard not to smile at the curves of the stern and prow, and the oars fringing the hull like legs. For Odysseus, sailing from cove to cove, a ship had been freedom, but I could not forget that this ship had kept me from my freedom for far too long.

We flew slowly. The air might have been cold or it might have been hot; I did not notice it any more than I noticed my own breathing. My thoughts had turned inward.

The future had always been a mirage, too hazy to make out, while I struggled through task after task. Now that I was released from the *Argo*, I was beginning to feel my way ahead. My emotions had not yet made the leap. *Death has not claimed you*, Apollo had said; I had not been torn apart, as the Oracle had predicted. Memories of a multitude of loving moments with Eurydicius had kept me fighting, and his care and support had strengthened me amidst the onslaught of sirens' visions: my own voice and my own words, brimming with the bounty of our love, had forced those creatures back. The fabric of our bond might hold, then. Instead of dying, I might thrive.

The lovers who defeated sirens. I could already imagine the ripe grapes of phrases, hanging on a vine, ready for me to pluck. *Love will help you pass into legend*, the Oracle had said: finally, I felt that I understood.

A swirl of cloud brushed my cheek as we shot higher. My father caught my eye but said nothing. We passed into a region of tiny clouds, spread out all the way to the horizon, puffs of luminous white displayed against a bronze mirror.

Thoughts hit me in a burst: I could begin planning my life with Eurydicius now. We could lay out plans for his shield-making, my poetry, and even collaborations with the Muses. We could structure our life together as a story is structured by scenes. For all the promise of big things, it was the little things I looked forward to: kissing the back of his neck, and keeping my lips pressed to the warm softness of his skin; trading stories about everything he had been doing and everything I had done, our voices mingling and interweaving, our fingers drawing pictures in the air.

It should not have been this easy to imagine Eurydicius rolling beneath me on my bed. I pictured my fingers removing his chiton. I could feel him gasp into my mouth, could feel the shuddering and subsiding of his chest beneath mine, so real that I could almost breathe in the scent of elm leaves, that gentle fragrance that lingered around him.

A vision came to me of the two of us sitting beside the lake, the sun drying our damp bodies, a few beads of water still threaded through his hair. Tiny droplets of pearlescent light crowned him.

Images followed quicker and quicker as we flew. If this was what it felt like to be free, I did not regret leaving the *Argo*.

'You may wish to grip me tighter.' Apollo's voice broke through my imagining.

'Why?'

'Because we are about to fly at five times our present speed, and it is tiresome to chase after plummeting children.'

The wind whipped my cheeks and brought a chill. We slipped into a bank of cloud, the swirls of vapour making all the world cold and thin and white.

Had my feet found Mt Parnassus' soil with ease, or had it merely been luck? I heard my welcome in the song of this earth and felt it in the touch of the breeze. My father extended a hand and let it hover, as if he were about to clap me on the shoulder.

'Remember what I have granted you.'

We held each other's eyes for a flash of a moment.

By the time he had disappeared into the clouds' embrace, I was already thinking of Eurydicius, imagining myself striding towards the lure of his bright hair.

Perhaps I should have known, when the oread greeted me without grumbling.

'What comes but once a year, yet flows all the year round?'

We faced each other. A bird cawed somewhere overhead.

'Spring.' It was strange to hear Calliope's reply pronounced from my own lips.

'And from whom do *you* spring?' The oread regarded me.

'Calliope, chief of the Muses,' I said, unflinching. 'Before her, Mnemosyne: eternal queen of memory. And before her, great Gaia: mother of all, root of all, creator from whose bounty all things grow.'

The silver frame of the doorway drew my gaze as it appeared, glistening in the air. The place where the oread had stood was empty by the time I looked back. I felt the resonance of her sorrowful look and tried to gather my spirits, putting on a smile as I climbed through the entrance.

My smile dissipated when the doorway did.

Caverns opened in the darkness around Melpomene's eyes. The sunlight seemed to dwindle as she fixed her gaze on me.

I should have known at that moment, too. Not Calliope, nor

Euterpe, nor even Erato, but Melpomene. Very slowly, I walked over the grass to her side.

'You have accomplished much, since we last spoke.'

It was too soft. Too polite. Not Melpomene's style of speech at all.

'Tell me now,' I said.

'Orphia?'

'I can see it in your eyes. I can hear it in every word. Whatever is wrong, I would rather know it now.'

'It will be best if we speak in the palace.'

The soaring ride on gryphon-back, over crags of limestone daubed with tiny pools; the view of the lake, striated with late afternoon sun; the descent towards the walled city with the poetry of grass and rock unfolding below me: it should all have brought a thrill. The welcome of my home should have melted away any discomfort.

We landed before I could put a name to the feeling that had stolen through my body.

'Word of your success reached us this morning,' Melpomene said.

The water-gardens stretched to our right, and it struck me that this was an odd place to land. The table where the Muses banqueted on sunny days stood to our left, covered with cups, jugs, dishes heaped with cheese, olives and figs, and one large dish of meat; but the food buzzed with flies. I turned to face Melpomene.

'Calliope created a feast when she learned you were returning. Euterpe let her songs wander through the corridors. And your husband, well … he turned pink, and asked if he could go out on the mountainside to pick flowers for you,' Melpomene said.

I felt the beginning of a vibration in my wrist, as if my very blood were shaking.

'Most of us liked his idea. Your mother disagreed. She did not wish to let him out on the slope with Apollo nearing Mt Parnassus. That was when Thalia stepped forward, and spoke of the purity of Eurydicius' love. Such love should be celebrated when the long-missed lover returns, she claimed. She offered to escort Eurydicius.'

A stronger vibration ran through me, but I tried to ignore it. 'You did not mind?'

'Thalia is my lover, not my possession.' I understood that well. Melpomene fell silent, and when she looked at me again, sea-beds glinted beneath her eyes. 'We were eating when she returned. At first, I did not recognise the man she carried. He lay half-exposed, and his hair flowed down, so that his body looked like an artwork.'

The thrumming of my blood made a wild music now, and nothing would stop it. I tried to breathe, but I could not seem to draw enough air; my lungs seemed to have closed, my chest tightening and tightening. 'Tell me,' I said. 'What happened?'

'I told you long ago that we all live in the shadow of tragedy.' Her pause lasted an age. 'The pair of them had been picking larkspur blooms on the slope. Eurydicius spotted one that he thought finer than the rest, sticking up alone amongst the long grass, and he passed his basket to Thalia and ran towards the purple flower. They were just below the higher forest. Moss, spiky cones and goat skulls covered the ground. When a grey snake slithered over roots and into the grass, neither of them saw it coming.'

Amidst the dappled light and shadow of the forest, you could never catch a glint of grey scales, and when the wind blew through the lush grass nearby, you could never hear the soft slide of death towards you, closer and closer. I had been there myself, and I knew the character of that place. Yet I could not speak; I could only force my head to nod, while sweat slicked my skin.

'Suddenly, Eurydicius clapped a hand to his ankle. By the time Thalia reached him, he was lying still, and his eyes … his eyes were looking at something beyond this world. She tried to work magic on him, but his skin had frozen. His lips remained silently parted. When she brought him back to us, I saw the two dots just above his foot, viciously red: a snake's triumph.' Melpomene laid one hand on my arm. 'He is dead, Orphia.'

I heard the words as one hears a speech in a dream, or birdsong through a hedge.

Melpomene gazed at me, waiting for me to say something. I could comprehend her words, but not their meaning; my mind could stretch to many things, but not this. This could not be real.

'What?' I said.

'The snake was too swift and cunning for him to flee.'

She was still holding my arm, as if she wished to keep me from breaking into pieces. She need not have worried. I was incapable of doing anything but staring at her.

'It was quick, Thalia told me. He died within seconds.'

The sun was shining. Water was flowing in the gardens to our right. After braving a dragon and soldiers and sirens, I was back home, standing in the Muses' city, and everything looked as it should look. Eurydicius could not be … I could not even get my lips around the word.

'He is waiting for me,' I said.

'He was waiting for you.' When I did not reply, Melpomene added, 'Calliope is overseeing the Muses and nymphs in preparing his body. She did not want you to see him like that.'

'No,' I said, the syllable dropping from my mouth.

'Orphia?'

'Stop them.'

The palace blurred into a series of impressions: footsteps ringing on stone, spears of sunlight jabbing from a window, a scent of roasting barley. I was surprised by how calm my mind seemed, even as we sped into the nymphs' work-hall, where bottles, brushes, chisels and knives lay unattended. I moved without hesitation to the far end of the hall, where a crowd encircled something on the floor. The group of Muses and nymphs turned to face me.

I saw my mother's face transform from a sorrowful mask to an angry one. 'Get her out, Melpomene.'

I strode into the midst of them all, without slowing. Melia and Balanos leaned over to stroke my arm, but when they saw the look on my face, they stepped back.

A figure rested on the floor. No smell of perfumed oil reached me. The anointing had not begun, then; those locks of soft blonde hair, splayed out and brushed, had not yet been decorated with a wreath.

'No,' I said.

This time, I spoke the word to myself.

'He was picking flowers for you.' Calliope's voice had dropped.

I knelt and touched Eurydicius' leg, running my fingers slowly from the knee to the ankle. A murmur ran through the crowd. I knew that my air of calm was unnerving the Muses and nymphs, but I examined his skin inch by inch, all the way down to the twin punctures on the ankle, crimson dots so small that they were barely discernible beneath my own shadow.

I gazed at them for so long that my knees began to hurt. Dimly, I registered the pain and pushed it away.

A spot of purple adorned his hand. I unfolded his fingers until I could remove the object; it was easier to focus on doing that than to look at his face. When I realised what I was holding, I placed it very carefully in my palm.

'He was going to bring it to me,' I said.

That simple, little, ordinary sentence hung there, solid and immutable as a grave marker.

I could look at nothing but the larkspur in my hand. The interplay of voices began around me, and I let them throw questions at each other, waiting for my mind to focus on something in all the din. Tasks. I had to find tasks to do. Could I tell his family? They were all dead. What of his friend, then – what of Jason? He was commanding the *Argo*, and he would not sail off course for Eurydicius. Not even a tragedy would keep him from seeking his throne.

There was no one to tell, then. That drove deep into my side, for there was no hope of distraction, now.

I rose, and the Muses and nymphs fell silent.

'I will not be followed,' I said.

My feet flew over the path to the copse, through slices of late afternoon sun, gilded and then shadowed again; I had the urge to turn back and fling myself down beside Eurydicius, but if I did so, I might never get up again. I burst through the trees and into the long grass. Stopping in a patch of roses, I gulped down air.

The soft fragrance of flowers serenaded me. This was not the precious solitude I had known – I felt an absence in my veins, like a tree whose upper branches have suddenly been hacked off. I understood that every year, every week, every moment was going to be empty of him. I would be alone in every garden and every chamber, for the rest of my life.

Sinking onto the roses, I rocked on the spot. I tried to scream. My tongue refused me; only a dry, rasping noise came out, something that was barely a sound. My palm unfolded to reveal the larkspur flower, crumpled and torn.

I could not say how long I stayed there, while the sky deepened in hue somewhere above the branches, a clear blue transforming to indigo. Mosquitoes began their dance. Time faded to a paltry thing; it dimmed and muted, allowing me to concentrate only on his face, which I mapped in its infinite moods: respect and awe, unfurling in his eyes as I spoke my poems; his blush as he caught my stare across the table; the intense focus on his countenance as he worked on a shield, fastening straps or tapping the surface; the joy that danced across his face as he kissed the skin of my inner thigh, as if to say: *I am the luckiest man in the world.*

I had lost the taproot of myself. There was nothing worth living for, in a world where Eurydicius had been snatched from my sight; nothing remained to sprout.

What was fame, now? What was poetry, without him? My dream of walking in the world and weaving poems about our love seemed a spiteful joke, now. I did not want to compose poems. I did not want to win renown. All the stories of Orphia and Eurydicius would turn to hemlock leaves in my mouth, and I would let my tongue wither.

I tried to remind myself that I needed to go on for him – that I needed to show the world how we had both loved, no matter what – but my mind could not seem to grasp my thoughts. They slipped from me like smoke.

My flesh hardened, and I became something new, thickening, so heavy that my body seemed impossible to move.

'Hera,' I whispered.

She arrived before I finished speaking her name. The grass rippled, and a rose dropped its petals at her sandalled feet, the flower quivering and then lying still.

'You suffer,' she said.

It was not a question.

'Great Queen of Heaven, I know your time is precious. I have only one thing to ask.'

She waited. With her ox eyes fixed upon me, I faltered, collecting my courage.

'I beg of you: release me from this suffering and from this world.'

'No.'

Her voice cut through me.

'One day, when your mind is a blade, we will speak again.'

A breeze swept through the grass, and petals fell where she had stood. I could not bring myself to move; constrained by the will of the goddess, I listened to the sound of my breathing. The shift in the world outside occurred slowly. My sensibility of the rising sun's warmth increased as my body returned, little by little, to my control.

It is not easy to force oneself upright when death seems more appealing than life. I thought of running towards Eurydicius, in the shadowy region of the Underworld that offers neither bliss nor torture, and living there with him forever, half alive, yet sated; the idea fell into my mind, and I seized upon it. A vision of his smile animated me. Somehow, I managed to haul myself to my feet and leave the copse. Every step was a hauling in itself, and it would not have surprised me if my insides had transformed to rock.

Calliope met me outside the palace. Her hand fell upon my shoulder.

'I knew that you loved him. I simply did not know how much.'

I love him, I thought. *Use the present tense.*

'If you would prefer, you may prepare his body alone.'

'I will not touch his body,' I said.

How could I explain to her that he had not stopped breathing, for me?

'Mother, I ask that the nymphs wash and anoint him today. His soul must not linger on without burial, drifting. The nymphs must lay him on his bed, in Thalia's tower, and dress him in his wedding clothes. Tomorrow morning, I will bury him.'

'Where?'

The two of us diving, then breaking the skin of the water, erupting into the air with laughter. My fingers tracing the warm curves of his body, in the shallows. My hands playing with his hair as we lay on the shore, picking at questions and paradoxes.

'Near the lake.'

My mother looked at me very closely. Eventually, she nodded.

She did not ask the question that I read in her eyes.

That day, I stared at the walls of my room, sitting on the cool stone of the floor. I refused the food that the dryads brought with a 'thank you' through the door. It was the only thing I said aloud. In private, I tried to force my lips to admit that Eurydicius was dead. Sometimes I tried phrases in the past tense. *I loved him. He was my husband. His heart was made of starlight.* Whatever the formulation, my lips refused to cooperate.

Sitting at my desk, I found myself repeating the only sentences that made sense.

Eurydicius is waiting for me.

Eurydicius makes shields.

Eurydicius kisses my ankle and works his way up to my inner thigh.

Eurydicius laughs when I wrestle him down.

Eurydicius helps women and poor farmers.

Eurydicius believes I can do anything.

Eurydicius listens to my poems with his lips parted.

Eurydicius cloaks me in his love when I face monsters.

Eurydicius is waiting for me.

The present tense had sustained me through my journey on the *Argo* and in Colchis. It had kept me alive when I thought I would die. And now I laughed, for I realised the sheer irony of my life – with all my determination, I had survived a blow to the head and fought off sirens, hoping to hold Eurydicius in my arms again, but it had never been *my* body that was in danger. I had focused on my own death. In doing so, I had ignored the thousands of humble threats that could strike Eurydicius at any moment.

Wolves, wildcats and boars: I had taught him to defend himself against those, yet my lessons had never covered a snake lying in the grass.

He was picking flowers for you. Calliope's words echoed in my mind.

That night, I screamed into my pillow again and again, a dry half-noise emerging, and in the sound I heard the rasping of broken bones and shattered things.

I do not know how I made it to Thalia's tower. By the time I had walked the short distance to her dwelling, my knees gave way. Melia and Balanos ran to catch me. I pushed my friends away, pressing my palm against the door, steadying myself.

His chamber welcomed me with thick fragrance. Roses perfumed the air, laid out on the small table, and all around the bed, anemone poppies daubed the floor, their blooms open like wounds. My feet resisted every step I took towards his body. I managed to look at his face long enough to be certain that it was him before my legs collapsed, and I fell with such a force that my hand missed the bed.

The floor met my nose and left cheek with coolness. I sobbed, not caring who heard me.

He deserved the greatest funeral games in the world: wrestling and archery and javelin hurling, and chariot races to make Athena jealous; but there was no time. I knew what I had to do.

Calliope held my hand all through the procession, the two of us following the plank that held his body, four Muses bearing it aloft on each side in a guard of honour. I felt my soul nearly splitting as I covered his body with earth. The soil fell from my hands in a stream, after I had crushed it between my palms; no clod would survive whole to bruise his face.

The second night passed no easier than the first. I lay awake, remembering the moment when I had slipped my finger between his teeth and laid a coin on his tongue, just before the Muses lowered him into the grave: a payment for the ferryman to the Underworld. Eurydicius had not deserved that. He should have been left untouched, still and perfect, to be admired forever. I wanted to scream and sob, but my lungs were drained of lamentation. I turned onto my side and stared at the wall again, wondering if a prayer to Hera would grant me a moment's relief.

I know what you are thinking. This cannot be fair.

'Eurydicius,' I said.

One word, but a million words within it.

Hundreds of questions surged to my tongue, and I wanted to voice them all; I struggled to choose one. It was unmistakeably *him* speaking, just as it had been in Colchis, and on the *Argo*. I was not going to waste this chance. The words came from me as if I were hearing my own voice through a viscous pool, a mixture of water and blood.

'Are you really dead?'

Yes.

Tears, making the room shimmer. 'Was it quick, as they say?'

So quick that I was looking down at the snake, and then my soul was lifting from my body. I felt nothing.

'I am glad the pain did not linger.' And at last, I began to cry. My nails scored the pillow as I pulled it tight, unsure if I wanted it to comfort me or smother me. I shook, calling his name over and over, and then I felt arms wrapping around my shoulders, soft and warm; they slipped over my back and linked beneath my stomach, and slowly, the gentleness of his grip changed to a firmer comfort, and I felt embraced, as if I were coming home to a bed of seagrass after walking barefoot and naked through a sharp wood.

It is a dark journey to this place. My boat ride was almost as bad as yours. Though no sirens were involved, for my part.

I bit back a fresh sob. *Do not joke!*

I know that this is hard, Orphia. Believe me, I know. But you can succeed for them: my mother, who is here; your mother, who is there; Gaia, too. And Mnemosyne. They are watching us and hoping you will not be broken. You must survive, Orphia.

'I do not know if I can endure life without you. Without seeing you, that is,' I corrected hastily, 'because I know you will be next to me, every day.' And as I spoke, I realised that I did know. There had been no effort to think, to believe. The fact had come to me with absolute clarity.

He would never go away. Somehow, I had been given this knowledge.

His touch made me calmer and stronger. Even as I absorbed it, I knew it was unfair of me to take this comfort without returning anything to him, and I reached out. Through space and magic and the thinning fabric of the world, I touched him, my hand twining with his. I felt him shudder, and then his warm lips pressed to my ear.

You can do it. I know you can.

'I hope you are right, for both our sakes.'

We are companions in misery, as in all things. I would soak up your pain, if I could. But I take courage from the love you showed

me in asking for my burial. You braved agony, pain, despair – no
word captures it fully – to give me the security of a destination.

His invisible self wrapped around me.

'I love you so much, my heart could burst and spill its blood.
I wish it would.'

I beg you, do not let despair vanquish you. You must live, Orphia.
I would gladly yield my body a hundred times more to watch you
survive each time.

The sentiment sucked the air from my lungs.

'Hold me,' I said.

And he did. The sun rose, and set, and rose again.

It continued to rise. From the window of my chamber,
I watched the first blush of pink changing to an angry orange,
the sun high in the sky by midday, ready to unleash its fury; and
by night, I watched the long fading of blue to indigo, streaks
of pink marking the transition. On the fourth day, Euterpe
insisted that I consume a piece of bread and a slice of cheese;
Erato foisted honey upon me and Urania pressed figs into my
hands. I chewed it all without tasting.

It hurt to look around my chamber and gaze upon the places
where he had knelt and kissed his way up my leg; where I had
straddled and pinned him; where we had lain side by side and
debated the characteristics of justice and freedom for hours.
There was a bright shard in my chest. When I tried to sleep,
I secretly hoped to hear from him again, but after a week of
bitter silence, yielding to the Muses' pleas, I dragged myself
into the palace corridors and began the inevitable.

In the largest hall of the palace, I had to grip the rail of the
balcony to steady myself. Here, again, I saw the two oreads
marching Eurydicius in, and he was kneeling. As his blindfold

was removed, our eyes met. Reimagining the moment, I felt the same sense of a vast beginning; how foolish it seemed, now. It was painful to stand in this place. Yet I wanted to luxuriate in the agony; to feel, and feel, and feel.

In every sunlit place and every shadowed nook, I had thought of him, or spoken with him. Passing the eastern garden, I saw us circling each other, my spear-head striking his shield. A second vision: I was dropping to my knee, beneath the almond tree that I had created, and trembling as I asked him to be my husband – lifting him into the air when he accepted, my smile mirroring his own. If it had not been a dream, it seemed like one now.

I drew a breath, yet I could not fill my lungs. Something seemed to scoop the air from them.

In truth, I do not know how I survived those days. The first assault of grief was followed by a second, and a third. Perhaps I survived by the simple act of hauling myself forward. My body was a sack of rocks, and it required more than mere physical strain to move it; there was a certain comfort to be derived from the immense effort of ordinary tasks, each deed turning into a labour, each small problem into a quest to be solved. Only when I sat still and allowed myself to feel did the horror of my life creep back over me.

Nothing distracted nor soothed, in those moments. No topic of conversation could be found that we had not turned over together; there was no joke we had not laughed at until our cheeks ached. How were you supposed to endure when the very reason for your endurance was missing? *Eurydicius would have known how to answer that*, I thought. I laughed bitterly.

My mother and the other Muses watched me, and I knew the nymphs were stealing looks at me between their chores. I felt the weight of expectation in their glances. No one said a word, but the need to look *better* began to prick at me; a friend's chastisement is not half so effective as the censure that one imagines for oneself. I was sure that I must appear an odd and pitiable figure: the woman who would not let go.

I pretended to begin work on a new poem. After taking breakfast with the nymphs, I would disappear into my room with my golden lyre, abandoning the instrument to my desk as soon as the door was closed. Sitting upright on my bed, I would speak to Eurydicius for hours, plunging into my feelings, telling him the many different ways I loved him. Hours turned into days. Days turned into weeks. Silence answered me; and yet sometimes, I thought I could hear part of a sentence, too faint to discern.

The fragments came again, and again. As I strained my ears to catch them, the sounds grew louder, until at last, I could hear a word. *Love.*

A day later – *brave.*

And when I focused every bit of my being on listening, I heard Eurydicius' voice speak in full clarity, at last.

Be brave, my love. I have been growing all the good things I can nourish in my mind: like perseverance, and faith in you. I send you the harvest, now.

It took every bit of my strength not to cry, but I managed it. 'I promise to sow my own seeds more wisely.'

Every day that followed, I was rewarded with the sound of his voice, and entranced, I would ask him questions, accepting the consolations that he gently offered, and lavishing him with love until he was called away to some duty or obligation in the Underworld. I never knew how long our conversations would last. Every fleeting word was to be relished; every familiar expression was to be adored.

'I am planting perseverance, too,' I told him, touching my fingers to my lips in the motion of a kiss. 'I hope it flourishes.'

One afternoon, before the first approach of soft-stealing dusk, I had settled down against the bark of a cypress when I heard the flap of wings nearby.

'Unshoulder it,' a voice said.

My mother dismounted, stepping smoothly onto the grass. Fury whuffled at my hand for a moment, then turned her attention to a nearby fir-cone.

'Unshoulder what?' I said.

'You do not have to bear this burden alone, Orphia. You never did.'

The mingling of rain and starlight in her voice struck me with a new power. Against the darkness of my grief, the radiant harmony of her words gilded my thoughts with a near-unbearable brightness.

'It seems unreal. He is so ...'

'So young?'

So alive, I had been about to say. I nodded.

'Some people erect kouroi: grave markers in the form of statues, showing the bodies of beautiful young men. These artworks preserve the lives of those who have died young, mortals believe. If you wish, I could have marble brought, and a sculptor—'

'No,' I said. 'I thank you for your care. But Eurydicius is not meant for a monument of cold stone.'

Her pause said more than any reply.

'What is it, mother?'

'I believe the time has come to work at your poetry again. The Muses will escort you to the nearest town, at the foot of Mt Parnassus, where you may perform. I understand that singing of love may seem too painful. But if you were to seek a new theme, Orphia—'

'No.' I was aware that I had interrupted her twice, now. 'I beg your compassion in this matter, mother. When I asked the

Oracle at Delphi if I should choose love or fame, she told me
that I would not need to choose. I thought I had finally worked
out what she meant. Eurydicius reached out to me across land
and sea – we cleaved to each other, and he supported me in the
face of dragonfire and siren-song. I thought I would sing of our
love when I returned, and we would share it with the world.
Maybe we would inspire others to love as we did. I hoped that
we would show women what it means to find an equal love,
and guide men to softness and kindness. Any fame that we
earned, we would plant like barley seed, to give nourishment
back to the world.' I let anger flare in my voice. 'But that future
has been ripped from me.'

. 'You were always aflame, Orphia. You blazed with action,
when Eurydicius flowed like water. Do you wish to put out
your fire, now?'

'I refuse to give up on him.'

I saw it again, now: the question I had read in her eyes when
I had agreed to bury him.

'Then what will you do?' she said.

And there it was. You do not experience many moments
where your answer might change the course of your life, and
recognising this one, I hesitated. Something had been brewing
at the back of my mind, in the long days since he was wrenched
from me, and now the mixture firmed and set.

'For a long time, I considered asking the gods and goddesses
to send me to the Underworld in Eurydicius' place, so that he
might live out his days here.' It felt good to admit it aloud, after
all the times I had turned it over in my head. 'But we would
still be apart, in such a case. Our misery would continue.' She
had to see my reasoning, if I was to persuade her. 'I considered,
too, taking a spear and plunging it into my stomach; yet while I
might join him swiftly, he would still be denied the opportunity
to live a full life upon the earth. His best years would still be

stolen from him. There is but one choice I can see, and I would pursue it with your blessing, mother.'

Calliope watched me closely. I drew a breath, pulling it into my core.

'I would travel to the Underworld and ask King Hades to return Eurydicius.'

The words changed from mist to earth as I spoke them. There was no taking them back, once voiced. Calliope sighed, but without anger.

'You guessed,' I said.

'I know my daughter's mind.'

She paced to the edge of the pond and gazed at the surface of the water. I had the impression that she was ruminating on something, rather than trying to come up with a response.

'Fitting that you should sit under the cypress,' she said, turning back to me. 'The tree of death and funerals. I find that another tree leaps into my mind, however. There is an olive grove at the foot of Mt Parnassus that stretches all the way to the Gulf of Corinth, a sea of green treetops running to meet that shining blue. Sometimes, I walk amongst the trees, watching the farmers. When an olive tree gets old or sick, the men cut it back, part-way, and wait for two branches to grow up anew; then they know that the tree will keep living.'

'What if only one branch survives?' My throat struggled to permit the words.

'Ah, but there are always two. The branches of the olive tree are natural companions. They understand each other because they are two halves of the same thing. On the surface, one may be gnarled and the other smooth, one twisted and the other straight, but they are of the same root, and deep down, they grow together. In doing so, they sustain the whole tree, until it sprouts leaves, bears fruit, makes oil, and nourishes our country – and the world.'

I pictured two branches, pushing up from a half-cut trunk.

'I watched the way he smiled when he looked at you, as if his lips were already ripening with praise. I saw how you encouraged his gentle heart, lending support to what was soft and honest and kind. Each of you nourished the other, without asking for anything in return, and in doing so, you sustained us all. You gave us all hope that love is possible, despite the way that men and gods behave.'

I thought of my father creeping into the mouth of a cave, stealing me from my mother's embrace while she slept. I thought of Zeus, disguising himself as a shepherd, seducing my grandmother and then banishing her to the Underworld. The love between Eurydicius and I was not part of the same tapestry as those cruelties: we had woven it with different threads.

'So I give you my blessing,' Calliope said. Her voice was rich and heavy, and in it, I recognised the weight of a pain that was all too familiar. I understood what it meant for her to let her daughter do this.

My heart was beating fast as an eagle's wings. *Breathe*, I told myself. *Let the air in.*

If this was how I would earn fame, as a woman foolish enough to seek out the Underworld, I did not care. I wanted him back – and I wanted to show the world what we meant to each other. For all the women, I told myself. For all the women who had no chance to sing full-throated and to love whole-hearted.

'It will not be easy,' Calliope said.

'To reach the gates of the Underworld?'

'To persuade Hades.'

She looked me in the eye. It was hard to tell what she knew of the realm that I had set my heart upon, but I guessed that it was enough for her to fear deeply for my life.

A ray of sunlight touched her crown. In the last remnants of sunset, the gold glinted. She looked as if she were made of the same metal, once malleable, now forged into something that all men bowed to.

'You must sleep well tonight. We have a journey to plan and gods to deceive,' she said.

I sat there, resting against the cypress for a long time after she had departed. The pink light gave way to a sickle moon, while the scents of pine trees and anemone poppies sweetened the air, deepening the evening. I remembered Eurydicius' words, spoken into the cool quiet of the copse. *If there were a thousand stars in the sky and you floated amongst them, I would see only you. The black infinity of night and a single bright point.*

There was no turning back. Not whilst he was hidden from me.

When I rose, the leaves of the cypress shone in the moonlight, and I saw them clearly for the first time in that silver glow: hundreds of tiny fingers, reaching out to me.

Twin streams thundered from the rock, pouring into the basin, transforming into jade and turquoise stillness where they settled. Even in the dense congregation of beeches, yews and hazels, the waterfall concealed itself with particular care: tall trees gathered around the water, layering their branches over the pool. As Calliope examined the vegetation, I crouched on a boulder and listened to the water's song.

She beckoned to me, and I followed her a little way to where the noise softened.

'The feeling of a place lingers in our memory, more than its shape or hue,' she said.

There was a weight in that idea.

'I believe that this is the best-hidden waterfall on Mt Olympus, not only because it is partway down the eastern side, far from the eyes of the gods, but because nature has enclosed it. You *feel* that you are safe, here.'

This was not a pause on our journey to the palace atop the peak, I realised. This was our destination. Of course, I had always known, somewhere deep inside myself, that if I made my plea before all the Olympians on the summit, Apollo would oppose me; but I had not wanted to admit it.

'I suppose my father will find an unusually creative way to forbid me to travel to the Underworld,' I said.

Calliope's face was stern. 'Not only him.'

My shoulders slumped.

'Did you think that even if you could bypass Apollo, you would persuade Zeus? That you would move him with your poetry, and he would just allow you to visit Hades – that he would permit you, a woman, to break the order of things?'

Silently, I admitted to myself that, yes, I had been hoping that.

'Male bonds always come first for men and gods. Have you learned nothing of authority, Orphia?'

I glanced at the smooth, unyielding surface of a boulder beside the pool.

'Women mean little or nothing to the gods unless they are desired, and even that desire brings calamity. If Zeus is trying to seduce a woman, he does not think of her happiness. Listen to me, Orphia. Listen well, for I will say this only once. Zeus and Hades may rule opposite realms, but they both wield their power with impunity, raping on a whim.'

The water roared beside us. In Calliope's face, I read no anger, nor even any real frustration. She had known what reception I would receive from Zeus and Apollo, I realised, and she had brought me to Mt Olympus all the same, to this strange waterfall, where the dance of yellow and green leaves concealed us.

I did not voice the question on my lips, but I was certain that she heard it.

What next?

A leaf fell and landed on my shoulder. A second later, another fell, and then another, and I noticed that Calliope was smiling at the sight. I picked up my bounty piece by piece.

'Beautiful, is it not? This is all Gaia's doing.' Calliope gestured around us, from the waterfall to the boulders, and then to the treetops. 'The goddesses remember the mother of all things. I have brought you here to pray, on the slope of Mt Olympus, because the goddesses' ears are still attuned to nature, far more than Zeus' are. There are places on the mountain that only those who respect the goddesses can find ... do you understand me?'

I nodded slowly.

'You will need to show devotion. And choose one goddess only. They like to feel special.' Her smile turned wry.

She clicked her fingers and a bottle appeared in her palm, not large enough to fit much wine or honey, but enough to pour an offering onto hungry soil.

Silence cloaked us again, and it occurred to me that Calliope was not asking me to abandon my quest; that she was not going to try to persuade me. I threw my arms around her, hugging her more tightly than ever. No words seemed adequate when we broke apart, yet I saw the small, involuntary motion that she made towards me.

'One more thing. If you reach the Underworld, never forget that Hades is Zeus' brother. You have heard what Zeus does with lightning, when he feels disrespected. Hades wields the same power, and the same cruelty, in more shadowed ways.'

'He will seek to trick me?'

'No.' She took my hand in hers. 'He will seek to make you trick yourself.'

One more embrace. I tried to carve her into my mind, depicting not just her physical self, but the way she strode into a room, and the essence of her voice, which was often rain and stars, yet sometimes ember and ash. She pressed a kiss to my brow, and when she disappeared, I realised that she had been bidding me farewell. A lump rose in my throat.

But you are going to come back.

The sound of Eurydicius' voice in my head made me jump.

'I missed your sudden interruptions,' I said, gazing at the waterfall.

Believe in the power of your every word. Not only your power to capture listeners, but your power to inspire them; to uplift them. To show them that the vulnerable can be strong as a thousand-year pine, if they wish; to bestow a spectrum of colour upon their world. That is how you will succeed.

He was gone before I could vow, again, that I would find him.

The sound of the water grew softer as I moved away from the streams, into the shade of a yew. Clusters of red berries leapt out between the leaves, their brilliant colour singing to me: poison-laden, yet dauntlessly alive. I marked a spot on the ground with my sandal. This was not the kind of prayer that could be said without accompaniment, so I poured a libation from Calliope's bottle, breathing in the rich scent of the wine as it splashed onto the earth.

I knew, instinctively, which goddess I wanted to summon. I knew which goddess set my whole person aflame simply by speaking; which woman gave me confidence by turning her firm glance upon me.

'Great Queen Hera, I pray that you will bless me with your presence.'

The rustle of leaves provided a reply. I lowered my eyes and waited. When I raised my eyes again, there was still no one before me.

This was a challenge, I told myself. It was a great journey I wished to make – terrible, strange, and dangerous, too, but great nonetheless. A simple libation might not be enough.

No birds adorned the lower branches of the yew. I could find no animal tracks in the surrounding forest. At last, a thin beam of sun illuminated brown scales near my feet, and I looked down at a shining body.

'Perfect,' I breathed, though I was not sure if I was happy or sad.

To sacrifice a snake in the hope of saving Eurydicius was the kind of poetic flourish that I could not have devised myself. The animal was a meagre streak, barely the width of two fingers, a pattern of dark brown splotches covering the creamy yellow-brown of its body. I held out my palm and the snake slithered onto it.

Against my warm skin, the scales felt unusually cool. Perhaps there was less life in this animal than in other creatures. Or perhaps I just wanted to believe that.

'Rest, little one,' I said, 'while I tell you of the weaving of wool.'

Its head drooped as I began to speak, and the rest of its body soon followed until the snake was a limp rag, its eyes glazed with the mesmeric effect of the hands of the women working the loom, my words creating the warp and the weights and the shuttle. I carried the sleeping creature to the waterfall and tilted my palm.

My chest heaved as I watched the snake float into the deepest part of the water. I kept up my recitation until the tip of the scaly body had plunged beneath the surface and the layers of jade and turquoise went still again. I felt like a loom-weight myself, my feet dragging me back to the yew.

The air trembled and a force travelled through me, lingering in vibration. A glory of peacock feathers burst out of the sky, and Hera swung herself easily onto the wine-drenched earth. The birds stood still, watching her. As always, I felt the urge to soak in the power of her eyes: a power that poured into me, that poured into all women and flowed between us in thousands of rivulets.

'Death for life. You understand.'

'I hope this sacrifice pleases you, Great Queen Hera.' I bowed my head.

'I said we would speak again when your mind was like a blade.' Her eyes roved over my face. 'And you have made your first stroke.'

The snake drowned itself, a voice in my head pointed out. *I did not execute it.*

Ah, another voice piped up, *but who put it to sleep and dropped it into the water?*

'Some would have expected a poet to take Athena, goddess of wisdom, to pray to. Others would have guessed Aphrodite, pinnacle of beauty. Instead, you chose me – as you always have.' Hera stepped away from her chariot, pronouncing each word slowly. 'The jealous wife. The immortal they call a scheming woman.'

Of course, I knew the stories of Hera punishing the women Zeus had seduced and raped, rewarding them with disfigurement or death; everyone knew those stories. My tutor had devoted hours to Hera's cruelty, and scarcely a minute to Zeus' assaults. Yet I also remembered how Hera had saved the washer-women and wives of the Whispering Isle.

A shadow fell across Hera's face. She walked to the next tree, turned, and paced back, fixing her gaze upon me, and I watched decisiveness spread over her features.

'When a woman cries out from Zeus' garden, after he has raped her and left her to bleed, the sound of her voice drifts across to my quarters.'

The peacock carved on one door, and the bull carved on another. I remembered.

'Zeus tells the gods that I persecute his victims. He has always been good at getting others to do his work. The gods tell mortals the same thing.'

As I looked at her face, I saw a struggle in her eyes. 'You don't persecute them, do you?'

'Even Zeus needs to keep his reputation amongst men.' Hera's mouth twisted. 'They will excuse a man's deeds if they can blame a woman. And who better than a wife?'

The air trembled again as she spoke.

'My private domain teems with wounded girls. They multiply, by the month. You see, I will not let him destroy them, even if he destroys my name.'

'We have all been deceived by the stories about you, Great Queen,' I said, letting my feelings pour forth, and knowing, somehow, that I should not try to check them. 'But no god or mortal could dim your light. All my life, I was drawn to your passion. I knew that even King Dorus was afraid of you, and when cruel men fear you, it seems likely that your power threatens theirs.' I took a breath. 'I never forgot that you saved the women, when my father burned the island.'

'Dorus was not unwise. All men with power should fear a passionate woman.'

I met Hera's gaze.

'And you, poet – you would follow your passion to the Underworld?'

'If I had a way to get there, and someone who might distract Zeus and Apollo ... then indeed, Great Queen of Heaven, I would go.'

'I see you do not hesitate to ask a favour.'

I smiled. 'Perhaps I learned boldness from one who speeds women to safety.'

'And what of fame? What of letting your poetry ring through the hills, for glory?'

'Fame is but dust and smoke without meaning to it. The Oracle declared that love and fame would combine in my life – and I must seek out the one whose soul inspires me, if I am to pass into myth. How else can I show the world that those like us deserve a free life? How else can I show women that they may choose – that they may work and love under the open sky?'

Hera's eyes did not lighten. 'Walk through the trees, and follow the gorge. When you find the right spot, stop. Offer a poem in return for passage to the Underworld – you will not have long, before the gods wake from my enchantment.'

I remembered the immortals freezing in the Hall of Starlight.

'How will I know it is the right spot?' I said.

'Remember your lineage, Orphia. It is called the Underworld for a reason. Beneath root and rock, the damp weight of soil and the smoothness of clay, you will find the entrance to the passageway.' Hera touched my cheek, and the sensation burned, white-hot. The lineage of powerful woman after powerful woman reverberated in my head like plucked lyre strings: the paintings of Gaia and Mnemosyne, calm and commanding, reappeared in my mind.

Hera snapped her fingers, calling the peacocks and the chariot to her side. I watched her mount it, feeling the whole world vibrate around me until she was gone from sight. The meaning of her advice sank in. I was not alone – I could never be alone, with the web of women connected to me. My community sang to me in the flow of the water, in the brightness of the yew berries, in the patterns of dappled sunlight and the smell of rain-sprinkled earth.

Yet it was more than Gaia's ancestral music that spurred me onward. The body keeps a rhythm of its own, and the sheer agony of grief led my flesh to beat its drum now.

I began to walk. One step, then another, then another. Surprising, how the littlest thing could feel like the beginning of something great.

'Eurydicius,' I said, 'stay patient. I will be with you soon.'

I know you will succeed. You can no more retreat than the sun can drop rain.

His voice came fleetingly. I could not say how, but I knew that his intonation was real, as gentle as the echo of a cithara's notes, and then I knew that he had departed.

I increased my pace. A gorge flowed away from the waterfall, branches layering overhead until it passed out of sight. Sunbeams danced on the surface of the water and foam unmade itself in waves, yet for all its beauty, the gorge burbled so loudly that my words would be drowned out. I turned away from the water, onto a narrow path that led upward.

A surge of excitement ran through me as I began to move through the trees and into denser foliage, to where branches blocked most of the sun. Something called to me. I walked and walked, feeling myself drawn onto a route parallel to the gorge, just as Hera had suggested. The river offered a constant companion, but the sound of its water softened, and only occasionally did the trees part enough for me to catch a glimpse of bright water and rocks. For the most part, I was alone with the scent of bark.

I had only turned the first bend when I glimpsed a flash of purple fire between the trees. The colour recalled the larkspur bloom that Eurydicius had clutched in his fingers, and I felt my legs freeze.

'Hello?'

My voice echoed through the forest. No reply came. Not even another flicker of purple light. Yet something had signalled to me, and I wondered if it could be my path to the Underworld: the flare of magical light had lasted only a moment, but I felt its power linger.

I tried not to think of that crumpled larkspur bloom.

Birds twittered as I resumed my walking, calling and responding to each other in an unmistakeable dialogue. Their song came clear and high through the branches, finches tweeting to woodpeckers and warblers talking to goldcrests, eagles calling to sparrowhawks and little golden-breasted nuthatches chirping to their companions. They did not fall silent, as I had noticed birds do elsewhere. I could sense the presence of a determinedly *living* world around me.

The forest shifted as I walked. In some places, thin trunks jutted up from the earth, while in others, the trees stood like pillars, thick and unperturbed, their roots sprawling onto the path. In some sections I walked over pine needles, stepping with delight on their spongy carpet, and in other sections rocks poked up from dirt like islands in a sea. Red and yellow leaves swayed on branches in some places, and in other regions still, green leaves took precedence, one layer of the forest giving way to another, a tapestry revealing the parts of its weaving. My feet passed by all manner of things: bursts of dark green ivy glinting against the soil; the ghost-faces of cyclamen flowers haunting the path with their pale pink blooms; a mushroom, almost undetectable in a sweep of shadow, its brown surface marked with darker brown spots. A colony of ants, a small red beetle, and many mosquitoes thronged around my ankles. At one point, I crouched to fix my sandal and found myself locked in a stare with a four-legged general.

She had placed one foot on a leaf, and appeared to have frozen. Her black scales glistened beneath brushstrokes of angry yellow. It was one thing to recognise a fire salamander, and quite another to stare it down, but my new companion did not show any sign of moving.

If she had any instinct to release her poison, she resisted it. I rose, still watching her, and edged around her tail, lifted from my grief for a moment.

Eurydicius, I am coming. The thought flowed from me without warning. A wave of power coursed through me, sending sparks to my fingertips.

The tree cover thinned, and after another stint of walking, a clearing opened up and I breathed in the rich scent of mule dung. Five of the animals stood munching grass, and only one of them bothered to glance up. I turned my gaze ahead, to where two tree-covered slopes met; beyond them, a peak raised its head, and now I saw the summit of Mt Olympus clearly, the stark lines of two points framing a curve that dipped down, as if Zeus had taken a bite out of the mountain.

It was unwise to linger here. As I slipped into the next part of the forest, I saw another flash of purple fire between two trunks. Excitement rippled through my blood.

My heels beat a rhythm on the path. They carried me over wayward roots and fallen logs. Despite the sun rising somewhere above the peak, the shade of beeches and maples covered everything, and I appreciated my mother's forethought in bringing me to this part of the slope – even if my father raged at me, I guessed that his rays could not reach me here.

Midday gave way to afternoon. Roots and leaves began to blur, and I had to crouch and hold my head until I could resume walking. It seemed an exceptionally long journey whilst Eurydicius was bound or confined in the lightless depths of the Underworld; holding back dark thoughts of torments, I clutched my lyre tighter. If only I could enter the same state of flow as when I created, when distractions slipped away and the petty cruelties of fear melted, I might be capable of reaching him sooner.

With one foot on a tree root, I halted.

Of course. Why had I not thought to do this before? Closing my eyes, I let rivers of golden words mingle with the darkness inside me.

My hand strummed the strings of my instrument, letting the lyre speak first.

'Most ancient one,' I said, 'I dedicate this poem to you, and I scatter it on your soil. A man walks through my verses. His presence is in every gold leaf that is illuminated before me, in every gossamer thread of a spiderweb, in every soft pine needle that carpets the forest.

'Like my grief and joy, he is perfectly balanced. He makes shields, the same things soldiers carry, yet he makes them for peace. He gives himself to me with softness, tenderness and compassion, but he can endure loss and pain with a strength that few mortals possess. He loves without restriction, beyond sex, beyond the rules of men. As the earth and sky are balanced, as the trees and water of the forest are created evenly, so is he.

'When I doubted myself, he sang to me. Every word from his lips was a song of awe – of belief in my art – of respect for my poetry. Every glance from his eyes was a song of desire, without a note of possession or cruelty in it.

'My feet will restore that song. I will not stop walking until Eurydicius is free. If my skin should peel and scatter, my bones will march on through the dust and smoke of the Underworld, until they reach the pure air of his soul's kindness.'

I let the last words rest, and the poem seemed to hang in the air. All the birds had ceased their dialogue. I realised that they were listening to me; that an unusual quality permeated the forest, as if the silence had developed a new layer. The burbling of the gorge faded. The insects halted their buzzing, and all around me the leaves hung still, so that for a moment, I was alone with the last words of my tribute.

Then the trees shook and shook. Pine needles poured down until everywhere was soft and spongy underfoot. Pine cones fell and arranged themselves to line the path; ferns reached out; cyclamens bloomed and stalks parted so that new life could push through; midges danced in the air; butterflies twirled around each other in a formation that dissolved and remade itself. The sound of hundreds and hundreds of bells rang through the treetops, and I recognised it as joy, offered from the throats of all the birds above me, their song pouring out a purity of delight that no human voices could have matched.

Allowing my lips to curve, I felt the unnaturalness of the motion. It had been so long since I had wanted to smile, truly and wholly. The world had changed forever on the day I had sped home from Jason's quest. Yet for just a moment, I remembered how it had felt when Eurydicius was next to me.

Something shifted near my foot. A few tree roots had pushed out further across the path, and looking up, I saw the trunks leaning over, forming a new path and pointing the way ahead. A clump of maple leaves fell and landed before me, and in that soft thud, I felt the encouragement of the forest.

My feet carried me over roots, leaves and mushrooms, my soles moving with a knowledge that came from somewhere deep in my blood. 'Gaia,' I called, 'I feel you.'

Larkspur-coloured light flared ahead of the next group of beeches, and my spirit leapt. More trees shifted as I ran, the path curving to the left, the branches enclosing it so that just enough sun filtered in to light my way. Something was *allowing me* to enter this part of the forest.

The new path came to an end abruptly. I stepped into a grove. Purple fire burst out around me, the flames spaced evenly between the trees, and staring around, I breathed in the magic of growing things.

Lichen clung to a log on my left. Moss tufted a limestone boulder on my right. Around me, dozens of spindly trees leaned at different angles, their leaves and branches layering over each other, and everywhere I saw green: jade coating the log, emerald covering the boulder, and a brighter lime in the canopy.

I drew a breath, feeling my body's deep anticipation.

'Listen to me, Gaia,' I said, facing one of the purple fires. 'I lifted Eurydicius off the damp grass and kissed him, on behalf of all women who love that which is soft. He kissed me back, on behalf of all men who love that which is bold and firm. As our lips met, we became thousands of people.' I tried to hone my expressions – tried to give voice to the twin streams of love and despair within me. Doubts thronged thick and fast into my mind. Perhaps the fire would flicker out. Perhaps I would fail, and be abandoned here.

The fire burned brighter, and a purple sheen tinted the leaves and trunks. I drew another breath. Launching into the tribute to Gaia I had performed at the inn, I poured all my passion into the praise, drawing on the skills the Muses had taught me, shifting my posture and strengthening my voice.

'I would speak to you now, great Gaia,' I declared, when I had finished the poem. 'You permeated the very air and soil at Delphi with your bright wisdom – a gift for those women. It is my shame that I, too, must ask a gift of you. Show me the way to the Underworld, great Gaia. Let me hold the other half of myself, and kiss his soft hair. Let us look at each other as equals – as few husbands and wives have gazed at each other in this land. Let me live again, if only for a moment, with my soul repaired.'

The air rippled. A brightness pierced the dim grove. For a moment, silence ruled, then a rhythm travelled through the earth beneath my feet. Softer than Hera's vibrations, yet steady as the hands of a hundred women pulling and straightening yarn, it gave out a magic that reverberated around me. It built, and built, and then suddenly, it was over – and I turned to find that I was no longer alone.

Ivy wrapped the limbs of a tall woman. Maple leaves pressed to her long robe, and roots twisted from her scalp, their colours varying so that she seemed to be wearing a rainbow of intertwining hair. The forest shimmered as she stepped towards me.

'Daughter of Calliope,' she said.

I wanted to touch her, but something told me to stay still. She laid a hand upon my own, and after a moment, I flipped my hand, our palms touching. The waves of her power built to a tide that swept through me and brought with it the glow of dawn, the scent of newly turned soil, the sound of ice cracking into many pieces, and the carving out of holes in a crag through the slow tenacity of erosion.

'Gaia,' I whispered.

Despite the power that flowed from her, she held my palm softly. Her eyes twinkled. As the wind rippled her robe. I glimpsed the curves of her breasts and felt a force emanating from her skin: the force that nourished every nurse, every mother, every father who had cared for their child. I sensed the milk of thought and the honey of feeling.

'Anyone would find it impressive, to hear a tribute in words that can uproot trees.'

'Generous mother of the earth, I owe you my thanks and my praise, for your fire.'

'*My* fire?' Her eyes twinkled again. 'No.'

I glanced at one of the larkspur-hued fires burning between the trees, then back at her.

'Your determination to find him. His love for you. They have run alongside each other, and as you walked through this forest they kindled a fire to light your way. Daughter of Calliope, I did not lead you anywhere.' Roots writhed on her head, the rainbow of colours shifting. 'I did not create the fire, nor the path.'

The flames still flickered around us. The presence of magic was strong in that purple light, and I wanted to deny what she had said; for how could I, breaking apart with sorrow, make something so pure and potent? Never once had I imagined that I could make magic *with* Eurydicius. I wanted to shout to him, through the soil beneath my feet.

'From a place of damp earth and flowing gorges, you made flame. Orphia and Eurydicius.' She spoke our names in a single breath. 'Of all mortals, you have created the most evenly balanced love, and thus, you are the happiest of lovers, even in grief.'

In her surety, I heard my feelings for Eurydicius reflected back at me in their depth and beauty. I felt the blessing of all elements of nature. Dropping to one knee, I looked up at her. 'Before, I called out to you, and now I voice my plea again. Show me the way to the Underworld, great Gaia. Let me seek him.'

'The way is there, for any who would find it.'

'Forgive me, great Gaia, but where?'

'I am no instructor. I provide my bounty.' Her gaze focused intensely on me. 'One who recognises the earth, who addresses the earth's creator and falls into the flow of her creative spirit: such a one can truly *see* the tunnel.'

I looked around, as if the entrance to the Underworld might appear between the trees.

'In all things, contrast will illuminate.' The twinkle returned to her eyes.

She motioned for me to rise, and kissed my brow when I did. The tide of her swept through me again.

'Will I see you, when this is over?'

I had not intended the question to ring with such desperation. The raw need of it made me sound like a child. But she was a mother. For most of my life, I had not known Calliope, nor had another woman to share my thoughts and emotions with; I had believed myself created by Apollo alone. My lineage was still a blessing I could scarcely believe. *Matrilineal.* The word ripened like a cedar berry in my heart. Now, I stood before the mother of all things, and recognised my great-grandmother.

'See me? Not in this way,' Gaia said. 'Your imagination has conjured my form, as it conjured this fire. But you will see me in every blade of grass, and every full nest. You will hear me in the keening of the wind, and in the clear cry of the oriole when it swoops.'

Finding the courage at last, I made to take her hand, thinking to convey my love and gratitude, perhaps to feel her force one more time. My fingers reached for empty air. I stared at the place where my great-grandmother had stood, and I knew at once what she had meant.

In all things, contrast will illuminate.

The world turned dark as I closed my eyes. In that void, I could hear the twittering of birds, building and enveloping me. I let it soothe my thoughts. Darkness came before a clear view. The birds stopped singing, one by one, until there was no sound but the faint rustling of leaves above me.

I opened my eyes. A tunnel yawned, beginning barely an inch from my toes, descending into the earth beyond my vision. My heart began to beat an uneven rhythm; in that hole there were no steps to climb down, only a sheer drop into a lightless place.

The choice was simple. Risk or cowardice.

Around me, the larkspur fires burned steadily between the trunks. I spoke Eurydicius' name into the breeze and clutched my lyre to my chest. Beeches and maples shivered and whispered in the language of root and leaf, until I felt their approval in that susurration.

The soil swallowed my body as I jumped.

24

The waves hit my cheeks again and again, and I gasped, straining to draw a lungful of the fetid air. The next wave surged over my head and I sank, clutching at strands of dark kelp.

Voices sang to me through the river, their melodies weaving around each other and buffeting me back, permeating my consciousness. Sounds of pain mingled. It was not the physical affliction of a wound that the singers bewailed, but anguish, grief, fear, regret: so many cruelties of emotion. Somewhere to my left, an old woman sang of losing her son, standing over his body on a black sand beach years before her own death and weeping onto his wet skin; a painter told of his sorrow at dying before he had finished his greatest work, a vase left half-coloured on his table. In rasping strains, a girl sang of dying in agony, strangled by her father's hands.

Intuition told me to open my eyes. The water stung me for a moment, but I perceived a myriad of tiny lights, constellations of red in the dark, decorating the water and imbuing it with power. I felt the pain emanating from those glowing dots. The river ceased its churning, and I moved between the lights, listening to each voice.

It seemed to me that I was not alone in my grief, at last. Listening, I reached out to the other souls, offering them the thread of my companionship through my thoughts. At once,

I felt them respond. Those glowing dots and lamenting voices lifted me, melting my isolation away, and I broke through the surface to breathe the air of the Underworld.

In all directions, I could see only darkness. Worse: I could feel the blackness as a warrior feels her enemy approaching from behind, hot breath gusting against her neck. Malice pressed against me. Searching for a landmark, I spotted two glowing coals on what I thought was the far bank of the river. I realised I was looking at two flame-red eyes.

'Hurry up, there! Into the boat!' someone cried.

I could have cursed all the stories that had fuelled my imagination. I had always imagined that the Acheron would be instantly recognisable: that I would find the river of woe at the edge of Hades' kingdom and board a boat to cross it. Yet here I was, floundering in the water that only shades were supposed to pass over. I was quickly realising that I had no coin to pay the Acheron's ferryman if he should catch me, too.

I peered at the glowing eyes. In the gloom, I thought I discerned the shape of a boat, bobbing by a shore that merged with the blackness.

There was no point in waiting. Grief lent me a kind of clarity. If I was to reach the gates of the terrible realm ahead, there was only one way forward: I *would* cross the river before that boat caught up.

I whispered, pouring my words of pain into the water, thickening the Acheron with a tribute to the souls within it. I did not stop to question my ability. Halfway through the poem, the river began to ripple, nudging me along in the opposite direction to the boat. As my body moved down the sorrow-rich Acheron, I thought of Eurydicius, and remembered the way he had once called out 'yes' when I spoke his name, a long, slow *ye-esss*, while his attention was focused on the surface of a shield, examining the indentation he had made.

In that moment, I could tell that he was not quite listening to me. Yet even though he was bent over his task, some part of him sensed the sound of my voice and responded. I loved those little things about him that no horror could steal from me: I loved the way he frowned as he contemplated and analysed; I loved the way he became one with his work in all its fine detail and beauty. I loved that he heard me.

And I hear you now.

I floundered, missing the river's flow, and water flooded my mouth, but I spat it out and called above the current's noise: 'Hold on!'

I could say the same to you. In that gentle tone, I could practically hear him smiling. *Remember, no matter what you do, Orphia, you can never disappoint that which is already yourself – your other half. Just feel your own glory.*

'For you, I'll try.'

I wish you could see yourself as I see you: a hero whose words shine like beaten gold, lighting up a path for others to walk on.

He was gone just as quickly as he had come, and I felt for a moment the emptiness of a world without his voice, a lifetime without him ever laughing or leaning into me as I wrapped him in my arms. It would not help me to falter. It would not help *us*. I pushed through despair and back into the flow of the river, returning to my poem, and with every line, I tried to take his advice: to believe that my words could gleam with a golden power.

A cry rang out behind me, and I looked back. Where the twin coals glowed, I saw the ferryman rowing his boat, sending ripples in my direction. My throat tightened. I urged the river with more and more force, until my knees hit rock and I clambered up, bruised, wet, but still breathing.

Faint light covered this region. I could see the rocky ground, and beyond it, the tall barrier of a wall. The very sight of that wall filled me with a dread that I could hardly bear, yet I forced myself to walk towards it, aware of the boat crossing the river behind me and the sound of my breath in the silent air.

As I drew closer to the wall, the light shifted. The gates in the middle emerged from the gloom as if someone were unveiling them for me, the vast size and thickness of those doors obvious at once, and the dread inside me grew, an intangible force, swelling.

Only when I reached the gates did I see what was crouching before them.

I looked from left to right, taking in three slavering mouths. A single body crouched. The great dog's paws scraped the ground, ready to spring.

I reached instinctively for a spear, as if one might appear in my hand, and the three-headed hound rose to its haunches. I reminded myself that I was not alone: Eurydicius, Calliope, all the Muses would be cheering me on as I faced this monster.

The beast lowered its heads and sniffed, warm breath rolling over me, and the weaker part of me wanted to retreat. A different part prevailed.

'You will let me through,' I whispered, sensing that the hound could hear me.

Another cry rang through the darkness, closer this time. The boat was drawing closer; one way or the other, I was about to be held to account as an intruder.

I opened my mouth, intending to speak words of calm and serenity, but finding none. Pain flew from my lips in a multitude of tiny spears; not only the sorrow of sudden loss but the dull exhaustion of endless grief. My invisible weapons struck their target, and I closed my eyes and waited ... and waited.

The wet surface of a tongue swept my face. When I opened my eyes, the dog gave a soft growl and stepped away – remarkably – to the side, leaving a path clear to the gates.

I heard the ferryman's cry again and ran towards the doors of solid stone.

They opened as I reached them. A heavy boom told me that they had closed behind me, and I inhaled the smoky air, looking around the vast space, waiting for my breathing to slow. I had breached the wall, now. Anxiety rose inside me, but mingling with it was a certain clarity: I *would not* turn back.

A bridge stretched before me, its narrow walkway dotted with tiny lights strung out like a necklace of colour. It was pocked with small holes where some of its planks were missing. I did not like the prospect of crossing it alone.

'Eurydicius,' I whispered.

No reply came. The hazy air shrouded me as I stepped onto the bridge. It burned my throat and stung my eyes, forcing me to take smaller breaths. As I moved forward, the bridge passed out of the smoke, and I could make out the walls of the realm, immense faces of raw rock greeting me on both sides. *Asphodel*, my tutor's voice repeated: the region of the Underworld that offered neither punishment nor happiness. I peered over the edge of the bridge, and immediately wished that I hadn't.

A grey domain unfolded below like a cloak bleached of all colour, a shadow of a garment. Something inside me churned as I saw the faint shapes of people amongst meadows of pale flowers. They were roaming alone, moving but never speaking, their outlines barely visible: always missing each other. I had not imagined a place could feel so crowded and so desolate at once. As I watched, two of them drew close to each other, but just before they came near enough to speak, they pulled away, as if an invisible wall had sprung up between them. The longer I watched those half-creatures, the more I understood why the dead were called shades.

The light shifted again as I walked on. Greyness gave way to a darker atmosphere, without the smoke of the first region. Here, my footsteps echoed, the soft slap of my sandals magnified by the silence. I whispered to Eurydicius that I was coming, and when again I heard no reply, I knew that our connection had been blocked. For a moment, the weight of utter loneliness fell upon me.

I knelt down beside one of the lights. A pale blue glow emanated from a small lamp, just enough to make the next few planks visible. I did not know who I should thank, so I sent a prayer to Hera, uttering it through gritted teeth.

The lamps allowed me to edge forward, but I had to watch where I put my feet; all around me the darkness thickened until I was walking through a soup, and the urge to call out to Eurydicius and reassure him – and myself – grew. A gutted feeling took over. I imagined the grinding of a world where Eurydicius and I could not even whisper to each other. Without each of us there to understand the other, would we cease to exist?

Only two choices seemed possible: yield to despair, or push past the fears that stood in my way, walking through smoke and pitch and the hot winds that threatened a spreading blaze.

I kept moving, one tiny step at a time.

A cry carried on the wind, sailing up to the bridge. It had scarcely faded when a scream followed it, a rasping voice hurling its agony into the depths of the Underworld. The sound made me stumble, for the pain in that shriek hit me like a punch to the stomach. Staring down into the tar-like depths, I caught sight of a circle of fire burning on a small plateau.

Atop a burning wheel, a man lay stretched out, strapped to the rim by his wrists and ankles. His skin bubbled with blisters. The fire left only his face unscathed, and as I stared, I recognised lips that had sneered at me and eyes that had burned with contempt.

I wanted to clamber down; to scrabble and slide until I could yank his ties loose. I wanted to drag him away. Could I spare enough time to rescue Ixion, this wretched creature who could not move to evade his torture? Or would Hades find me and cast me out before I could reach Eurydicius?

Teetering on the edge of the plank, I wondered if I could land safely on that plateau. A woman's voice cut through the air.

'I did not take you for a reckless fool.'

She was standing with her arms at her sides, perfectly still, a few paces before me. A moment ago, the bridge had been empty. My gaze swept over her simple gown and up to her face, which was etched with a frown.

'Anyone who climbs down into Tartarus, thinking to return alive, is most certainly a reckless fool.' The hard lines of her posture warned me not to try a retort.

'Tartarus,' I echoed.

Had I dreamed it, or had she really spoken the name of the cruellest region of the Underworld, where the souls of the damned prayed for a second death just to be released?

'Yes. The place from which none return. Do you really think you can rescue that man, Orphia, daughter of Calliope?'

Ixion shrieked again. In the darkness, his wheel began to turn, a sudden spinning of fire on the plateau, and I heard another cry of agony, flaring like the flames.

'Come,' the woman said, extending her hand towards me. A lamp appeared above her palm, floating there, so that she looked exactly like the portrait in Calliope's chamber, and I realised with a shock that I was looking at my grandmother. Her skin paled for a few seconds, then brightened again, and I wondered how much of Mnemosyne's spirit Hades had stolen.

'I am honoured to be your descendant. If the bridge were not so feeble here, I would get on my knees,' I said.

'No kneeling is necessary for a poet ... or a granddaughter.'

'If I cannot rescue Prince Ixion here, how can I rescue Eurydicius?'

Her face softened, and her lamp wobbled a little. 'That must wait.'

There was hope in that reply. If Mnemosyne knew why I was here, then maybe, just maybe, I would make it all the way to my husband, and lead him by the hand from this nightmare of smoke and flame. My grandmother beckoned me forward, and we passed over the rest of Tartarus until the shrieks and cries faded, giving way to a mingling of shouts, the sound growing fainter and fainter. When silence took over, I could still hear those screams in my mind.

I tried to focus on the wonder of finding another piece of my family. Calliope. Gaia. Mnemosyne. It was extraordinary to think that I had met my elders now: that it was not Apollo alone whose blood swirled through me, but a whole chain of women. I felt stronger upon looking at the woman before me; almost capable of braving those screams.

'How much do you know of Queen Persephone?' Mnemosyne said.

'Little of her character. But I was taught that Hades carried her off to be his bride.'

'It sounds romantic, does it not? *Carried her off.* As if she wanted to come.' She kicked a stone off the edge of the next plank and it disappeared. 'Persephone's mother, Demeter, railed against her abduction – and the act that would surely follow. When Zeus ruled that it was lawful, Demeter's black rage bubbled inside her like a fountain. In full fury, she told Gaia, and the earth goddess rent the ground, cracking and cracking it until the soil was too treacherous to walk on. Whilst the ground split, Demeter refused to let the trees bear fruit.'

The ingenuity of it crept over me. Without land to farm or fruit to pick, the people would have starved; they would have cried out that the chief of the gods had abandoned them. Zeus' heroes could not have completed their quests without food, either. I had to admire the mind that had targeted Zeus where it hurt: in his reputation.

In front of me, Mnemosyne slowed her pace.

'Demeter and Zeus reached a bargain. Now, Persephone dwells in the Underworld for half of the year. She walks on the earth as goddess of spring for the other half, free to love and laugh. Unlike me.' There was no rage in her voice, and I could not tell whether she was angry, sad, or merely pensive. 'Have you guessed why I am telling you this, Orphia?'

'Because you wish to warn me?'

'Because Hades asked me to tell you the story of his conquest.' Mnemosyne reached the end of the bridge and glided smoothly onto the ground, stopping in front of a pair of small gates.

'You see,' Mnemosyne said, 'when women work together, they succeed. Hades believes that his abduction of Persephone is the story of one man getting his way. But perhaps ...'

'Perhaps it is the story of two goddesses joining forces?'

'You are quick-witted.' She stepped back, clearing my way to the gates. 'Persephone will like you.'

I waited, and waited. She did not move. 'I have lived most of my life without knowing I had a grandmother,' I said. 'Will you come with me?'

'The thrones of the Underworld lie beyond these doors. I can go no further. All of your family walks with you, Orphia,' she added, taking my hand and squeezing it. 'We are not here because of the blood running through your body, but because we have chosen to be your family. Our support is no accident.'

'And I choose you.' Tears blocked my view. 'I had not guessed that love would shine in the darkest of places.'

'That is where love does its greatest work.'

She let go, and watched me pass. The gates opened to admit me, a sliver gradually widening, allowing me to see a haze of smoke ahead. When I looked back, Mnemosyne stood just before the end of the bridge, her lamp bobbing beside her, her body unmoving.

What was it that Erato had said? *You will find your way to all kinds of places, and there may come a time when love is the only thing you grasp in the darkness.*

Gathering my strength, I straightened, and stepped forward into Hades' private domain. I entered the room at a steady pace, not striding but not hesitating either, making my way through swirls of grey smoke and ash flakes that fell from somewhere above. Heat blew against me in a solid wave, turning my eyelids into a molten slurry. Surely, my skin was going to sear off; my lips would crack and peel back any second now. Somehow, I pressed on, until the grey plumes parted and I glimpsed two thrones rising from the middle of the floor, the ash avoiding their occupants.

'You should kneel, and thank me for my generosity in receiving you. You have been granted permission to walk here, where others burn.'

The speaker shifted in his chair, looming over the pile of small white boulders that were stacked almost to his elbow. Against the smoothness of his dark locks, his crown of bones looked almost beautiful, if you could forget the ribs and vertebrae that nestled on his head, strung together by some intangible thread. His high cheekbones stood out like slashes through the smoke, while his eyes were sunless oceans, unrippled by my arrival.

From the throne beside him, a woman rose. 'My love,' she said, 'let our guest sit, not kneel. She has come a long way for this audience.'

A snap of her fingers, and a chair appeared, carved with a design of entwined flowers. I sat, and felt a sudden coolness, the wind no longer inflicting its violence upon my face.

'Thank you, great queen,' I said, looking up into Persephone's eyes.

'It is my pleasure. Perhaps we should consider how you made your journey all the way to us.' She radiated kindness, even as the black flowers strung through her hair and the dread power of her voice gave out a different kind of aura. I had the impression that she was speaking to Hades, even as she looked at me, and he gave an infinitesimal nod, motioning lazily with one hand.

'Orphia, the greatest poet in all Greece, defeats our guardian Cerberus, yet never lifts a hand,' Persephone said. 'The three-headed beast lets her walk right through our gates. Such an event has never happened in all the ages I have dwelt here. A miracle, would you not say, my love?' Persephone turned to her husband.

Hades scowled. 'A petty trick. Somehow, she fooled the beast.'

'On the contrary. The hound is as quick-witted as ever. I say our guardian cannot help seeing her as a shade – for this woman is so stricken with grief that she seems less than half alive. So strong is her love for the shield-maker that his very absence saps her vitality. And yet this same grief fuels her determination, I think.'

The kindness in her eyes told me she spoke the truth. I was as good as dead to the guardian-dog of the Underworld. I almost wanted to laugh: such was my pain that I seemed a walking corpse, even in the house of death.

'She charms the Acheron with her poetry, speaking her sorrow in phrases that burst into luminous power, and swims fearlessly down the river. She walks over the bridge, past the Asphodel fields and the pits of Tartarus, to reach us here. So deep a feeling. So rich a pain.'

Did she truly understand how I felt? I could not help but hope. My will had brought me this far. I would take whatever grains of faith I could find, to keep my resolution firm.

'Come closer, woman.' Hades beckoned me. I walked over and knelt at his feet, hoping that this was what he wanted. I could not tell if my submission had pleased him. My gaze fixed on the pile of boulders beside his throne – boulders which were not boulders, I now saw, but gaped with eye sockets and shone with teeth. The chipped ends of incisors made me recoil.

'Do you like my skulls?' Hades said. 'They belonged to those who attempted to trespass here. Cerberus has had many a good meal. Tell me, woman, do you think my wife is right about the power of your grief?'

'I could not say, great king.'

'Then you cannot be very special or clever, can you? Where are your golden words now, hmm?'

'They desert me in the face of your wonderful majesty.'

He smiled and tilted his angular face in my direction. 'Rise, then.' I clambered to my feet. 'Those muscles are impressive. On a man, they would be handsome. On a woman, they suggest something quite unnatural. A desire to attack, perhaps?'

'I have brought no weapon but my tongue,' I said.

'And I see that you have sharpened it.'

The idea of hurling a verse at him tempted me – I could describe, for the first time, what I had encountered when I returned from the *Argo*: Eurydicius' body, lifeless and pale, lying on the floor; the crimson puncture marks on his ankle; the purple larkspur flower I had pulled from his hand; the red daubs of anemone poppies around his anointed body, perfuming his death-bed. I thought of screaming at Hades of how I had crushed the clods of earth until they poured in a stream of grains onto my husband's face. I could launch my grief at him in a hundred different verses, each more furious than the last. The idea dangled before me. I reminded myself that I had not come here to clash with Hades.

I would make this god nothing more than soil to walk over.

'My love.' Persephone walked to his side and touched a lock of his dark, shining hair, twirling it around her forefinger. 'Countless people weep for their beloved, yet never make it so far as Orphia, daughter of Calliope, has done. Why not hear her out? She has not attempted to sneak past you to find her husband. She came here honestly, and you do not punish the honest. If you are not moved by her plea, then you may send her back to the upper world; if you *are* moved, then you will have proof of her talent and the power of her love. That will be reason to reunite her with the shield-maker. After all,' she leaned down, looking at him, 'surely it is almost impossible for a poet to move the sovereign of the Underworld?'

She let go of his hair, and I saw the flowers strung through her own hair brighten a little, as if they had gained a small burst of vitality. She pointed to my golden lyre, and I unstrapped it and brought it forward tentatively, placing it on the ground and glancing at Hades.

'You are right. It is almost impossible,' he said.

The light played upon the lines of his cheekbones, and though smugness infused his expression, it was hard not to be affected by the sheer beauty of that face. Somehow, I forced myself to recall what I had determined to say. I dipped my head and picked up my lyre.

It was the easiest thing in the world to run my fingers across the strings, pulling a plea from them before I had begun my own. Music spread through the air like warm honey. As I played, I forgot the ash and the smoke and absorbed the music's life-force, merging with the sound.

'Great king of the Underworld,' I began, 'great queen of springtime and darkness, I sing to you of love. I do not come to slay your harpies or your furies, nor to smite the heads of your peerless hound. I seek revenge on no one, and demand no riches. But if you will hear me, I will share my sorrow with you.

'I walked here in search of my husband, who once waited patiently for me on lofty Mt Parnassus. While I aided the Argonauts, he wove a cloth of encouragement around me, reaching me across land and sea. Ever since we first laid eyes upon each other, he has offered me support and belief: faith in my art, and faith in myself. He gave the world nothing but gentleness and lavished me with respect and care. He was picking flowers for me when a snake, envying our union, thrust its fangs into the tender flesh of his ankle.

'I thought I would bear my sorrow through endurance. After his death, I tried to return to my work. Yet the force of that same love he showed me in life came to bear upon my spirit. I know that you will understand this, for I have heard the tale of how King Hades sought out Queen Persephone, wild with passion, and took her in his arms, carrying her here out of love. Such an act could only be born of nobility of sentiment. You too have felt love's grip.

'I, Orphia, implore you to unbind my Eurydicius from this realm. Loosen the bonds around his wrists and ankles, whether they are real or magical, and allow him to live out his days in the upper world in all their ripeness, before he returns. For we all return. You are our ultimate sovereigns and we cease our striving at last when we arrive at your gates.

'If destiny binds *your* wrists, and forbids you to show my love mercy, then I will never return from the Underworld. You may keep us both, and delight in our deaths.'

Silence cloaked us all. The flowers in Persephone's hair reached towards me, straining to unbind themselves, a flurry of crimson and violet. Everywhere else, I felt the absence of movement: not only in my immediate surrounds but in the ashen meadows and sunken pits beyond my sight, where I could sense Ixion's wheel grinding slowly to a halt and the screams of the tortured petering out, leaving an unease in the realm's atmosphere. In the sudden stillness, the tears that had appeared on Hades' cheeks were diamonds, too bright to be real.

'My love,' Persephone said, 'I, too, weep at Orphia's plea.'

'Get away from me, woman.' Hades batted her hand away, the clash of their palms making a loud slap.

I held my position, clutching my lyre, determined not to speak until I was addressed. I could feel Hades glaring at me, could sense the force of his anger, searing me, and guessed that his new tears had prompted it. Like Zeus, he had not expected to cry. All the more urgent, then, was my memory of Eurydicius sobbing against me after he learned of his parents' deaths, nestling into my side; I reminded myself that my husband had been brave enough to let his sorrow flow without shame, despite the contempt and cruelty meted out to all men who dared to feel. He had shown me a side of himself that the man sitting before me, staring furiously into my face, would never permit himself to reveal.

'You know well the laws of the Underworld. Mortals are forbidden to enter. Your very presence before my throne is a defilement of my rule,' Hades said.

'Perhaps it is a blessing,' Persephone put in, 'for now you will be on your guard against any others, knowing that it is possible for Cerberus to fail. Orphia has helped us, in showing us where our protection needs improvement. If you send her back at this moment, it will be no different to her leaving a little later; so let her go to her Eurydicius first.' She dropped her voice slightly. 'Her plea has moved you where no man's cries ever could.'

Hades rose from his throne. 'Do you think that *you* can set rules here? I would wager that you have forgotten why I brought you here. I made you my wife, and wives obey.'

'You are wise to reproach me, my love.' Persephone dropped quickly to her knees. 'My true sovereignty lies in blessed Elysium, the realm of sun-tinged fields and rivulets of crystal, where the virtuous dead greet me.' She shot a look at me, for less than a heartbeat's length, before returning her gaze to Hades. 'Here, I am but your loving servant, as everyone knows.'

I waited. Hades' gaze moved from me to his wife, and his lips curled into a cruel smile. 'I see that you know your place.'

'I ask you in supplication. This poet could charm the stars themselves, and she has moved me, a woman, to tears. My love, can you help her?'

As she spoke, she pressed her head to her husband's knees. He reached down and fondled her hair, that vicious smile never leaving his face. 'Very well,' he said. 'I find myself in a kindly mood. She may return with Eurydicius to the upper world – on one condition.'

I dared not speak.

'She must lead him out of the Underworld without looking back, or she will have to leave him here forever.'

My throat tightened. It was as if my body could not cope with taking in air whilst his words sank into my mind. I looked to Persephone, who caught my eye and nodded; a simple gesture, but one that made me take courage.

'I accept,' I said.

Hades clicked his fingers, and the ash and smoke cleared to leave a path to the gates of the throne room, the twin doors opening without touch. 'We will make our way to the region near the entrance,' he said. 'Mnemosyne, who remembers every shortcut in this kingdom, will find your husband.'

'Can I go with her?' I asked.

Hades turned the full force of his elegant beauty upon me, angling his face towards me. 'Why, woman?'

'I would look upon my love, at least once, before I must turn my back and walk away from him.'

'If you do so,' Persephone said, 'I will need to check you both over at the meeting point. I am zealous in defence of justice. If you think of smuggling a bell to him, for instance, to mark his steps with sound, you must think again. An obedient woman does not cheat a king.'

There was a twist in the word *obedient* as it left her lips – the slightest twist, barely audible, if you were not listening carefully. Hades did not seem to mark it. 'You think well,' he said, smiling at Persephone. 'I permit you to search them very thoroughly.'

He turned his gaze to me, and that smile transformed to a snarl. 'Get out of my sight.'

25

We walked swiftly along the bridge, our footsteps the only accompaniment to our breath. Once we had passed some way from the throne room, I took Mnemosyne by the hand, and my voice came out low and raw. 'They have permitted me to see my husband.'

'I know.'

'Are you not pleased for me?' *Grandmother*, I wanted to add.

'As pleased as one can be, in this place.' I had the impression that she was holding something back. We turned a corner, and I stared, for there had been no pathways leading off the bridge before, just a long, narrow walkway of rotten boards; and yet here we were, pushing through a tangle of vines. Flowers brushed against my cheeks as I squeezed through the plants: pale silver flowers, soft and ambrosial in their scent. On the other side, we stood in almost complete darkness, a few streaks of light revealing an expanse of rocky ground.

I faced my grandmother and took in her unworried countenance.

'How did you hide a whole section of the Underworld from me?'

'Not only you. Everyone who glimpses the turning from the main bridge forgets that they have seen it, immediately afterwards. Unless they have the goddess of memory with them, of course.'

At a click of her fingers, a lamp appeared in the air beside her. 'Come.'

We picked our way over rubble and between boulders to where a steep hill rose. Mnemosyne's fingers curled around my arm. 'There is something you must understand.' She fixed her gaze on me. 'When Calliope told me how you protected Eurydicius from a wild boar, I knew that my granddaughter was strong and loving in equal measures. I made my choice, then. I will not say that it was easy to make the decision to defy Hades, but I prepared myself long before your husband arrived here.' She waved a hand around us. 'And not only with this region.'

Possibilities danced before me, twirling in circles. 'What should I know?'

'Only that I have preserved his memories. No doubt Hades thought it would be best not to tell you that the shades drink from a stream deep in the Underworld, a dark river we call Lethe. Its water allows them to forget their lives.'

I tried not to show the horror I felt; the thought of finding Eurydicius with all his memories stolen hit me so forcefully, I could not speak.

'I made sure that Eurydicius was not taken there, but to another place: a pool I keep for those who wish to feel and to remember. There, I let him drink, until the magic of oblivion could not touch him. I led him to this region, where I cast a spell to keep him suspended in a kind of dreamless sleep. Hades does not know this, you understand.'

I stepped forward and embraced Mnemosyne. The light wobbled beside her, throwing beams of silver over her forehead. Something occurred to me as I let go of her. 'Even in the hold of your magic, his mind found its way to me.'

'Do you speak of witchcraft?' Her eyes narrowed.

'No spells were needed. We have been in conversation ever since he passed from the upper world. It is thanks to Eurydicius' urging that I stand before you now.'

'Then the kind of magic you share is rarer than any I know.' She laid a hand upon my forearm. 'Do not waste it.'

I realised that she was waiting for me to move. Staring up to the summit of the hill, I saw a single light shining there, shrouded in a layer of smog. I looked back at Mnemosyne, and she nodded.

My palms hurt from grabbing the tops of rocks to steady myself, and by the time I reached the top, the pain seemed a marker of my efforts to find him. I welcomed it. Stepping onto the hilltop at last, I emerged into a pale mistiness: the smog cleared in the middle of the ground, and I nearly shouted. For a long time, I had been telling myself that this moment would come and that I would do what seemed impossible, but I had never truly allowed myself to imagine what it might feel like to see him at last.

There are times when the need for urgency is plain, yet even as you recognise it, something more primal in you resists moving, willing you to sate yourself with emotion, like a bucket that needs to be filled from a very deep well. An ache ran through me and I dropped down beside Eurydicius' body, my knees landing on soft petals. A carpet of roses covered the rock's surface where he lay, and a wreath of pink roses decorated his hair – the same wreath he had worn as he walked towards me at our wedding.

His locks flowed out behind him in rivulets of gold; even the crowding smoke could not dim his beauty, and the heat left his skin unblemished. Relief overwhelmed me. Vines twined over his legs and body, and although most of his sapphire wedding chiton had burned in the Underworld's heat, the lower part remained tied around his hips – so at least he would have some modesty, if I could bring myself to act.

Something raw and powerful writhed inside me. I forced myself to remember why I was here. I was not going to let sheer misery overwhelm me, nor the foaming wave of love wash me aground here until I could only stare at him, clasp him in my arms, and whisper to him. But I wanted to. I wanted to hold him until our bones became dust.

With the slightest touch, I traced the line of his upper lip, running my finger from one side to the other, working his tiny smile into my memory.

Was it unusual, for the dead to give off heat? A gentle warmth lingered on my finger even after I had removed it. A tear dropped onto my knee, and I could not stop another from falling; I pressed my lips to his brow and kept them there while more tears fell. I kissed his neck, his arm, his thigh. I had to tell myself that this would not be the last time; that I could not luxuriate in his scent and shape.

'We will speak again in the sunlight,' I whispered.

Lifting him to his feet, I propped him against me for a moment. I felt grateful for my years of training in combat as I hefted him bodily, tucking one hand beneath his thighs and supporting his back with my other hand. 'I will die before I give you up,' I said, louder.

Perhaps this was how my fame was destined to be earned – not in polished verses, but in the struggle to steal him from Hades' domain – and yet a ripple in my chest told me that love had not sapped my poetry, but strengthened it. The very sight of him inspired me. I would show the whole world what an equal love meant and brighten my words until they scintillated, if I ever made it out of here.

Grey smog blocked my way to the edge of the hill, turning every step into a treacherous gamble, and only by remembering the love of Calliope, Gaia and Mnemosyne did I make it out of the smoke cloud and begin to descend the slope, their belief in me driving every step. Partway down, I stumbled on a rock and thought that I would fall, and we would both crack our heads, a bloody finale after all that labour to get here, yet I managed to right my balance and carry on. With smaller steps, I shuffled my way to the foot of the hill.

Mnemosyne's lamp bobbed a greeting, guiding me through the darkness.

'Careful,' she warned, as we neared the circle of vines and silver flowers.

I stopped before the door, judging the distance I would need to duck. 'I can get him through.'

'That is not my concern. Nothing angers Hades like the sight of a woman carrying a man. If you lift him, you show what all women might achieve – with training and practice.' She flexed the fingers of one hand. 'I could cast a spell, to move him along … now that I need no longer keep this region hidden, my power may be fully restored.'

'I would rather carry him myself.' My words came out stiffly. I did not want to let go of him, no matter what power Mnemosyne could offer.

I walked on before she could protest.

A journey through the Underworld should terrify, or, at the very least, appal. Our walk back over the chequered planks of the bridge brought the cries of the tortured drifting up to my ears, but muffled, as if blocked by my own emotions. I could feel Eurydicius' thighs against the palm of my right hand, and a wave of disbelief passed through me at the knowledge that the sweetest man in the world was propped against me – that he was in my grip once more, and he was not cold, nor drained of memory. I wanted to savour every moment that I held him.

Mnemosyne tapped my shoulder when we passed out of the greyness of Asphodel and approached the first region of the Underworld. My footfalls seemed louder, though perhaps it was just that the swirls of thick smoke consumed all other noise. Mnemosyne took Eurydicius from my arms and stood him upright on the bridge, and I fought the urge to grab him bodily. Every second that he swayed on the planks was a torment.

'Hmm.' She examined his person. 'We cannot keep him suspended when the task begins. If you try to lead a sleeping man from the Underworld, Hades will cast aside your bargain. He will claim that you tried to twist the terms.'

She began to chant, the quiet hiss of her words obscuring their edges. Silver dust glimmered around Eurydicius' head, lending him a glow that was eerie and not at all comforting to watch; he shivered, floated a little way into the air, then gasped and floated back down. His eyes opened and fixed upon me.

'Orphia.' His voice was sunlight on a frosted lake.

I scarcely dared to believe that he was speaking. I wanted to grab him around the waist. I wanted to shake him gently, to make sure that he would not vanish.

'Eurydicius,' I whispered.

'You risked everything.' His words came out tinged with gratitude.

'To do nothing would be to risk everything,' I said, closing the space between us, wrapping one arm around his neck and stroking him.

'I caused this. My own foolishness brought me here. Orphia … all I want is for your poetry to ring in halls the world over, and for you to gain what you deserve. Go back to the world. Forget about me, and—'

I pressed my lips to his.

Could I map his soul by drinking in the bright warmth of him? Perhaps I could heal the wounds within my consciousness by kissing him until I knew the taste of his palate, his teeth, the underside of his tongue.

When I felt the sunlight of his adoration pouring into me and dissolving every piece of my pain in a single rush, I knew the answer. I no longer ached. I was sunlight, too.

'This is too high a price,' he whispered, as we drew apart. 'Orphia, you worked so hard to make your poems shine. Tell me you have not risked your legacy by pursuing me here.'

'I have done what you would do.'

My throat throbbed with the joy of addressing him at last. I wanted to seize him again. I wanted to smell the soft fragrance of elm leaves upon his skin, and kiss him behind the ears; to hear him murmur my name again. I wanted to murmur other things in return.

Mnemosyne moved between us, turning to face me. Her frown was obvious even in the gloom. 'You must both be silent. There are no second chances here, Orphia.' Her gaze sharpened. 'It is because I love you that I ask you to come forward meekly, and do as he says.'

By *he*, I knew she did not mean my husband.

Ash and embers dropped around us. I led the way over the rotten planks and out of the smoke haze, stopping about twenty paces from the tiny platform of rock that lay between the bridge and the outer gates. Inhaling, I faced the rulers of the Underworld. Hades stood with his arms folded, smiling with a flint-honed calm. Persephone wore a frown, as if she were trying to look polite and landing somewhere between anxious and fearful – her clenched fists spoke of a different emotion.

I felt the air crackle, as if sparks of the Underworld's fire leapt between us all, yet I knew that it was fear I felt. I pushed it out of my consciousness as hard as I could, yet my body tingled; the danger of the moment infused my very skin.

'How pleasant it is to end this disturbance at last,' Hades said.

I shot a glance over my shoulder. Eurydicius had halted a pace or two behind me. A few strands of hair danced over his brow, the breeze unwilling to leave his beauty untouched.

Persephone approached me and extended a hand, and I felt a wave of warm air wash over me; not the noxious, smoky air of the Underworld, but a gust that carried the gentle touch of a mother. She nodded at me, and moved on to check Eurydicius. After she had performed the same spell upon him, she leaned in slightly, and I thought I saw a pinch of something silvery pass from her fingers to his lips, but it happened so quickly that I could not be sure if I had imagined it.

Had she silenced him? Was that Hades' order – to make sure my husband could not help me? Or was this some spell to ensure his compliance in following me?

Putting on the same polite, strained expression as before, she rejoined Hades and nodded. The king of the Underworld turned his lightless gaze upon me.

'The rules are clear,' he said. 'You will lead Eurydicius from the gates without looking back. You will not touch him. You will not speak to him. If you break my orders, he will remain with me forever.'

In the silence that followed, I stared at Eurydicius and tried to drink in every bit of him – to glean one last look at his gentle expression before I turned my back on him. In that moment, I wished that we could hear each other. *I would give up my last breath for you at the end of the world*, I thought. Our gazes locked, and the fraction of a nod he gave told me he was not afraid.

'Open the gates,' I said, turning back to face Hades and Persephone.

Hades snapped his fingers, and the great doors of the Underworld opened behind him, affording me a view of the hound's hulking body and the glimmer of the Acheron's surface.

'Excellent,' Hades said. 'A poet who wins the gods' praises will succeed in such a meagre challenge. Her sight is clear. Her ears are keen. Her conviction is unbending.'

I set my foot on the next plank, waited long enough for Eurydicius to draw near, and took the first step forward. As I walked into the first region of the Underworld, I heard my heartbeat, an anvil-song, quickening with each pace.

26

I had thought that the first step would be hard. My body moved with natural force, driven by the memory of carrying Eurydicius through the Underworld; I recalled the warmth of his thighs, the touch of skin much softer than my own. He gave me strength, in his very fragility, and I knew that beneath the delicate surface lay a power that outstripped my own.

I was going to save this exquisitely kind creature – the man who had worried about *my* happiness when I found him in the Underworld. I was going to make my way out of the gates, because the thought of what would happen otherwise was too much to carry.

The smoke lessened a little as I passed onto the plateau, but the taste of that haze never left my mouth: an ashen miasma that I inhaled as I moved. The promise of fire lived in that smoke, yet while flame threatened me, I too threatened to become flame. My embers refused to die.

Step after step, heavy and firm, my feet slapped the rocky ground. I wanted to look back at Eurydicius more than I had ever wanted anything: to know that he walked behind me, that I was not betraying him with each perilous footfall. Somehow, I managed to keep moving, focusing my gaze on the immortals before me.

Hades stared directly at me, breaking into a smile, and I did not like to see him so pleased. Beside him, Persephone's brow furrowed much more deeply than before, and I liked that even less; but I was still walking, was I not? There had been no trick, had there? And I could see the way out in front of me, clear and unmissable, the doors open wide enough for even my broad shoulders.

Everything seemed as it should be.

More lines dug trenches on Persephone's brow as I drew nearer. She and Hades moved out of my path.

Just a few more steps. Just a few more moments and I would be free at last, to live together with Eurydicius as one: two hearts with the same passion, differently expressed; two minds with the same capability, differently directed. Two beings with the same understanding of each other, the same acuity that pierced each other's souls – we would embrace again in the sunlight.

Persephone made the slightest movement with her lips as I drew level with her. Her forehead scrunched, and an inquiry leapt to my mouth. I caught it just in time. Yet as I took my next step, my foot slipped, my mind troubled by her desperate expression, and I threw out an arm to balance myself. The lyre tumbled from my hand.

A clang of metal against solid rock pierced the air. The noise assaulted my senses, and I bent, and picked the lyre up; as I held the instrument before me, the last of the echoes tapered out, and I realised that I was surrounded by utter silence.

Not quietness. Not a pause in a melody of background noise. There had been no muffled sounds anywhere since I had begun to walk; the only noise, aside from the lyre falling, had been that of my own footsteps.

My resolve thrashed inside me.

I glanced sideways, taking in the visages of Hades and Persephone. They wore the same expressions as before: Hades coolly pleased, Persephone's face scrunched, anxiety deepening in her eyes.

'I am almost at the gates,' I said.

Hades smirked. My remark evidently did not merit reply.

'And all this time, I have heard one pair of footsteps, not two.'

His shrug dared me to turn the statement into a question. Was he trying to scare me into silence? The fear on Persephone's face scared me most, for I had never seen a goddess look like that.

I paused. For a moment, I thought about trying to project a question to her. That might be too great a risk, if Hades could hear me. The tang of river salt and black honey infused the air, surprising me, until I realised that I was breathing in the scent of my own fear.

I wanted to reach backward and take Eurydicius' hand; to grip those slender fingers until my knuckles ached.

Her sight is clear. Her ears are keen. Her conviction is unbending.

Why had Hades mentioned my ears?

If I kept moving, and Eurydicius did not walk behind me, I would lose him to the Underworld, a ploy of promise writing the end of my story. How could I trust without the sound of his steps?

Was the hope of saving my husband an illusion? Could you set your belief down, like the coin on a corpse's tongue, and assure yourself that it would stay in place?

Looking across, I caught the haunted aspect to Persephone's eyes. It struck me as a mirror of my own trepidation, and in that moment, I knew that I might cede all chance of fighting for Eurydicius if I walked from this place, but on the other hand ... I could stay, and wield my lyre.

I could let my words fly like spears.

If Hades was playing a game with me, I could not win by playing within the rules. I had to break them at once and fight him until he lay supine, pinned by the tips of my words. *He will seek to make you trick yourself*, Calliope had said – and where was the noise of Eurydicius' feet?

This was a test, to see if my ears were keen enough.

No. To see if my *wits* were sharp enough.

Should I challenge Hades over his deceit, then? Strike him down with rhythm and imagery?

I wanted to believe that I could do it.

Do not turn, I told myself. Questions pursued that thought, hot and angry. Had Jason not deliberately omitted the fact that Apollo would be at the inn? Had Zeus not worded his concession to Calliope carefully, so that the gods could block her way? Had King Dorus not broken his promise to shelter me? Had my own father not lied to me about my birth? I saw a bouquet of falsehoods, handed to me by gods and mortal men; every one of them had sought to trick me, except for the man I led forward now. It was right to conclude that Hades would deceive me – was it not?

Turn, I told myself.

If I was right, I would be justified. I would have the right to rain down my words upon Hades; to run back to Eurydicius and steal him away. Smoke swirled with vicious tenacity into my lungs. The day Eurydicius had handed me the necklace rushed back to me, and I remembered taking the sun-warmed metal in my hands and studying the star that hung from the first chain. *The brightest jewel in the she-bear constellation*, I had told Eurydicius. My fingers reached for it, now, beneath my armour.

He had kept me on a firm path, through dragonfire and siren-song. Now, I had the chance to be his guiding star. *Do not turn*, my conscience said. *Do not waver.*

Where was the sound of his feet?

My mind called up the second chain, where two stars dangled from one link, their tips joining, forming a single pendant. *Two souls may touch and be joined, some philosophers claim.* I thought of the larger star's tip touching the smaller star's tip so that they appeared fused, and I imagined a god with lightless oceans for eyes grabbing those stars and tearing them apart.

Before me, that same god watched me approach.

I stared at Hades' lips, pressed together in an exquisite yet venomous smile, and remembered the way that he had pronounced 'woman', spitting the word at his wife, at me.

If you keep walking, I told myself, *you will never be able to fight.*

I turned.

Eurydicius' pupils widened as I looked into his eyes. His lips parted, but made no sound. I only faintly registered Persephone's horrified cry and Hades' half-bitten-off laugh; instead, I focused on my husband. Even through the shock that twisted my insides, I saw the sorrow on his face quickly give way to something else.

He whose justice extends widely.

No anger, no reproach, no disappointment surged in Eurydicius' eyes; only something soft and gentle eddied there.

I grasped his hand. His delicate fingers interlaced with my own. I reached to pull his body against me, gripping him by the neck, drawing him into my embrace until I could smell the sweetness of his skin. His lips found mine, and I tasted them before he transformed into smoke.

Even as he evaporated, he regarded me with a radiant forgiveness.

'No!' Persephone cried.

'Why moan, woman? He will enjoy himself in Asphodel. Well,' Hades stroked his chin, 'perhaps enjoyment is not the right word. But an eternity in the grey meadows is still not Tartarus.'

I was moving, though I did not know how. My legs stumbled forward. In my mind, fury danced with disbelief, and pain cavorted with confusion – and amidst it all, the thought pushed through that I had to reverse this decision, somehow. Looking into Hades' eyes, I discerned only contempt.

'You tricked me with sound,' I said. 'You dared to ...' I could not finish, for anger exploded in my mouth and set my tongue ablaze.

'No, idiot woman. I changed nothing. Your husband is a shade. Shades make no sound when they walk – or did your bleating Muse-mother forget to pass on that fact?'

That was what Persephone had wanted to tell me, I realised at once: the frown, the urgency in her eyes – she had feared that I would not consider *why* Eurydicius walked silently. She had feared that I would be tricked by Hades' self-assured demeanour; that I would miss the second loop, the double stitch in his plan, and yield to distrust. And now, while my lyre shook in my hands, I knew that there had been a third stitch, just to make sure: Hades had silenced Persephone during my test. She had watched, unable to call out.

Snuffing out the voices of women. It was how they set up the game so that we would lose, even as we convinced ourselves that it was our fault. If we could shout for help, then we might take the hands of our sisters, swim ashore, and manage to win.

I raised my lyre.

It all happened so quickly that now, as I look back, I still cannot quite be sure which one of us moved first. My hand was about to pluck the strings, ripping out a melody and hurling it at Hades, and my lips were already forming the first line of a poem when something hit me. I staggered, my free hand flying to my throat. It was as if all the blood in my body had welled up to block the passage of air.

Crumpling, I tottered forward, shooting a glare at Hades, but when I tried to speak, the only sound that came out was a rasp, like dry reeds scraping against each other.

Hades pointed a finger at me and smiled. His crown of bones gleamed, pale and lustrous in the smoky air, as he raised his hand and sent me soaring over the rocky ground.

I gasped and hacked, clutching my lyre. Cerberus raised his heads as I flew over him, and the Acheron glittered darkly below me while I flew back, back, in the direction from which I had arrived, my lungs still straining for air, my tongue seeking words. Ripples appeared and disappeared on the river, and I flung out my arms, unable to slow myself.

I had the strangest feeling that I was being expelled from my own life's story: that the ending was being snatched from me, and I was to be written over by Zeus' brother, the man who had carried off a woman for his pleasure, who had seen my muscles as a threat.

Smoke filled my mouth. The ferryman shouted something at me from his moored boat. I was already shooting up the tunnel that Gaia had made for me in the earth, back up into clear air, screaming my refusal to the blue sky, the wisps of cloud, the flood of pitiless sunlight.

The thump must have set every leaf in the forest trembling. By all rights I should have died, landing face-down on the solid ground. I could feel no spikes of pain in my arms; no stickiness at my temples, either, and against all odds, my lungs heaved. I dragged myself to my knees.

'Eurydicius,' I whispered.

No reply came. But the sound of my own voice was clear enough, once more.

In my mind's eye, I saw Eurydicius dying again, this time from across the cavern. My other self kissed him, and he vanished in my arms; the one person who had been real to me throughout every unreal twist in my life's thread, evanesced in wisps of smoke.

I was a fool. An arrogant fool. To believe that Hades would have kept Eurydicius back, ripe for the plucking – to assume that I could fight the king of the Underworld and seize my husband! I had thought so highly of my wits that I had believed them superior to Hades'. But Hades had followed his own rules perfectly. The trick had lain in his words, and in the spaces between them.

Her ears are keen.

I deserved to be trapped in the Underworld. Not Eurydicius.

A sob tore through my throat, but crying did not interest me. There was only one thing that would be useful to both of us, now that I had squandered his only chance of returning to the earth's surface.

Be a sprouting tree, I told myself. *Be root and rock and branch. Force yourself to find a way to where you need to be. For him.*

The roar of twin streams told me where I was, and I dragged myself towards the waterfall. I seemed to have lost the ability to walk easily, but no matter – I would haul myself, whatever the pain.

'Hear me, anyone who would listen,' I croaked, and I was relieved to hear my voice sound clearly again, ravaged though it was. 'I have walked in the realm of the dead and broken, and I have brought you back a tale.'

Stones scraped my legs and knees, hard enough to draw blood, yet they did not succeed in serrating my skin, and somehow I knew that the rocks refused to hurt me. Poetry poured from me, golden rivers of words merging, and I shaped and honed my account as I spoke, throwing everything into my description of Eurydicius kissing me – Eurydicius forgiving me – Eurydicius turning into smoke.

Beyond the slick boulders, the waterfall still poured, forming a deep pool before the gorge began to run downhill. It was easy enough to climb over the nearest boulder and slide down into the pool, kicking away from the rocks and swimming into the middle. Perhaps it had been this easy for the snake I dropped in, with only the cool essence of water surrounding it before it drowned. Ever so slowly, I closed my eyes and stopped moving.

The purity of death is something you can almost grasp as you sink beneath the surface of a pool. Nothing blew through my mind; nothing stirred up the husks of memories. I was losing air. I recognised this, and yet it seemed right. This was the easiest way; the swiftest way. Compared to the agony of striving with a blade, all I had to do was let myself fall, and I would find him.

My lungs stopped questing for air. For a few blessed moments, it seemed that death had arrived. Then something like a geyser erupted underneath me, and I flew.

Life filled my lungs and propelled me angrily upwards. I shot out of the pool and landed on my back, gasping, coughing up spit and water onto my chest. Above me, the sky peeked through a tapestry of branches.

'Damn you,' I whispered, glaring at the leaves.

He was waiting for me, in the smoke-filled caverns, amongst the ash and grit. Maybe he was sobbing as he circled around the other shades in Asphodel, his cheeks bejewelled with tears, his eyes bright with the last glimmer of hope; and I had failed him.

Clambering to my feet, I moved further down the path beside the gorge, to where the water flowed faster, surging over a bed of rocks with the hard edges of boulders on either side, a litany of thrusting points. Here, I could tumble to my death, and the force of the gorge would carry me away. The thought of stone ribboning my arms did not stall me. The prospect of rocks peeling back the flesh of my thighs did not halt me. Drawing a deep breath, I gave a final poem to the air, pulling grief from my throat, and jumped.

The water slapped my sides for a moment. A churning disrupted the flow all around me; the geyser-like force threw me up from the gorge, and I was shouting, spraying water all around me, screaming as I landed on soft soil on the other side of the rocks. 'Damn you! Let me die, that I may live!'

One last try. The water's rejection came even more swiftly this time.

He was still fading before me, evaporating into the smoky air of the Underworld. I could see his expression as if we were both still there, in that moment. The bounteous forgiveness of his gaze forced me to draw another lungful of air.

I rose, picked up my lyre, and trudged in my half-sodden chiton to the yew tree where I had prayed to Hera.

The same clusters of red berries dangled from the branches, beneath thick fringes of green leaves. I plucked two fat berries and a handful of leaves.

'Not the way I would have chosen,' I whispered.

The fruit sparkled in a beam of sunlight that had snuck through the branches. I sent a silent promise to Eurydicius and slipped the berries and leaves into my mouth.

Anger pulsed through me as my mouth spat them back out, my jaw moving against my will.

'Fine,' I said to the air, even as I took in the unchewed leaves and the still-intact yew berries. 'I will seek out every danger on this mountain, if that is how it must be. Is it you, Gaia, or is it some other deity who denies me death?'

No one answered. Seething, I set off along the narrow path that led into the forest, not caring if I stumbled. It was not long before I passed the mushroom I had sighted in the shadows, and a quick inspection told me that poison lurked in that small brown cap. My fingers closed on the stem and yanked it from the ground, clutching it so firmly that my knuckles whitened.

I almost got it to my mouth before the wind knocked it from my fingers.

My love, I thought, hoping he could hear me, *I will not abandon you, even if the whole of nature conspires to keep me alive.*

A long wander through trees and over spidering roots, past pale flowers, bark draped with tresses of ivy, and leaves gilded by distant sun brought me nothing but more defeat. I made to slam my head into a rock and found myself repelled by a sudden breeze. I provoked a wildcat with a stick, only for it to rub against me and mewl into my leg. Mushrooms and berries flew from my fingers, or came flying back out of my mouth. I even found the same fire salamander again, and made a plea to her to release her poison, but she stared at me with unwavering focus, refusing to move. The moistening of her eyes made me suspect that she had heard my poetry.

The last animal to offer me hope slithered over the roots of an oak and curled around my sandal, its grey scales sliding against the leather. I almost laughed as I looked down at the snake. The irony of this was too much. 'Go on,' I whispered.

A hiss escaped the snake's mouth and it slithered on, disappearing into a clump of leaves, the undergrowth sealing it from my sight. This time, my protest came out as a sigh.

If I had never tried to save him, perhaps it would not hurt so much. I had tried and failed, and the layer of pain that added was like an iron door that pressed down upon me, pushing me into dense earth, into a lightless world from which I could only imagine the sun of his smile, the pure glow of his voice. Every wrong done to him was my fault. His parents' deaths – because I had caused my father's wrath. The snake's bite – because I had brought him to Mt Parnassus, and then abandoned him. His fate in the Underworld – because I had thought I could bring him back to the upper world. Hope flitted from my grasp, and I felt pain hollow out my body.

Of course, he might hate me, now. If I ever glimpsed his face again, it might be contorted with a new-grown loathing, born of the realisation that I had wrecked his life. But even that did not stop me from lying down and praying to Hera, one more time, to grant me death.

The silence of Mt Olympus answered me. I looked up at the branches of the oak and something wet filled my eyes. Crying was his right, I told myself: not mine. The tears flowed all the quicker, for that, and I sobbed out the lines I had first spoken in the Hall of Starlight, raw emotion obscuring some of the words.

'Tell me, Muse, of a man like water, who came close enough to the sun-girl that she could see him ripple in the light. Tell me of his yielding smile, of the doors that opened in his eyes. Tell me of all the worlds, real and unreal, that they might have explored, and tell me of how he was snatched away.'

Silence, again: then, after a moment, the chiming of a thousand bells came ringing through the treetops and branches, on and on, swelling until the sound filled every corner of the forest. The birds echoed my sorrow back to me and amplified my agony a thousand times, and I lay on the soft earth, listening to the song of my own despair, letting my tears flow.

Nature was crying for me. And because nature pitied me, I was condemned to cry.

There were no plants left to try, and no animals left to provoke. Whatever poison lurked in the undergrowth, it was not going to yield itself to me, so I faced the canopy of the trees with renewed strength, allowing the tears to ebb.

'If you will not kill me, great Queen of Heaven, time will do it for you. I will lie here until my body starves, and my mind will sharpen itself until it is ready.'

For the moment when I am reunited with him, I did not add.

I lay there for a day and a night. When the light of dawn filtered through the treetops, I wandered a little, speaking my grief and playing the lyre, but not seeking food. A patter of feet made me aware of the badgers, wildcats and dormice that followed me without a hint of animosity. Whenever I ceased to speak, they clustered around me, eyes shining.

Hunger nested in my stomach when I slept again. The third night brought a desperate thirst which overpowered even the solid presence of starvation inside me; I felt a strange power in the honing and focusing of my will as my flesh wasted away. My only other comfort was my golden lyre – the sight of it reminded me that every joyous moment in my life had truly been real.

As my feet wandered, so did my sense of time. I could no more count the sunrises and sunsets than I could remember where on Mt Olympus I was. Oaks and beeches blurred with the quicksilver flash of the gorge's water, while the gloss of silver moonlight on leaves melted into the pink and lavender drapery of dawn. The more my days flowed together, the more my vision of Eurydicius brightened, until I was content to sit for hours in the heat of the afternoon, picturing his face, tracing every line of his soft eyelashes in my mind. Every few minutes, one of the things he had said to me would repeat itself.

I wish you could see yourself as I see you: a hero whose words shine like beaten gold, lighting up a path for others to walk on.

Believe in the power of your every word.

You are the most remarkable person I have ever known. Every detail of the moment you first spoke to me in that courtyard is carved in my mind, as if you had scored it there with a blade.

I knew I was listening to a hero, and her magic was not cruelty but poetry.

Before you, I lived in greyness.

I was sitting in one such reverie when a sound pulled me from my thoughts: a glistening of notes in a single voice, like rain mingling with stars.

'The Muses did not think I should come.'

I opened my eyes and looked into Calliope's face.

'Euterpe thought it would break me to see you like this. Erato said the same. But I gave birth to you, and I suffered your abduction. I am less breakable than they think.' She extended a hand to me. 'It is your flesh that needs salvation.'

She clicked her fingers. A bunch of grapes dropped from the air and I cupped my hands just in time to catch them. The dark globes of fruit heated my skin. I knew at once that these were no ordinary grapes, and I knew, too, from my mother's expression, that I would be unwise to refuse this gift.

'I want your physical form to be full and strong when you see him again.'

I looked into her eyes for a long moment.

'Faced with a desperate daughter, most mothers would wail and beat their breasts, begging their child not to die,' Calliope added. She plucked a grape from the bunch and placed it, loose, in my palm. 'But I know you are chasing the one thing that will make your days burst with colour again.'

Colour ... compared to a world bleached of life. The eye sockets of the skulls beside Hades' throne gaped again in my memory. Teeth shone, in that pile of white pates: teeth that would never again work to form words.

Voiceless. That was how Hades liked his women. Persephone knew it better than anyone; yet had I not seen her look in my direction when she conceded to her husband? And had I not seen her drop a pinch of something silver onto Eurydicius' lips, as she checked him over? Perhaps I was reaching too easily for any scrap of hope, as a starving man clutches at bare branches.

Calliope took the loose grape from my palm and held it against my lips. 'Eat, Orphia. You have another journey to make.'

We held each other's gaze for a long moment. At last, she smiled, and I managed the slightest of smiles in return.

The fruit tasted sweeter than any I had ever known: not a cloying sweetness, but a deep and healthful flavour. As I devoured more of the grapes, I felt my stomach warming. The heat of the grapes travelled through me from my hair to my toes, and only now did I realise how cold I had become while I denied myself food; heat and fullness swirled within me, and with them came a harder power. For the first time in many, many days, I felt as if I were living in my own body.

You were right, mother, I thought, projecting the words to her. *Strength of flesh brings joy to the soul.*

It is joy I wish for you, Orphia.

She did not smile to match her words. Staring at her, I understood. The reality of what we would both go through came plummeting to land upon my shoulders. All this time, I had been thinking of being *with* Eurydicius, not of all the people I would be *without*. And chief amongst them loomed my mother, standing before me now, her gold-flecked chiton and her heavy golden crown exuding majesty, yet not half so elegant as the lines of pain on her face.

'It will be worse for us than for Demeter and Persephone.' My words came out in a whisper. 'At least they are allowed to dwell together, mother and daughter, for half of the year.'

'It will.'

'Why do you not stamp your feet? Or seize me by the shoulders and shake me until my teeth rattle?'

'Would it console you, Orphia, for me to make a show of anger?'

'Mother! Why must you—?'

'Deny you the opportunity to hurl your fury at Hades? To scream that it is all his fault? To shout of how he treated Eurydicius unjustly, and gave you no fair chance? That is the way Hades works: he deceives, and he controls. To fall into anger or despair is to grant him the victory.' She directed her stare to my face. 'And are you a woman who grants victory to selfish men?'

I lowered my head.

'Look me in the eye and answer me.'

Her voice smoked with ember and ash once more. I met the flint of her stare. 'No,' I said. 'I step over them to seize glory.'

Her nod made me stronger. Taking my hand, she walked me towards the sound of water, a little lower on the mountainside. The gorge silvered the slope, trickling over boulders and broken rocks, passing under the arms of branches and running on to where thicker walls of greenery obscured it from my view. Calliope stopped very close to the nearest boulder, peering down at the gorge. While she stood there, shrouded in contemplation, the voice of the water carried to me; it seemed to whisper soft and sorrowful things, but amidst its melancholy offerings I spied a few bright shards of hope.

'To be reunited with him, you must surrender your own life and any chance of wandering over the earth's surface, of dancing on a thousand mirrors with grains of sand glinting between your toes as you leap along a beach at midnight ... of greeting the sunrise from the middle of a clear lagoon. Bitter and sweet at once – is it not? But will you taste that fruit?' My mother turned to face me. 'Do you truly want love at that price?'

'I would pluck the stars and moon from the sky and live in eternal night, if it meant that I could hear his voice and live side by side with him.'

'And fame?'

I drew breath from the bottom of my lungs. 'I would strive for fame, yes. But not if fame is hollowed out, a shell left to me. If I were famous in every village in the world, if kings and queens raised their cups and cried my name, and women named their daughters after me, but it was all without Eurydicius ... what kind of life is that?'

'It might become your new life.'

'I call it a greyer existence than those shades in Asphodel endure. I could never call it a life at all. Fame cannot merely be a cauldron or a tripod – I cannot chase it as a prize made of bronze or gold, to hoard for myself. It is a river, on whose waters my stories of love and hope may be carried, flowing downhill to all parched souls. I cannot nourish them if I let go of my own love ... and I cannot give to them if I would yield up my own hope.'

Calliope sighed and took my hand once more. She rubbed my palm between hers, adding to the warmth that the magical grapes had given my flesh, and when she was done, she stroked my cheek with a single finger.

'Do not think that I will leave quietly,' I said. 'I will call to him full-throated, with words so clear that women will hear them across the world, not only now but in centuries yet unborn. They will learn that they too can create. They will learn that an equal love is possible, and that they, too, deserve a lover who seeks to raise them up to the sun-glossed clouds. I yearn to show them that they can live without the barrage of open barbs or closed fists. I will speak the two of us into legend, if I have to draw each letter from my own marrow. I will become poetry as I die.'

'Then I give you my blessing.'

I knew what it cost Calliope to speak those words, and not only as a mother. I heard the dust of long battles in her voice, the crowns of heroes clinking on her tongue. The Muse of Epic Poetry, the chief goddess of the arts, had given me the training most poets could only dream of, and here I was, telling her that I was abandoning a life above the earth. Perhaps she understood – as I guessed and hoped – that fame could outlive something so paltry as flesh.

'Not far from here, you will find a place where water pours over rock and makes a pool of such clear green, you could

mistake it for an emerald. Death will greet you there, even as
I say farewell.'

'Sharp rocks and soft mushrooms refuse to let me die,
mother. Salamanders and yew berries deny me the bliss of
death. Why should that place be any different?'

'Because you are going to seek the mad women there:
the dancers in fawnskins, the weavers of ivy, the handlers of
snakes, the women who have torn kings into pieces one limb at
a time. Come.' She held out her hand. 'Let us find the goddess
who will help you.'

27

In the cold stone of my chamber on the Whispering Isle, the word maenad had sounded in my ears for the first time. I had repeated it several times after my tutor had left, listening to it roll off my tongue. *Maenad. Maenad. Maenad.*

I turned it over in my head as I trudged down the slope, stepping over roots and rocks, remembering the phrases my tutor had used. *Violent, deranged women. Driven by Dionysus' lust.* Above all else, I remembered a simple fact: the word maenad meant a woman who used her voice. *Raving one.*

My legs ached as we pushed our way through overgrown trails. The trees here did not cover the earth with shade nor glisten with dew. Dry leaves and twigs littered the ground. A wave of air rolled over me as we turned a bend, its wild purity washing against my cheeks, and from somewhere ahead, a waterfall's melody flowed, never ceasing.

Calliope beckoned me to where the trail forked, guiding me away from the well-worn earth and onto a narrower path. Mint sprouted on the side of this trail, its soft, fuzzy leaves merging with the low bushes. Pale pink cyclamen flowers grew from beneath a rock, their petals shaped like bats' ears; as I bent down to peer at them, I imagined the wreath of pink roses nestling on Eurydicius' hair, in that lifeless place below the earth.

'Can you sense divinity?' Calliope paused. 'We are almost at the spot where the maenads come to bathe.'

I watched her inhale a deep lungful of the clean air.

'Men call this river Vaphyras. It used to be called Helicon. Either way, the river itself is a god, and gods need offerings if they are to let mortals walk in their presence unharmed.'

'I have nothing to give.' I spoke softly.

'So long as you have your voice, you have something to give.' Calliope's countenance was a storm-struck sea.

'Once you have made your offering, you will need this.' The bottle she pressed into my hand cooled my skin. Its neck felt smooth. I did not need to ask who it was for, nor what my mother expected me to do.

She turned and led me down the thin trail to the very end, where I could see light shining beyond the branches. When she stopped, I heard the raggedness of her breath. 'Remember that I am proud of you,' she said.

'You have been the greatest mother I could ask for.' My voice cracked. 'You gave me instruction, but also choice.' I put down my lyre and seized her in my arms, stronger than before, forgetting the force of my body. She let me hold on until I had ridden out the pain.

'Remember.'

Her hand found my cheek when we parted. She mouthed the word a final time before she vanished. *Remember.* Wind surged through the space where her body had been.

Warm tears painted my cheeks. I picked up my lyre and pushed through the layer of branches, clearing space enough to duck, moving headfirst towards the light – if I just kept moving, maybe I could outrun my grief, and do what I had come to do.

I liked this waterfall at once. I liked the way it poured down on the right side of the rock, and I liked the way the first pool trickled down to a second pool, the water flowing on the right there, too, the asymmetry of it carrying all the way down. It seemed all the more beautiful for not being centred.

Light bathed me as I stood beside a boulder, staring down at the series of pools. The source of sun was no mystery, for this waterfall opened to the sky – Vaphyras did not wish to conceal himself, it seemed.

The river-god poured from somewhere up high, and flowed downhill between rocky walls that rose on either side. His basin only allowed a narrow space to welcome the sun. Looking up, I saw a slice of the peak, revealed to me through the pines, and although I knew we were only a little way up the mountainside, I felt as if I were gazing straight at the gods.

Could Zeus or Apollo see me? If my father knew what I had done, and what I was about to do, would he wreak his vengeance upon me – or would it be someone else who suffered? Would Calliope, Euterpe or even the nymphs be scorched to ash?

Clutching the bottle in one hand and the golden lyre in the other, I edged down. The sharp sides of the boulders threatened to tear my skin, but the slim path formed by stones and mud permitted me to move past them. A strip of earth bordered the main basin of the waterfall. I clambered down and perched on a small log, listening; the flow of the waterfall came without a pause, as if jugs were constantly emptying their contents.

Drawn by something in that sound, I walked to the main pool and peered down. The green of the water was not jade or turquoise, but a clear emerald, as Calliope had promised, turning to a deeper seaweed green on the right side. At the edge, the water became almost transparent and the flat stones beneath appeared like coins. A ripple set them shimmering. For a moment, again, I saw myself placing the coin on Eurydicius' tongue, and felt the brush of his teeth against my fingers.

I knew that burying my husband had wounded my soul. My spirit had weakened until it nearly dissipated. Yet while I listened to the water and watched it flow into the basin, I began to hope. Slightly lower, where the main basin gave way to small rocks and the water trickled over them to the next level, the river made a softer bubbling noise.

If the maenads were murderers, as my tutor had claimed, then it could not be a coincidence that they frequented this spot, where the river flowed as soft and clear as a hymn. The air struck my cheeks, purifying my skin.

'This is where the mad women come to bathe,' I told the river-god. 'Am I not a mad woman?'

I heard Eurydicius' reply, in my own imagining: *Let us be mad together.*

I began to laugh. *Yes,* I thought, *I am mad: mad with sorrow and mad with desperation. Grief and love have made me mad enough to try to cheat death.* My laugh transformed to a sob, and I gripped my lyre tightly, bending over. So deeply had I grieved in the chambers of my soul and so forcefully had I hauled myself up, day after day, that I sensed I could create poems even richer with pain and joy – that I could touch every listener. Such was the irony of it.

I could reach them as I took death into my embrace.

Yet I remembered what I had told Calliope. Fame was a river. And I might let my nourishment flow with greater force from beyond this mortal realm.

I gazed at the waterfall. Whatever men said about the wailing of mad women, I was beyond wailing. I would be mad with creation. Mad with action. Mad with determination.

Lowering myself onto a wet rock at the side of the waterfall, I strummed my lyre and began to speak. Pain gushed from me, and I shaped it with my tongue. The whole poem seemed

scarcely a verse: there was something more in me, something
heaving, pushing upward.

'Tell me, Muse, how love grows like a stalk, seeking the air
in which it can blossom. Tell me how a lack nourishes love – a
lack of expectation, a lack of pressure, a lack of control. And in
that air, a flower grows.'

The rushes around the waterfall danced, and pine trees
bent their branches in my direction, scattering their needles.
Maple leaves carpeted the earth. I stopped strumming, and
something nudged my foot: a skink pressed its glistening body
against my sandal, its tiny eyes staring up at me. A pair of
woodpeckers flapped down from a pine branch.

Dipping one hand into the pool, I let the water run over
my skin. A gentle emotion flowed over my fingernails and
knuckles. It was familiar and new at once, for although I had
felt the sympathy of goddesses, I had never felt sympathy from
a god. I was tempted to yank my hand out.

Vaphyras immersed my fingers with his quiet care.
The jug-like pouring of the waterfall carried on, cleansing
my spirit as well as my flesh, and I thanked the river-god
in simple words. Stepping back from the basin, I held out
Calliope's bottle.

Let us find the goddess who will help you. My mother's voice
echoed inside my head.

I poured the contents onto the earth. The heady smell of the
wine mingled with an ambrosial scent, rising all around me,
and I began to pray to the first goddess I had ever worshipped.
The soft thump of a chariot came from behind me, and I
turned.

'Some would be displeased. But I am proud that you have
come to die.' Hera stepped towards me. 'You prove yourself a
passionate woman.'

I knelt, not minding the slick of wet earth against my calves.

She snapped her fingers and armour appeared by her side, along with a helmet, a spear and a shield, dangling in the air. 'Take it,' she said.

I hesitated.

'You wish to know why you need armour.' She tilted her head towards the path.

At first, I heard only the gusting of the wind, slapping my cheeks. But as I strained my ears, I began to hear footfalls – a great many footfalls, from a group marching towards us. I heard the tapping of sticks, too. Before I knew what was happening, Hera's hand curled around my waist. The two of us shot into her chariot and soared above the waterfall, the armour hovering magically beside me, the spear flying into my right hand while I clutched my lyre with the left.

We landed behind a bush, up high. Next to us, the water poured over the rock. We appeared to have stopped atop a rocky ridge, and below us the basin appeared as a clear green jewel. The pouring of the waterfall drowned out the footsteps, yet now there came a swell of song, rising above the water. A multitude of voices harmonised within that song, and the sound made me shiver. Melodic threads wove together, each voice coming in at the right moment to keep the song flowing, and I realised that I was not shivering in discomfort. That cold prickle on my skin was born of admiration for artistry, something I had not felt since I left the Muses' city – in a flash, my mind leapt to the poems I had composed for Eurydicius, about women who strove and laboured for things that seemed impossible.

I looked quickly at Hera. She put a finger to her lips. The peacocks settled onto their haunches in front of us, folding their tails.

The song grew louder as the women emerged from the tree cover, climbing down to the waterfall. Sunlight glinted off wreaths of ivy leaves, oak leaves and bryony flowers on their heads. Their long hair flew freely over their shoulders as they moved – and what a range of hair it was, from grey locks to brown and black and yellow. Swarthy women walked beside fair-skinned women. Big women walked with thin women. Hard-bodied women walked beside delicate blooms of women – and a few of them looked to be between woman and man, or seamlessly blended elements of both. I even spotted a pair of boys.

A company of maenads of all ages, living in the hills alone, without soldiers to protect them ... was I dreaming this, or had I fallen under some immortal's spell? Would Eurydicius say this group was a threat or the promise of my salvation? Either way, I knew, he would have believed that I could speak to them – he would have reminded me of the power that dwelt in my voice.

I had never beheld such costumes. The maenads all wore fawnskins, the thick fur cloaking their shoulders. Beneath the animal skins they wore chitons, the kind that I had worn my whole life, but which only men were supposed to wear: a short garment rather than a long one. I could see why they favoured it. Their ankles and calves were flecked with mud, and the scratches on their legs spoke of long hours of walking.

Snakes curled around the necks of some in the company, licking their cheeks. These vipers seemed tame as newborn lambs; the maenads paid them no heed as they sang.

The dancers in fawnskins, Calliope had said. *The handlers of snakes.*

They climbed easily, leaping over rocks and roots. Each carried a staff in their right hand, long and straight, wrapped with ivy leaves and crowned with a pine cone, and I recalled an old lesson: *the maenads carry a thyrsus, a staff to show their devotion to Dionysus,* my tutor had croaked. He had not mentioned the throbbing power that emanated from those wands. As I watched, the magic of the thyrsus washed against me and coated my skin in the scents of pine sap, wet soil, and new-grown ivy. The song carried through the air all the while.

These singers breathed majesty. I felt it in my blood and bones. Something in that song made me hope for pain, and for what might come beyond it.

Below me, the company spread out beside the waterfall, setting down the gazelle and sheep carcasses they had transported on their backs. Still singing, they raised their staffs to the sky. My body braced; if they invoked their patron god, Dionysus ...

I glanced at Hera. Her hard gaze betrayed no concern.

The singing stopped, and the maenads strode up to the rocks that fringed the basin. One tapped her thyrsus against a jagged rock. Where she struck, a crystal-clear stream sprang up: the water glistened as it arced through the air. Another tapped her staff against the earth, and a fountain of white milk gushed up. A third woman tapped the pine-cone end of her thyrsus against a tree, and a stream of honey came oozing from the bough, sparkling as it caught the sun, purer than any honey I had ever seen.

The woman who had tapped the tree tilted her head up at the sky.

'Hera!' she called, and her companions took up her chant. 'Hera! Great Hera!'

I glanced across at Hera again. A smile curved her lips.

'Your blessing flows like milk. Your protection flows like honey. As you offer us freedom, we offer you devotion!'

One of the maenads brought forward a pomegranate and cut it open upon a rock. The speaker squeezed the juice of the pomegranate onto the earth.

'Hera!' the company shouted, as one. 'Our lives belong to you!'

Then, smiling, the maenads sat down. Some shared berries and nuts amongst the group. Some twined new strings of ivy around their thyrsus. Others wove new wreaths of oak leaves, and many discoursed in pairs. Four members stood, one on each side of the group, staring at the trees. These guards carried no spears, but clutched their staffs; I began to suspect that a sharp tip of iron might be hidden beneath the pine cone on the end of each thyrsus, or at the very least, a honed point. With an unpleasant jolt, I remembered why I was here.

'A disappointing lack of madness, would you not say?' Hera's voice cut through the waterfall's burbling.

'They are not mad.' I turned my face to her. 'They are women who live together.'

'To Zeus, that is madness enough. What could women wish to do in each other's company?'

Erato would have laughed at that. A pang struck me at the thought of the Muses on Mt Parnassus.

'My tutor once told me that the god of wine protects and controls these maenads. Yet it was not Dionysus' name they called,' I said.

'You have heard them chant and shout. Only mad women would use their voices so freely, men said: *raving ones*. So the first maenads claimed that name.' Hera's words crackled. 'They spread word in the cities and towns that Dionysus gave them voice and purpose, and that theirs was a blessed madness. You see, if you are going to invoke a god's name to ward off men, you must choose a god that men respect. Dionysus is the king of debauchery. I need not explain to you what soldiers do when they are drunk on his wine.' Her look could have equalled a panther's glare. 'The maenads call their actions sacred mysteries. They claim that Dionysus will punish any who try to come near them. But it is not Dionysus who blesses them.'

I stared at a pair of maenads who were drinking from the fountain of milk. My gaze focused on the stone from which the stream gushed. Rock, earth and pine ... the mountain answered these singing wanderers.

'Great Queen of Heaven,' I said, 'you are wise beyond all Olympians. Since I came here to die, I would know – what purpose drives these maenads to Mt Olympus?' *And what help do they offer me?* I did not add aloud.

'They are women who have suffered, and others who have suffered like women.' Her gaze turned upon me, and it seemed to pierce me through. 'It began with a pair of women who had been beaten by their husbands and used most cruelly in their marriage beds. They ran away to the mountain and prayed to me. Lying naked on the grass, they showed me the marks on their bodies and told me what their husbands had done. So I protected them from the sight of gods and men.'

She was silent for a moment.

'Excepting certain men,' she added.

I followed the line of her pointed finger, to the pair of young men chatting while they wove their wreaths. They were, I noticed, just past that tender age when youths might meet an older man to show them the ways of the world ... or do as he pleased with them.

'All mortals need society,' Hera said. 'I sent those first women companions: others whose husbands or lovers had used them brutally, sometimes with fists and objects, sometimes with lies, insults and cruel demands. They formed their own tribe and learned to hunt and to gather plants. I showed them how to make a staff that can kill, and I instructed them to disguise it with Gaia's bounty.'

Ivy leaves and pine cones, but not for Dionysus. The thought gave me a prick of satisfaction.

'The women here no longer bear children for men. So when I see new cruelties amongst mortals, I send more of the abused here to renew their tribe.' Her mouth twisted. 'There is no shortage of eligible members. I have made them invisible to my fellow Olympians – that was the easiest part – and against mortals, I have created enough of a shield that no large group can find them. Yet sometimes a powerful man slips through my spell, by great cunning. Such a man is always determined.'

She paused, looking down upon the group. 'In those cases, the maenads have a plan.'

I studied the shape of the thyrsus in one woman's hand, noticing how well the pine cone concealed the tip.

'I think this is a life you could plunge into.' Hera's tone had softened, though it never smoothed all the way to mellowness. 'A group living on the mountain alone. Self-sustaining; self-protecting. You could compose your poems here and sing them in the fresh air. Death would not find you until you were old.'

'It might.'

'I would see to it that it did not.'

I looked down again, drinking in the sight of the maenads, noting their easy way of touching each other, without shame.

'It is a beautiful life,' I said. 'But it is not for me.'

I knew that she was expecting an explanation. Goddesses did not wait long.

'I fell in love before I ever left the Whispering Isle, great Hera. So deep and so rich is the joy that Eurydicius and I give each other, I cannot imagine any kind of happiness without him. He believes in my art when I, myself, doubt it, and his faith in me never wavers. I have never met another person who offered such support, like a pillar that props up a vast hall, as if its essence were stronger than paint or stone ... he inspires me to splash colour through my words; to make them as bright as he imagines them to be. And when we love one another, everything fits with ease. He receives when I give.' I drew a breath. 'It is because of such love that I carry such pain now. When I lose him, I lose half of myself.'

'It is a misfortune, then, your love.'

'It seems that way, if you only think of the pain. But when you weigh that pain with the joy … I do not think it balances to misfortune,' I said.

Hera stared at me. 'Put on the armour.'

A sinking feeling passed through me.

'You have lived as a man. Now you must dress as one,' she added.

After I had donned everything but the helmet, Hera stepped back to survey my figure. 'When I say you have lived as a man, I do not mean that you think like one. I mean that you have seized the opportunities of a man; and for that, I praise you. Not because women are weak. But because women are denied so much.' Her fingers wrapped around my wrist. 'You have seized the chance to pursue greatness, Orphia. Will you prove that you can truly weave love and fame together, with the last breath in your body?'

Her words sang through my veins. I felt their salt and iron, the tang of their potency. 'I told my mother that I would speak my love into legend,' I said quietly. 'Perhaps I aimed too high.'

'When you think of Eurydicius, do you still believe that?'

Such a simple question. Raw and succinct, stripped of all rhetoric. If I answered it, I would have to bare the part of me that I was still ashamed to acknowledge.

I wanted to compose poems for Eurydicius. For us. I wanted to make him famous, and I wanted to make our love famous. Right now, I wanted to compose the greatest poem ever made and speak it for him – and for all the women who might hear it, one day, and imagine themselves weaving words into poetry: living not as servants to men, but as equals.

After gazing at the maenads sitting below me, I looked back up at Hera.

'Never hold back your ambition. For him, or for yourself.'

'My voice will go unheard.' In speaking those words, I felt myself admitting my fear, letting it ring in the sanctum of my own conscience.

'Such words as yours, plucked from heart's blood, can never go unheard.' Hera's smile brimmed with mystery and satisfaction. 'Speak as you die,' she said. 'Speak, and pour forth the greatest poem you have ever imagined.'

I knew it, then, with all the sparkle of river pearls; I saw it as clearly as the sun on mountain snow, before the first thaws begin. I was not giving up my poetry or my art, with this choice. I was making sure they endured.

We did not need to say farewell. I feared what would happen if I touched the queen of the gods, so I climbed out of the chariot and knelt. Warmth soothed my forehead, and I started against the press of flesh; Hera let her hand linger for a moment, the heat of her palm blessing me.

When I rose, she pointed to the steep slope that led down to the basin, picking out a narrow opening between ferns.

'Follow the path there. Once you put the helmet on, you will need to move without hesitation.'

She did not need to warn me. I was no longer the kind of woman who looked back.

A vapour swirled above the ferns and rocks, wafting the perfume of lilies, brushing my cheeks with the softness of peacock feathers and the faintest touch of pomegranate juice. The nectarous effect of the spell faded as I climbed down, and halfway down the rocky side of the waterfall, I felt it dissipate. I ducked behind a boulder.

I heard my own breath, gusting in my ears, forceful as the wind that blew past me. My fingers curled around the spear, and I clutched my lyre in my left hand. Since the spell had lifted, Hera must have left the ridge; I was visible, now, and entirely alone.

No, I told Eurydicius, trying to project my thoughts as I had done before. *Not alone.*

With every fibre in my body, I sent the force of my love to him. I hoped that he felt it.

If I could not pull him back through wet soil and tree roots and caked dirt to stand upon the earth again, I could make sure the earth never forgot him. If it was my destiny to meet him in Asphodel, then let my end be with a song – and let that song shake every refuge of gods and men. Let their sanctums fall.

Sunlight glanced off my armour as I descended the slope. The sparks of gold made me stare down at my breastplate, skirt and greaves, and I propped my spear against my side for a moment. I adjusted my helmet, settling it firmly so that the slit lined up with my eyes. Steadily, with steps that thumped against the earth, I approached the waterfall. The guard at the edge of the maenads' group looked up as I emerged onto the strip of soil. Her lips parted silently as she took in my armour.

Remember, Calliope's voice seemed to repeat in my head, ragged with feeling. *Remember that I am proud of you.*

It would have been easy to hurl the spear, but I did not move my arm. I stood, facing the company of maenads. Silence cloaked us all for a heartbeat's length.

The nearest guard tapped her thyrsus on the ground and chanted. The other guards rushed to her side. Behind them, the maenads stopped their weaving and talking and rose as one, clutching their wands and facing me. The tapping of wood against soil and the earth-shaking chant of more than two dozen voices filled the air; the water slowed its movement to a trickle, as if Vaphyras was listening.

Still, I did not move. The maenads circled me, peering at the muscles of my calves and arms as if to verify that I was a soldier. I waited until their chant built to a roar. Anger and anguish merged in that chant, until one woman tossed her thyrsus into the air and caught it.

'Their bodies, not our bodies!' she cried. 'Defend and tear!'

'Their bodies, not our bodies!' two dozen voices echoed. 'Defend and tear! Defend and tear! Defend and tear!'

I brandished my spear high, then lowered it and closed my eyes.

The maenads, my tutor had warned me, could tear off an attacker's arm at the shoulder: a mad woman, possessed by a god, could rip a man's limb from its socket. I felt four hands grasp my right shoulder, now, and a battle-cry broke over my head. *Two mortals working together*, I thought, *not a single god*. Other hands tore my spear from my grasp and pummelled my back; still others clawed at my helmet. A wrench jolted through my gristle and blood, and I slammed into the unshakeable knowledge of pain.

I had believed that I knew injuries, after all the blows from spear-ends and shield-rims that I had endured on the Whispering Isle. Hindsight teaches with a cruel efficacy. Those blunt knocks had not been wounds – they had been rehearsals. This sundering of bone and fat was the whole story, pain moving from the place where my right arm had been ripped away, coursing through every nerve in my body, every muscle, into places I had not known could feel pain; and although I tried to immure my scream within my mouth, it burst into the air.

Somehow, through the haze of agony, I managed to raise my left arm enough to pull my helmet off and toss it onto the ground. I opened my eyes to a mass of fawnskins. The maenads charged at me before they could notice my face. In their rush to seize my fallen arm, they did not take in my female lips and cheekbones, and I let my fear drop away. I began to speak.

When I had imagined the greatest poem I would ever compose, the pinnacle of my art, I had imagined crafting verses the way Eurydicius crafted shields: examining each bump and indentation in my phrasing, checking that the rhythm was sturdy in some places and light in others, running my fingertips over metaphors and images. As I opened my lips, now, golden rivers flowed through me without the need for shaping and checking, and time tapered to an instant. Words I had spoken on my bed, words I had sung in the Hall of Starlight, words I had revised and honed and arranged – they all burst out again, gushing into the air. I did not have to think, for I already knew this story.

The comfort of his conversation, never vaunting. The way he had followed my threads of inquiry to probe the mysteries of the sciences and arts with me. The press of his lips against my ankle, like a prayer, anointed with unspoken devotion. The way that his forehead crinkled when he was trying to solve a problem. The softness of his earlobe beneath my finger, slender and small: a sculptor's masterpiece.

I remembered the tears shining in the corners of his eyes as he spoke of the raid on his parents' farm. Yet he had refused to take up the idea of retaliation. *One vengeance for another*, he had said. *A wheel turning, and so many lives flattened beneath it.*

After Hades threw me, choked and flailing, from his domain, I had thought to wreak my revenge on the king of the Underworld, but whenever I recalled Eurydicius' words, I felt the futility of such retribution.

Now, I let the vast bounty of Eurydicius' forgiveness flow from my tongue into the world, glossing fields and oceans and the sharp tips of crags, striping the mountain where I stood, until the tree trunks basked in beams of scintillating gold.

I spoke of the gentle ripple that had passed across his face as he evaporated. I spoke of the smile that curled his lips as he lay on a rock in the Underworld. I spoke of those same lips, months ago, pressing kisses to the toughened line of my scar. After I had described the beautiful oddities of his features and manner, my words transformed to lyrics, and my voice to music.

Slipping into the flow of passion, I sang of weaving my words like wool, until they formed poems as strong as a skilled woman's cloak. I sang of hurling them before the immortals in the Hall of Starlight, pouring my own voice back at the laughing gods even as they mocked me. I sang of the fear that had gripped me in foreign lands, beside a dragon and in front of winged sirens, and I sang of Eurydicius telling me to go on – of his faith glistening in the darkness of each moment.

With every new breath, I wanted to tell the world what it felt like to love a man as an artist, as a wooer, and with the power of Hera. I wanted every woman to know what it felt like to be loved without a man's control – without his possessive cruelty – without his authority. I wanted everyone to see what it meant for two people to esteem each other equally, even beyond death.

And so I sang of climbing the hill in the Underworld: of stepping over a carpet of crimson and white roses, through the swirling smoke, to where Eurydicius lay. I sang of pressing my lips to his brow and thinking that I wished to keep them there until we both became dust. I sang of hefting him into my arms and carrying him along the narrow bridge, past Tartarus and Asphodel, gripping his shoulders as if I could never let go.

Your forgiveness. Your adoration. And your compassion. Those, I hold to my breast. Let me die as a woman aflame, and merge with your gentle water, I thought. *Let us show the world what love and poetry truly mean.*

As I sang, the golden rivers of words broke free of the darkness in my mind, slipping out of the grasp of fear and restraint, surging into the fresh air. Streams of poetry arced towards the sky. They twirled above me and divided into dozens of curls, dancing above the treetops, dipping down near the basin and flitting over the soil. They redivided, then transformed: I saw a pair of golden horses, champing in the sky, their bodies glossy and muscular; a bear danced with another golden bear, both tottering on their hind legs, roaring their happiness to each other; and in every animal that my words created, I felt a heart beating in time with my verses, a mind brimming with the phrases of my love.

A fork of crackling light flashed inside my skull. The raw power of it slammed into me with a force that could only be Zeus', and I battled to hold myself still. As soon as the lightning retreated, another force struck me, this one curling around me in tendrils of icy pain, with all the lightless malice of Hades' smile. I looked up at the golden animals of my poetry – dancing for Eurydicius and myself, for our agony and our joy – and I held firm, keeping my feet planted on the soil.

'You will not choose my fate, nor any woman's,' I whispered. I repeated the words softly, over and over, until the freezing tendrils uncurled from my limbs.

A movement caught my gaze. Two maenads approached me. They chanted and tapped their staffs. If I had offered them my forgiveness, they would not have heard a word of it: they were already tearing my lyre from my grip, tossing it towards the trees.

Four arms reached down and grasped my remaining shoulder, and I braced. The bliss of anticipation blotted out my remaining fear.

Eurydicius would see me, if only for a short while: we would find our way to each other, and I would wipe the tears from his cheeks.

I felt my left arm coming loose. Hot blood sprayed over my thighs, and I saw the pieces of my body as if I were a goddess, looking down from a height at some mortal's dismemberment.

I glanced left and right, glimpsing the bloodied stumps at each shoulder where my armour ended, but something moved inside me and shielded me from shock and anguish.

Bliss. The thought of seeing Eurydicius again guarded my mind from the horror of the present moment. The thought of spreading my poetry across the world, for him and for others, kept my mind firm. Harnessing all the strength left in my body, I knelt.

'I forgive you,' I said, loud enough for the maenads to hear, had they not been chanting. 'I forgive you for killing me, and I thank you for delivering me.'

The circle tightened. Voices rose in a single melody, startling sparrowhawks from the pine branches, shaking butterflies from the bushes. I knew what my attackers were spurring each other to do. Letting all barriers fall, I whispered of Eurydicius and myself, myself and Eurydicius, my self in halves, myself whole. I whispered of scalding love and bone-cold death and blood-rich grief. I whispered of love, again, and the word itself broke, unable to hold its meaning under the weight of my emotion, splitting into shards and circling my head, *l o v e*, each fragment a letter that glistened like a rainbow, vibrating with defiant life.

Even as four maenads moved to grab my head and take hold of my jaw, I turned my eyes to the sky and spoke the last line of my poem.

I am coming, I told him. *I am coming to you.*

The last thing I saw, before the maenads twisted my head from my body, was my lyre soaring up and entering the sky, its strings transforming, burning against the blue, a constellation of stars.

The earth shuddered and welcomed my blood.

28

Imagine a river diving into soil, parting clay and root and rock, surging into slim cracks and carving out channels with the force of its own grief. Imagine a torrent of water gushing into the hidden chambers of the mountain. On that river surges a head, carried like a crown at the foremost point of the flow.

Imagine that blood wends its way through Mt Olympus, borne on Vaphyras' waters. The river-god shepherds the head with care. The stump of the severed neck heals as it bobs along; its skin folds over and seals itself, yet some of the blood has already entered the water. The red liquid sings as it passes through earth channels and rock. The head sings, too, its lips moving to the rhythms of grief and anticipation, voicing its love to the world in a myriad of phrases, dark hair trailing behind it like lyre strings.

Calliope hears these poems, as she rests in her palace on Mt Parnassus, and she gathers the Muses around her. They listen to the head sing, and they smile.

Although Calliope never lifts a finger to intervene, she stands atop her tower every day, listening and listening. Sometimes, the nymphs think they hear her singing a reply.

Imagine, far away, a temple. Its altar blazes with orange fury. Pillars ignite, and the stones of the temple floor crack under the heat of flame, disintegrating, melting away. From the heart of the fire, a woman runs, her hair burning, her body a pyre without need for wood. She never screams as she falls.

The Oracle dies with her hands pointing upward, mouthing a single, calm word. *Bounty*. Around her, Delphi collapses and blackens, crackling and smoking, and you think to yourself: this is how a god grieves.

Yet though Apollo burns Pythia to her bones, he cannot burn what is braided by women's tongues. Two thousand years later, in the temple that his followers have rebuilt, visitors to Delphi will still remember the Oracle; they will look down at the spot where vapours once hissed up from the temple floor, and they will listen.

Imagine a river still questing through the mountain, searching for a green and gentle place to emerge. Stalks of grass tremble and tears of dew shimmer at his presence. Vaphyras shoots up through the carpet of leaves and vines, flowing between black poplars and oaks, pouring onto the earth at the foot of Mt Olympus. He transports the head of the poet who moves all Greeks, the one whose lyre sits amongst the stars. But you know that already. You know whose death he mourns.

Birds cluster around the river, listening to your head sing. Ivy crawls down towards the water, listening, too. Lizards scuttle through the undergrowth; kingfishers dart over the water, nightingales flit through the boughs, and damselflies flit across the grass. You watch as Vaphyras settles into the woods' embrace and wends a course between the trees, trickling his grief over soft mud.

Later, Zeus will call this place Dion, after his own true name. The woods will become a sanctuary in honour of his might. Yet the travellers who walk here will not hear thunder rumbling – they will hear leaves, bark, birds, spiders and insects singing, and in that song, a thousand souls will weep, crying the name of Orphia.

Imagine the last of your blood soaking into the earth. You watch from somewhere above the trees, disembodied, your spirit burning as brightly as the stars, and you hear the sigh of soil as your life-force flows into the ground and begins to nourish roots. Leaves drop to the earth. Bark and branches yearn to join you. Through the soil's whispers, you learn that Gaia is spreading word, using the scent of anemone poppies and the voices of owls: telling mortals that the blood of the poet Orphia emerged from the mountain here.

As Gaia works, Vaphyras dwells on your final poem – the love that even language could not contain – and he stirs from his pool and picks up your head, guiding it with the same tender care away from Dion. You sing as he carries you towards the sea.

Still Calliope listens, and still she does not intervene. Often, very often, she smiles.

Imagine a deep and lightless expanse, cleansing you. Imagine monsters approaching you beneath the waves, hearing your poetry and drawing back, crying salt tears into salt water. Imagine that your head keeps floating, lamenting Eurydicius through the vast darkness of sea and foam, all the way to the pebbled shore of an island.

You enter a cave. Here, at last, you rest: Vaphyras surges back out to sea, leaving you on a rock ledge within the airy cavern, facing a circle of light. From darkness you speak the words of new poems. Your odes to Eurydicius reverberate and bounce out into the hills and fields, and soon a trail of people winds its way to your cave, bringing offerings of honey and figs, the pilgrims gazing with awe as they listen to the story of Orphia and Eurydicius. When they return to their farms, these people plough their land with sorrow and yearning. Their trees droop with fattened peaches. Some of their fruit tastes like ripened joy, and some of it tastes like the nectar of melancholy, whilst in their groves, the olives turn dark and lustrous in the sun.

Whenever the farmers taste the oil from their lands, a look

of pensive mystery comes over their faces, and they pick up a lyre or cithara and begin to strum, filling the air with melody, pouring their thoughts into aching words.

It will be said that the people of Lesbos – for that is the island's name – bear the gift of poetry in their veins. You feel a tremor in the island's heart as a poet called Sappho is born. You observe her composing verses which ring through the world until her name entwines itself with the silken threads of passion, sex and love: themes you know well. Like you, Sappho is a woman. Like you, she has desired beyond what is expected of women – traced the soft curves of another's waist with her gaze, and led the way to kisses. And like you, she dares to speak of her own life: to shape and hammer and hone her poetry until the world must recognise its truth. Her truth.

You cannot express, yet, how much that means to you.

Imagine that Calliope flies to Lesbos, soaring over farms and villages and olive groves, dipping down towards the dark mouth of the cave. Your ears prickle as she glides into the dim haven. Her gaze sweeps rock ledges bedecked with offerings: your offerings, from farmers, fishermen, wives and daughters, glistening amongst the shadows. Behind Calliope walk eight goddesses. Euterpe smiles to see you, and to your surprise, Melpomene drops to her knees, bowing her head to you and laying down her sword.

Your mother carries your head from the cave. You do not feel the rush of air from flying, nor the jolt of transportation. The Muses place you in your chamber on Mt Parnassus, where you sleep for seven days and seven nights, until the soft fragrance of elm leaves wakes you. At your request, Calliope carries you around the Muses' city, holding you so that you see every tower and every tree, and sing of Eurydicius in every spot. When the sun lowers itself into the sea and a blanket of black wool covers the sky once more, the Muses bear you to the side of the lake.

Above you, the stars begin to prick the dark cloth with gold. One constellation shines brighter than all the others, a cluster of dots laid out like strings.

Lyra, Calliope calls it. The lyre constellation. The instrument of Orphia, honoured in the heavens for eternity.

The earth comes away slowly near Calliope's feet, even with eight Muses digging. You watch the soil being churned up and heaped aside, and you are sure that if you still had a heart, it would be beating faster now. When the Muses reveal Eurydicius' body at last, Calliope lowers your head into the grave and caresses your hair, making sure that you lie beside him. You glimpse the lyre blazing above you before she closes your eyes. Dirt begins to pour onto your brow.

Imagine that you view the earth like an eagle. You are not sure how. Through some kind of grace, after your burial, you watch the Muses casting their magic into a chunk of marble, straining until the substance whittles itself into a slab with a scene upon it: a woman stands, her chiton exposing her muscular thighs, her lyre clutched in her hand, while beside her a man sits on a tree stump, listening, his face a picture of rapturous love. The pattern that frames the scene is neatly etched. The names next to the two figures send a shiver through your incorporeal self. *Orphia. Eurydicius.*

The Muses do not measure grief in monuments alone. Each day, they stop by your grave and speak to you and Eurydicius, sometimes together, sometimes unaccompanied, and these tiny acts of remembering build and build, paying you a bounty of love and respect. Your mother and her eight sisters whisper your tale into the ears of poets all across Greece. They whisper that a love between equals is possible; that souls can join and form a bond to last beyond the agony of grief, even beyond death; and that a woman can speak of her life and dazzle the world. They whisper of Orphia and Eurydicius: poet and verse.

They whisper, too, of the woman who defied the rulers of Mt Olympus and the Underworld, and walked her own way steadily, step by step, hurling her love at the sky.

Imagine that your legacy spreads and spreads. The rich build temples for you and the poor make household shrines. A cult springs up across Greece in your name, until your life and death are so glory-hung that men worship you in mystery rites, hoping to free their souls from physical bondage. In some thickets and forests, it is said that women and outcasts perform their own Orphic Mysteries. Some believe that these people are mad. Gossips say that daughters and wives speak of the pain they have endured and the love they know, working their phrases over and over in new rhythms, trying to memorialise their agony and their ecstasy. Rumours abound that they are training each other to become poets.

If you know their secret, you do not sing of it where kings and fathers can hear.

Sometimes, these poets feel a rush of happiness after a performance, an unexpected joy in the work they have laboured so hard to perfect, and they sense, in their lungs and throat, a glow like the touch of sunlight on a still lake, which they come to describe as a blessing from the poet Orphia. When they return to their work, they find their spirits refreshed. They compose with a queer energy, as if the voices of many poets speak through their lips.

Imagine the wrath of gods, turned upon your body. Hades and Zeus order that Apollo must destroy your grave and deny your soul its journey. When Apollo arrives on Mt Parnassus, he senses that your spirit has left the earth: the burial has succeeded. Even without your limbs, you have been given the proper rites, and the devotion of the Muses has sent you somewhere beyond soil and clay.

Where are you?

To mortals, you are everywhere. The story of Orphia, her poetic skill, her love for Eurydicius and his equal love for her, her quest to the Underworld and her plea that moved King Hades ... her final song, a force of love so powerful it flung her lyre into the night sky and turned the strings into stars to light the hopes of poets ... this tale pulses through the ground and carries to every corner of Greece. It flows to other lands, seeping into the very air.

All around the world, people gasp and cry at your life and rejoice at your fame. Dauntless women, quiet men, and others still feel your story reverberate inside them and settle in their veins.

Poets old and youthful, women, men and others, draw inspiration from you as they learn to speak of their own lives, their own loves; to tell their own stories. Those who love beyond sex hear your melodies. Unrecognised poets grow in number and practise their art until they, too, know fame. They radiate hope as they pluck strings, singing of great feats and of greater pain.

For in hearing a story, we bind it to ourselves. We understand it in a way that is real to us, like a sunrise inking the sky with pale pink outside our window, presented for only us to see. The story of Orphia and Eurydicius flows from ear to ear, and as mortals absorb it, they learn not only what it is to die, but also what it is to be fully alive. Desperate people who hear the tale begin to nourish hope that they will find love: a bond so fairly balanced that the pain of life will be worth it, and their joy will weigh evenly against the agony of their grief. Their hope renews your tale.

A story is a legacy, more than gold or marble can ever be. A story gives and gives. It creates new tales and poems and songs, and its children heave with the birthing pains of art.

But you have not reached the end of this story.

I awoke, gasping, in a bath of light. It took a moment for me to stretch my arms and legs, marvelling at the fact that they were attached to my torso; that my flesh was warm and supple and strong. When I had allowed myself the pleasure of simply being in my body, I stood up. I could not tell if the light was truly light or some magical trick, yet I seemed to be standing in a long, featureless corridor. I began to walk.

It is strange to move through a mass of light that rises almost to your knee; stranger still if the light looks silver, instead of the natural golden glow of the sun, and if it slips away from your body as you walk. I seemed to be parting a sea with my calves. My naked state did not bother me, for I could see nobody before me. The silver glow filled me with a warmth that felt soft and cleansing, and in the air all around me, a soft fragrance of elm leaves swirled.

The corridor ended in a round room, its ceiling curving upward into a dome. The sea of light stopped at this room, leaving me to walk across the floor, bare and breathless, my soles making no noise on the polished stone. No sooner had I stopped than a length of cloth dropped from the air and wound itself around me: a gold chiton covered me to the knee, sparkling like a harbour at night. The material contained its own glow, and this was not the anger of sunlight but the steadfast compassion of stars.

I felt the soft support of sandals beneath my feet, and I took a step away from the centre of the room. The wall opposite me shivered like a mirage. Two doors appeared in its surface, and I paused, looking from left to right, while a queer tremor ran through me, like a hope that I did not understand. On the left door, two pomegranates gleamed in red paint, while on the right door, a crown of bones shone in brilliant white.

'What do you see, when you look at those two portals?'

Persephone's voice reached me before she appeared.

When I glanced to my right, she stood watching me. Tiny flowers bloomed in crimson and violet splendour amongst the strands of her hair; not a single black petal lingered, and the trenches on her brow had disappeared, replaced by tiny lines around the corners of her eyes.

'Queen Persephone,' I said, 'is this another trick?'

She smiled, and a new flower unfurled itself behind her ear. I returned my gaze to the doors, reminding myself that I had come this far because I would risk anything.

'I ask again, Orphia. What do you see, when you look at those two doors?'

'On the right, Hades' mark.' I pointed to the painted crown of bones. 'And on the left, your symbol.' I pointed to the pomegranates.

'Opposites, some would say.' Her face seemed to glow. 'I call these doors the gateways to our interpretations. Very few reach this place without passing through the Underworld and hearing the screams from Tartarus. But when Queen Hera, Calliope, the Muses, Gaia, Mnemosyne and even Aphrodite lent me the support of their magic ... it was quite astounding what they could do.' Her smile deepened. 'I do not believe Hades and Zeus ever saw them as they carried you to the entrance-way.'

There were gaps between those words. A tide of gratitude washed over me at the thought of my mother and all the other goddesses who had worked to bring me here, but I forced myself to concentrate on what Persephone had *not* said.

'And Eurydicius?' My voice wavered.

'Would it please you to hear that he, too, has partaken in a journey? I shall have to take the credit, since it had to be done under my authority ... with a little sleight of hand, of course.'

I saw it in my mind's eye: the moment after she had checked

Eurydicius over; the silvery dust passing from her fingers to his lips.

'You did not think I really doubted his honesty, did you?' she said.

I stared at her. 'Was he in pain as you moved him?'

'Far from it. The magic of the virtuous is painless and soft. But it can only transport a shade to a kinder place if that shade's life has been virtuous, too.' She looked at me with a slight pity, as if she could see the emotions jostling in my breast. *Eurydicius. A kinder place.* I gazed at the pair of pomegranates painted on the left door.

If I had avoided Tartarus, and I was not in Asphodel, then I had to be ... I must be ...

'I think you already suspect the nature of this place,' Persephone said.

In the Underworld, her words had rung out clearly. They had rung in my head many times since, but I had only nursed a faint imagining of what they might mean. 'I guessed that you were speaking to me when you proclaimed that your sovereignty lay in blessed Elysium, the realm of the virtuous dead,' I said.

She took my hand in hers. The touch of her palm reassured me.

'Virtue is a single word. Perhaps more than anyone, you know how a single word can yield more than one meaning, as a single farm may yield barley and olives and milk.' She nodded to the opposite wall. 'When Hades sees virtue, he sees raping and slaughter. He praises the conquests of kings on foreign soil.'

The crown of bones seemed to shine even more brightly.

'Behind one of these doors lies the place where Hades sends the shades he finds virtuous. It serves as an extension of his territory. The other door ...'

She had let the sentence trail off.

'The other door leads to your Elysium,' I said.

I had already begun to move. I was halfway to the door when Persephone clutched my wrist. For the longest moment of my life, it seemed that she was going to stop me; but then she laughed, and the sound rippled.

'This time,' she said, 'you must be the one to walk behind, and be led.'

She pushed the door open with both hands and crossed the threshold at a stride, her hair streaming behind her and scattering petals onto the grass beyond. It was easy to follow her: so easy that I almost failed to notice the door disappearing as I passed through it. The flowers in her hair burst open and swelled in the air of our new destination. I felt my senses opening, too, slowly and steadily, like smaller buds.

Beams of sun caressed my face. A warm breeze gambolled about my heels, and inhaling, I gazed out at a vista of orange-glossed fields, the grass burnished by a soft, tentative flow of sun. Rivulets of crystalline water descended from round hills in the distance, snaking through the meadows as if some unseen hand wove a pattern of silver over golden cloth. A rustle drew my eyes to the clusters of trees, beneath which birds, butterflies and beasts of all kinds played. Amongst the menagerie, I spied a pair of peacocks resting against each other.

Persephone led me by the hand. I was grateful, for without her prompting, I do not think I would have been able to move; the feeling of Elysium's pastures washed through me, permeating my skin, infusing my blood with a song of joy, and I longed to absorb it.

Shapes moved at the sides of the rivulets ahead. I followed Persephone at a swifter pace, my sandals barely touching the grass. As we neared one of the streams, the shapes became people, and I heard them chattering and conversing, laughing and singing, so occupied with the joyous exchange of thought that they did not notice us. I halted.

'So many,' I said. 'There are so many of them. They look so ... untroubled.'

Adults gestured as they spoke; elderly people sat against the trees; children dipped their hands in the stream and youths bathed in its crystalline water. Injured friends hobbled along the bank, supporting each other. Weather-beaten farmers and sharp-eyed artisans grinned and laughed together. I could not have imagined a clearer contrast to the pale and insipid shades of the Asphodel fields.

'Yes,' Persephone said, softly. 'So many people choose the path of peace, instead of the way of destruction. Understand, Orphia, that these people did not stay silent and let cruelties unfold around them when they were alive. They spoke up. They created. They defended. They aided others in their work. They took risks, not for gain, but for good.' She looked into my eyes. 'We lead through our choices, and in time, our choices lead us. They escort us to our final home.'

She pointed at something behind me, and I turned. Near my ankle, a silver thread hovered, extending all the way back to where the door had been: a thick, glimmering cord of poetry and magic, whose presence I sensed as much as saw. Persephone flicked her finger and the thread moved swiftly, coiling into a bundle at my feet.

'This is where I leave you, Orphia. You must weave the thread of your own story.'

She lifted our hands so that we were pressed palm to palm, our fingers fused for a perfect instant, gilded by the sunbeams.

I watched her walk slowly away. She looked at me and smiled before snapping her fingers. The door appeared, showing a painting of two pomegranates on this side, too, and she pushed it open and passed through.

Immediately, the door vanished, and a faint ripple of crimson and violet marked the place where it had been – and then that, too, was gone.

On every side, the sun-tinged fields of Elysium offered me a wordless welcome. I advanced slowly past the first group of people, my eyes roving along their number, finding no familiar face. A pair of grey-haired women waved as I passed them, and I waved back. I kept walking, past another crystalline stream, and another, staring at every person who was lounging in the shade or skittering along the banks. As I journeyed, I felt anticipation filling me as wine fills an amphora, leaving me heady with the sensation of surety. The pain of leaving Calliope still lingered, but regret no longer dwelt in my person.

Home was finally near. Not a home of place, but the home of his voice, his touch, his respectful and exalting words. I could feel the nearness of him in every lungful of the sweet air that I drew, as if I were breathing in his love for me anew, swelling, my soul flourishing under his adoration. The silver thread followed me as I walked. It stopped when I did.

My lips formed his name, and yet only a rasp came out, a noise so slight that the syllables within it could barely be discerned. Ahead of me, next to a ribbon of crystal water, a man turned from his conversation with a pair of elderly women. He looked straight at me. A beam of sun fell on his face, and tears sprang into his eyes.

He ran as I ran. We matched each other's strides without knowing how, without needing to know. His hair flew over his shoulders, wafting a familiar scent: that of the bright yellow flowers I had once seen surrounding him on Mt Parnassus. Amaranthos. The everlasting.

The space between us closed to an inch, and I flung my arms around his waist and pulled him to me. His body felt solid under my touch and I knew, at last, that he was not going to dissolve. I held him so tightly that I was sure the ground beneath us would sunder and we would fall through to a chasm of silent darkness. But it did not. I rubbed my nose against his, and he laughed, his eyes still shining.

Lifting him up, I bore his weight easily as he wrapped his arms around my shoulders; yet even as I did, I felt a new density to him. Not a heaviness of flesh, but a heaviness of soul. I could feel the weight of everything he had held back from me since he died, a burden of pain so great that I staggered, fighting to regain my footing. He had been bearing this alone. He had been carrying a mountain of fear and sorrow and grief, without ever asking for my comfort, and he had ensured that I would not be burdened by his pain atop my own. Now, the touch of our bodies let truth flow between us.

I lowered him and ran my fingers through his hair. The way he smiled at me made me feel that I had never really died; that I had never felt despair.

'You lack shields,' I said, trying to keep a sob from my throat.

'You lack a lyre.'

'I can endure without those strings. There is only one thing I cannot exist without.'

Pressing his mouth to the back of my hand, he kissed each of my knuckles in turn, and I felt the sadness in him ebbing, giving way. He straightened and looked me in the eye. 'Nobody needs shields, in this place. That is how I knew it was my true home.' He beckoned me, and I followed him to a patch of shade beneath a twisting giant of an oak. Crouching down, he passed me instruments from a pile. I examined a cithara, running my fingers over its taut strings, and stroked the length of an aulos, enjoying the smoothness of the whittled reed and the fine detail of the carved flower on the side. I did not need to ask who had made them.

Finally, he held up a golden instrument. I stared at the lyre. It hummed with the magic of words yet unsung, and in its crossbar, a line of graceful letters spelt out my name.

'I admit, I have worked at it longer than my new friends think necessary. But it is never quite perfect, as it should be, for you.'

My tears flowed without cessation. I did not attempt to wipe them away as I threw my arms around him and brought my mouth to his. The taste of him strengthened my spirit. 'Thank you,' I whispered, when I finally pulled back, allowing myself a long glance at him, drinking in his whole and unbroken form.

'You stare too long.' He dipped his gaze. 'Does my appearance displease you?'

'The opposite.'

A wrinkle crossed his brow. 'I thought you might not recognise me, after everything you endured. I feared ...'

My throat tightened. I waited, until I was sure he was not going to continue.

'I would know you in pitch darkness,' I said. 'I have known you in a grave, where the earth kisses our bones and caresses our flesh, even now. I will know you after death, always, at the end of the world.'

The streams on his cheeks glistened. I reached for the lyre and took it gently from his hand, feeling it thrum and vibrate. Golden rivers of poetry flowed through me, and I looked at him, waiting, hoping for the consent that would grant me the beginning of a new journey. I prayed silently. Beaming through tears, Eurydicius nodded.

I summoned all my memories of our bond, from the very first moment I gazed upon him, without whittling them down in the slightest. The rivers inside me merged to a single torrent. The flow turned molten, burning fear and sorrow from my mind, and I opened my mouth to speak.

'Tell me, Muse,' I began, 'of Orphia and Eurydicius.'

Author's Note

Readers immersed in classical texts may notice that I have made a choice about chronology in *Orphia and Eurydicius*. This decision concerns the timeline of the events of the *Iliad* and the *Odyssey*, in relation to the events of the *Argonautica*.

As we engage with and reimagine classical texts, we make choices as writers for the purpose of the particular stories we wish to tell – and in this case, writing about a poet, I had the idea of poetic tradition in mind. I had the choice of either taking Homer's and Apollonius' stories in the order of their recording, or in the order of their updated timeline.

The latter might seem like a simpler choice. Apollonius provided a prequel of sorts. I could write of Orpheus'/Orphia's adventures among the Argonauts as preceding the Trojan War and thus accept the prequel's timeline. Jason and his heroes would come first; Achilles and Odysseus would come later.

However, I was struck by the sense of poetic tradition that would emerge if I conceived of the poet Orphia learning from, engaging with, and even questioning Homer's stories. If Achilles and Odysseus came first, and Orphia was contending with these golden-age tales of war and violence, there was a sense of the real-life reckoning with these stories that poets of Apollonius' time (indeed, Apollonius himself) would have most likely had to undergo, as well as those of us writing afterwards. Just as Homeric myth left a legacy for Western literary tradition, it leaves a legacy for Orphia to contend with. I liked this idea most, so it was my choice for *Orphia and Eurydicius'* chronology. I hope, then, that readers will understand this as a choice, not an accident.

Acknowledgements

This book is dedicated to my brother, John – my other half, biggest supporter and closest friend. His encouragement for my writing gave me the will to continue, many times over. I am profoundly grateful for John's depth, his wit and his selfless acts of kindness over so many years. Our conversations and adventures are etched upon my heart. I miss you every day, John.

I am grateful to my parents for their support and love throughout my work on this novel. Their unwavering encouragement has been a rock amidst bushfires, lockdowns and the undulations of a global pandemic. These haven't been easy years. I'm thankful to have parents who care deeply and share the bonds of family in our most difficult moments.

Thank you to Roberta Ivers for taking on this book at HarperCollins and for believing in it. Your enthusiasm for *Orphia and Eurydicius* has been a warm support, and I'm delighted that it has a publishing home. Thanks to Vanessa Lanaway for her kind comments and thoughtful suggestions during copyedits. Thank you, also, to everyone at HarperCollins who worked on this book in any capacity – I appreciate the many hours of effort that go into producing a novel and am grateful for your hard work.

My gratitude to my agent, Julie Crisp, for helping this book to find a publisher, and for continuing to champion it. Thank you for your efforts on my behalf.

I'm thankful to Andrew Davis for designing a beautiful cover for this book. Thank you for incorporating elements of the story and creating a luminous ode to poetry, grief and unconventional love.

Deep thanks to my early reader, Rosamund Taylor, a superb writer and a steadfast friend. I treasure your kindness and insight.

Orphia and Eurydicius draws upon my experiences walking on the slope and summit of Mt Parnassus; at Delphi and in the ancient olive grove below; on Mt Olympus, including on the slope, at the Orlias Waterfalls, at Enipeas Gorge, and at Dion at the mountain's foot. To spend time in these locations in Greece, soaking up the sights, sounds and smells, was an experience I will always treasure. It forms a fundamental part of this book.

I am fortunate to have had the help of guides during my research in the mountains: Kostis and Eleni on Mt Parnassus, and Christina on Mt Olympus. Their expertise helped me to visit places that were hard to reach on both mountains. Special thanks to Kostis for sharing some of his father's doctoral knowledge of the endemic plants of Greece, and for the up-close tour of olive cultivation.

The archaeological sites at Corinth, Athens, Delphi and Dion provided many rich opportunities to walk around locations from the ancient world, and observe the ruins and geography first-hand. I am also thankful to have spent time at the Archaeological Museum of Ancient Corinth, the Delphi Archaeological Museum, the Archaeological Museum of Dion, the Acropolis Museum, and the National Archaeological Museum in Athens.

My thanks to the traveller and geographer Pausanias, whose *Description of Greece* was my companion as I moved around Greece. The author's detailed guide to each location provided me with insight into how these places might have looked at an earlier time – as well as some wry and colourful observations.

Thanks to the classical authors Euripides, Homer, Ovid, Virgil and Apollonius of Rhodes, for gifting the world with rich literature about the myths featured in this book.

I'm grateful to Greek-Australian poet Dorothy Poulopoulos for her advice on gender-flipping the names of Orpheus and

Eurydice. Thank you for considering the poetic ring of different versions in English and sharing your wisdom.

My gratitude to the writers from The Bunker who have been supportive and kind during the last few, rough years.

Profound thanks to the close friends who have stuck by me and encouraged me on my writing journey. I'm so grateful to you for the kind words and the willing ears. Special thanks to those who strolled with me in our permitted five-kilometre radius during the lockdowns – Anthony, Belle, and Tristan, in particular – and to Shyamala for our extensive and exuberant chats. My endless thanks to Jenna, who is always warm, witty and wise.

Thank you to A for giving your love so easily that it seems effortless.

Once again, to John: thank you for being my light.